Trials of the Elected

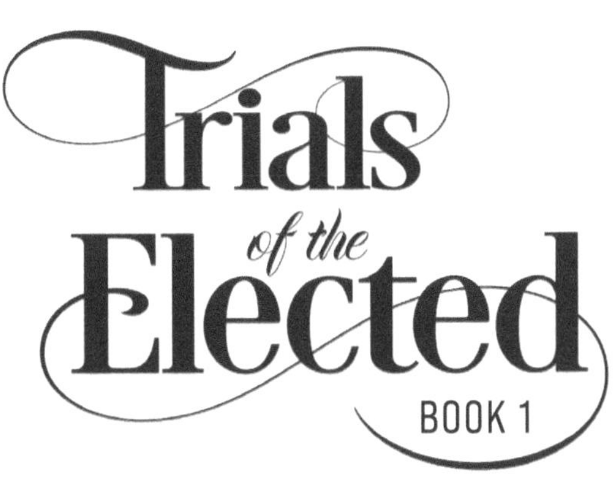

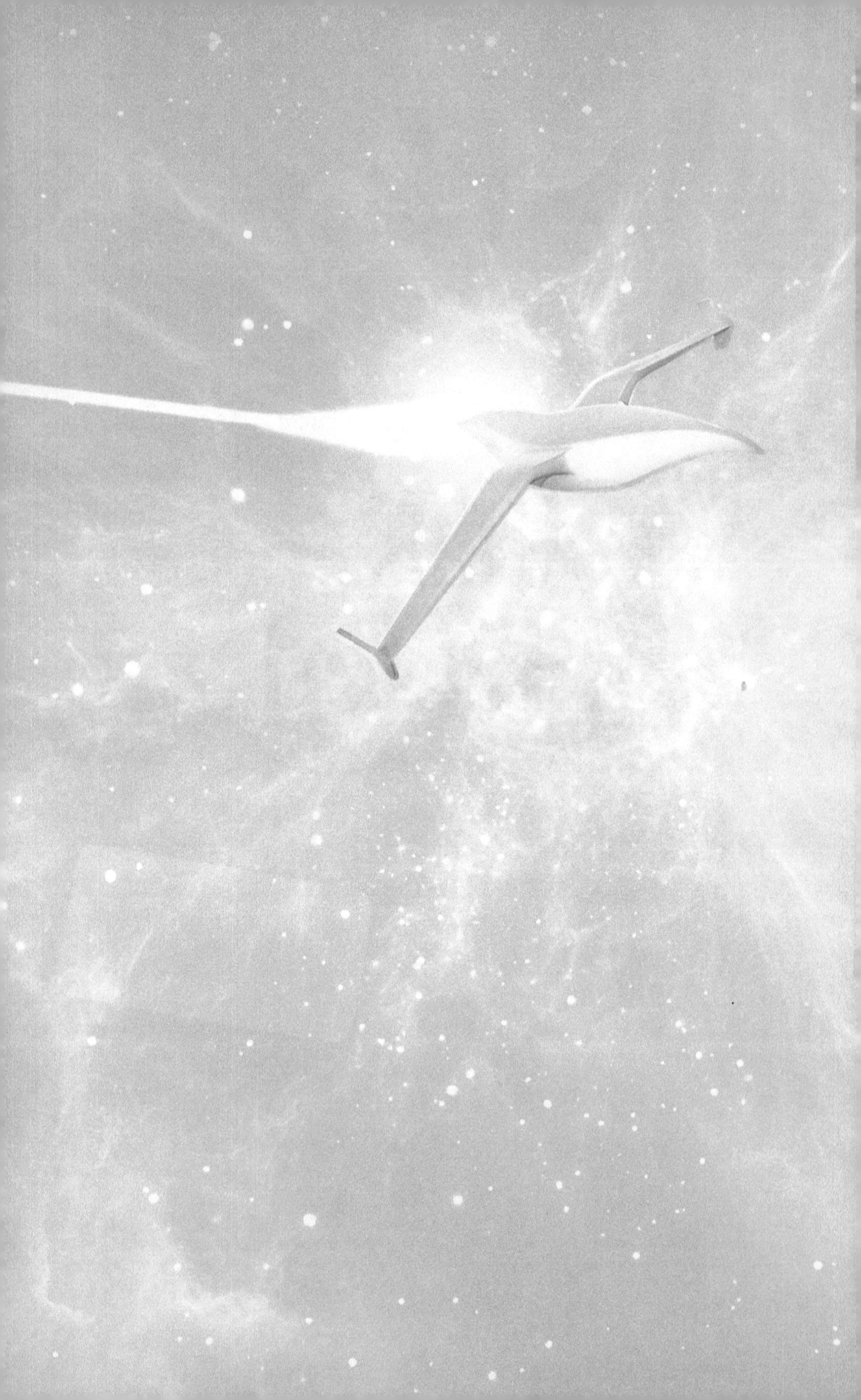

A HOME AMONG THE STARS

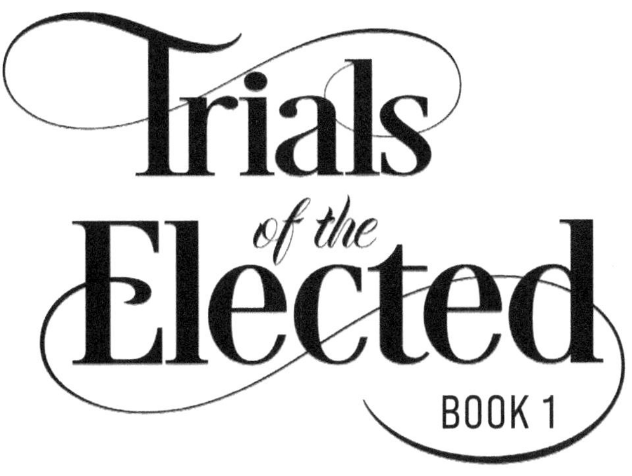

Trials of the Elected

BOOK 1

JAMES CATLIN

Decaslin Publishing

All the women in my life…
Mom, who helped me develop an imagination.
Diana, my wife, for helping me develop my talents.
My seven daughters, for reading and demanding
that I give them more.

Prologue

All that begins is set forth by intelligence.
All that succeeds is wrought by persistence.
But to what end?

The Divine drew near Far'el and allowed him to observe the scene unfolding on Earth.

"Far'el, it begins."

"So soon?"

"Yes, the enemy stirs."

"Will they prevail?"

"There lies nothing within which is prepared to confront the blight which comes."

"Then what can be done? You have said it is forbidden to interfere directly."

"We must introduce a new element into the mix."

"Is that not risky?"

"Yes, but if we do nothing, the conclusion is foregone."

"Where will you look?"

"Come, I will show you."

"Here…? How will one of them cope?"

"They are indeed more primitive, yet the scourge that comes will threaten even this far."

"Has there ever been an intrusion of such magnitude?"

"Yes, Far'el, the last such incursion was long ages before your ascension."

"So many to search through…"

"The choice has already been made."

"So quickly?"

"Yes, all that each of them can become is known unto me."

"Then this one is prepared…?"

"This one…is like all others, capable of the best and the worst, untried and ignorant of the limitless possibilities within. This one possesses great promise."

"Just one…alone?"

"Alone? No, unless wisdom is abandoned."

"But…"

"Far'el. The blight which approaches does so subtly, slithering like a serpent, hidden in the shadows, biting covertly at unwary heals until ready for the final strike. It is filthy, cunning, and dangerous, fearing to reveal itself too soon for it is well aware of its own weakness. Herein lies time to prepare."

"To teach?"

"To harden the weapon through trial and fire. Watch and learn, Far'el, for a time will come when you too, will face such problems."

"I stand ready."

"Good."

A stiff breeze lashed the falling snow in Jared's face like a multitude of tiny, biting insects. His anger had subsided slightly, though more due to the cold than to an improvement in his mood. He had known catching the ride with his sister Sandra had been a mistake, but he had wanted to avoid making his father go out in the storm. His demand to get out of the car while still several miles from his apartment had given her even more to gloat over, knowing she had ruffled his feathers. Jared couldn't understand why she had changed so drastically from who she had been before graduating high school.

Crossing Seventh, Jared glanced up at the clock on the credit union across the street and noted that only half an hour remained of Thanksgiving, and he wondered just what he had to be thankful for. There was a time when he had looked forward to the holiday, but that had changed over the last couple years. Despite Sandra spouting that he was just running away, Jared felt it was time to put some distance between himself and his family. Except for his two nephews, he didn't think he'd miss much.

Jared had not followed in his mother's staunch faith, and knew she was disappointed, but at least he wasn't antagonistic, like Sandra. He wondered why she even bothered coming to the family gatherings considering her views, particularly on men. What had made the evening especially bad was that Sandra had broken the news to their mother that Jared had broken up with his girlfriend, Janet. He had no idea how the snipe had found out about it, but it had opened the flood gates. Jared's mother considered Janet a stabilizing influence and was bound to see them married. He had wanted to wait until after the holiday to tell her, and Sandra was lucky her father had firmly instilled in Jared the precept that a man must never hit a woman.

Stopping, Jared leaned for a moment against a telephone pole and shook the snow off his beanie, readjusting it around his ears. His small pack was not usually a burden, but he was growing tired as well as being upset. He rubbed his eyes, righted himself and set off again. All the evening's events might not have played so heavily upon him if it wasn't also for the void that had grown between himself and his father. Jared had done well in school, primarily to please his parents; particularly his father. The older Chandler had tried to steer him toward the honorable path of military service. Yet when the time came, Jared discovered he had no desire to follow the same course.

His acceptance to West Point had been secured by the last few months of his senior year, but he chose instead to go to college and study industrial arts. The once congenial relationship with his father quickly became one of stoic indifference and aloof conversations. Though he hadn't thought about it at the time, taking a couple years off after his junior year at the University of Colorado had only aggravated his father's disappointment, and fueled Sandra's fire that he was a loser.

He sighed and glanced up at the night sky.

Yep, I definitely think it's time I blow this town.

He passed the auto shop where his car was being repaired. It would be good to have it back in the morning. At the corner, he decided to stop and get a snack at the all-night convenience store. He shook the snow off as best he could before he entered and headed directly for the store's rather poorly stocked deli section.

The elderly clerk smiled ruefully at him as he passed the checkout counter. Jared took off his gloves, picked up a turkey and Swiss, a drink, and a bag of chips. He set them on the counter and withdrew his wallet.

Again, the old man smiled. "Bad storm to be out in."

"Yeah," Jared replied with a deep exhale then watched a news blurb on the TV behind the counter as the man scanned the items.

"What you think of all that?"

Startled he asked, "All what?"

The man flung his thumb over his shoulder. "The killin' in the Middle East."

Jared glanced back at the TV. "Don't really pay much attention to it. Got enough of my own problems right here."

The man paused, then changed the subject. "Get a chance to spend some time with your family?" The man asked sincerely, and Jared noted a wistful undertone.

Jared's smile was only half-hearted. "Well, I did, but the holidays aren't what they used to be. I mean, you know, like when you're a kid."

"Yep, things change, but don't let that push you away. Time will come when those changes won't seem so bad. Not when you're all alone." He was still smiling, but a deep sadness was in his eyes.

Jared looked at the man, puzzlement creasing his face.

"That'll be $6.84."

Jared handed him a ten and collected his change. "Thanks."

The old man gave him a nod and a smile.

Jared donned his gloves and set off again. The snow was falling harder now, and his visual range was down to about fifty feet. He made it to the sidewalk as a small red sports car pulled up to one of the convenience store pumps and then it all vanished into the coming white out.

He walked for some time before stopping in the covered shelter of a bus stop. The wind was fierce, and his cheeks stung from the whipping snow crystals. His attention was caught by three loud pops that emanated from the direction he had come. They were very definite despite the howling of the wind.

He wondered what they were, but his thoughts were interrupted when a reddish object flew past him at high speed. Though only a blur in the dense snow, he knew it was the red car he had seen only minutes before. For an instant Jared thought he should return to the store to see if anything was amiss.

No, no thanks. I met my social quota for the day.

He had not gone more than twenty feet when the high-pitched whine of an engine caught his ear, coming closer. His first instinct was to run, but he could not see anything. He remained on the sidewalk, knowing he might otherwise run right in front of it.

With alarming quickness, a gust of wind hit him square in the face, instinctively making him close his eyes, but instead of bitter cold, the air was warm. In surprise he opened them again to find himself looking at a perfectly clear area as if magical forces were keeping the snow at bay. Fear gripped him, for in the clarity was the revelation that the vehicle with the whining engine was headed directly for him. It was spinning wildly out of control, flashing him alternately with its headlights, then tail lights. His mind told him to run, but his body was responding as if he was caught in a bubble of molasses.

Jared's eyes widened in disbelief and focused on something behind the car. A swirling dark blue-violet mist at the rear of the vehicle seemed to be digesting it with each passing moment.

He heard a scream but could not tell where it came from. He glanced down into the car's window and saw the unmistakable terror in the eyes of what appeared to be a doomed man. Jared wondered if he had that same look the instant the car vanished completely.

In the brief moment that followed, Jared's thoughts flashed through a series of faces that brought tears to his eyes. Terri, his older sister, had always been close and he regretted his earlier thought that there was nothing he would miss. If this was indeed the time of his death, he knew he would miss them dearly. What was it the old man had said? That one day he would not mind the changes. Well, that day had come all too soon. Lastly, his mother and father's images danced for an instant in his memory before his attention returned to the strange phenomenon as it enveloped him, and all turned to blackness.

CHAPTER ONE

Alone

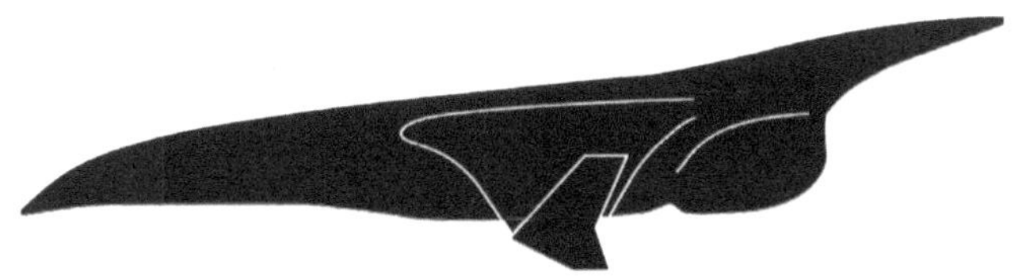

"Knowledge is a gift we give ourselves, though it is often difficult to acquire. It's true value cannot easily be calculated. Understanding is a dividend received from the investment of time used to seek knowledge. Wisdom is the final payoff of the gift and the dividend, when combined with common sense, courage and humility."

CONSCIOUSNESS RETURNED and brought with it sensation. Jared breathed deeply and filled his lungs, holding it to stretch his chest. His mouth felt dry and in need of brushing. He was on his back on a firm, though not uncomfortable surface.

Not my bed.

The thought came slowly as he tried to clear the fog from his mind. He shifted to his right to get comfortable but was stunned when his face hit something hard.

"Ugh!" He lay back for a moment massaging his nose. After the stinging subsided, he felt along the smooth barrier and discovered he was completely sealed in.

Panic engulfed him. He couldn't sit up or turn. He suddenly couldn't breathe, and claustrophobia overtook him.

He settled back and took several deep breaths until his heart resumed a normal rhythm. He took one final deep breath and glanced at his watch.

11:52 November 28.

"Alright," he said aloud. "There are a couple of possible explanations for this. I could have been kidnapped and my captors are keeping me in some kind of container, or perhaps I did something really stupid and I'm now in solitary confinement."

Being in total blackness left his last possibility unsaid, though the idea that he was in a coffin was actually the most believable. He contemplated for a while whether it might be possible for a soul to be trapped in a casket with its now lifeless host, particularly if the soul was in denial about its fate. He was thus engaged when he realized there was a small lump near his hip and found it to be a soft container. After a few minutes of fumbling around he realized it was his pack.

His earlier train of thought was tossed out as he concluded that in none of those scenarios would it have been left with him. No other logical idea came as to why he would have been so confined.

"Okay, so it's some kind of box."

His anxiety grew again slightly at his acceptance of the only fact he had.

"Damn, it's almost as if I'm in some old refrigerator or something like that." He pushed hard on the top, and it only reinforced his belief. It would not budge. He felt too warm, so took off his gloves, and unzipped his coat. It helped lessen the growing claustrophobic feeling.

What bothered him most was that his short-term memory seemed to be blank.

He whispered, "All right, take a deep breath and calm down. It's not likely I have much breathable air left, so I have to stay calm." He shut his eyes and slowed his breathing.

Okay, I'm not dead. I'm just locked in a small rectangular box with no apparent way out. What options do I have?

After a few moments he remembered the contents of his pack and smiled. He reached down along his left side, pulled the pack up and unzipped the main compartment and searched for the flashlight he always carried.

Several small items fell out before he found it, but he ignored them for the present, withdrew the small slender instrument and pushed the switch. The beam of light did not hit an opaque surface but extended a considerable distance beyond, revealing a ceiling above. A transparent barrier covered the top and right side allowing him to see that there were at least two other similar containers in close proximity to his. They sat several feet off the floor on solid pedestals and each had a small control panel which appeared inoperative.

Where the hell am I?

He continued to stare at what details he could make out.

Looks like some sort of laboratory storage facility.

The two containers seemed to be occupied, but Jared was unable to make out clearly what was inside. For all he knew they could be animals.

Am I having a nightmare? Uhm, nope, that's just wishful thinking.

He moved the light over his head and discovered a small panel with a single button at its center and a strange imperceptible symbol above it.

Well, it either opens this thing or calls room service.

He looked all around the outside of the container again to make sure he was alone, then reached above his head and pressed the button, figuring either option would reverse his situation.

He jumped as three quick clicks followed by the hiss of escaping air filled his ears and several small lights illuminated the corners of the container. Once most of the noise stopped, he heard a deep-toned pop, and the lid slowly opened upward and back to his left.

Cold immediately hit his entire body and filled his lungs. He sat up slowly and tried to rub the chill out of his arms. He zipped his coat and that helped considerably, but the low temperature left him feeling even more concerned as to his possible circumstances. He knew he would have to find a way out of the room soon, before he froze to death. He swung his legs over the edge, slid on his gloves, and adjusted his stocking cap. He leaned forward and dropped a few feet to the floor. He stumbled and swooned, finding himself weak and unsteady. Breathing was becoming difficult, so he pulled his gym shirt around his nose and mouth.

November in Colorado could often be very cold around Thanksgiving, but he had not felt this kind of cold since he was a teen on winter vacation in Alaska, at the February Fur Rendezvous celebration.

For a moment his curiosity overcame his need to escape. He moved closer to one of the other chambers. A chill ran down his back making him even colder than he already was; it contained skeletal remains.

He tried to maintain his sense of humor. "Okay, I guess this means there's no room service."

There were twenty-four containers in all, and besides his, four others were occupied. He sighed and turned his attention to finding a way out.

He walked to one end of the room where he saw an average-sized door with no doorknob. A small panel was mounted to the right of the door at chest level.

He pressed each of the panel's three buttons—nothing. He looked around and noticed more of the strange symbols above the control panel. He pushed on the door, but it didn't budge.

Jared returned to the open container and sat down. He took his shoes off and tried to rub some feeling back into his now very cold feet.

He put his shoes back on and approached the door again.

After some thought he tried to move it from right to left with no success. Frustrated he shifted to the other side and heaved with all his might.

Caught by surprise when it opened he fell forward crashing to the floor. Scrambling to his feet he cautiously stepped into the dimly lit hallway. Long bluish lights tapered where light gray walls met the ceiling. There were no windows.

If this were some kind of government facility, I don't think they'd have the hallways so dark, unless it was little used or abandoned.

To the right, the hallway extended a short distance and was a dead end. To the left the hall continued out of sight into the darkness with no apparent openings.

Everything was cold.

Jared checked another door directly across the hall. It opened into a room like the one he had just left. It too had twenty-four containers, though all were barren. He exited and continued down the longer portion of the hall.

His footfalls were loud on the cold, hard floor despite his efforts to step lightly. He was hungry and tried to locate the people who ran the facility. He walked about sixty paces, came across another door, and stopped in front of it.

He removed his gloves and tried to slide the door to the right. This one appeared to be locked or broken, so he continued. Ten more doors on the same side of the hall lay evenly spaced, and Jared tried each one. All but the first opened easily and revealed that they had at one time been someone's living quarters. Except for the tattered remnants of bedding, nothing else remained. After the same results at the last door, he became very discouraged.

At the far end he found a stairwell leading upward. He hesitated only a moment then started up. The next level proved to be just as dark and deserted.

Not far from the stairwell he came to a large series of windows that looked out into the blackness of space above, and dark gray/ black rock in front of and below him. His mind fought the reality he stood facing, but it was plainly clear he was not in Colorado.

Several bright stars cast enough light for him to see that no vegetation grew anywhere. Numerous possibilities flashed through his mind such as, he was in some type of virtual reality simulation or perhaps even on some kind of drug. He had no idea how long he stood there staring out into the starlit vista, but his legs started aching, so he continued on.

Maybe I'm in some kind of enclosure designed to look like outer space. But why?!

He looked at his watch and grimaced. "11:52, November 28. Damn. I have no idea what day it really is or how long I've been here."

He searched his thoughts for several seconds and finally his memory began to return.

"Thanksgiving, it was Thanksgiving, and I had just returned from the c-store."

He went to another door and opened it. "Empty."

Then moved on to the next, but his thoughts were running rampant now.

No, I never made it home. That car passed me then I saw...

He stopped cold.

"What was it?" he said out loud.

He entered another room and glanced around. The bed here was made as though the room's last occupant had intended to return. The bedding was in fairly good condition, so he gathered it up, along with a dull knife he found in a small desk.

His stomach growled so he proceeded to the next level. As soon as he stepped out of the stairwell, he saw another row of observation windows leaning at a slant over the dark, rocky landscape giving him an even better view of the surrounding star field. Limited light from the distant stars revealed that he was looking out into a huge canyon, the base of which was far below.

I must be on some kind of station in outer space. He took a deep breath. *That's impossible.*

Many of the doors he found had odd symbols on them. The characters were graceful with similarities to Arabic and Asian script, though Jared doubted they were either.

His stomach growled again and his desire to find food now became urgent. The largest room on the floor contained many tables and what appeared to be a kitchen area, but he had no idea how the food would be prepared.

He was unable to access one door. He was sure it was a storage room, the one place he needed and hoped desperately contained food. It was also the first that still appeared to have power.

Jared had refrained from touching any equipment or devices, preferring not to push his luck. He had no idea what might happen if he pressed the wrong switch, but his gut was moving beyond the complaining stage into full-fledged cramping.

He collapsed to the floor. His stomach was in spasms, and he was extremely thirsty. He had been blessed with a high metabolism, allowing him to eat far more than he would have been able to otherwise, but now it was becoming a curse. With nothing to put in his stomach and his body's high demand, he knew he was starving faster than someone with a normal metabolic rate.

After about half an hour, he decided to set up a place to be comfortable until he found a way out of his predicament. He struggled to drag a stiff mattress from one of the rooms and placed it in a corner of the dining area then gathered more of the tattered and worn blankets.

He felt the spot was centrally located and afforded a view out the windows from which he would hopefully see some form of rescue. He also wanted to be close to what he thought was a food storage room because if it wasn't, he would not last long. He pulled a table next to his corner. He set his pack on it and began to inventory the contents.

Everybody knows when you're lost you always check your supplies.

In addition to the flashlight, he had a small first aid kit, a package of wooden stick matches, several rubber bands, some stamps, four empty candy wrappers, a T-shirt, a pair of briefs, his pocketknife, fingernail clippers, and the sandwich, chips and drink he had purchased at the convenience store.

"Great! I'd forgotten this was in here." He unwrapped it and took a bite. He stopped chewing and looked at the sandwich. "How long's it been in there? No way to know," he shrugged. "Doesn't really matter I guess." It tasted good.

He stopped as thoughts of home surfaced. His mother was in the forefront of those memories. She had always been so confident in her path through life. Her admonition had always been to pray in times of trouble for help from God, but Jared had begun to drift away from religion during his last couple years of high school. He had not attended any kind of theological meeting since leaving home. Yet now he found himself compelled for some strange reason to pray to a being he wasn't sure even existed. Prayer had been a daily occurrence in the Chandler household. He remembered his father's tales of life in a prisoner of war camp and how his faith was what saw him through the terrible time. Now he was, in a way, like his father had once been, an isolated prisoner in a situation which motivated a part of him he had long since thought dead. He had been taught that prayer brought comfort. He had no idea how it could do so, but regardless of his viewpoint, he was able to sleep after he had finished talking to whatever unseen beings might be there to listen.

Still hungry when he woke, his chest felt as if he'd been kicked hard just below his sternum. He was dehydrated. The air was cold and dry; his lips and knuckles were chapped and even cracked in some places.

To start his second day, he put two marks on the wall to indicate the day before when he first left the glass case, and the second for this new day. Five blankets had provided enough warmth to sleep somewhat comfortably, but when he got up he was freezing. He was well aware that if the place had breathable air, other systems might still work. It was time to take some chances, push some buttons.

"If this really is an asteroid, I doubt it has its own gravity field, which means that's still working too." Jared scratched his head and realized he not only needed a shower but wanted a hot one. "This place must have some kind of operation's center."

No such facility existed below so he headed for the stairs. He stopped just short of the stairwell and looked at two sets of flush mounted doors. On one side of each set were two buttons labeled with more unfamiliar symbols, though in this case Jared had little doubt as to their meaning. *Elevators.* They were inoperative and the one on the left had a metal sign secured to the two doors with large fasteners straddling the separation line.

The top of the stairs opened into a large octagonal room of which five sides were windows. The sixth aligned with the elevators below and, here too, one set was sealed. The seventh had a hall extending back into the rock. From this vantage point he was quite sure he was on an asteroid. What appeared to be a huge set of doors like those used for hangars were set into the rock on the opposite canyon wall. He estimated that the doors had to be three or four hundred feet long and a third that high. An overhanging outcrop of black rock prevented them from being visible from the windows on the lower levels.

But he was starving so he hurried down the connecting corridor.

He had little energy, and he figured the cold was adding to it.

The hall was short, with only five doors: two left, two right, and one on the end. Starting on his right he slid open the door and peered inside. A small office with a desk, two chairs and two freestanding cabinets lay covered in dust. On the desk sat what was obviously a computer terminal, but it had a very artsy designed casing and a keyboard which was definitely not like any he had seen before. Jared quickly riffled through the desk drawers turning up some faded papers that fell apart when he touched them, a pair of writing instruments, and what Jared assumed was a very beautiful pistol.

He stashed the items in a pocket and left the room. The next compartment contained numerous empty shelves except for several rolls of clear, wrapped paper and two electrical cabinets. Beyond the door at the end of the hall, Jared discovered another narrower stairwell up another level. Behind the fourth door he found what he was searching for: a large room containing eight workstations with computer terminals, control consoles and two tables. The power was actually on for several of them, but frustration soon took over.

This is pointless.

Jared sat back laying his head in his left hand, he had never felt so totally alone. He slowly stood, arched his back and turned to leave. He abruptly stopped, holding his breath. He heard an unmistakable sound. With caution he moved toward the door and withdrew the alien weapon. He peered out the control room door, seeing nothing. All the other doors remained closed.

"Hello!"

Like they would understand me.

He was stopped short again when a light flickered to his right.

With slow deliberate steps he moved to investigate, holding the pistol in front of him. In the middle of the octagonal observation area, he could survey 360 degrees but saw nothing. He took a deep breath and tried to relax, then moved back toward the hall.

Suddenly he jerked around to a dull popping sound. He dropped to one knee and brandished the weapon menacingly. He smiled. Outside the windows a shimmering cascade of metallic dust billowed away from the station's wall.

"Meteors" he breathed softly. "These windows must be…" He was startled as another of the small rocks impacted directly on the transparent barrier and shattered into dust. He swallowed. "Very durable." A moment later another larger one hit above, beyond his view.

But then his head snapped around one hundred and eighty degrees to a sound that was definitely inside. Frazzled, he moved slowly back toward the control room, his steps unsteady, hands shaking. Confused, he stopped about ten feet from the first door.

"Where's the SWAT Team when you need them?" he quipped. "Alright, can't stand here all…"

Something moved directly above him, and he attempted to back away, but his arm was caught in a long black tendril. Shifting his trajectory didn't help as more of the tendrils entangled his torso and legs. Flailing wildly only worsened the situation as the weight of the mass forced him to the floor. Aided by an adrenaline rush, and angry at having been caught off guard, he struggled fiercely and managed to extricate one of his legs.

A sharp pain erupted in his neck as if stung by a wasp.

"Aaarh," he bellowed in pain and slapped at anything near his neck. Again, he felt the sting, but this time it was near his spine, low on his back.

Finally, he flung the last of the mass off his upper torso and used his remaining energy to pull free. After putting several body lengths between himself and the creature, he rolled to face his attacker. Part of it still hung suspended from the ceiling while the rest lay coiled on the floor, unmoving.

"Maybe the struggle killed it," he said breathlessly, staring at it in the dim light through a haze of weary eyes. His breathing slowed and he squinted, looking closer at the mass. He closed his eyes and laughed.

"Cables…and wires."

The following day it took more than three hours to find something he could use as a crowbar and another hour of useless effort before he gave up trying to open the door in the mess hall. Jared turned away from the unyielding portal and stared out the window across from the dining room.

"I could just throw the metal bar through the window and end it all."

His father came to mind, as did some of the images his stories evoked of time spent in a POW camp.

"I guess this is not that bad." But he was about at his limit of endurance. Anger gripped him and he drew back and threw the metal bar at the door like a javelin. It hit the wall just below the control panel with a loud clanging 'thung.'

Jared's eyes widened as a small amber light on the panel illuminated. Stunned, he froze but then rushed toward the panel. He carefully pressed the first of three buttons. A click followed and he tried to pull the door open but was unable to get a grip on the small lip at its edge.

He pressed the second button—click. He figured he'd just re-locked it. Before he could press the top button again the amber light went out and he was left once more with an inoperable door.

"Ahhhh!" he bellowed. "Alright mother, I prayed, now what do I do? Where's the help you said would come?" he walked over and slammed his fist against the window.

"Where's the point in all this?" Jared had never been one to easily lose his temper, but he'd never been in this kind of situation before. His stomach lurched. Exhausted from lack of food he returned to his warm bed and tried to forget about his aching abdomen.

Several hours later he awoke to sharp shooting stomach pains. He curled into a fetal position trying to reduce the sensation he felt. He had no idea how long he'd been in the transparent container; he might have gone without food far longer than he'd originally thought.

He suddenly froze and stared into the darkness. Fear swept through him. He fumbled about for the flashlight but couldn't find it. Was something else in the room? Yellow eyes stared at him from across the dining room. For several tense minutes he stared back staying as still as he could, thinking he might be able to intimidate whatever it was. He remembered that he'd left the weapon and flashlight on the table several feet away and he clenched his teeth. Mustering his courage and pushing the varied visions of Hollywood-inspired aliens out of his mind, he slowly moved to the table and armed himself. With the weapon in his right hand and the light in his other, he stood erect and aimed.

Suddenly, the two yellow orbs merged into one.

He shook his head but that did not bring the second eye back. Fear left and logic returned as it dawned on him that he was looking at a control panel. He snapped the light on and ran toward the door.

"I've got to get a grip, there's no one else here."

He stopped before getting to the wall, fearing he might terminate the miracle of power to the door. He touched the top button. As soon as he heard the click, he moved his finger over the bottom button and said a quick prayer. "Please God, let this work."

The amber light went out and Jared dropped his head in anguish, not even caring that he was barefooted on the ice-cold floor. Suddenly, his head snapped up to a low grumbling sound. After several tense seconds, he watched the big door begin to move outward. He sank to the floor and wiped the moisture from his eyes.

According to his best calculations it had taken thirty-seven hours before he found something to eat. It took another half hour to figure out how to heat the frozen items. The tables were made of fireproof material, as was nearly everything else in the complex. He resorted to burning two of the blankets he'd collected. Fortunately, they burned slowly with a good, hot flame. Jared placed the frozen meal into a metal pan and stuck it directly in the fire. At this point he neither cared what the food was, nor how old it was. If he had to die, he'd rather go with a full stomach.

Using his T-shirt as a potholder he checked the pan's contents three times before it was completely thawed. Using his pocketknife, he put a small amount of the greenish, yellow mash in his mouth and chewed briefly before swallowing. It had the texture of sweet potatoes but a taste like corn, which made him thankful he didn't have to survive on something disgusting. Hopefully this wasn't the only thing in the storage room, but he'd make do if it was. He had no trouble finishing off the entire loaf of corn mush, as he chose to call it, even though he knew it might make him sick. Getting ill from eating too much too soon couldn't be any worse than what he'd already endured.

During the following weeks Jared found many things that were useful, but nothing that would provide a way off the asteroid. Now resigned to his situation and having convinced himself he was alone; he was able to live with less stress.

He found six containers of fresh water in the storage room. He had rationed the precious fluid, but now only one remained. It was the beginning of the seventh week, and again, he was worried. Food was no longer a problem as the locker had enough to last for a very long time, but not one of the plumbing fixtures on any of the levels produced even the smallest amount of water. He had traced the plumbing from several rooms but kept coming to places where they ran into the natural rock, and he could not find where they began again. He knew there had to be a water storage tank somewhere as he couldn't imagine the asteroid would have a natural source of its own. The number of rooms he found indicated that the station once had a crew complement of between eighty and a hundred permanent residents, so a large reservoir would have been required.

There was another area of the base he could not access and that grated at his mind, but he ignored the feeling as best he could. He had explored every square inch of the five levels, and he didn't know where to look next. The elevators were useless, and he couldn't find any stairs leading to the other area.

To take up some of the time, Jared began to keep a journal of what transpired since his arrival but had little to write about now that the place was fully explored. Living in near total darkness had not bothered him so much when he had things to do, but now that he had so much idle time on his hands it was getting on his nerves. He rarely used the flashlight anymore as his eyes seemed to have adjusted to functioning in the dim blue light that filled all but a few rooms. From time to time, he wandered through the halls like some half-awake specter looking for a soul to steal. He hoped he would find something he'd overlooked.

He tried several ways to learn at least something about the language of the former inhabitants but had no baseline to begin with. It might be possible if he could just get the computers working, but so far he'd had no luck there either.

He headed back to the dining area to turn in for the night. As he passed the place where the metal bar he had thrown weeks before had hit the wall, he stopped and pondered the sound it had made. He had not messed with the exterior panels that covered the excavated asteroid but suddenly realized they might hold the key. He smacked the panel again just to verify that it did sound hollow, then moved to the next one down and repeated. The second panel sounded solid and did not yield at all.

Jared retrieved the metal bar and jammed the tapered end into the seam of the panel then leaned into it with all his weight. Several good pushes later the edge snapped away with a series of small loud pops. The panel seemed to be made of a fiberglass-like material and was anchored into the rock by long, flush mounted fasteners driven deeply into the stone. Another series of pops and the panel broke free, throwing Jared to the floor. Behind the panel lay a deep alcove where two small pipes converged into a larger one, then entered the rock near the ceiling. It appeared that these aliens had used the rock itself as pipe except where bends or connections were needed. Jared calculated if the pipe remained straight, it would follow the wall and perhaps lead him to water.

He began hitting every panel along that side of the hall leading away from the large row of windows. He tore away several panels that sounded like the first but found no more than shallow voids where possibly a bit too much rock was removed during construction. Three panels from the end of the hall, he tore away a section that revealed three pipes exiting the rock. He tapped the last two hallway wall panels firmly then moved into the stairwell to try there.

He estimated the stairwell was eight feet across, about the same deep, and the wall had three paneled sections running from front to rear. Due to the nearby steps and handrail, he had a little more difficulty getting panels off, but was soon looking down a long, narrow, rough-hewn corridor. Without hesitation Jared strode into the cave-like passage and turned on his flashlight.

About two hundred feet along, the passage opened into a huge cavern in which was built an equally large cistern containing millions of gallons of water. "Lesson one, don't give up." He spoke softly, wondering if some higher being might be listening after all.

With the water problem solved survival was no longer an issue, but the effects of isolation and long periods of boredom were increasing. Eleven more weeks passed, during which he had torn off nearly every wall panel, leaving the elevators as the only obvious way to get to the other part of the station. He was no longer holding out any hope that someone might show up to reclaim the place, nor did he harbor further thoughts about this being a secret Earth outpost in space.

He had somehow been ripped from Earth and marooned. The question of 'why' continued to plague him, but he felt he might never have an answer. Two more weeks and his internship into being truly alone would be in its fifth month. He was almost ready to hold a celebration to reward himself for not yet going crazy.

"Okay, so I've got water, food and a place to sleep, but the scenery is getting old." He let another burst of the cold-water wash over him. "It's a wonder I haven't caught pneumonia doing this." He had become somewhat accustomed to the cold of the place and managed as long as he dressed well. He had, however, finally tired of being unbathed and found a way to release some of the water from an outlet near the reservoir. His weekly sojourn to the vat was both a blessing and a curse. Cleanliness was the blessing, but the cold blast of frigid liquid left him with the shivers for hours afterward. He often wondered what kept the water from freezing solid but that was another mystery he might never answer.

On his way back to his living area to climb beneath eight layers of blankets, he paused at one point in the hallway and stood looking at the floor. "If I was building a place like this and I were digging different levels, there would definitely be interconnecting tunnels," he spoke through chattering teeth. "If they're not along the wall, then what about the floor?" Jared pursed his lips then hurried back to his residence to get warm and prepare for his new campaign toward escape.

If it hadn't been for the warm blankets he'd found, he knew he would have been dead long ago. He spent a good deal of time under them warming his chilled bones and muscles. Several of them actually seemed to amplify his body temperature and hold the heat for a good while after he got up. It was right after his showers that this characteristic was most noticeable. Once a week he built a large fire using some of the blankets, packaging and other combustibles he had found. The fire not only helped his spirits but was a wonderful way to quickly dry his wash. Cooking now took far less material since he had determined what was needed to thaw and cook the food in the storage room. It wasn't until the following morning that he actually found the desire to leave his bed and descend down two levels below.

The floor panels were securely mounted, so dislodging them required a great deal more effort. By the end of the first day, he had only five panels ripped up and no sign of any passage. Looking as far down the corridor as he could, he estimated there must be about two hundred. A grimace crossed his face as he rolled his shoulders to flex sore muscles. He considered going to the other end as the adage, 'it's always in the last place you look' came to mind but decided to just take it methodically. He also knew there were panels in the various rooms that could push the number to well above three hundred.

"Well, it's not like I have any other pressing business."

It was the hope that salvation might lie on the other side of the installation that kept Jared working each new day. When not tearing up level one's floor, he began doing stretches and calisthenics to relieve periods of inactivity and to keep warm. On the third day of his twenty-seventh week of isolation, Jared finished his exercises and headed down to the first level. He had to step carefully as nearly half the length of the hall was exposed, leaving only the joists to walk on from the stairs.

Hopping from the last exposed joist to the next intact panel, Jared picked up the pry bar and with a deep inhale, jammed the pointed end under its edge. He was surprised when the panel's lip popped free with little effort and a smile creased his face. He pulled the bar out and with renewed excitement slammed it into the panel a few inches along. The bar severed the fasteners, slid in and downward like he had shoved the thin cudgel into butter. Just as abruptly his eyes widened as it hit something with a resounding ring that echoed in the hall.

"Hm," he grunted, and pulled the bar out. His last effort was followed by a hissing sound, and his face changed from surprise to concern. The hissing continued, followed by a popping sound like that of a metal container being filled with too much pressure. Jared moved a few paces back from the sound, and after a moment the panel began to bulge upward.

"Oh, crap!" He took another step back as popping sounds alerted him the remaining fasteners were giving way. With shocking suddenness, the panel blew apart and the pieces shot out in all directions. One caught him on the thigh leaving a painful gash in his leg. He stood there for a moment in shock before his eyes again registered alarm.

The panel directly below had begun to bulge, and he knew it was time to vacate the area. He realized he would never make it to the stairwell so turned and ran. One after another the panels buckled. Within moments, each succeeding segment violently exploded upward with increasing speed. Jared's slight head start was rapidly losing ground to the oncoming devastation. Shrapnel pelted everything, shattering the light panels on the ceiling, and pockmarking the walls. As he neared the room he had been in when he first found himself on the asteroid, he cut right, hoping he could make it through.

Jared's foot left the panel in front of the doorway just as the pressure ripped its fasteners away cleanly. His body was only partially through when the panel caught his foot and flipped him head over heels. His hip collided with the doorjamb as he cartwheeled, then he slammed into the floor. He groaned as the last few panels erupted, then silence.

Jared coughed and rolled onto his back.

"Oh, Jeez."

He lay there for some time before he checked his stinging forehead. There was a large bump, and a trace of blood crossed his fingers.

"Great." His attempt to sit up brought twinges of pain from his hip, and he gritted his teeth. Dust filled the air, and he coughed several more times.

Jared's leg was painful but still had good mobility. He forced himself to stand, walked to the door and looked out. The panels were all torn up. Not one was intact. In some places, chunks of the flooring were imbedded in the wall or ceiling, and he found it a good reason to give a half-hearted smile; only one had hit him. He used the new projections to make it from one joist to another, which was now even more difficult with all but a few of the blue lights eradicated. It took him nearly an hour to traverse the entire length of the hall. By the time he reached the stairs, he was exhausted. Finding out what had been revealed by the day's events would have to wait for later.

It was almost a full week before Jared felt well enough to descend again to level one. His hip was still sore and stiff but not like it had been just after he'd suffered the injury. Carefully stepping his way down the hall, he came to the place where the destruction had begun. Jared counted as he moved from one section to another, shining the flashlight downward each time. At the fifteenth the light illuminated a roughly hewn hole that had to be nearly twenty feet deep.

"*Yes!*"

He smiled. Inhaling the cold air deeply he silently told himself not to get his hopes too high. It was at this point he realized he hadn't brought anything to climb down with.

After returning to the third level, he decided not to attempt to enter the hole until the following day. As he passed the long row of windows, he noticed something outside a short distance from where the rock met the structure. Dim light from the nearby star allowed him to see an outline that was smooth, but in the blackness, there were no details. He chalked it up to one more of the little mysteries about his situation and departed, logging it away for later.

When he woke up he stretched his leg then went through his exercise routine. According to the marks on the wall, he had been in his prison for roughly six months. After dressing, he ascended to the fourth level and cut about a thirty-foot section of the electrical cable that was still hanging from the ceiling. Satisfied, he headed down to continue his quest.

In his pack was a container of water, all the items he had brought from Earth, the pistol he'd found in the office, two of the frozen food loaves and three rolled-up blankets for warmth in case he needed to sleep elsewhere. Due to the torn-up flooring, there were numerous choices for anchoring the cable. It took him awhile to secure the stiff material but once it was done, he gathered up his supplies and prepared to enter. Shining the flashlight downward, he again assessed the depth and condition of the passage then dropped down into the black hole.

When he reached the bottom, he used the flashlight again to ascertain his situation. Moving around in the dim light above had become easy, but here in the passage it was totally black. There was another problem compounding this foray into the unknown. Despite his careful and very limited use of the device, it was dimming more each time he used it.

The passage continued descending in the general direction of the canyon wall. It slanted mostly downward, but occasionally the path jogged back up toward the surface. Smooth-floored areas connected numerous rocky natural caves where footing was tentative at best.

In about half an hour he stepped from one of the excavations into an enormous cavern, and his eyes widened in amazement.

"Wow."

An eerily green glow filled the chamber, which appeared to be produced by some phosphorescent substance on the walls and ceiling. In several places tools and other equipment stood silently waiting. Before him a sturdy bridge spanned a deep, seemingly bottomless chasm. A smooth path had been cut through this cavern and a toppled scaffolding sat a way off to his left.

"The air's thinner here." He felt a tightening in his chest

"Amazing, somehow the life support system is even keeping all this supplied."

Several minutes later the path stopped at a door set into the rock. At first its heavy appearance led Jared to believe it might be to an air lock, but upon closer inspection he found the source of the cavern's air supply. A constant breeze of cool air came from a vent plate set into the rock above the door. Jared tapped the buttons on the adjacent control panel.

"Nothing, no surprise there." Unlike all the doors he had seen, this one had a lever at its center. It was hard to get it to budge, but then the door swung easily outward.

He stepped through, finding himself in a small unremarkable rectangular room, with a wide hallway leading into darkness. Beside him were two sets of elevator doors, one of which was sealed, closed with a sign affixed across the parting line.

Curious, he wasted no time moving on. "My ride outta' here might be just a…ugh."

He tripped over something on the floor and the flashlight clattered ahead. He retrieved it then scanned around to see what caused the fall. Two metal strips inset into the floor about three feet apart ran along the length of the corridor.

"Looks like some kind of railway."

Jared had not expected the corridor to be so long, but after a few minutes he was beginning to understand why the hall had rail-like grooves in the floor. A short time later he stopped and stared out a set of windows that overlooked the canyon's wide bottom. He could see a portion of the command center above and to the left on the opposite cliff face, and assumed the rail was for some form of shuttle. He looked in both directions from the center of the window area and estimated he had only traveled about a quarter of the hall's entire length. A short while later he came across a cart-like vehicle with seats for up to ten individuals, confirming his suspicion of the rails. He chose to ignore it, continuing toward the other end.

He passed another set of windows, stopped and flexed his gloved right hand. It felt clammy and he took a deep breath.

A grin creased his face. "It's warmer here."

Finally, after nearly half an hour, he entered another rectangular room with two sets of elevator doors and another of the sliding doors across from where he entered. The area was also illuminated by the dim, blue lighting, and he turned off the fading flashlight. He checked the elevators; they were not working. He tried the door and found it opened into a stairwell. There was no hesitation before he began his ascent to whatever lay above.

Twenty-two flights later the stairs ended before a door with a small metal plate fastened to it bearing a single line of unreadable characters. The portal opened into another long hall, lined on both sides by a series of doors. Those on the right were obviously for the movement of cargo and consisted of numerous overlapping panels, spaced about twenty feet apart. He saw no latches or controls, so he ignored them.

To his left the doors were wide but no taller than those in the command center and operated the same way. He stepped through the first door and saw various types of machinery but wasn't sure what purpose they might serve.

In the next room he found much the same except there were spherical objects on the wall with a ringed hole in them. Jared whipped out his flashlight, illuminating what was obviously a light-equipped helmet.

Hopefully the light works.

The clear lens was intact, but Jared could find no button or switch with which to turn it on. He put it on to see how the thing would fit and was stunned to see the area in front of him suddenly light up. He shielded his eyes from the unaccustomed intensity and smacked his thigh with his left hand in celebration of the discovery.

"Ahhhh!" His earlier wound was healing but objected to the abuse. He gritted his teeth and paused to let the pain subside.

He took a deep breath and then counted nineteen other helmets hanging neatly along one wall paired with several well-worn coveralls. Two benches and several lockers were full of small construction tools, supplies and safety gear.

In the third room, he stood in wide-eyed wonder at neatly arranged exercise and weight training equipment, very similar to those one would find on Earth.

"Oh yeah, good-bye boredom."

He now had something to do besides explore or sit around staring at dark walls, thinking about his mortality and life expectancy. So far, the day had brought several pleasant surprises.

Might be time to relocate. Only drawback is that no matter where I choose to live, I'll still have a lot of walking to do.

Four of the other five doors on the left side of the hall contained stored items just as the first had. The last room, which was also larger than the others, contained what appeared to be a machine and fabrication shop. Several of the machines had been abandoned while in the middle of a project. A lathe-like device had a partially turned shaft on it, while another had been etching out a cavity in a rectangular piece of metal. Jared couldn't be sure, but from what he could see it looked as though the stylus used was some type of laser. He felt in no hurry to look at all the items in detail at the moment, so left to check the door at the end of the hall.

Once through, the light from the helmet illuminated a large room with railings at the far side and a solid wall some fifty feet away to his left. He walked in and looked around the corner to his right and found he was on the opposite side of the large cargo doors. He moved to the railing and looked around. The beam of light revealed part of a vast room with a metallic surface approximately twenty feet below. He aimed the light upward; he could barely make out another smooth surface high above. Straight in front of him showed him nothing. There was a gap in the railing that led to a small platform about four feet square, which extended over the area below.

A flight of creaky stairs led down into the darkness and the first step was loose. Here, though still cool, the temperature was far more pleasant than that in the living section.

"Yeah, definitely time to move."

He decided to suspend his explorations and retraced his steps back toward the main complex. His memories drifted to Earth and his home. He did miss his family, and even Sandra would have been welcome if she somehow appeared. His whole desire was to return home, and yet he often found himself asking why. At these times Sandra was on the other end of the scale again, along with the day-to-day drudgery of work and bills, dealing with girlfriends and other problems. He shook his head and shoved the thoughts of home away as he entered the long corridor to the hangar. He paused again at the transport vehicle and after looking it over decided to try to get it working, otherwise this trip would get very monotonous.

The next day Jared lowered himself over the edge with one of the cables. He had little trouble reaching the bottom and began his search of the area in earnest. He was able to make out a sliver of light some distance away and headed in that direction. He came across a large, long object supported by five sturdy struts. Though his helmet light would not illuminate the entire thing he was quite sure he had found a spaceship.

Still, more curious about the distant light, he proceeded in that direction and found that an incredibly large, heavy composite curtain separated him from what was on the other side. Giving up on that for the moment, he completed his inspection of the area he had access to and found two more large vessels. He paced off the perimeter to determine how big the hangar was and came up with a rectangle that was 345.5 paces wide and 816.5 paces long.

He roughly calculated that the hangar was one thousand feet wide and close to twenty-five hundred feet long. An area at one end that was elevated about fifteen to twenty feet prevented him from adding it to his measurement. The three ships took up very little space in the hangar, being only about one hundred and fifty feet or so long and perhaps sixty feet wide. From what he could see, they were ugly with few symmetrical lines. They looked like a squat collection of containers affixed to a central thick spine with a personnel compartment on one end, and propulsion units on the other. The engines looked akin to something dreamed up by Hollywood special effects with piping, conduits and tanks exposed, though a few places did have some plating. The front section was the only portion that was entirely plated and looked as if it had been cannibalized and stuck on to replace whatever had been there originally.

At least he had found something to get him away from the deserted station if he could just find a way to operate them.

Over the next two days, he explored numerous small rooms, and on the third day found one full of control panels and computer consoles. He spent the remainder of the day studying the panels, buttons, switches, and the few schematics within the room. Several of the panels had power as some small green, amber, blue, and orange/red lights were illuminated. None of them would respond to his touch, however so he sat down to try and get a reaction from the computer, with no results.

Several more days passed as he divided his time between more searching and spending time in the control room. He was planning to go back to the other side to take a shower and restock in the next day or two and was hoping for some results before going. Suddenly, a deep humming sound began filling the entire area and he leaned back, away from the computer. It was not loud enough to be annoying but sounded like a deep purring from an enormous feline.

He had been trying combinations on the keyboard. He stood and walked toward the wall with all the panels on it. Several of the amber lights were flashing as were one of the blue and two of the orange/red ones.

He had no idea what the different colors meant to these people, so had no way to know which buttons not to push. He chose to go for it. Clenching his left hand, he pushed one of the buttons next to the uppermost amber light. He heard what sounded like evenly spaced, giant-thumping footsteps echoing through the hangar and two very loud explosive popping sounds.

Jared closed his eyes tight waiting for the whole place to explode. He opened them slowly to light filtering into the small room and he was pleased to see hundreds of circular fixtures mounted on the ceiling far above, filling the hangar with bright, white light.

The following day while Jared was again trying to get other systems running, he heard a loud series of pulses and dashed into the large hangar to see what was operating. To his surprise and joy the large curtain was retracting. It suddenly stopped with a raucous, grinding clamor, leaving a gap about fifty feet wide. Before him was the most incredible sight he had yet encountered.

On the hangar floor was a huge white vessel with the silhouette of a stylized bird. It looked about half again as long as a 747, with an equally scaled wingspan and three to four times the volume. It rested on its winglets and turned-down nose, with its tail rising into the air. No sign of an entry point was visible across the fuselage nor were there any seams, panel lines, or even a view port. The surface of the vessel possessed no markings of any kind and when Jared touched it near the nose, it felt silky, smooth, and warm. Tapping on the surface produced no sound whatsoever and he noticed it gave a little, like the flesh on his forearm, but was otherwise firm.

I wonder if this could be a creature instead of a ship.

He dismissed the idea.

It surely would have awakened by now.

In the weeks following the great discovery, Jared found little to celebrate. He desperately wanted to find a way to access the white ship but was losing hope. He had looked around the interior of the three ugly freighters and as far as he could tell they were operable. If he had a choice though he wanted to try and take the white ship, as it seemed far more advanced and much easier to look at.

He doubted that those who had built the station had also built the white ship, and from the way it was sitting he figured they had found it and somehow towed it in. It didn't appear to be damaged, but the strangest thing Jared noticed was that it cast no shadow nor did any shadow show up on its surface.

About a month after he got the hangar lights on, he figured out how to operate the small personnel lift, which allowed him to get to the upper level of the hangar without climbing the cable. Further along the upper deck he also discovered that part of the floor was a cargo lift used to get items up to the eight large cargo bays. About that time, it occurred to him that if he did finally get off the outpost, he would need resources to barter or trade so he began collecting all the items that might be of value. Now, collections of cases and equipment sat between the white ship and the three freighters where they could be loaded easily into whatever vessel he eventually chose to take.

Fortunately, a few days later he opened another of the doors along the perimeter of the main bay and found eleven vehicles that would have been used for servicing and loading spaceships. The first one he tried to start seized up and he figured it was because he had done something wrong. However, he did the same with a second one and it worked fine; that is, until he ran it up under one of the freighters. No matter how hard he tried, he could not get it unstuck.

After that debacle he took several days to practice, well away from anything else, until he felt fully competent on the oddly configured controls. The six tugs, as he chose to call them, were small, one-person vehicles with permanently attached, long trailers with many ball bearing rollers across their surface. They were not unlike those he had used while working for an air transport company.

Of the remaining five, two were very large with elevating platforms which he left untouched until he had learned all he could about the smaller ones. The last three were larger than the tugs but about half the size of the huge lifts and resembled forklifts. After spending training time on one of the vehicles, or moving cargo around, Jared spent time walking a perimeter around the white ship trying to figure out its secrets.

Upon moving to the hangar, he continued his habit of marking the wall to keep track of time. One morning, he rubbed his eyes and rolled toward the wall to look at the date he'd marked the previous day. He had used November 28th as his first day of reckoning after escaping from the glass container.

The thought had occurred that he may have been in suspended animation—if that were true, he might have been in that box for years, if not centuries. He hated the idea because it meant his family might be long dead, and not even an Earth to go back to.

He sat up, made another mark and sighed. Two more days would be the beginning of his ninth month on the dark, cold rock. He tried not to think about the fact that he could be stuck on it for many years, or maybe forever.

He gathered his dirty laundry and prepared for his weekly trip to fill his water containers and take the bone-chilling shower that he hated, though better than suffering through his own smell. After the first few weeks of being marooned, he started to realize just how firmly entrenched he was in the things his parents had taught him.

They would be proud of me for not giving up, making do and staying somewhat civilized.

He felt he could appreciate far more what his father had gone through while a prisoner of war, at least the isolation part. He gathered more cargo for the first half of the day and now he was tired. He would have no desire to work after his shower and preferred to spend at least part of one day a week clean, and just resting.

Before leaving for the other side of the canyon, he returned to the hangar floor to get one of the water jugs he'd left. The floor of hangar one, near the ugly freighters, was cluttered with the considerable amount of material and crates he had gathered from various locations. He had to walk around some, duck under others and in one place, to avoid a lengthy detour, actually climb over one grouping to get to hangar two.

In the distance he could clearly see the white ship, unchanged from when he'd found it.

He headed in that direction, hit the crown of his head and swore loudly. He rarely used vulgarity, as much from his mother's aversion to it as to the fact that he felt it far more intelligent sounding if he expressed himself in a more articulate fashion, even when angered.

Math and formal literature had never been his strong point, but he cared how he sounded to other people. In his opinion, those who felt the need to use such expletives did so because they had precious little else in their vocabulary to use as ammunition in getting their message across.

After chastising himself, he rubbed his head and started forward again, looking up to make sure the way was clear.

He stopped short and did a double take at a small change he noticed.

The white ship was in his line of sight and a rectangular, shadowed area had appeared on its side just ahead of the wing. Jared walked closer and discovered it was an opening.

Immediately forgetting any thought of going to the other side of the canyon, he ran toward the vessel. Though the nose was resting on the floor, the opening was still nearly two stories above the surface. He would need one of the large lifts to get to it. He had only driven one of the large vehicles twice to get familiar with its controls, but he did not hesitate to use it now in his excitement.

As usual, it took time to get the behemoth started and he worried, fearing the opening might disappear just as fast as it had appeared. Once he got the vehicle started, he drove slowly to avoid any mishap. His impatient desire to get inside the vessel, and the care needed to do no damage to anything, including the ship, left him with a dull headache by the time he pulled to a stop about twenty feet away.

An enclosed cage was all that existed for an operator's compartment, and it rose with the cargo platform. Jared raised the deck, estimating the height of the opening, slowly moving the vehicle closer. When he stopped, the platform was about six inches away from the white hull and a bit less than a foot below the threshold. Cautiously peering through the doorway, he half expected some strange alien creature to spring out and maul him to death.

"I think I've seen one too many science fiction movies," he breathed, addressing the ship. The interior was well lit and as white as the exterior, also showing no sign of shadow or detail, except for a number of doorways. From the opening he walked down a short hall about four feet across which opened into another long hall extending both fore and aft. The longer hall was wider, with a higher ceiling. To his left were three doors, one at the end and one on either side. He chose to check the one at the very end first. When he got within a few feet it snapped open so quickly it startled him.

Inside was a room which narrowed gradually, but was void of any furnishings, equipment, or windows. Jared walked aft through every other door he could find, except one that would not open, and found the interiors the same.

Returning to the front of the empty hulk, Jared paused to consider what might have happened to leave such a magnificent ship in such a state. He considered the possibility that the builders of the station may have found their way on board and, unable to get it to operate, had stripped it. If that were true it would be a great disappointment. While this thought was filtering through his head, he placed his hand on the smooth wall. A sudden jolt blasted through him, and he was thrown back several feet, landing on the floor.

Jared blinked several times and rubbed his head. His ears were buzzing, but he forgot his own discomfort to focus on the room again. It was now filled with consoles across the front and along both sides. A center console extended from the front one about six feet and even more amazing, he could now see out into the hangar.

A calming, gentle, almost imperceptible hum permeated the interior. Four high-back chairs completed the furnishings, but he found it difficult to focus on anything due to the whiteness of it all and the lack of contrasting shadows or colors.

As he was leaving the room, he noticed there was no longer a tilt to the floor.

He returned to the exterior opening and found it was now about eight feet above the lift. If he wanted out, he'd have to jump. Unable to see underneath the ship, he had no idea whether it was sitting on the surface or hovering, either way, there was no motion. The nose was now raised high off the floor. He re-checked the many rooms and found that they too had become fully furnished. He was still unable to access the door at the very back of the ship, but another opening had appeared which had not been there before. A set of stairs led downward into a cavernous area he was sure was used for holding cargo.

He spent a short amount of time walking its perimeter, but nothing of interest was contained within. Returning to the front upper deck, he wondered how one would operate such a vessel when the consoles showed no obvious controls, switches, or lights. With the absence of shadow, it was even difficult to see the chairs, everything blending into the background. It was mostly by touch he confirmed they were there.

Jared decided to call the room "The Bridge" and moved forward to sit in the front left seat. As he did so his hand touched the console, and again he felt the shock pulse through him. This time however, it pounded in his head more intensely and he stumbled, falling to the floor.

A wave of nausea swept over him, and he struggled to the outer door. For some reason he did not want to vomit inside the white ship and jumped to the lift platform where he tossed what little was in his stomach. Several minutes passed while he collected himself and took a number of deep breaths. Though not feeling well, he raised the lift back to within a foot of the door and stepped inside. Again, he felt the nausea well up in his throat and he backed out.

"Okay, so what do I do now?" Jared stated irritably, though it dawned on him that the words he spoke sounded strange.

"The Companion needs rest."

A disembodied and androgynous voice seemed to come from everywhere.

Jared froze. "Who's there?" he asked in definite English but received no reply. He tried again. He didn't know how, but he was using words both familiar and alien at the same time. "Who's there?"

"I am One."

"Okay, that tells me a lot."

Is the ship talking to me?

He sighed. "Why do I feel sick?"

The voice emanated again from somewhere inside the vessel.

"The Companion is experiencing the effects of post neural interface transfer shock which seems to be aggravated by the phased magnetic plasma envelope."

"Um, I just woke up?"

"The Companion needs rest."

"Gotcha, I'm off to rest," Jared said, indicating his intent by pointing his thumb over his shoulder before turning away and getting into the operator's cage.

Orion Comparison 2

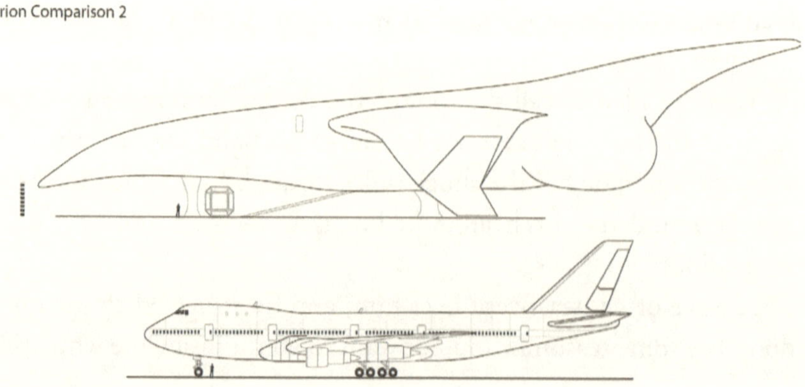

CHAPTER TWO

Discoveries

*"Live not by expectation, for to do so is
to set oneself up for disappointment."*

Jared had no intention of going to sleep, planning instead to head for the main control center on the opposite side of the canyon. He was brought up short as he reached for the lift's controls, noticing he could now understand the writing on the dashboard. Several minutes went by as he tried to puzzle out this new development and the more he thought, the more crowded his mind felt.

Suddenly excitement hit him, and he hurried to discover more about the facility, where he was and perhaps why.

Once back in the main station he stopped momentarily to read the sign across the elevator door. It read:

DANGER

ENVIRONMENTAL SEAL INTEGRITY
COMPROMISED. DO NOT ACCESS.

During his walk along the canyon causeway, he found he now had no problem with German, which surprised him considering how callously he'd paid attention or studied. Incredibly, another language was now open to him, and it might very well lead to his salvation from his cold prison. A word sprang into the forefront as he wondered about the people who had once lived here and spoken it.

Ilirian.

"Ilirian," he said in a reflective whisper. "Hm."

As he reached the landing of the stairs at the command level, it occurred to him that the voice had addressed him in neither English nor Ilirian. He opened the door and moved across to the large windows gazing with more interest now.

"Adari," he spoke as his eyes fell on one of the distant stars. "That's the second one. Adarian, language of the Adari." It also dawned how he had gained access. It had been a single word in English, spoken in pain and frustration in the right place, that had caused the white ship to open. It seemed the download was a dual exchange. However it worked, Jared was learning new languages, and learning them fast.

He chuckled, "Shyr'st, the Adarian word for open." Pronounced with the emphasis on the "Sh," it came so very close to the expletive he'd used when he'd hit his head.

Turning about, he walked the short hall to the command center and sat down at the nearest operating terminal. The keypad had ten keys corresponding to numerals representing the values zero through nine, and eight keys which had computation symbols on them. Four of the symbols indicated now familiar basic math operations, but the other four were far more complicated. Thirty-two other keys, slightly separated from the numerical pad, made up the Ilirian alphabet. Nearly two dozen others, primarily punctuation, made up the rest of the keyboard.

Jared tried numerous key combinations with no luck. After the forty-third invalid entry prompt his earlier enthusiasm had faded.

"Well, I may know the language, but not the technology." He sat back and rubbed the bridge of his nose. "Maybe I should go get some sleep." As he pushed himself out of the chair, he noticed a cord draped over the back of the monitor. He pulled on it and found the other end to be a microphone.

"Great, now all I need is music and I can do Karaoke." He said the last word loudly and with sarcasm. He placed the microphone back in its holder and turned away. He brought himself up short and turned back, eyes doing a double take on the screen.

"...and do Karaoke."

Invalid command.

Jared picked up the microphone. "I wonder," he said, moving it close to his mouth. "Um, computer?"

There was no response and no change on the screen.

"Oh, come on, does everything here have to be so damn cryptic?" Scanning the device's surface for a trigger button, he found a small flush pad that activated the microphone.

"Computer...?" Jared stated tentatively.

Terminal CS-5 online

When the words appeared on the monitor, Jared sat back down. He had no idea how to construct commands the computer would consider valid.

He threw up his palms. "Huh, let's try. System Access"

Ready

At this prompt Jared's spirits instantly blossomed but then fell just as quickly as the prompt expanded.

Terminal 5 is a secure command I/O. please provide access clearance code.

"Ahhh." Jared grunted in frustration then shouted out the first numbers that came to his mind. "12/20/1980."

Access code verified. System ready.

Jared stared at the screen in disbelief. "No way! Huh, man this situation gets more bizarre by the minute."

He shook his head. "How can my birth date be the right code?" Jared forced the anomalies aside and focused on getting more information. "Station Status?"

Specify

"Where's the crew?"

Only one crew member accounted for. Remaining crew disposition unknown.

So, the station's computer considers me a crew member.
"Last log entry?"

Specify Log

"Commanding Officer's Log."

Searching.... Accessing

> Station Chief's Log, Cycle 4765/7/17. News reached us today that the Drakstrad has fallen. No member of the royal family apparently survived.
>
> Civil war has broken out on many of the Commonwealth's worlds. All area exploration operations have been terminated and all government ships and personnel recalled by the Hanshakar. I'm sure the Nurians, Tirodyn, or Kelovi will try to take advantage of the chaos. I expect that's part of the reason for the recall.
>
> The last serviceable ship is ready to depart but doesn't have room for all remaining personnel. Four of my staff and I have volunteered to remain behind and enter cryo so the others can return to their homes. The scheduled fuel transport ship did not arrive on time, and I doubt it will get here at all. Three old Hedmar TR-745 class freighters arrived two days ago, out of essential supplies, and two with many system failures. Their crews are also returning with the Eirgon.
>
> The captain of one of the freighters was not at all happy about leaving his ship behind. He said he had a lot of valuable salvage aboard. I suspect that he

has more than just salvage, but that matters little now. It's also quite a waste that all our new replacement parts and supplies will never be used.

Finally, I regret that we weren't able to discover the secrets of the recovered alien spacecraft. This will be my last log entry. I hope rescue comes soon. I fear that many will suffer in this great disaster. Farewell....

End of Log

"System Access"

Ready

"What is the current date?"

Cycle 4869/3/09

"What is the Drakstrad?"

Ruling class of the Ilirian Commonwealth

"What is the Ilirian Commonwealth?"

Three hundred twenty-seven planetary units ruled over by the Drakstrad.

"Current status of the Ilirian Commonwealth?"

Unknown

"Historical data."

Time period

"Most recent."

Local, Regional or General

"General."

Political, Geographical, Demographic, Social,

"Stop! Damn, just give a political overview."

Accessing historical database, general political summary of the Drakstrad. Existing data has not been updated for 104.4 cycles.

"Run last update."

Running . . . the beginning of the Ilirian Common-wealth coincides with the beginning of the current Ilir-ian calendar. As of 4765/5/12, Thoris Hulnmar Riovan, Imperial High Seat of the Drakstrad, has ruled over the Ilirian Commonwealth for the past 27 cycles. The Drakstrad Counsel consists of 24 individuals directly descended from Tyaron Hasis Myrstrad, who became the first Drakstrad ruler or the heads of the 24 houses created during the Commonwealth Charter Conven-tion. Those houses are known as the Havasra.

Jared repeated the translation of Havasra into English in a curious whisper, "Gold court."

At the time Myrstrad took power, the Ilirian Common-wealth consisted of 23 member worlds and one col-ony. Current planetary membership is 327. Estimated population is more than 1,708,571,000,000. Estimate resulted from Census of 4760, though it is deemed unreliable.

The current Commonwealth is divided into 24 regions, each one overseen by one of the members of the Drakstrad council. Council members are called by the title of Thal. Governors of planetary systems are cho-sen by the region's Thal, although must be approved by both the Council and the High Seat. Members of the Council must be able to trace their ancestry back to one of the original 24 member worlds. To rise to the High Seat, a Thal must undergo the Shi-dai Su'lar.

The Commonwealth has three major political neighbors.

1. The Tirodyn Triarchy lies 4.700...

"Stop!" Jared realized after listening to the brief history that he didn't know anything about what the Commonwealth was like at present. According to the last log entry of the station chief, the Drakstrad's current ruling family had been killed. He thought it unlikely that all those with royal blood had been eradicated.

After such an event, it was likely many of the member worlds would be at odds with each other. Transportation, manufacturing, and other industries might be far less than they once had been, which might account for no rescue vessel ever reaching the outpost.

"Are there any inventory lists for property and stores on the station, or cargo on the three transports?"

Inventory lists for government property do exist. Lists are filed by type. Please specify type and value level. Manifests for cargo on board freighters are not available.

"Are the printers functional?"

Print station two is online. Print station one is not currently connected to station system. Print station three is out of ink.

"Print list pertaining to food stores and locations."

Printing.

The old printer began discharging paper, noisily rasping as it operated. Jared picked up the end and noticed that smears and blank areas occurred frequently but most of the list was readable. Satisfied with what he was getting, he turned his attention back to the computer.

"Display base floorplans."

Specify Level

"Command level."

Improper designation

"Level one."

Displaying.

A multi-colored schematic of the floor one level above Jared's current location appeared on the screen. It showed the equipment rooms for the communication's array and several defense turrets. Also included on level one were two emergency docking modules.

"Level two."

Displaying.

Level two was larger than the one above. It included the main observation area, station chief's office, the main control room in which he sat, a conference room, a latrine, a storage room, and an equipment room.

"Skip levels three and four, show level five."

Displaying.

This had been the level he had first been on after escaping from the cryo chamber. The two rooms, each containing twenty-four casket-shaped containers, were identified in red except for five which were in yellow, and one of those had a blue dot at its center. The four skeletal remains stood undisturbed, and the schematic listed all but one of the devices as offline.

Jared had thought earlier that the computer considered him to be one of the crew. The fact that his birth date had matched a valid security code made him even more curious as well as feeling eerie.

"List the five personnel assigned to cryosleep."

Searching.

Taldimar. Sulas/ Station Chief (M).
Ner'yol. Lanys/ Assistant First (M).
Ozvar. Sha'thra/ Assistant second (F).
Cyan'dlyr. Gyas'red/ Security First (M).
K'yasta. Valia/ Maintenance First (F).

"Status of each person on the list."

Taldimar. Sulas/ Station Cheif—Cryo system Malfunction. Deceased. Ner'yol. Lanys/ Assistant First—Cryo system Malfunction. Deceased. Ozvar. Sha'thra/ Assistant second—Cryo system Malfunction. Deceased. Cyan'dlyr. Gyas'red/ Security First—Current location. deck two room one. K'yasta. Valia/ Maintenance First—Cryo system Malfunction. Deceased.

Not just weird. Unbelievable.
"What is the system status on Gyas'red's cryochamber?"

Cryo unit 353-791-04, status: currently inactive, malfunction in life support regulator in 27 em–har if reactivated.

"The computer thinks I'm this Gyas'red Cyan'dlyr. I'm not... Gyas'red..." Jared sat confused. "Gyas'red, Jared...no way! Cyan'dlyr...Chandler...what the hell is going on here?!"

Jared stood; eyes blurry from fatigue. He snatched up the list, started out of the office, then stopped.

"The computer has me listed as this Gyas'red so won't likely have any clue as to how I came to be here. I not only got zapped here, but I also took some other being's place in a failing cryo chamber on a dead space station."

Jared had thought this was a bad dream at first, but that had changed to grudging acceptance. With the discovery of the white ship, he had become excited, but now he was questioning reality.

He walked out of the room. His head was spinning from lack of real sleep since finding his way onto the white ship. Perhaps things would be easier to deal with after a good rest. He headed toward the stairwell and as he passed the windows on level four, he again saw the smooth-lined silhouette jutting out from the dark rock. He decided to come back after he had rested and check it out with a pair of optic-magnifiers he'd found during his searches. After his long trek back to the hangar area and despite how tired he was, it was some time before he fell asleep.

Jared awoke several times, and each time struggled to get back to sleep. He finally gave up and feeling somewhat better he retrieved the pair of optical magnifiers and headed back to the long row of windows. It took him a minute or two to find the spot. Placing the optical magnifier before his eyes, he set the unit against the transparent wall and adjusted the magnification and light amplitude. What came into view was so startling he almost dropped the device.

Outside, embedded nearly halfway into the rock face, was the back end of a little red sports car. It took some time to remember all that happened that long ago night, and he wondered what had become of the individual driving it. He finally decided he didn't want to know.

He returned to the hangar and stood at the railing. He gazed out over the expansive area. On the far side of the room sat the white ship like some huge, alabaster sculpture. He turned to his right, walked to the lift, set his pack on the floor and pressed the down button twice. The small, railed platform lurched slightly then began its slow descent. He looked off to his left where he could see the massive hangar doors which provided access to the asteroid base's docking facility.

They would be his last big obstacle before he could leave. Just before the lift reached the bottom, Jared picked up his bundle and hopped off. Behind him the platform hit the floor with a jolt causing a reverberating echo throughout the immense room. Without looking back, he strode toward the far side.

Piles of crates, boxes and equipment now surrounded the white ship, waiting to be loaded. The two vehicles had been invaluable in unloading the three freighters and gathering other cargo from the several storage compartments around the hangar bay. He gazed at the alien craft. Describing it as 'awesome' seemed an understatement. It was unlike any other machine made for travel he had ever seen. The shape of it was fluid, its outlines graceful and no shadows touched it, as if light passed directly through its hull. The landing gear were merely extensions of the smooth underside. The gentle, almost musical hum that emanated from all around it seemed to be calling him, as if to say, "Come home."

It was a strange sensation, but not uncomfortable or alien. The most intriguing thing about the vessel was that even though he could see out from inside, there was still no sign of a window on the outside. Placing his bundle on top of a nearby crate, he climbed into the cab of one of the two loaders and turned on the power. Then getting out, he climbed onto the loading platform and pushed a lever forward. The platform rose upward, carrying him toward the main hatch. He released the lever, stopping a few inches below the opening.

He stepped inside. "Ship?"

"Ready."

"Who am I?"

"You are the Companion."

"Companion?" Jared puzzled. "Who are you?"

"I am One."

"What does that mean?"

"I am One."

"Do you have a designation?"

"I am One."

"One," Jared repeated at the same time. "Yes, I know. Okay, so do you have a name?"

"Is a name of importance to the Companion?"

"Well, I guess so," Jared hesitated. "Yeah, it is."

"Since it is of significance to the Companion, I will assume a name. What name would the Companion select?"

Jared stood in silence considering.

What should I name it? Enterprise? No way. Some place out of history. Bunker Hill? Nope, too long. Wait. Mythology. Uh huh, constellations!

"Orion?" Jared waited a moment for the ship to respond.

Nothing.

He began again. "I am One…"

"Ready."

"I have decided to name you 'Orion'."

"Name 'Orion' has been added to memory. Elaborate on Orion."

"It is a word used on the world of my birth to describe one of what we call 'constellations'. Constellations are groupings of…"

"Constellations are groups of stars and other astronomical phenomena which form patterns in the terrestrial heavens, and for many centuries have been used for terrestrial navigation. Designations for these patterns are derived from Greek mythology. That one which is called Orion is named for a mythological giant who was handsome and a mighty hunter."

Jared felt the name fit. A white giant that was awe-inspiring and would most likely prove very much like the great bird of prey it resembled. However, he was shocked that the ship knew about the Greeks.

"Orion?"

"Ready."

"How do you know all that?"

"It is contained in your memory files."

"You didn't just give me knowledge of the languages then; you downloaded my memories."

"Yes, a concurrent data transfer."

Jared felt invaded, violated for a moment before realizing that such a feeling was pointless. Whatever its motivation, the ship had helped him. "What now?"

"Specify."

"Where do I go…? I mean, do I have a room? How do I get my stuff on board? I don't know where to start."

"There are no restrictions on Companion. You may choose living accommodations and arrangements. Access for oversized objects is found on lower level."

Jared realized he had no difficulty intermixing English for words that had no Adarian equivalent. For some reason he knew Orion would only speak in Adarian and also preferred to be addressed in that language as well.

A search of each room revealed there were no sharp angles or corners. Walls, floors, and ceilings flowed together as if the entirety of Orion had been poured in some gigantic mold. Cabinets, chairs, beds, tables, consoles, lockers, and numerous other furnishings were all part of the same whole fluid mass. On the port side of the main hall, just aft of the bridge, was a room Jared selected for himself. It contained a sleeping surface which was similar in dimension to a standard, full-sized bed. It was also quite comfortable considering it was made out of the same material as the hull. The head of the bed was against the forward wall. About six feet separated the foot of the bed from the opposite wall out of which extended a number of shelves and two sets of four drawers. Another door next to the bed on the forward wall led to a small bathroom with shower, sink, storage cabinets and a waste disposal chute.

Another door directly across the hall opened into a space set up as an office. A large white desk near the aft wall, three chairs, several cabinets and a console completed the room's decor. Jared stood for some time, taking in the sight. Living in a ship that was all white on the outside would be no problem, but nothing except white on the inside might become quite disturbing after a while.

"Orion?"

"Ready."

"Is it possible to change the color inside this ship?"

"Yes."

"Please change the color to green."

The entire inside of the ship began to flow with color as it ran through the spectrum and finally settled on a bright green hue.

"Can colors be selected for localized areas?"

"Yes."

"Change the color of this desk to a dark, wood brown."

"Define wood."

"Ignore the wood part, just make it dark brown."

"Specify area."

"The surface and down the side to here," Jared said, indicating the point where the desktop flowed back under to the supports. The color began to flow again until a glossy dark brown tone had replaced the green. "Please return the rest of the ship back to its original white." Again, the ship ran with color, and then back to white, except for the desk which had remained dark brown.

"Cool," Jared said, then stopped with an exhale remembering his sister Sandra's view of his fashion sense and related subjects. He knew that here her opinion mattered little but it still irritated him. "Okay, so I'll take a bit of time to think about what I'd like instead of just throwing colors on the walls like an adolescent finger painting.

He shrugged. "I'll have to play more with this later."

Back in his chosen room he undressed quickly and started the water. After nine months of freezing cold showers, he was impatient and wasn't going to wait any longer. He entered while the water was still tepid. His muscles relaxed and tension eased as the hot water flowed over his body. The shower, being all white, was a little disorienting. Jared was at times unable to distinguish where the walls and floor joined in the steamy air. Dropping the soap twice, and then finding it again proved interesting, since it was also white. "Argh, Orion make the shower floor blue."

"Complying."

The crew of the outpost, having departed in a great hurry had left many personal items behind, including toiletries, for which he was very thankful. The skin on his hands was quite wrinkled when he finally stepped out. While drying off he realized he had no clean clothes and was loathe to put what he had been wearing back on. So, for the next half-hour he walked around wearing only the towel.

Jared found he had little trouble shifting back and forth between Adarian, Ilirian, and English. Preferences had also developed quickly as to which forms of measure he wanted to use. No word or idea expressed a unit less than one myir in the Adarian system of time measurement. Jared wasn't sure yet how long a myir was, though he felt it was quite long. The Adarian language had been downloaded into his head, but only very few details on their culture. The smallest whole unit of measure for distance in Adarian, the ald, was also considerable. He drew these conclusions from the few facts he did know. Speed seemed to be the only exception to the rule having very minute increments though Orion measured it in percentages instead of something like miles per hour. He did not know how the ald and myir correlated to measurements on Earth, but he planned on finding out when the chance arose. The ald seemed to be used primarily for distances in space and any distance less than an ald was indicated as a decimal.

Orion's laundry facilities were in the forward area of the medical room. After depositing his only set of clothes in the opening that was clearly a washer, he retraced his steps and began looking around. He stopped next to the first of two exam tables and placed his hand on the surface which was firm but had a leather-like feel to it. Aft, he could see the entry to the restrooms and decontamination showers. To his left just fore of the door to the hall was a U-shaped desk sporting a computer terminal. Aft of the door along the inner wall sat the two consoles used to operate the medical scanner. Mounted on the ceiling between the two exam tables was the housing for the diagnostic mechanism with several hanging attachments. On the outer wall were three narrow, hospital style beds with integrated monitors. The medical facility was well laid out and though not large had ample room for the care of at least five patients. Two transparent supply cabinets rounded out the furnishings. Turning from the exam table he entered a small room next to the laundry, which was a surprisingly well-stocked medical pantry. Back in the main area, he paused glancing at everything. He felt a bit bewildered.

Except for some of the Xaxilor design elements, all this could easily fit in any hospital, laundromat or bathroom on earth.

From there he walked aft for a quick look into the hygiene area and stopped at a counter on the back wall between the toilets and showers. "Orion, what is the function of this?"

"An incinerator for disposing of contaminated garments and other forms of biohazard."

"Good to know," Jared chuckled, "I'll remember not to stick any extremities in."

"There is no danger to lifeforms, operation is disengaged until companion is clear of event horizon."

Jared smiled, raising his hand, thumb up, "cool." With a shake of his head, he exited the medical bay and headed toward the bow.

The next door on the port side led into a square room with more Xaxilor items. What were obviously space suits hung on the aft wall, four in all, and there was nothing truly alien in their design, coloring or material as far as he could tell. "Orion."

"Yes Companion."

"When I first came on board none of these items were present, where were they?"

"In storage."

"Storage, how does that actually work?"

"While active functions are dormant due to a lack of suitable companion, all non-native elements are put in a shielded magnetic field storage mode. This allows the lowest power output to be used during dormancy."

"Were you conscious this entire time?"

"Yes."

"Wow, didn't that get a little tedious?"

"No, programming does not provide for such an unproductive use of time."

"I guess that's a plus," he said, eyebrows raised, then looked at the EVA suits on the wall. "Do you have the ability to dock with other ships?"

"Yes, docking orifices can be initiated at almost any point on outer surfaces with the exception of bow and stern focus points and directly around the core."

"Ok," Jared stood in silence for a time letting all that sink in and realized he had a lot more questions, but for the moment felt a bit overwhelmed. "I guess I'll label this the EVA room."

"Designation noted and logged."

"Thank you."

"You are welcome, Companion."

It felt natural to speak to Orion as if it were a person, though he couldn't put his finger on the reason why.

Lockers, formed like almost everything else on the vessel and from the same material as the ship itself, lined the outer hull wall and the one to the right of the door. Everything was white except the obviously Xaxilor equipment. It was still difficult for his human mind to wrap itself around the idea that he was literally standing inside a construct made from solar plasma. Approaching the row of lockers along the outer hull wall he touched the surface gently. The same warmth that permeated the rest of Orion was present here too. After a moment of reflection, he turned to the rear wall and approached a Xaxilor bundle, "Orion."

"Yes, Companion."

Jared placed his hand on a metallic clasp, "Would you change the color of the lockers so they are similar to this?"

The now familiar swirling of colors began and its rainbow of hues shifted until the white was replaced by a shiny chrome finish. "Is this satisfactory?"

Jared grinned, "Very, but I think the mirror finish is a bit over the top. If possible, can it be toned to look like…" he trailed off wondering how to explain what he had in mind.

"Are you referring to brushed steel?" Orion asked.

Jared was caught off guard, "How did you…?"

"Simple color, material and textural references were recorded during the first neural transfer."

Jared smiled broadly, "Nice," and watched as the surface dulled as much more subtle swirling effects left very realistic brushed marks. Standing in the middle of the room he took in the new aesthetic and his smile deepened. *So cool.*

Most of the lockers were empty, except for two which each held a tool that was the most alien looking device he had yet come across. He lifted one out and found it was surprisingly light for its bulky size. "Orion, what are these?"

"Plasma torches."

Jared closed the door and moved to his right, opening the remaining four lockers which held various small storage containers.

More things to look through at a later time.

He turned his attention to the opposite wall. Neatly folded into transparent covers were two large bundles made out of a canvas-like material. On the face of one he read the Xaxilor inscription: **MULTI-CLIMATE SHELTER.** The rest of the wall was covered with a variety of other tools and small survival equipment.

He paused in the main hall before heading into what Orion called the power room. This room was located at the aft-most portion of the vessel. A large orb hovering in the center of the chamber pulsated with swirls and eddies of light. Occasionally he could see streamers of color flow through the orb, but they didn't last long.

"Orion?"

"Ready."

"I assume this is the source of your power?"

"Yes."

"Why is there a dark haze surrounding it?"

"A polarized magnetic containment field has been erected which protects the Companion from being damaged."

"Okay, anything else I should know about this room?"

"Yes, this room is sealed from access when power levels exceed 0.0001 percent. Power cannot be increased to exceed that point until Companion departs."

"You mean that everything is running on less than one ten thousandth of a percent right now?"

"Yes."

"Wow. What is the maximum speed Orion can attain?"

"531,040.8957 alds per em-har."

"Okay, first things first," Jared spoke in Adarian. "I may know these other languages, but I need references based on my native tongue."

"Specify."

"Why didn't you just access all this from my head when you dumped the languages into me?"

"High speed data input and concurrent extraction is dangerous to most biological entities. Standard waiting time before additional input or extraction is .015 myir."

"In other words, fragile brained. That's nice to know. Okay, I know it's not working, but on my left wrist I have a device used for measuring time on my home world. Can you scan it, and determine how it correlates to the Ilirian and Adarian time scales?"

"Yes. Scan complete. Malfunction corrected; device is now operational. Define markings, indicators, and their significance."

"What was wrong with it?"

"Energy cell was depleted."

Jared was impressed. "Okay, the three hands measure seconds, minutes, and hours. Seconds are the smallest increments, and the fastest moving indicator is called the second hand. The surface of the device is broken down into sixty small marks and twelve larger.

Jared spent several more minutes explaining how time was measured on Earth. Orion had an answer for him a few seconds later.

"Results of comparison ready."

"Let's hear it."

"One Adarian myir is equal to 8,786,674.2 hours. One Ilirian em-har is equal to 93.2 minutes or 1.553 hours. One al-em equals 55.92 seconds or .932 minutes. One em equals .5592 seconds."

Let's see if we can narrow this down a bit.

"Sounds good, but can you convert the myir from hours to years?"

"Yes, how many hours represent a year?"

"What is 24 multiplied by 365?"

"8760."

"That's how many hours there are in a year."

"One Myir is equivalent to 1003.045 years."

"Is that the smallest measurement of time in Adarian?"

"Yes."

"Adarion's must be long-lived."

"Yes."

"Okay, now to find out how an ald measures out," Jared spoke in Ilirian to avoid an input from Orion, then back to Adarian.

"If one em-har equals 93.2 minutes or approximately one and a half hours," Jared paused, "I need to know how many miles equal an ald." He paused again. "But where do I get an accurate example of a mile or even a foot for that matter? I suppose I will have to settle for as close as I can get. Orion?"

"Ready."

"Are there any other Adarian measurement units beside the ald?"

"Yes."

"What are they?"

"The Tal which is equal to 1000 Ald and the Sya which is equal to 1000 Tal."

"Okay, let's just stick with the ald for now. What is the best way to get a measurement of part of my anatomy?"

"Use of the medical scanner will produce the best results."

"Right," Jared said as he headed back to the medical room. "Okay, what do I do first?"

"Activate the scanner, power relay is on the main console."

Jared walked over to the two consoles and studied the pathway diagrams. He recognized a symbol from the Xaxilor language he had been gifted with; activate.

He brought the unit to life when he touched the smooth surface. Colored traces of light flowed along the pathways lighting up each junction they came to. As one of the tendrils of light reached a symbol meaning link-function, another icon on the second console lit up. He moved to the second console. The character for *standby* was illuminated and next to it the icon for *activate*. He touched *activate* on console two again and sent the tendrils of light racing across its surface. Each flowing offshoot ended at an icon. There were nine characters representing numerous anatomical groupings. The first was listed as General External and the remainder were Respiratory,

Circulatory, Digestive, Reproductive, Neural, Muscular, Skeletal, and Aural. Each of the primaries had sub-groupings assigned to them.

He selected 'General External' and moved back to the main console. He surveyed the icons again and found one labeled 'Statistical Profile,' and touched it. "Is that the appropriate setting?"

"The Companion has chosen wisely."

"Okay, I guess I have to get on the table now."

"The selected anatomical part must be placed on the table."

Right, just detach it and flop it on the table.

Jared climbed onto the table and sitting with his legs crossed reached up and took hold of one of the two handles of the scanning unit. "I assume I hold it over the 'selected anatomical part' and depress the button on this handle . . .?"

"The Companion has determined the correct procedure."

"Thanks."

"You are welcome, Companion."

A very polite ship.

Jared extended his left foot and turned it, so it lay flat on the surface with the arch upward. Moving the scanner over his foot about twelve inches above, he pressed the trigger. A brief hum was all that indicated that something had taken place.

"Scan complete."

"How can I take a scan of my height?"

"A statistical scan of the Companion's height is already cataloged."

"Oh," Jared chuckled. "Great, that means I don't have to lay here taking pictures of my naked self."

"That is correct."

"Okay, can you break the scan of my height into 73.75 units?"

"Completed."

"Now label the whole units as inches."

"Completed."

"I wear size eleven shoes so my foot scan should measure out to about 11.5 Or 12 units."

"Incorrect. Foot scan is 11.00031 based on units derived from height scan."

"Okay, I guess my shoes are a little big." Jared slid off the table and headed for the bridge. "Are my clothes ready yet?"

"No."

"I've got to get some new clothes."

"Yes."

Jared grinned.

Blunt, very blunt.

"Now one foot equals twelve inches and..."

"Incorrect, one foot is equal to 11.00031."

"What?" Jared stopped walking. "Oh. No, my foot which is part of my anatomy is 11.00031 inches long, but the unit of measure my people use, which is also called a foot, is an even twelve units or inches long."

"Understood and cataloged."

"Now, starting with the base unit or inch, and twelve of those units equaling one foot, and 5,280 feet equaling one mile . . ."

"Define feet."

"Feet is . . .um, the plural form of the root word 'foot'."

"Understood and cataloged."

"Anyway, 5,280 feet or foot units equal one mile," Jared resumed walking. "How many miles are there in one Ald?"

"1,800.000067."

"1,800 miles per ald. Okay, so what's the maximum speed of the Orion in miles per hour using the time system I told you about earlier?"

"637,249,098.587611 miles per hour."

"Whoa! And that's the fastest you can travel?"

"It is the greatest velocity that can be achieved in normal space."

"Normal space. You mean there's another type of space?"

"'Normal space' is the designation of the plane of existence in which Orion and the Companion originated. Another plane of existence, which is the exact opposite, occupies the same space, but is permanently separated. Between these two planes is a boundary called Null Space. Without the Null Space barrier, the two opposing planes would cease to exist. Accessing null space requires complex calculations, an ability to generate a protective envelope around the construct entering null space and producing a stable rift in the fabric of space. Velocity cannot be altered while in null space. Maximum speed of vessel upon entry determines speed of vessel while within the null space boundaries. Upon transition, velocity is increased by a multiple of ten and sustained while the protective envelope is maintained. Time spent in null space is limited only by the constitution of the occupants."

"You mean null space is dangerous for entities like me?"

"Yes."

"How long will I be able to stay in null space?"

"Effects of null space will be significantly reduced to Companion due to type of phase field used. Estimated time Companion can currently remain in null space without adverse effects is 47.5 em-har."

"About seventy-two hours. Okay. I have only one other question I'd like to ask for right now."

"Proceed."

"The symbols on the med scanner are Xaxilor, is that where it was manufactured?"

"Yes, on the planet of Onru'illakmala." Orion pronounced the K gutturally.

"Is that the reason I was given knowledge of the Xaxilor language?"

"Correct."

"Is Onru'illakmala part of the Ilirian Commonwealth?"

"No."

While pondering all he had learned during the last hour, Jared made his way to the bridge. Orion was beautiful on the outside and full of marvels on the inside. He wondered if anyone on Earth had ever even dreamed of such a ship.

Would it someday be able to take me home? If Null Space travel was indeed possible and he could find out where Earth was, could he return? Question was, did he really want to try? Not long ago he would have said yes. But now?

"Garment cleaning cycle completed."

"Great." Jared jumped up from the seat he had taken moments before and walked to the laundry. As he was removing his pants from the cleaning chamber another wave of curiosity overcame him.

"Orion?"

"Ready."

"Why am I able to see out of the bridge windows when there is no way to see in from the outside?"

Orion tried to explain the technology of what it called its selective optical image system. Jared might know the language, but knowledge of Adarian science had also not been downloaded into his mind. Most of what Orion said was not understood. He hoped the vessel, however, did not know he was clueless. The conclusion he drew from the technobabble was that Orion could see where it was going and the window-like screens on the inside showed a reflection of what the brain like core saw. This allowed the companion to view outside, but also allowed the vessel to avoid anything it deemed a hazard.

As Jared dressed, he considered what to do next. Getting the cargo on board would be a good start and there was plenty to load. Once dressed, he headed for the lower level and asked Orion to explain how the cargo elevator operated. Describing the size and orientation of the aperture desired was all that was required before raising or lowering. After choosing maximum extents then walking to the center of the deck, he said the Adarian word for 'lower' and rode the elevator down. Using one of the loaders he began to place some of the larger items onto the elevator.

He tested the throttle after starting the vehicle and periodically during operation as had become routine. He also made sure the brakes functioned properly. For a vehicle in excess of one hundred years, it worked remarkably well. The only component on this unit that gave him problems was the lifting mechanism which seized occasionally, and he had to use a pry bar to loosen the complex chain. Fuel was the only factor he was really worried about. The loaders used large power packs instead of gasoline and he had several on hand, but the chargers no longer worked, and he had no idea how long a charge lasted. Four em-hars passed as he concentrated on loading the largest of the items. He stopped working only after his stomach had begun to grumble. Keeping busy made him feel less of a prisoner and more like he had some control over his life.

Eating his first meal aboard was not as quickly accomplished as he'd hoped. The food processor was easy enough to understand though it seemed a bit inferior to the rest of the technology on the vessel. The problem was selecting something it could prepare, that he could stomach, and had the needed ingredients available. Also, Xaxilor in manufacture, the unit was programmed to prepare food tailored to a Xaxilor's tastes. He tried several dishes before settling on the fifth for two reasons: the first being his stomach, which was beginning to complain violently; and the second, the stores of supplies were limited. Fortunately, it wasn't as bad as his first attempts. As he cleaned up, his thoughts drifted to what the previous occupant of the ship may have been like. The ten dishes he'd found were triangular in shape with rounded sides and corners, about twelve inches across at the widest point and looking as if they'd been made out of mother-of-pearl. A like amount of tall drinking cups, serving implements and utensils made of the same material completed the collection.

"Orion."

"Yes, Companion."

"Can you show me an image of a typical Xaxilor male?"

A shimmering globe of energy coalesced a short distance away floating in midair. Within the orb an image formed. Jared was stunned. The figure was that of a man, and except for his significantly impressive physique, would not have otherwise stood out in any Earth city.

"Unbelievable!"

He read a little from one of the books he'd found, but soon tired of its slow pace and headed for his sleep room. On arriving, he tried re-decorating the room. However, he soon realized he would have to get some samples to give Orion an idea of what he wanted. He returned to the room about twenty al-em later and deposited the contents of a sack on the floor.

"Orion?"

"Ready."

"I would like to add color to the room. I have collected samples of colors and textures as reference. Is that acceptable to you?"

"Yes."

"Alright, let's decorate."

He knelt down and picked up a small rectangular box made of some type of wood. "This box is made of wood, I believe, unless it's a synthetic. Can you identify its composition?"

"Yes. Organic vegetation, a material found on many planets with oxygen-rich atmospheres. Easily combustible, fibrous cell structure."

"Okay, please simulate wood in a medium brown on the exterior of the cabinet here and the chest of drawers. The shifting colors he had seen earlier returned, though they seemed to last longer. When the wood color and grain pattern had finally come to a rest, he continued. The walls he left white, but the floor became a rich forest green and the sides of the bed he decided to match with the other furnishings. The mattress portion of the bed looked like the canopy of some tropical forest when he was done and lastly, he had the ceiling changed to beige. Though he would probably change things from time to time, he was quite pleased with the outcome. He tossed the now clean but worn quilt over the bed, undressed and climbed in. The bed shifted slightly, adjusting to his shape, and sleep overcame him quickly.

CHAPTER THREE

Complications

"Tribulation sets the wise to action, the foolish to despair."

DARKNESS.

Where am I?

Jared felt claustrophobic, a stark memory flaring from his first moments on the asteroid.

Am I back in the…no…

His senses told him as he reached out there was no barrier of any kind. He swung his right arm out until it encountered a solid surface. The darkness was absolute so he could not see his extremity or what he had touched, but running his hand up and down he decided it was a wall. He reached directly left and encountered nothing, so he leaned a bit in that direction and found another surface. With one arm out in front he took a step.

Nothing.

A hallway perhaps.

Keeping his arm raised, hand up with his fingers out he took a few more tentative steps. The anxiety that had first arisen faded somewhat. He wondered if he had an option, so he reached out and found the surface he had first touched and turned around. Several steps in the opposite direction revealed the answer. He could only go one way. With a mental shrug he turned around and slowly began to walk. A few moments later his left shoulder hit a wall, *okay, so not quite 180 degrees.* Being so close to the left side he switched arms and continued letting the fingers of his left-hand trail along the smooth surface. After a time, he noticed that he could vaguely make out where the wall met the floor.

Are my eyes adjusting?

The thought vanished as a moving point of light appeared in the distance and he stopped. At first, he thought it might be someone or something coming from the other direction, but it did not grow or diminish in size.

No use in just standing here.

He moved on again, both hands by his side as he was no longer in absolute darkness. By the time he was closer to the point of light many more had appeared further on. The first bright spot danced about in lazy arcs like a will-o-wisp. The odd thing was that it did not seem to be restrained by the walls as he was. On occasion it came close, and Jared simply moved his head out of its way. Feeling no sense of danger from the miniscule orb he continued. "No" came from all around and even through him. There had been no sound and yet the impression on his mind had been certain. With more light around from the growing number of illuminated globes he had to duck out of the way more frequently. Twice more he sensed the pleading "no" being repeated. Each occurred when he moved further on and away from an orb. With the points of light becoming more numerous he could make out further details. The walls were indeed black as were the ceiling and floor, made from smooth glossy material. He drew up short as something new met his gaze. On the left side wall, an indistinct dark shape moved. A few steps brought it into focus. *I'm constrained in the hallway, the orbs bound by none, but this shadow of a being is tied to the wall.*

Jared wasn't sure if this last thought had been his or if it had been placed there by something else. He watched for a moment to see if the shadow's slow movements had a purpose. They didn't.

The hall seemed to go on forever, but the number of orbs kept increasing as did the odd wraiths on the walls. After a time, the slow undulations of the apparitions became more animated. With a start Jared realized he was moving. To make sure his mind was registering correctly, he looked down and found his legs were unmoving. Something was pulling him. He realized this because he was passing the orbs and wraiths quite quickly now. Reaching out to try and slow himself, he found no purchase on the smooth wall.

Could this be some form of black ice?

His mind shifted from a curious confusion to concern as he now noticed a definite slope to the floor.

His momentum was slowly increasing and a short time later the dance of the orbs had gone from a playful swirl to a panicked frenzy. The movements of the dark wall flowers were frantic, as if they were running out of time. Unlike before, the figures were trying to capture the points of light and at that moment Jared slid past an orb quite close to his face and he again heard the distinctive, "No!"

This time, however, the hue of the light was not white, but golden, and he heard not an impression but a voice, childlike and terrified. To his right, as he continued to try to halt his advance, he saw one of the shadow figures catch an orb and both vanished immediately.

Is that my way out of this?

Forgetting his increasingly unsettling momentum he began to look around for an orb that he might reach. There were none, but not far away he saw the single golden orb that had passed him moments before. It was beyond the furthest wall, so he leaned left and pushed off hard. There was no resistance, and his forward trajectory shifted slightly, and he hit the opposite wall with a jolt. He focused, trying to will the golden orb closer with his mind, but it remained beyond reach.

He saw another shadow and orb vanish and happened to look ahead. The hall was no longer angular, but tube-like and in the distance, there was a disk of blackness that seemed far darker than any he could have ever imagined. It was toward this that he and the glowing orbs were rushing. Why the wraiths themselves were not being drawn into the black maw he had no clue. Very swiftly the black disk had become massive and unlike the few orbs that had vanished when caught by a dark shadow, those ahead of Jared appeared to be pulled apart and vibrated in agony. At that moment the golden orb shot passed his head and he made a grab for it.

Jared sat up abruptly and wiped the sweat from his brow. He'd never had a nightmare so strikingly real, nor so vividly memorable. Despite the bed's warmth he stood, stretched, and shook off the foreboding feeling that lingered. After he dressed, he headed for the bridge. He sat in the left front chair and thought about how to open the bay doors when he was ready to leave the station.

"Orion?"

"Ready."

"Is it necessary for me to be able to pilot this vessel?"

"No. It is only necessary for the Companion to properly communicate needed instructions. Manual control is possible if the Companion wishes."

"Can you show me what I need to know to operate this ship?"

"Yes. Educational simulation on standby. Please indicate parameters."

"Um, like what?"

"Parameters include time limits, starting and ending points, conditions encountered, and difficulty of elements encountered."

"Wow, a full-blown video game," Jared grinned. "Okay, time limits, fifteen min...uh, al-em, start on a planetary surface, end with a successful landing at a random target, conditions and difficulty, uh... easy."

"Confirmed, but a successful landing will depend on piloting competence."

"Right, um, okay, now show me the controls," Jared said.

"Primary command controls are located on the left side of console."

"Am I in the right place?"

"Yes. Directional controls are located on the center console. Place right hand on surface of console at center. Moving your hand forward results in a downward attitude. Movement to the rear results in an upward attitude. Right or left movement results in a path deviation in the indicated direction. Pressure applied with outer most digits will initiate roll function. Length of hold will determine the angle of roll. Moving your hand in a diagonal direction will result in a combination of maneuvers.

Vertical lift is located to the right of directional controls. Forward thrust is increased using the left hand on the pad. Speed increases exponentially across each colored band. Once desired speed is reached, the hand may be removed. To the left of the thrust pad are the defensive controls. Shield at top. Weapon at bottom.

"Yeah. I think I've got it. Begin simulation."

"Complying."

The screens suddenly showed an alien cityscape followed by a simulated voice speaking Xaxilor.

"Transport vessel 735, you are cleared for departure."

"Uh, okay, understood. Transport 735 lifting off."

Jared smiled and increased the vertical lift slightly. The Orion jumped off the ground and shot straight up.

"Whoa! gotta go easy on the controls."

Jared eased off to hover in place. He eased the thruster forward one half of a colored band and Orion advanced slowly.

The beautiful but unusual cityscape filled the view screen, and Jared was soon caught up in sightseeing. Tall, elegant buildings with graceful spires rose into the sky to great heights. Six pillar-like structures to his left with many windows, were arrayed in a circular pattern, and rose straight upward. About mid-way, they arched inward and joined to a huge disk near the center.

Jared turned toward the edifice to get a better look. Orion slid sideways less than gracefully under Jared's hands as he pulled out of the turn toward the structure. After adjusting to avoid a collision, he increased the attitude of the nose. The disk at the top of the curving supports was a multi-story building with many windows and numerous docking platforms. Three ships about twice Orion's size were each docked to one of the gantries, hovering high above the ground without support.

"Transport vessel 735, you are off course and entering a controlled area. Turn port to compass heading 093."

That caught Jared off guard. "Sorry. I'm going to…um. Executing turn now."

Jared tried to sound competent. He had not expected the simulation to be so detailed and accurate. Coming out of his second turn, he again over-shot and was still slightly off course though no voice piped up to accuse.

"Orion?"

"Ready."

"Is there a course I am to follow for this simulation?"

"Course setting to Shanlar orbital transfer facility is 136 degrees to outer marker. At outer marker reset to 195 degrees and adjust attitude to positive 79 degrees."

"Thanks."

"You are welcome."

Direction indicated on the console to his right was 131 and attitude was at +1.15. As gently as possible he turned the ship to starboard until the readout read 136. It became readily apparent why ships were required to follow this course. None of the structures along this route were very tall on either side for some distance, which presented few obstacles.

"Orion…"

"Ready."

"Why don't the ships just travel vertically until they are clear of all the buildings in the city?"

"Defensive shield dome restricts altitude within city precincts."

"How big is the exit opening?"

"Shield gate is .00025 ald across and rises vertically .0001 ald."

"Okay, that means 1800 miles times .00025. I never did like mathematics. Let's see. 1800 times .10 is 180 so .01 would be 18 miles and .001 would be 1.8 miles, ugh, so I'd say between one quarter and one-half of a mile." Switching back to Adarian, Jared asked Orion for the answer.

".45"

"Okay, so closer to half a mile. That should be sufficient."

"As long as you do not deviate from course 136 by more than one degree."

"Gotcha."

"Define unknown term."

"It means understood."

"Cataloged."

"Distance to shield gate?"

".00053 ald."

"Is the shield gate open?"

"The shield gate is currently closed."

"Do I need to request to have it opened?"

"If flight clearance code has been filed with traffic control, gate will be opened automatically when vessel enters threshold area."

"Has the clearance code been given to traffic control?"

"Yes. Now entering gate threshold."

"Transport 735, this is shield-gate control."

"This is 735, go ahead."

"Shield gate is open, and you are clear to proceed."

"Thanks control. 735 out." Jared was beginning to feel a little more comfortable in his communication skills. No evidence of a shield existed visually but the outer marker was clearly identified by a line of colored lights running transverse to his flight path. "Orion, what was the new heading?"

"195."

"Thank you."

"You are welcome."

Jared turned starboard 59 degrees, increased the angle of assent by 76 and increased speed to .55 percent. "Orion, what is our current speed in miles per hour?"

"450."

"What speed is needed to break free of the atmosphere?"

"12 to 13 percent power."

"In mph please."

"20,954 to 26,193"

"Are we at a point where it is safe to increase to escape speed?"

"Increasing power for escape velocity is recommended."

"All right, here we go . . ."

Jared slowly pushed the throttle forward, carefully watching the digital readout. Control functions on the Orion were extremely sensitive, which left little room for error. Each band across the face of the throttle pad was about a quarter of an inch and he guessed there were between 75 and 100. The pad itself was about 25 inches long and 6 wide. Reaching 12.5 on the indicator, he stopped and withdrew his hand.

"Orion."

"Ready."

"How many increments is the thrust pad divided into?"

"110."

"Why 110?"

"0 through 0.9 are fractional for easier transition at slow velocities. 1 through 20 increase speed by a factor of 1.25, 21-70 by a factor of 1.16, 71-80 by a factor of 1.08, 81-95 by a factor of 1.02, and 96-100 by a factor of 1.01. At 1 percent power velocity is equal to 1.000009 ald per hour which is 1800.00067 miles per hour. Preparing to leave an atmospheric envelope. Stand by for transition."

"Is there anything I need to do?"

"Maintain current heading. Distance to transfer facility is 0.26 ald."

"What is the orbit speed of the facility?"

"12 percent."

"While we are within an atmosphere and attempting to dock anywhere, would you please make the default response for speed and distance in miles per hour?"

"Yes. Adapting memory protocol. Update complete."

"Thank you."

"You are welcome."

"Distance to facility?"

"4,902 miles."

"Orbit speed of facility?"

"20,954 mph."

"Our current speed?"

"23,573 mph."

It was about this time that things began to unravel.

Results of the first simulation were not as good as he'd hoped. Orion informed him that his reaction time was low, and his directional control was dismal. Okay, so he hit the landing target sideways at excessive velocity. He was also given low marks on his comm skills. Not that he was really concerned about it, but it would be good to know if he ever had to pilot a ship other than Orion. Despite the crash, Jared felt good. Optimism was beginning to seep back into his psyche and his energy was high. Much of the afternoon was still left and he felt he could get a good deal of the remaining cargo onboard.

"Orion."

"Ready."

"Would you scan the hangar area and about 100 feet beyond?"

"Scanning complete. Unable to effectively scan entire area due to density and composition of planetoid."

"Great. Can you tell me anything about the area on the other side of the unopened door off your port side?"

"Scan complete. Enclosed compartment with estimated 47.79 percent of space occupied. Movement detected."

"Movement. You mean there's something alive in there?"

"No. Movement is not a biological organism. Motion is constant and rhythmic."

As he stepped off the cargo ramp Jared's eyes drifted to the one large door, he'd been unable to open. He ran his fingers over its surface. It was the same temperature as the rest of the hangar and when struck, sounded exactly like any of the other doors in the hangar of the same size. Since Orion's sensors were able to determine it was an interior door, no danger existed from the vacuum of space. However, despite Orion's assurance that there was nothing alive behind the door, Jared's imagination conjured up images of robotic nightmares. He would still have to be cautious when he finally did get around to opening it. Leaving the last mystery that remained in the hangar, he walked to where the loaders were parked.

Although the loaders were powered by energy cells, they still produced a deep grumbling sound. For a time, he considered taking one with him but decided against it due to their apparent age. He wasn't sure he could trust them to function efficiently. After six medium-sized containers had been successfully placed on Orion's lift, the loader jammed. Having become used to the repetitive glitch, he patiently got out, grabbed his crowbar, and began shaking the stubborn chain. He gave the metal links a hard jerk and felt the entire hangar shift beneath him. A groan reverberated throughout.

He lost his balance, and as he grabbed for the strapping holding the crate to the loader's lift bars, it snapped. He fell backwards crashing to the floor and narrowly escaped being crushed by the falling container.

It burst apart on impact, and many of the thin plastic canisters inside ruptured. The golf ball-sized metallic spheres scattered all over the floor.

Jared rubbed his head. He noticed many of the balls continued to roll and one of the balls seemed to be picking up speed as it rolled away.

That's strange, the floor still looks level.

He watched curiously as the ball continued on, then noticed several others heading in the same direction. The first ball ran into a large metal barrel and exploded. Though small in size, Jared knew the blast would be more than enough to kill someone. Several other explosions followed as other balls found similar barrels. He looked around and saw a number of the balls had rolled up against the large, inoperable door. Many were also resting against the tires of the loader and Orion's landing struts.

He did not have any time to think more about the subject because another blast set off a chain reaction. Like falling dominoes, ball after ball went off, heading in his direction. He scrambled to his feet and ran toward Orion's lift platform. He knew without looking that the loud bursts behind him were rapidly getting closer. Several of them went off at once right behind him and he threw himself toward the platform.

Jared waited for several al-em after silence returned before looking up. Glancing around he found Orion was undamaged and there seemed to be little damage to the containers. The loader though would need four new tires before he could use it again. His back felt as though he'd been stung by numerous, vicious insects and when he sat up, his buttocks hurt.

He asked Orion to raise the lift and carefully made his way to the bedroom. When he removed his shirt, he found it pitted with tiny holes as were the seat of his pants, and tiny bits of shrapnel were embedded in the soles of his shoes.

"Orion?"

"Ready."

"Do you have any idea what caused the jolt in the hangar area?"

"A shock wave produced by an instability within the asteroid. Exact cause unknown."

"Is it falling apart?"

"Unknown. Unable to effectively scan entire area due to density and composition of planetoid. Recommend departure within 45 em-hars."

"I understand. Is it possible for you to scan my back? I can't exactly do it myself."

"Overview of exterior surface is possible. Primary scanners are unsafe to use on biological entities for periods in excess of 1.3 em. Detailed analysis of complex interior systems requires periods in excess of danger threshold."

"All I want to know is how bad my back is and what to do about it, if you can do that in 1.3 em then proceed."

"Scan complete. Posterior quadrants two, five, and six have been subjected to multiple micro-particle impact. First three layers of tissue have moderate abrasions and is heat damaged."

"What do you mean by 'quadrants?'"

"Companion's structure is divided into eight quadrants. Diagnostic data has been transferred to medical data files. Video display can be viewed from that location."

Jared headed for the med room, then spent several moments studying the display. The schematic showed the skull and neck as quadrant one, the upper torso as quadrant two, the left arm, three; right arm, four; lower torso, five; pelvic region, six; and legs, seven and eight.

"Why wasn't I wounded more severely? I saw what those firecrackers did to a number of barrels."

"Utilizing a modified magnetic field and infusing it with highly charged plasma vapor created a localized shielding. All dangerous fragments were converted into micro-particles as they passed through the barrier."

"You put up a shield to save me?"

"Yes."

"Thank you."

"You are welcome."

"Micro-particles huh, I guess it was like being hit briefly by a sand blaster." Jared figured his back, and cheeks would be sensitive for a few days but was not going to let that get him off schedule. With the outpost beginning to deteriorate noticeably, it would be wise to leave soon.

Only one loader remained usable so he would have to be careful. He knew he could finish loading the following day. He decided to relax for what remained of this day and he began by showering to wash off any of the micro-fragments still clinging to his hide. Initially the warm water stung, but before too long was very enjoyable. The small spheres had nearly killed him, and he was thankful that the ship had the ability to act on its own.

On the other hand, the little bombs presented him with a means to get the door open if he used them properly. When he managed to get around to inventorying all his loot, he would have to watch out in case any more of them were in other containers. He stepped out of the shower, toweled off, then headed for the laundry room with his tattered clothes in hand.

With what remained of his shirt and pants freshly laundered, he left Orion and began an inspection of the hangar. Many of the small, metallic spheres still littered the deck, most gathered along the walls. He picked up one of the small broken canisters to make sure his earlier observation was correct, that the rectangular box was made of composite material. Next, he went to the small room where he had put a number of empty shipping containers of various sizes. He chose one with a volume of about two square feet, then began to pick up all the little spheres he could find. After nearly two hours of searching the hangar floor between and under crates, he felt he had found all he was going to. With the clean-up accomplished he began to look for a way to use the box of dangerous orbs to open the jammed garage door.

He set the full box of balls down next to the inoperative door, then backed away to ponder how best to carry out his plan. He thought of several movies he had seen in which explosives experts used what were called 'shaped charges.' They gave him a course to follow. It had probably been foolish not to access the deck plans for the hangar area when he last used the station's computer, but after Orion's report on the facility's stability he had no intention of returning to the upper levels. He had considered running one of the loaders into the door to break it down. But that would leave a large obstacle in his way, not to mention placing him near the door for whatever might be inside to pounce on him. The second choice was to use one of the two Xaxilor plasma torches in the ship's EVA room, but that too could possibly place him in danger, along with the fact he had no idea how to use it, yet.

With the floor clear, he climbed into the remaining loader and fired it up. Unlike the other loader and its troublesome chain, this one had a bad axle. It made a loud, continuous grinding noise and rough vibration whenever it moved. He wasn't able to go very fast, so the rest of the loading was slow.

The fifth pallet he loaded was the first one he had removed from one of the old freighters. Several of the cases lashed to the pallet were damaged. One large container had a broken hinge and torn corner, which revealed the contents. He was stunned to see a great quantity of various, flat metallic disks with intricate detailing on them. He took a handful and gazed curiously at the gold and silver hued coins.

Why would the transport ship be carrying such a large amount of money? Maybe it had been the outpost crew's payroll.

He placed the last large container on the lift platform and glanced at his watch. Over eight hours had elapsed, about twice the time he estimated it would have taken with the other loader.

The Ilirian terms 'em-har', 'al-em' and 'em' kept popping up in his mind each time he checked his watch. Converting the hours to em-har in his head was now easy, a result of the shock Orion had hit him with. He backed up the ponderous vehicle and moved it slowly away from the ship.

With all the cargo finally loaded, he could now spend time figuring out how to get the weight equipment on board. His only option at this point was to get the large freight elevator on the far side of Hangar One to work. So far, however, the thing had refused to operate, and Jared had no idea what was wrong with it, let alone how to fix it.

Several minutes later the heavy piece of equipment groaned to a stop and Jared climbed down from the cab. Faint tendrils of smoke wafted up from the front axle and Jared could feel heat near the hub of the wheel. He took a deep breath and turned his attention back to Orion and the now uncluttered floor of the hangar. He glanced first at the box of excessively powered firecrackers, then toward the opening connecting the two bays.

He had two problems left to solve, but hunger and fatigue required it wait until tomorrow. Having finished loading he was one step closer to leaving as well as being prepared to provide for himself. He figured that a lot of the items he had chosen to load would be worth a good deal for trade or salvage. He walked quickly back to the ship and headed for the galley.

Part way through his meal another rumbling jolt shook the outpost. It was violent enough to make him jump up, but Orion reported that though it had been more intense than the first, structural integrity had not yet been compromised. He sat down and finished eating. His attention was not on the food, but rather why within the last few days the outpost had begun to deteriorate.

One possibility was that when he messed with the computer system, he'd fouled something up before being enlightened by Orion. Numerous other such thoughts crossed his mind as he walked back to his quarters and entered the shower. In spite of all his rising fears he slipped into bed fairly confident Orion would get them out of danger if the need should arise.

As soon as Jared awoke, he dressed and headed for the galley to grab a quick breakfast, eating the last of it as he left the ship and walked to the jammed door. The box of dangerous marbles had been undisturbed by last evening's tremor and Jared set to work to create a blast directing shield around the case. After punching a hole in the container's lid and removing one of the balls, he sealed the box as best he could, leaving one orb partially exposed through the top. Around the composite box he stacked ten half-inch metal panels and braced them with some of the surviving barrels. He then filled them with the heaviest debris he could find. For a trigger he chose to use a wrench.

Because of the incident the day before, he felt it wise to test his plan before getting too close to the full box with a metal object. A good distance away from his intended target he placed the ball into another box then covered it with a small section of the composite. Using some cord and a makeshift tripod he suspended the wrench over the container and, after moving to a safe distance, lowered the wrench slowly. As he had hoped, the cord went slack and nothing happened, indicating that to detonate, the two had to come into direct contact. With the test out of the way he felt confident in rigging the rest of his bomb.

The container that held the collected explosive spheres was about six inches from the big door and set securely against the circular shaped barrier. With the blast barrier in place, he laid the small composite panel over the hole in the container's top. After making sure the cord was securely attached, he set the wrench on the panel so when it was pulled out, it would fall through the hole. He would have preferred to use the tripod, but the blast shield made that more complicated. If it worked as planned, the wrench would contact the exposed sphere when the panel was pulled from between the two.

Retreating back to Orion, he moved to the center of the lift platform and instructed the ship to raise it 90 percent of the way. Satisfied he was safe if things got out of hand, he pulled the cord. The first ball detonated, immediately setting off the others, producing an intense thundering boom. The concussion from the collected spheres made Jared recoil despite being tucked away inside Orion. All the barrels were blown outward from the blast area far enough to be out of Jared's range of vision. The heavy metal panels had effectively directed the brunt of the explosions force but, like the barrels, had been thrown away from the door though not quite as far. He'd watched as one had cart-wheeled end over end in its rush outward from the epicenter.

From his vantage he could not see the entirety of the door but was able to make out a wide gap where it met the wall on the left side. He watched for about half an hour before exiting the ship. In a surrealistic way he felt like some actor in a sci-fi horror film heading toward a gruesome end.

While inside Orion he was fine. As he moved toward the damaged door, fear rose. He had faced dark unknowns numerous times in the past months, so the feeling was not as bad as it had been at first. He had questioned his courage in the beginning as thoughts of doom and fear gripped him in his initial exploration of the outpost. Now, however, he knew it just made him more alert to any danger that might pop up. He was sure as long as he didn't freeze up and fail to act, he would be alright.

Gripping the crowbar firmly, he approached the blast site. The door's lower five panels were blown inward, making an opening roughly two feet high and two wide. It was quickly apparent that the door was considerably thicker than the others in the hangar. Insufficient light penetrated the small hole not permitting him to see, but there was a consistent grumbling sound coming from within. It was constant and sounded mechanical, so he discounted the hostile alien theory and prepared to investigate.

Selecting two portable high intensity light units from the vehicle maintenance area, Jared crudely attached them to long poles and slid them into the opening. When the room lit up it revealed a large vehicle. He knelt, crawled inside, then detached one of the lights from its pole and began to survey the room.

It was larger than the other garages. It extended back some distance and had another door at the rear, though a collapsed ceiling on the right side partially blocked the small access. A huge boulder lay against the large door's track. If there was time, he would check the back door later. He began inspecting the vehicle. It was not another loading vehicle as he had thought it might be but appeared to be for travel on the outer surface of the asteroid. With the damage to the door there was no way for him to extract it, so he ignored it, and set about searching the remainder of the room.

Due to the density of the asteroid, the cave-in had not produced small rocks or dirt. A series of fissures ran the length of the visible ceiling and the chunks that had fallen were long and jagged. The sound he'd heard when he first entered was still going and as he neared its point of origin, he realized it was definitely mechanical.

Near the rear door he was finally able to see part of the device. Partially crushed under one of the large rocks was a cylindrical body on a tracked suspension. At what Jared assumed was the front was a series of slightly tapered augers noisily rotating, most likely one of the tools used for excavating the outpost and stored here. The boulder must have activated the drilling bit when it impacted several days before.

He breathed a sigh of relief and dismissed doubts of whether or not he was alone. Trying to stop the boring machine seemed a waste of time, so he turned and tried the small door. Like the larger door, it had been wedged solidly shut by the shifting asteroid.

He looked around and noticed several large tools along the wall opposite the cave-in. They had been hidden by the vehicle when he first entered. One of them was a large saw with a mean looking blade—he pulled it off the shelf and inspected. As with all the other equipment he'd found, with the exception of the computer, it had no power cord. A search revealed numerous power cells, seven that fit the saw, but with only one still having a charge. Interestingly, the saw had two multiple wire combinations leading to a band on either side of the blade just inside the teeth. Cutting depth was limited to about fifteen inches and when Jared turned it on, a bright, glowing band appeared at the teeth. Lowering the cutting tool so the blade contacted the workbench he was pleased to see it cut cleanly and easily through the material. He shut it off and glanced at the small door. He smiled knowing it would also stand little chance against the voracious tool. For now, the door would have to wait, as he was more concerned about getting the weight equipment onto Orion.

Jared jogged across the nearly half mile width of the hangar and came to a stop next to the wall leading up to the balcony. He searched again for a control to lower the elevator, but it appeared as though none had ever been installed.

Suddenly, he spun around and looked back across the hangar. Only Orion's nose was visible from where he stood, but if he could get the ship into Hangar One, he could load the weight machines directly into the cargo bay. He estimated the ceiling was more than high enough. The opening in the partition was wide enough for the hull, but getting the ship's wings through would be a problem.

He wasted no time in getting back to the ship and headed for the bridge.

"Orion?"

"Ready."

"Is there some way for you to cut down the exposed partition on the left without causing too much damage to the surrounding structure?"

"Yes."

"How?"

"By using a focused beam of plasma energy."

"I'd like you to do that. There is one more thing I need but have no way to get without your help."

"Understood."

"All right, let's do it."

"Complying."

Jared felt the ship begin to rise slowly and dashed forward, climbing into the left front seat. He looked through the view port and watched as Orion gained altitude and pivoted around to the left. Once the vessel had stopped with the opening in the partition directly ahead, a brightness flared up outside; but he couldn't see where it came from. Suddenly, an intense white beam lashed out, striking the partition to his left…and cutting into the segmented plates that made up the massive retractable curtain wall. He chastised himself for not thinking of this before blowing the large door the previous day. Once enough of the segments had been cut from the track, they began to fall to the floor. Jared assumed the curtain had been used to seal off one side of the huge hangar if needed but couldn't quite figure out how that would have worked. From inside, the noise of the destroyed segments hitting the floor was absent, but he watched as several of them laid waste to the aft portion of one of the Hedmar freighters. Residual chemicals exploded and though not a catastrophic blast, debris flew in all directions. The other two vessels were far enough apart to be spared from the inferno.

"Indicate final destination."

"Off to the left, over by the raised deck area," Jared instructed. "Can you see where I'm pointing?"

Jared felt foolish for asking the question, realizing Orion could not likely see as he did. Orion's answer, however, surprised him.

"Yes."

"Wow, great, over there then, my big friend."

Orion had no problem reaching the balcony level but had to change its starboard wing configuration to get the hull close to the ledge. It was an odd site to see the ship's right wing jutting into the wide alcove where the line of cargo doors met the long hall back to the main complex. The winglets had disappeared and Jared was sure the wing was, at that moment, shorter than it had been. Even more surprising was that Orion had formed an access port and ramp that was level with the balcony and about three times the width of the main hatch. Once he stepped out, the reason for the alternate aperture became apparent. The first step was a doozy. After marveling at the oddity of it all he set off to get the gym equipment.

He had been surprised to find that the weight machines were a great deal like those he had used on Earth. Two reasons for the similarity crossed his mind. The first was that he had indeed been in the cryo chamber for a long time and somehow people from Earth had made it into space, along with him, which seemed improbable the more he thought about it. More likely, the people who built this outpost, being very similar to the people of Earth with comparable muscle structure, had designed devices to work the same muscle groups; two units for working the legs, two for the arms and upper body and one for the lower torso. Insufficient time was available to disassemble the units and that wasn't something he wanted to tackle anyway. The solution he finally settled on, after looking for a piece of equipment to move them with, was to drag them out with a winch if he could find one.

The solution to his problem had come as things usually had since his arrival at the outpost, by accident. When Orion had revealed itself after Jared's second shock, it had not given up all its secrets. Jared had mentioned the word 'winch' out loud in Adarian, and though he was not directly addressing the ship, a device appeared in the cargo bay's floor. After seven em-har and a short lunch, he succeeded in getting all five units on board. His reward for the work was a headache and ringing ears from the clamor the floor panels made as each unit was moved across them. The floors in the outpost might be made out of a composite, but that didn't prevent them from complaining when being gouged.

The weight equipment was loaded and secure well within the 45 em-har that had been recommended. As soon as Orion was back in its original place, Jared's curiosity led him to investigate the small doorway in the large garage. Several sets of protective eyewear hung on pegs near the tools. Jared grabbed a pair and put them on. He stepped up to the door, started the unit and began cutting. First upward on the left side, the glowing blade sliced easily into the metal. Near the top he turned it horizontally and made a crosscut. About this time the unit began to lose power, so Jared quickly made another crosscut at the bottom. Power failed completely as he cut vertically into the right side. The last cut had only gone a foot, and the door remained immovable.

He returned to the main hangar and removed one lift prong from the small loader. Securing the hook to one end of a cable, he then attached the other end to the heavy loader. After jamming the hook through the left slit he returned to the loader. The vehicle vibrated considerably as power was applied, but after a few moments it lurched violently; the door had given way.

He hopped out and grabbed one of the maintenance lights and set off into the corridor. For some distance the hall was in good shape but when he turned a corner, he saw more evidence of the asteroid's instability. The hall, split about halfway up the wall, had shifted sideways leaving only a crawlspace. If he hadn't noticed a faint red glow ahead, he would have turned back. On hands and knees for about forty feet he was finally able to stand again and looked into a room full of computer consoles, monitors and control panels. He descended the five steps to investigate the room.

When he read the control labels on one station, he noticed a particularly persistent red flashing light. He went over to it and his jaw dropped when he read the flashing message:

WARNING!
CORE FAILURE IMMINENT
CONTAINMENT CHAMBER AND SHIELDING
COMPROMISED
ESTIMATED TIME TO FULL OVERLOAD:
17.23 AL-EM

Jared ran. He crawled so fast he scraped his knees. With about ten feet left to go another jolt shook the station and the rock slab above him shifted again. When the motion stopped, he felt the rock against his back preventing him from crawling further, so he pulled himself along as fast as he could.

Just as he got out another shock rumbled through the facility and the entire hangar seemed to groan under its influence. He ran toward the main hanger, but he hadn't gone far when he heard a crash from behind.

He didn't look back; he knew the hall behind was gone.

He ran as fast as he could, darted around the loader, and made for Orion. Out of breath he stumbled onto Orion's cargo lift and yelled. "Shy'vas' and make it quick."

The lift rose quickly as if Orion sensed the danger. Before it stopped Jared was on his feet and running toward the bridge.

"Orion! We have to get out of here now. The core is going to explode."

"Confirmed. All systems ready for departure."

"What weapon power setting will be needed to blow out those doors?"

"Stage two plasma burst will be sufficient."

"Will blowing the outer doors cause any dangerous debris for you to fly through?"

"Possibility does exist."

"Can you use your shields inside the hangar?"

"Yes."

"Good! Raise shields and fire."

Just off the tip of Orion's nose a ball of energy began forming and rapidly blossomed until it was about twenty feet in diameter. Jared entered the bridge just as it reached its full size and brightness. It was so intense he shielded his eyes with his hand.

The plasma burst forth, hitting the hangar doors, and turning them into glowing scraps, some of which flew back toward Orion. Jared slid into one of the two rear chairs as Orion surged forward toward the opening. Items being sucked out into space bounced off the invisible shield as the ship rushed past.

When Jared could see only space around him, he stood and headed for his chair. Halfway there Orion jerked violently due to severe turbulence, and Jared was thrown back against the rear bulkhead.

Rapid pressure loss from the doomed station had caused the power core to detonate early. With already weakened core shielding, the overload of energy began its outward expansion. The asteroid shuddered momentarily then came apart along numerous faults and fissures. Huge chunks of the planetoid shot outward propelled by the fury of the core's demise. Pieces far larger than Orion came dangerously close, but the ship maneuvered deftly until its speed carried it out of harm's way.

CHAPTER FOUR

The Void

*Is there anywhere in this never-ending black void,
any reply to the question which for countless
civilizations through time has gone unanswered...*

Why am I here...?

ORION, ITSELF UNDAMAGED from the incident, accelerated away from the dying outpost, but Jared had been caught off guard.

He gripped his left arm. "I've been knocked into walls a few too many times in this room."

"Observe safety protocol."

Jared rolled his eyes. "Go figure."

"Complying."

Jared looked at the ceiling and shook his head.

Too literal.

"Incomplete request, specify parameters."

"It was not meant as a...just forget it."

"Complying."

Jared walked slowly trying not to move his arm too much when the full realization that he was actually free of his prison hit him. In spite of the pain in his arm, he felt relief and excitement. Whatever the reason or method that brought him here, he felt a strong desire to find answers. Perhaps he would find that there was no God, and that what he did really made no difference in an endless, mindless, eternal galaxy.

For now, he chose to try and remain true to what he had been taught, though more from a logical standpoint than that of a spiritual one. Even out here, so far from all he knew, there was something comforting in believing that this life was not the end of his existence.

A sharp pain brought him out of his musings as he opened the med room door. Activating the scanning unit, he pulled it down with his right arm and laid his left on the table. Only one pass was required to tell him what he already knew, though worse than expected. The smaller of his two forearm bones was broken in two places and the larger had a small fracture. He had a bump on his head along with several hefty bruises.

In conjunction with the report of injury was a recommendation of treatment. Orion indicated that even though the device was of Xaxilor manufacture, the data indicated was for Jared's physiology. Directed by the data, Jared opened one of the drawers along the same wall and withdrew a cylindrical apparatus. Included on one-half of the device were instructions on how to open, apply and remove. A splint-like instrument of Xaxilor manufacture with 'Ska-lakovlik Nilkaska Rityalk' written boldly at the top, which roughly translated meant bio-structural regenerating accelerator. The instructions indicated it would also accomplish the setting of bones, if necessary.

Opening was achieved by setting the touch meter to '0' and depressing a tab along one side. Beautifully crafted, the instrument opened smoothly and possessed a padded interior. Laying his arm onto the bottom half as the instructions indicated, he then folded the top closed and listened for the auto lock. A noticeable click let him know the lock had engaged and he depressed the activate switch. Pressure from the cushion inside made his arm hurt briefly as it tightened and formed to fit his appendage. The pain subsided as the device also administered an anesthetic to the area. A reddish light indicated the regenerating accelerator had started and was accompanied by a slight warming sensation. Use of his left arm would be severely limited for about six days, but the only task he had planned on starting was to inventory what was in the cargo bay. Six days was a lot better than the six or so weeks it would have taken on Earth, and he could start inventorying the smaller stuff one-handed.

Nine months, seven days had passed since Jared found himself on the deserted outpost and he had changed in many ways. He had added sixteen pounds of muscle and at two hundred thirteen pounds was in the best shape he had ever enjoyed. The mental connection between himself and the Orion grew stronger each day. Being called 'Companion' no longer seemed strange, and the feeling of being totally alone was gone. To someone else it might sound strange, but the vessel had become his friend, and was someone he could talk to and count on. Though he was far from fully knowledgeable about the ship or its systems, he felt they could work quite well together.

With his arm resting on his lap, he sat contentedly for the first time since he found himself on the asteroid, looking out into space from his chair on the bridge. It no longer seemed so oppressive, so overwhelming now that he could concentrate on other things besides survival. Having loaded every item that might be of value into Orion's huge cargo bay, along with the coins, probably meant he would not have to worry about money for some time. The large quantity of Drakstrad currency had been on one of the freighters, but it had not been on the station's inventory list, nor had nine large pieces of equipment, most of which he could not identify.

It's time to go meet some aliens.

"Orion."

"Ready."

"What is the nearest inhabited planet to our current location?"

"Sha'Lural."

"Sha'Lural," Jared repeated. "Then that's where we'll go."

"Course calculated and executed."

"Good night, Orion." Jared stood and left the bridge.

"Good night, Companion."

Numbness in his arm woke him early. Since he could not fully work out, he did what exercises he could, then showered. Once out, he stopped by the laundry, dropped his tattered clothes in the wash receptacle and headed for the galley. Having become more comfortable in the use of the processor, he was able to make breakfast quickly. Rushing was no longer a need or desire, and he ate slowly, trying to enjoy the unusual cuisine.

Later, as Jared reposed in his bridge chair, he spent several hours gazing out at the star-filled void, hoping to see something of interest. Except for the fact that he could not identify any constellations, space looked the same as it had on any night from Earth.

So much for sight-seeing.

He'd found a book that morning by an Ilirian author named Kaldrio Mind'yurel. The book told a fictitious story based on Iliria some six thousand cycles ago. Whether or not it had any basis in fact, Jared didn't care. It had begun well, and he didn't feel like working, so spent the entire morning reading. By the time he decided to get lunch, he still had seen nothing but blackness outside.

After he ate, he headed for the cargo bay to delve into the inventory. Selecting an area closest to the door to temporarily store what he chose to keep, he began opening the small containers. Replacement parts, electrical components and tools made up the bulk of what he found. Useless to him, but they would likely be of great value to others. He found one case full of explosive metal balls in their plastic packages. Placing the other items that had been on top in another container, he set the dangerous box securely off to one side. Four hours later he retired to his room and fell asleep.

The following morning, he began redecorating the interior to an Earthlier vibe. Being stuck on the outpost had been dark and often depressing; Orion on the other hand was bright and with a little adjustment would be quite homey. As he had done to his quarters, he began to add color to the various rooms.

For the bridge walls and ceiling, he chose a flat, silver-gray overall. The floor became deep gray, and the consoles a charcoal gray, with maroon trim and framing. For the chairs he had Orion simulate fabric on the front and back in a light gray with maroon trim. Sides, being harder and smooth, were given the darker charcoal hue, like the consoles. Accents such as light emitters, which were simply exposed areas of Orion's natural material and window framing, he made silver.

Moving to his office, he decided to give it the corporate wood look that many on Earth would refer to as the 'old money' look. Orion changed the floor to resemble deep-pile carpeting. A pale red-brown shade covered the walls with fancy decorative trim at the baseboard and along the wall near the ceiling. Also added was a large oval view port that allowed him to see outside.

He left the office, stopped in the hall and gave it a coat of medium gray with maroon trim. He asked Orion to add an oval view port in his quarters as well. Portions of the vessel that were currently unused he changed to varying shades of gray, just to cut down on the brightness of the white. The room across from the galley in which he had put the weight equipment was given beige walls, a large view port, a climbing wall and a tiled marble effect for the floor.

For the galley he chose to use more lively colors, like might have been seen in a 1950's or 1960's diner. Tiles again were used on the floor but colored red and black and the walls were white, though not as bright as Orion's natural state. The tables, benches and chairs were black with red and white trim, while the counter surfaces in the prep area had small black and white tiles. After that had been accomplished, he trimmed the whole place with gold. Perhaps a little gaudy, but who was going to complain? In the bedroom he left the walls white but again flattened the shine.

In the medical room, he tried to complement the tan and black of the existing Xaxilor equipment. Doors on the cabinets in both rooms became transparent to resemble glass with silver hued handles.

Bathrooms received a little color, particularly his, which he decorated in green and white with bamboo accents, and tile on the floors of the showers. He then went back through all the used rooms a second time to make fine adjustments. Lastly a green and silver braided stripe running the length of the main hall was placed at waist level on either side. Achieving the results he wanted took the entirety of the day and despite his efforts there were still some small details he was reconsidering.

By the third day Jared began to comprehend the vast distance of space more fully. He had wanted to see it, but he thought there would be more to it. Unlike the movies on Earth and the astronomical photos he had seen, it was just vast and black, with millions of points of light. He believed he was still within his home galaxy. At least, he could see a white band like the one that gave the Milky Way its name. One thing was for sure, regardless which galaxy he was in; he was far closer to the galactic core than he had been on Earth.

"This is nuts," he finally decided. "It'll take way too long to get there at this pace. Orion?"

"Ready."

"Please take us into null space."

"High acceleration imminent, please observe safety protocol."

"Complying," Jared replied playfully, climbing into the command chair. "Restraints applied."

"Confirmed. Initializing NSPD-Null Space Phase Drive. Primary phase field at 25%. Energizing for hyper boost. Navigational data recalculated for NS tracking. Primary phase field at 50%. Accelerating to 60%."

Jared felt the ship surge forward as he was pressed deeply into the command chair.

"Acceleration at 100%. Thrust settings to 80%."

Another burst of speed caused a wave of disorientation to flow through him.

"Primary phase field at 75%. Increasing thrust settings to 100%. Velocity nearing maximum for normal space operation. Implementing NSGN. Primary phase field at 100%. NSGN optimal. All systems ready. Null space gate calculated and confirmed. Node burst in five, four, three, two, one. Node burst successful. NS gate open. Forming phase field envelope. Phase field established. Phase field locking onto NSG. NS transition in five, four, three, two, one."

The transition itself, from normal space to null space was silent and smooth except for Orion's continuing status reports.

"Null space transition complete. At current velocity destination target eta is five days Ilirian time cycle."

Total black enveloped Orion as it plunged into null space and

Jared felt a slight twinge of nausea. The complete absence of stars added to the odd sensation of being in truly alien surroundings. Because of his queasy stomach and slight dizziness, he decided to lie down. He began to realize why humans or other similar life forms would have trouble spending long periods of time in null space. Orion informed him that the initial experience would be uncomfortable. Even though he still felt odd an em-har later, the sickness and unsteadiness had passed. Orion also explained the slow changes the body of biological entities went through if in null space for too long. Neural functions deteriorate and become erratic, cell structure begins to slowly lose cohesiveness and sensory organs degenerate. Not considering all the physiological effects, the psychological impact of perfect stillness of the ship and absolute nothingness outside would become quite disturbing.

Sitting in the command chair reading, sleeping, and sporadic meals due to nausea had comprised his activity during the following few days. Orion had indicated that continuing efforts were being performed to further calibrate the phase field to reduce the unpleasant effects. For Jared, however, enough was enough, and he asked Orion to drop out of Null Space. Orion complied and though Jared had expected it to be a similar scenario to the NS insertion, Orion simply let the phase field fall apart, and the ship reappeared in normal space. Almost instantly the worst of the unpleasant feeling vanished. Jared gazed out of the view screen for several minutes welcoming the reappearance of the stars.

"Orion."

"Ready."

"Is it difficult on your systems to access null space?"

"No."

Jared reclined the command chair as he continued to scan the star field. "Are there any interesting phenomena near our current location?"

"Several."

"Please list them."

"The Kyan-Tlar Rothan is 17,769,926.347 alds (31,985,867,425 miles) distant. Composed of gas and dust particles encompassing an area of 72,379,103 cubic alds. Course variation is .0251 by .00037."

"A nebula, okay."

"Triovass is a free roaming heavy density planetoid. Distance is 712,005 alds. No magnetic or gravitational fields. Rotation minimal. One estimated rotation is completed in 90 cycles Ilirian. Composition 99.3574 percent rhylom and less than one percent other trace elements. Course variation is 175.93012 by 23.00981."

"What is our current ETA to the Sha'Lural colony without re-entering null space?"

"Specify velocity setting."

"80 percent."

"Nine days Ilirian."

"Just out of curiosity, how far is it in miles from here to Sha'Lural? You can round it to the nearest hundred."

"121,636,397,300 miles."

"How much time will it add to our ETA if we deviate to within viewing range of the Kyan-Tlar Rothan."

"Eight days Ilirian."

"Orion…"

"Yes."

Jared thought for a second then asked, "Can you delete the Ilirian qualifier from your responses?"

"Yes. Why?"

"I know the default system you use and therefore, unless a specific system other than the default is required, repeating it is unnecessary."

"Confirmed, Companion. Increasing logic rating reference for Companion. Additional data download probability is now at 65 percent."

"Just exactly what does that mean?"

"Specify."

"Never mind, I'm not sure I want to know," Jared frowned. "Eight days is a bit more than I want to take so I think we'll skip it."

"Understood."

Jared kept busy for the next seven hours by continuing the inventory of his cargo, stopping only for lunch, and to play a quick tactical war game of Rilo-ta'non-cyns with Orion. Since all the large items had been inventoried at the outpost and the remaining few could not be identified, he concentrated on the packed crates he had yet to open. He had Orion scan each of the remaining containers before opening to verify there wouldn't be any unpleasant surprises. Several of the crates contained numerous circuit boards, which he matched by type and serial number and repacked with like units. Two more contained tools of varied style, size, and design. Occasionally he would come across an item he wanted to keep and knew might one day be useful. Another had eight weapons inside and a routing document that listed them as Hyrolon MK3 10vr assault rifles. Also were several boxes of spare ammo clips. These were the first weapons he'd found but had yet to find any ammunition. Except for the small side arm in the outpost commander's quarters and three power cells, he had no other protection if he left Orion.

The most impressive object he came across was a golden-hued necklace with an intricate lace pattern. The filigree, when the ends were held, formed a crescent that was thickest at the bottom. Six gemlike stones symmetrically inset sparkled in the low light. The two end parts would not latch together and had sharp needle like protrusions. At first, he considered tossing it into the box he was using for damaged items or junk but chose to keep it. The metal could be valuable and perhaps it was an antique. One other box held numerous items he found of great interest: a few Ilirian novels, theatrical videos, and historical books.

Before having dinner and retiring for the night he placed the items he chose to keep in his office. The necklace he put in a drawer of the desk, the tools onto a low shelf, and the books and videos onto various other shelves in the wall unit. During his first meal after returning to normal space, he discovered that food also tasted better in the real world. Choosing a meat and gravy dish, he ate slowly, pondering again many of the questions and mysteries that surrounded him. As he walked back to his quarters, he considered the cylinder on his arm. One more day and he would be able to remove the bone healing device and begin to get some serious work accomplished along with resuming his morning workouts. Stars outside the view port in his room were a pleasant change from the smothering blackness of null space. Quite a change considering he'd thought them disappointing after the first three days he'd been free of the outpost.

The following three days were uneventful, and Jared was able to get a great deal more of the cargo inventoried. In his estimation, the inventory was about 60% complete. After several more times of being annihilated in the game of Rilo-ta'non-cyns, he was beginning to think he didn't like the game, nor would he ever be very good at it. He spent several em-har each night before going to sleep reading one of the Ilirian novels. However, not knowing Ilirian history or anything about the culture, most of it was very difficult to understand. Considering the technology he saw on the outpost, the novel was probably set in a time period long before the Drakstrad came to power, sort of a medieval on the other side of the galaxy book, or a biblical story with a science fiction twist.

Five days out from Sha'Lural, Orion woke Jared mid-way through the night and informed him a small vessel was un-powered and drifting near their position.

"Orion?"

"Ready."

"Is there anyone alive on board?"

"Detecting one active biological unit."

"Distance to contact?"

"848,189,731.572 alds."

"How far off our course is it?"

"Course deviation required .00000031."

"That's not bad. Okay, we'll check it out. Uhm, Orion? How many alds difference would that be from the same starting point if we stayed on course?"

"Calculating, insignificant distance—4,860,000.181 alds."

"Adjust course toward the vessel, 90% power."

"Confirmed Companion, course recalculated, accelerating to 90%."

"ETA to target?"

"1.9 hours."

"Good. Inform me as soon as we arrive. I'm going back to bed."

For the second time since he'd arrived in this new reality, Jared dreamed. It was very strange and dark. He had a difficult time seeing his surroundings. He vaguely remembered someone or thing beside him moving quickly along a path. Then suddenly, he was drifting alone in space.

Slowly spinning he rotated and a planet came into view, green with blue oceans and cloudy skies. The planet swung out of sight; a distant ship came into view. As he continued to rotate the planet came back into the frame of what he assumed was some type of environmental helmet. Half a rotation further, the ship was partially obscured in a bright ball of light. Again, the planet appeared, but as it centered in his view, it exploded. Chunks of rock flew outward in all directions, and as he rotated back toward the ship the debris flew past his shoulders. A moment later the ship exploded. Consciousness returned and the sensation of suffocating faded. He lay there for some time wondering what the dream might mean, if anything. It was not particularly scary or disturbing, nor was he prone to having dreams that meant anything, so it was soon forgotten.

Jared lay in bed, musing, when Orion informed him they'd entered communications range with the small ship.

He got up and headed for the bridge. "Well, I guess we'd better contact them."

"Channel open."

"Adrift vessel, this is the Trader Ship Orion, please respond…" Jared's transmission received nothing but silence. He waited for almost a minute before trying again.

"Adrift vessel, I repeat, this is the Trader Ship Orion, please respond…"

"All right, all right, keep your clothes on."

Jared couldn't help but chuckle. The individual who responded sounded old and cantankerous.

"I hear ya, who'd ya say it was?"

"This is the Trader Ship Orion. My name is Jared Chandler."

"Mine's Weese, Brodan Weese. What 'cha doin' out here so far?"

"I could ask the same question of you."

"Don't get uppity with me, boy. I've been out in these parts longer than you've been sniffin' air."

"Whoa, I simply meant you're a long way from any outpost or port."

"You're right! And it weren't my choice I got out here either."

"Well, to answer your question, I am not from the Commonwealth. This is my first trip here."

"From outside? Ain't never met an outsider before. What'cha look like?"

Jared's face broke into a wide grin. "I could ask you that same question."

"Now don't start that again."

"Would you like some assistance?"

"Well, if you're offering, I'd be more than happy to accept."

"What seems to be the problem?"

"About ten days ago, I got shanghaied by pirates. Old Gutless here managed to outrun 'em, but they fired a tracker at me, so I just had to keep running. Was clippin' along at near full speed for seven days before the engines blew. I was lucky I didn't go up like a daystar having a panic attack. But I lost it. Been drifting for the past three. Never figured to meet anybody out here. Expected I'd either starve to death or run out of breathable air. Just been spending the last little while writing my obituary. Worse thing is I've been drinkin' water for the last 4 days. Ran plum out o' ph'lem."

Jared chuckled. "I'll pull alongside and see if I can help."

"Sounds good. Looking forward to meeting ya."

"Orion?"

"Ready."

"Do we have the capability of docking with the other ship?"

"Yes."

"Can you locate an accessible hatch?"

"Hatch located."

"Proceed with docking please."

"Complying, docking maneuver initiated."

The docking maneuver took about five minutes and was completed without incident. Jared heard nothing as Orion connected with 'Old Gutless'.

"Orion to Old Gutless."

"Watch it there, only I get to call it Old Gutless!"

"Okay, so what should I call your ship?"

"Wicky."

Jared's eyebrows shot up. He shook his head and stifled a laugh. "Wicky? Okay, is that your ship's name?"

"Stop your cacklin'. Wicky was a fine woman and best darn co-pilot I ever had. Good bond-mate too."

"How about I just call you Trader Weese? You are a trader, aren't you?"

"Sure am. Old Wicky may be gutless, but she sure can haul a lot."

"Docking maneuver complete, air seal confirmed," Orion informed Jared.

"Our airlock is connected to you, Trader Weese."

"What? I didn't feel nothin'."

"You may open your airlock at any time."

"I ain't opening my airlock until I confirm it!" After a short pause. "Wow! It is connected. I didn't feel nuthin'. Woa-K, I'm heading back to the airlock. See ya there."

"Orion, terminate comm link."

"Link terminated."

Jared opened the main hatch and waited for the grumpy old space cadet to open his side. The clamor that accompanied the opening of Old Gutless's airlock was intense. Hissing air, scraping, squealing latch mechanisms, rusty un-oiled hinges, and other miscellaneous popping, clanking and rattling sounds attended the happening. The Wicky wasn't much better looking than the three freighters he had seen at the outpost, except it looked as if all its components had been manufactured at the same time and for the same vessel.

As the airlock thudded against the wall, an elderly man with a scraggly, unkempt beard and worn, wrinkled, leathery-looking skin came into view. Jared had to smile because the old man obviously was also missing many teeth and his jaw sat higher when his mouth was closed, which caused his lower lip to protrude significantly. His attire was worn and faded, but there were no unpleasant smells in the ship's air.

Initially Jared noticed a concerned look on Weese's face. The old man's countenance changed shortly after he first saw Jared.

"Guess you ain't no strange alien," Weese grunted as he walked up to where Jared stood. "Darn unusual vessel ya got."

"How many strange aliens have you encountered?" Jared asked curiously.

"Ain't never seen one and never want to," grumped Weese as he fumbled with a circuit box near the air lock. "Okay, its secure. Whar' ya headed anyway?"

"Sha'Lural," Jared answered and noticed Weese screw up his face worse than it already was.

"Klal!" he spat. "That's where them bunch of guren dung jumped me."

"Guren dung?" Jared asked quizzically.

"Pirates," Weese spat again.

Jared nodded and shrugged. "Oh."

"Well, come on in and I'll figure out what it is I need."

Weese led the way from whence he'd come. The hall was cluttered and narrow but at least the headroom was sufficient. The walls were tapered inward at the top and bottom. See-through grating vaguely resembling a honeycomb covered some areas of the deck. It wasn't very far from the airlock to the living area, which was also quite small. Weese's sleeping area was no more than an alcove above and fore of the galley with a small common area to the left, over which were two other alcoves. Ahead of that was the bridge, where there was just enough room for three chairs and the instrumentation. Nearly every square foot of the Wicky's interior looked as though it had been torn apart. Missing panels and cabinet doors left wiring and pipes exposed. Parts and circuitry lay scattered everywhere except the bridge. Numerous bottles, which Jared assumed had at one time held Weese's valued ph'lem lay mixed in with the mess.

Weese cleared the small table in the center of the common area with a single swipe of his arm. Plates half full of a recent meal, papers, a couple of books and some circuit boards piled together into a large plastic box.

"Pull up a seat."

Jared found the nearest chair, straddled it, and rested his arms on the back. He continued to survey Weese's home, and it did indeed look as though the old man had given up and was preparing to die. Now, however, he was carefully going over his lists of damages with quiet vigor. A photo-image of an elderly woman was hanging near Weese's sleeping alcove and Jared figured it was Weese's late love, Wicky.

Occasionally the ship would produce an irritating series of buzzing, clicking or sputtering sounds, which Jared hoped did not portend disaster. Deciding to remain quiet and not aggravate the old space dog, Jared waited for nearly a half em-har before Weese looked up from his lists and note-taking.

"Alright, boy," he said in better humor than he had been earlier. "I got my list, show me the goods."

Jared rose from the chair and stretched. He smiled, then stepped toward the hall. "Right this way."

Jared waited for the old man to pass and then followed. They made their way back to the air lock and entered Orion. Weese was very impressed by both the size and layout of the vessel. He had never been on a ship that was maintained so well and Jared didn't have the heart to tell Weese that the ship maintained itself, not that the old spacer was likely to believe it. He would have probably been very suspicious of the Orion if Jared had left the interior white. After giving Weese a brief tour of the bridge, galley and med room, they descended into the cargo bay.

When they entered the cargo area the look on the old man's face amused Jared.

"You got a lot more 'n I figured," he said quietly. "Where do I start lookin'?"

"That depends," he pointed to his right. "Electrical components such as wire, cable, circuit boards and modular units are in those crates. Tools and diagnostic equipment are in crates there. Pipe, fasteners, adhesives, conduit, and panel material are on that side of the room. If you have an item not in those categories let me know and I'll see if I can find it."

"Hoo Wa, I think I just might find what I need." Weese chuckled and began searching through the crates of electrical parts.

The old man spent over three em-hars going through various stock and found nearly everything he wanted. Most importantly he found what he needed to get the Wicky operating again. Most of the damage inflicted had been circuit overloads and cable breakage. He wanted to fix his food storage locker and alcohol still, but Jared had no refrigeration unit nor the unusual parts. He gave Weese ample dried food supplies for his trip back to familiar space. Since Weese flat out refused to return to Sha'Lural, Jared gave him a bit extra so he could make it to Yuali'rod.

The old trader was more than happy to accept Jared's invitation for a hot meal. Conversation was limited due to Weese's desire to begin the repairs. They ate very quickly, and as they walked to the Wicky, Jared began to probe for more information about Sha'Lural.

"Is pirate activity really that bad at Sha'Lural?"

Exasperated again Weese said, "Don't know exactly how bad it is. Was my first run out that far. Was supposed to be a good payin' contract too."

"So, you never even had a chance to pick up the cargo?" Jared was surprised.

"Nope."

"Why would they go after an empty ship?"

"Well, I doubt they'd a' known whether I was empty or not, but they didn't ask no questions, they just started shootin'."

"How many ships were there?"

"One, but that was enough for me, Wicky's a good tug, but ain't got much as far as defenses. Never needed 'em before."

"Can I help you with any of the repairs?" Jared offered.

"You willin' to help?"

"Sure. I'm not trained in electronics or star drives and the like but I have worked with sheet metal and composites."

"Ha, Wicky, looks as if we're gonna be outa here soon," Weese said enthusiastically. "Think ya' can install some cable and pipe sections?"

"Not a problem as long as I have a schematic to refer to."

"Good, the tech manuals are in that cabinet there." Weese indicated a set of metal shelves with perforated doors. "You'll need one for section 6 and one for section 11."

Jared walked to the cabinet, pulled open the doors and began searching for the appropriate volumes. Proper filing was obviously not one of Weese's concerns. The books, which were in bad condition anyway, were simply crammed onto the shelves haphazardly. Some had partially torn pages sticking out and others had missing covers or backs. After several minutes he succeeded in locating volume three, which covered sections six, seven, and eight and volume four, which covered sections nine, ten, eleven, and twelve.

Weese was still sorting through the components he'd brought from the Orion when Jared sat the books on the table.

"Good." Weese looked up briefly. "I'll show ya' where them two sections are shortly."

"Right." Jared pulled up a chair.

"Most of the damage is in the engine room." Weese did not look up. "Had ta put patches over several leaks an' shut down the port side coolant pump." He paused as he switched circuit boards. "Took a bad hit on that side and it blew most of the circuitry to the regulator. I was runnin' both engines on full for a good while. They sure was hot when I finally shut 'em down. Much longer an' I'm sure lefty would'a' blown."

"Any hull breeches?"

"A few but I patched them quick."

"You did that while being chased?" Jared smiled. "Multitasking, nice."

"Naw, I had one trick to use," Weese chuckled. "'Bout two cycles ago ah salvaged an old military wreck. Its Autonav system was intact and in good shape, which is rare 'cause they're usually one of the first ta go when damage occurs ta the bridge area."

"They're that delicate?"

"Compared to most of the other systems, yeah." Weese stood and gathered together the circuit boards he had selected. "C'mon, I'll show ya where ta start."

Jared picked up the two tech manuals, nodded his head and followed. "So how did finding the Autonav help you elude the pirates?"

"Well, the autonavs on these Hedmar KL-5 boats are good, but no one ever meant for 'em to do any more than maintain travel in a straight line. Wicky's old, and was about due for a system overhaul, so finding it was a blessin'. Kept me from havin' to shell out a lot for a new one." Weese stopped at a bulkhead conveniently and clearly marked 6.

"This is where you start." Weese pointed to a section of pipe that was broken and twisted. "I figure it broke here due to over pressurization before I got the pump shut down, but the alarm never went off." He rubbed his head.

"I guess having to pay full price for a new Autonav is a form of piracy," Jared joked.

Weese, however, didn't hear or was ignoring the remark. Jared decided to ask one more time. "What was the main difference between your old Autonav and the military one?"

"I told you, maneuverability."

"The Autonav improved the ship's maneuvering?"

Weese furrowed his eyebrows. "No, it's advanced AI did the maneuverin' for me so I could take care of the damage control."

"Ah."

"Okay, got ever' thing ya need? Good. The damaged pipe will likely be a Mk-3 or Mk-4. I got those stored in bunker seven." Heading aft, he added. "If ya have any questions, holler."

Jared was going to ask a question but reconsidered, not wanting to sound too ignorant. Instead, he began to search the manual for the port side coolant flow system at section six. Part one of the manual covered section six and the coolant schematic was near the end. An overall view of the entire system covered two pages, which indeed answered his question. The port side pump was located in the front of the ship while the other was in the aft on the opposite side.

Never having seen a real spacecraft he had wondered why the ship would need a coolant pump so far forward if the engines were in the rear. The coolant cycled around the entire ship, circulated by the two pumps. The system provided coolant to the four main thrusters, two braking thrusters and twelve directional thrusters. The following page detailed the portion of the system between bulkhead five and six. Each space between bulkheads was about twelve feet long and had two six-foot lengths of the pipe per section. After noting the location of the pipe, he studied the manual for several minutes.

He picked up the wrench and two clamps Weese had left. Two thick pegs on the clamps fit into hard points just below the pipes and reinforced the mountings so he could apply the necessary amount of torque. The forward coupling refused to budge. Finally, having to resort to placing his feet firmly against the wall and using his body weight, he succeeded in loosening it. Less effort was needed to break the seal on the aft end. Twisting the couplings off the rest of the way by hand took little effort. Residue of a thick yellow-orange fluid ran out of the pipe and a thin layer of sludge coated the inside. Jared shoved one of several rags from the box into one end of the old pipe and leaned it against the opposite wall. Referring back to the manual, he determined the required procedure for installation of the new piece. Ensuring that the threads were straight and not exceeding the maximum torque were the only critical steps he had to worry about.

Jared picked up the approximately six-foot-long section of the new pipe and examined it. Weese had probably done so, but he wanted to make sure there were no cracks or other damage. Threads on one end and a flange on the other showed no signs of dents or fractures. He slid the coupling he had removed from the old pipe onto the new one and tested it for fit. The manual indicated the necessity of using an approved gasket material between the couplings, pipe head and threads. Another search through the box revealed an odd-looking spray can labeled Flexi-seal, which was on the manual's list of accepted substances. Fortunately, the smell of the gasket material, though irritating, was not enough to make Jared feel ill. He assembled the aft end first where the threads of the new pipe fit into the coupling on the back pipe then slid the coupling on the new pipe over the end of the front one. After hand tightening the couplings, he began looking for a torque wrench.

Unable to locate the needed tool in the box of things Brodan had given him, he headed toward the engine room. Missing floor panels at various locations along with other equipment or parts lying about created an obstacle course. He entered the largest room he had yet seen on the Wicky and found Weese's lower half protruding out of an opening near the rear most bulkhead. Not wanting to startle the old man, he made sure he didn't touch him.

"Trader Weese?"

"What?"

"I need a wrench with a torque meter to finish tightening the couplings on the coolant pipe."

"Well, you can't have one," Weese said, as if Jared were a child asking for candy. "'Cause that was one of the items on my list you didn't have." He paused, grunting loudly and then swore. "Klal, stubborn piece of junk. You still standing there? What else you need?"

"Nothing," Jared said as respectfully as he could. "I'm just preparing to re-enter the hall of the *damned.*"

"You talking to me?"

"Nope, just admiring the decorating," Jared began his trek back to section six. He stopped to look at section eleven and discovered he would have to crawl over one of the large equipment units to get to the cable he needed to replace. Back at section six he used the standard wrench and tightened the couplings as best he could. After repacking his so-called tool/supply box he headed back to section eleven.

The piece of equipment blocking easy access to the damaged cable looked like a complex series of relays, circuit breakers and valves. Space at the side was too small to squeeze through but would allow him to reach items from the box, so he set the container down close to the aft side. Whoever designed this barge never meant for it to be operator maintained. Placing his foot on a wall strut and pulling himself up while trying to avoid causing damage to the unit made the effort awkward. Most difficult was that the maneuver required turning so he could get his feet in first, then find a handle to hold before sliding into the alcove. Once in, he found there was sufficient room to work comfortably. Using the manual, he located the ends of the cable and detached them. The ruined cable was burnt and frayed near one end and a black carbon score on the side wall indicated it had actually caught fire. Weese had indeed been lucky because any one of these damaged areas could have proved fatal.

Jared had no idea whether or not Orion had any such cables, conduits, relays, or pipes. The ship had no apparent panels or access points. Well, at least none he had yet seen. Snapping the new cable into place proved difficult since the old one had dissimilar end connectors, and the new one had the same type.

Jared was irritated.

So now what? I'm sure not going to crawl out of here, just to have the old fart tell me to figure it out myself.

He connected the end he could and again referred to the manual. The book indicated the cable should have matching connectors so he decided the problem must lie in the section transition plug attached to the bulkhead. This would require replacing the transition plug and the cable aft of where he was, which meant entering an alcove in section twelve. Not to mention, he didn't even know if Weese had another section of the needed cordage or another plug. The company who built these freighters had obviously designed them to use standard modular components. Each of the sections between bulk heads were of equal length except for the engine room and the bridge, though the section shapes varied greatly from one to the next. Sections five, six, eight, nine, eleven and twelve were narrow to provide recesses for the modular pods the vessel utilized to haul cargo.

Getting out of the tiny compartment was far easier than getting in. He returned to the engine room where he found Weese sitting on the floor working on a bulky component that looked like a huge camera lens. "Is that the flow regulator?"

"Yeah, and several of the valve plates are bent."

"Can you fix it?"

"Should be able to get them straight enough to last until I can get to a repair facility."

"That's lucky."

"No, that's experience," Weese said confidently. "What ya need now?"

"Well, the transition plug in bulkhead eleven does not match the new cable connector, so either the plug needs to be replaced, or a different connector needs to be spliced onto the cable."

"Klal, that's the piece I fixed all of them cycles ago and forgot about. Took me ten days to get all the individual wires matched up. I'll be working on this for a while. Think ya can check to see if ya have one on your ship? I used the only two I had back here to fix damage to the engine power and control lines. The manual can give you the part code."

"No problem."

"Good. Did'ja get the pipe in?"

"It's tight, but I have no idea how close it is to specs."

"I'll check it before I start the system."

"Okay." Jared turned to leave. "Is there anything else I should look for while I'm at it?"

"Not that I can think of, but I'm sure something will turn up."

"That's what I'm afraid of," Jared said under his breath as he walked out. Stopping at bulkhead eleven, he picked up the manual, tucked it under his arm, then continued on to the airlock.

Happy to be back on-board Orion and its clean, spacious surroundings, Jared took time to grab a snack. His clothes were covered with dust, grease, and coolant so he tried to avoid coming into contact with more than he had to. From the galley he headed directly to the lower level. Having an accessible interior cargo bay was far preferable to the set up the Hedmar freighter used. Rather than spending time going through the items he had already inventoried, he began looking in crates he hadn't previously investigated. Opening the manual and reviewing the system part listings revealed that there were three different plugs that could be used. EIR-213-7983-2a was the default part manufactured by Hedmar. Also useable was the Shyldrom–Nyclar PFC-77353-2 and the Zyenricon triflow energy jack, series five. Special mounting modification had to be provided for the Zyenricon jack however and Jared hoped it would not be the one he came across.

Two em-har and sixteen cases later Jared had found no part matching either the descriptions or the faded drawings contained in the book. Sitting back against a stack of crates he pulled the remainder of the pastry out of his pocket and took a bite. He lay his head back and closed his eyes as he chewed. It occurred that he should ask Weese what the regulations were concerning traders. He would probably need a license to trade and a registration for Orion. He'd have to be careful, because if pirate activity was bad, someone might be suspicious of where he got all this stuff. Difficulties might even arise from the fact that he was not a citizen of any of the worlds in this area of space.

"Orion?"

"Ready."

"Are there any other vessels besides us and the Wicky in our area?"

"No other vessels in sensor range."

"How are you doing?"

"Specify."

"Um, give me a system status report."

"All systems except sensors are at minimal output levels. No anomalies or malfunctions."

"Thank you."

"You are welcome."

"Guess I should get back to work."

"Indeed."

Flustered by Orion's remark, Jared knitted his eyebrows.

The ship occasionally made statements Jared wasn't sure how to take. He shrugged off the feeling and resumed searching. He wasn't sure what he was looking for at the moment, but inside the next crate was an excellent find. For some time, he had wondered how he would defend himself off the Orion if the need ever arose. Now, here lay ten handguns and four rifles which utilized rechargeable power cells instead of metallic slugs. He had the assault rifles but no ammunition for them, and the one handgun he possessed had few rounds to go with it. The manifest listed the pistols as Wykar Series seven SR-479 power pulse side-arms and the rifles as Wykar pulse series rapid fire assault guns. It also indicated that the weapons were for military issue only. Four, multiple cavity recharging units were also included in the shipment. Securely closing the crate, Jared carried it to the area where he stored the items he had chosen to keep. As he returned to the search, he determined to find a suitable area on the main deck to store his belongings.

Another em-har passed and he was beginning to tire of what was a seemingly fruitless task. Leaving Weese stranded out here was out of the question and Jared doubted the man would leave the Wicky. To avoid having to spend many more days drifting in one spot, finding the simple receptacle was a must.

"Companion."

"Yes."

"Weese has entered."

"Thanks," Jared sighed and got to his feet.

"You are welcome."

Weese was about halfway along the main deck when Jared found him. The old spacer's countenance was quite cheerful, and he smiled as Jared came into view.

"Ain't found nothin' yet, huh?"

"No," Jared said, beginning to show some irritation of his own. "There are about thirty more crates so I'm trying to maintain some optimism."

"Bah. No bother if ya don't. It'll just take a little longer ta fix."

Jared turned his head away and raised his eyes toward the ceiling.

Great, just great.

Then he closed them.

Please, if there is any being on a higher plane out there, let me find the part.

"You okay, boy?" Weese looked concerned.

"Yeah, just fine."

"Well, let's get back to lookin'."

"Actually, I think I need something to eat."

"Hoo wa, that does sound good. You gonna make another meal like ya did earlier?"

"Sure."

Weese grinned impishly. "Great."

As they ate, Weese answered Jared's questions happily through mouthfuls. Jared wondered whether he had never learned manners or simply stopped using them after being so long alone in space.

"Yuali'rod is a lot further than Sha'Lural. How long will it take you to get there?"

"Oh, 'bout seven weeks I s'pose. Lot more if my JFG gives me any trouble."

"JFG, what's that?"

"Jump field generator," Weese said as he stuffed another bite. "Allows a ship to jump forward for brief periods of time and sure does git ya closer to your target faster."

"What do you mean by 'jump forward'?"

"Don't know what it means for sure, just know it works." He burped and continued, "That's just what most call it. If ya want details, you'll have to find an engineer."

"I'll remember that," Jared nodded.

Weese had not taken his eyes off the food since Jared set it down. Holding any more questions until Weese was finished allowed him to eat a little faster.

I wonder if a jump is similar to Null Space travel.

Weese stuffed his last bite, and Jared began his questions again.

"Why does the JFG only work for brief periods?"

"Huh? Oh, well I'm not sure if they can work for long periods or not, but if ya stay in a jump for too long it sure will mess ya up."

"In what way?"

"Twists up your insides and messes with your head."

Jared feigned a grimace as he stood up to clear the table.

Stomachs full, the two men began searching the cargo bay with vigor. Weese was a bit more cheerful than Jared but getting this over with was a good motivator. Several times the old man stopped to inform Jared he'd found an item of high value. Jared had responded by placing an empty container near him. Box after box yielded many surprises and items of value, but nothing that came close to what they were looking for. With only five cases remaining Weese found two torque wrenches and Jared offered him one. Weese expressed his gratitude briefly before delving back into the box. One of the two last boxes was full of one hundred and sixty cycles old Flura's sauce which Weese said was probably worth ten to twenty thousand credits.

"What exactly is Flura sauce?"

"You really are from outside aren't ya'?"

"You doubted me before?"

Weese looked a bit apologetic. "A little skeptical, maybe. Last time a new world with an indigenous race was found was over six hundred cycles ago. That's what the history texts say, though there hasn't been much new exploration for about two hundred fifty cycles. I think the Drakstrad was havin' a tough time keeping the territory it controlled from comin' apart long before the actual fall. Anyway, Fluras is made from the tiny eggs of the Flura'kat, which is found in the oceans of Andrios. Considered quite a delicacy on most worlds. Well, that's it for this crate."

Weese began replacing the unneeded contents.

"Caviar."

"What?"

"Oh, sorry. That's the word used to describe a similar food on my home world. Fish eggs." Jared finished emptying the last crate and sighed. "Well, that's it."

Weese raised his brows. "I'll get started on the splicing in the morning."

Jared decided to leave the box he had unloaded as is until later. He walked Weese back to the air lock, wished the old man good night then headed for the laundry. With his dirty clothing taken care of he retired to his quarters for a hot shower. He had no desire to be waiting here any longer, but if he had to, he could continue the inventory.

He stood soaking for some time before getting out and decided it might be fun to try and grow a beard but settled on a goatee. He had grown one once when he was 18, but Sandra had given him so much grief he had shaved it off. He still had no idea why she found them so distasteful. Shaving everywhere except his chin and upper lip, he brushed his teeth and climbed into bed.

Jared awoke feeling good until he remembered he might be sitting at this location for some time. Breakfast went fast and an em-har later he couldn't even remember what he'd had. Instead of inventory he began moving his personal stash up to the main deck. He neatly organized weapons and equipment in the EVA room. The remainder he put into two of the unused small sleep rooms. On his last trip he tried to lift a box that was quite heavy and dropped it, scattering the contents all over the cargo area.

"Damn!" he spat through clenched teeth. He decided he'd had enough and headed toward the exit. An object to his left caught his eye and he bent to pick it up. There was no mistaking it, a Shyl-drom-Nyclar PFC style connector.

Relief raced through him, and he suddenly felt better. Without a second thought, he took it immediately to Weese.

"Morning boy," the old man said cheerfully. "Nice ta see ya with a smile on. Things ain't so bad after a good sleep."

Jared revealed the elusive part. "It's even better than that."

"Hoo Wa!" The old spacer yelled and jumped from his seat. "Ain't that the best of luck!"

"No, growing experience," Jared joked.

Weese considered him for a moment, then smiled and took the part.

"Ever wish there were an easier way to access these areas?" Jared asked.

"Ain't never had a problem," Weese leaned over as he spoke and released a switch on either side of the frame, pulling the unit entirely across the narrow hall. Jared hoped he didn't look as foolish as he felt. Weese stepped into the open space and began loosening the fasteners that held the receptacle in place.

"Can you disconnect the cable from the other side?"

"Sure." Jared moved into section twelve and spent several em figuring out how the latches worked. He had no intention of asking Weese. It might be a stupid ego issue, but he wanted to leave without being remembered as too dense to figure something out. A loud snap accompanied the release of the second latch. Jared looked to see if Weese had noticed, but the old spacer was concentrating on extracting the fasteners. Once inside he had no difficulty removing the cable and waited several al-em for Weese to get the last fastener undone. Reassembly took less than half an em-har after which Jared assisted in repositioning the units into their respective niches.

"Are there any panels which cover these?"

"Was once, but they got so dinged up cycles ago that I tossed most of 'em. Less of a hassle this way too."

"Aren't you worried that there might be exterior damage which could cause problems when you start the Wicky up?"

"Oh, I know there is damage to the hull, but I won't know if it'll cause trouble if I just sit here."

"Guess that's true, but could I take a look and let you know?"

"Sure, ya could but what good would it do? You have experience workin' in a weightless environment and usin' EVA equipment such as torches and the like?"

"No."

"Alright then, stop with the ideas. You've been plenty of help already. So, let's say good-bye and part company so's I can get back to civilization." Weese headed back to the common area at a lively pace.

"Okay," Jared chuckled. He figured that Weese was worried about the start up too but was also too proud to admit the fact. Letting the old man lead the way back to the airlock, Jared asked a few last questions. "Any ideas what Sha'Lural is like?"

"Probably not unlike most other Commonwealth colonies, which means if you can get past the pirates, it will be a fair place. The Drakstrad usually ignored planets much different than Iliria or that required domes or such, except for mining. I read somewhere that they tried using huge devices to alter the atmosphere of a planet a long time ago, but the cost was just too high."

"One other thing I was meaning to ask you. How should I go about getting the necessary licenses and registrations for myself and my ship to operate as a trader?"

"Now that is one good thing about being out here near the colonies. They're usually hard up for transport even at the best of times. If ya' treat em real friendly you should be able to get a license and registration for a greatly reduced fee."

"Will a Sha'Luralian license and registration be valid in the Commonwealth itself?"

"Should be, and it'll be easier to get into the trader's guild if ya already have a license 'cause they aren't too keen on competition from non-member traders."

When they reached the airlock, Jared asked, "So, there are some who won't join the guild?"

"Yep."

"Why?"

"Not sure. Guess they don't like to pay the annuals." Weese stopped next to the airlock door and gave Jared a slight wave. "Perhaps I'll see you around."

Jared thought about offering to shake Weese's hand, but Weese had given no indication that such gestures were used in his culture. Waving seemed to satisfy his need for salutation. The clanking, rattling and hissing noises once again accompanied the moving airlock door. Halfway through its arc, Jared had Orion secure the hatch and went to the bridge, waiting for Weese to notify him that Wicky's air lock was sealed and ready for separation. It would be interesting to see what other classes of ships looked like and if any resembled designs dreamed up on Earth.

"Weese to Orion."

"This is Orion. Go ahead"

"You ready to let me go yet?"

"Any time."

"Then cut me loose."

Jared switched to Adarian. "Ohval'tya Wicky anasri, You are free and clear, Trader Weese."

"Understood and thanks."

Jared took control of Orion, turned slightly to starboard and accelerated slowly away. Once at a distance he stopped. He figured he would give Weese some breathing room.

"I'll wait here in case you have any problems."

"Suit yourself. Wicky out."

"So long."

It took about fifteen al-em before Wicky showed any signs of life. A faint glow indicated that something was happening in the Wicky's main engines. Jared didn't worry. He figured it was probably a warm-up sequence.

Then suddenly the four exhaust nozzles burst to life and the small freighter began to move. The vessel turned across Orion's path and began to accelerate away. Jared decided before Weese was too far away he'd give the old spacer a view of real acceleration, though he had no idea whether the man would be watching or not. Placing his head against the back of the chair and telling Orion to reduce the gravity on board, he shoved the accelerator forward one quarter of its length.

Weese was indeed watching as Orion was one moment sitting still and the next gone from sight and sensor. That boy may not look alien, but Weese still had his suspicions, and the ship certainly was, as far as he was concerned. He also figured the beautiful ship had plenty of defenses, which meant the pirates were likely to get their come-uppence and that was one thing he wished he could see.

Jared sat for some time in the command chair reviewing the last two days. He would be in the Lural system in five days if he stayed in normal space or could drop it to eleven hours if he chose to use Null Space. Weese, on the other hand, had a seven-week trip to Yuali'rod and that was if he risked full speed using his jump field generator.

CHAPTER FIVE

Sha'Lural

*"It is far easier to conquer than to maintain control over
any group of intelligent beings. The reason for this is:
it is nearly impossible to change the customs and habits
of the conquered to those of the conqueror, and will almost
assuredly result in the eventual withdrawal of the conqueror,
or more likely, the destruction of the conquered."*

*Alaran Safarak,
Supreme Shakar,
Drakstrad Military Forces*

O RION GAVE JARED a report on the approaching system. Lural was
a yellow star slightly smaller than Earth's sun with four satellites. The closest body to Lural was called Enar-tho'lural. Enar in
the Ilirian tongue means death. Sha'Lural had originally been called
Sha–tho adom'lural. 'Sha' meaning bright one, 'tho' meaning near
and 'adom' meaning warm, thus being called 'bright one near warm

lural'. The two remaining planets had received simple numerical designations and except for a mining facility on the third planet, were unsettled, large, unremarkable, low-atmosphere rocks.

Sha'Lural had been one of the last few planets the Drakstrad Commonwealth had colonized before the great fall. Orion informed Jared that the planet possessed a circumference of 23,921 miles, with two large continental masses and three smaller, covering 17% of its surface. Only three cities and numerous small agricultural towns were developed and those only on the second largest of the continents.

With not much else to do, Jared spent his morning working out. After a warm shower, his stomach led him to the galley. He was very appreciative that the food processor was so easy to use. He simply had to input his choice, and the device would prepare it. Many of the items it had in its memory had tastes like Earth food. Some, however, were very strange. This was one of the devices that was a total mystery, because it did not actually create food. The food storage lockers had to have the required ingredients, which the processor would select and then prepare. The dish he had this morning was somewhat like steak and eggs and he had a double portion. He hadn't been able to fill many of the food lockers from the outpost's supplies, so they were mostly empty now. He knew filling them would have to be one of his first priorities.

By the time Jared arrived on the bridge, the fourth of Lural's planets was looming large on the view screen. Its distance from Lural was nearly as far as Neptune was from Sol, though it was much larger. Orion passed close enough to magnify the view of the planetoid's surface so Jared could see it in detail. In their own way, the immense ice fields and formations of jagged rock were extremely beautiful. Someday he would very much like to view the planets of his home system, especially Earth, and see how they compared.

The two smaller satellites orbiting it were marked with numerous craters and fissures. After passing number 4, Jared left the bridge and headed for the cargo bay. As he passed his quarters he stopped, a look of curiosity crossing his face.

"Orion?"

"Ready."

"Do you know what 'music' is?" Jared asked. Not having heard music since leaving Earth, and despite the few Ilirian books, Jared found himself suffering from periods of boredom.

"Variable tonal resonance?"

"Uhm, possibly, I'll give you a demonstration." Jared began humming a familiar tune, shortly after which the same sound was heard reverberating throughout the ship. "Yes, you've got it. That's music."

"Understood."

"Okay, can you download similar information from my memory synapses?"

"Scanning individual data groups is possible periodically, but any input or extraction can cause potential side effects."

"What kind of side effects?"

"Short duration extraction can cause neural discomfort. Extended can result in permanent neural damage."

"Okay, let's try a short one and see how it affects me."

"Understood. Please designate which of the 6,523 data groups."

"Whoa . . .! 6,523?!"

"Confirmed."

"Uh, choose one at random please."

"Accessing data unit 5.

"Whoa, Stop, Please," Jared winced, hearing what he assumed was himself as a child, screeching out *Twinkle, Twinkle, Little Star.* "Is it safe to try another?"

"Yes. First scan required approximately one ten thousandth of an hour."

"Wait, why did you default to my native language with this response?"

Orion queried, "Does the companion really wish to know?"

"Ya, I do."

"First scan referenced in Adarian was less than .00000…"

"Okay, stop. Whoa. I really don't want to know. How about data unit number 5,000?"

"Accessing."

Shortly after the ship spoke, an exact duplicate of a 1990's pop song began playing throughout the ship. Jared smiled broadly. It would help a great deal to keep himself from going nuts during long periods of travel.

"Orion?"

"Ready."

"I do not feel any change; can you tell if I was injured in any way by this experiment?"

"No neural strain was detected during the extraction."

"How many songs do you think you can safely download at each short burst?"

"Calculating—depending on each track's length, between six and eight. Recommended rate is once every eighteen em-har."

"Cool, make it so. Hopefully that won't cause any problems, but if you suspect it does you may stop at your discretion."

"Confirmed. Additional micro data group extractions at eighteen em–har intervals."

Jared continued his way toward the cargo bay moving rhythmically to music he'd not heard in a very long time. One song did not last very long, though he had it repeated twice. Soon he would have quite a collection.

He entered the cargo bay and began going through the containers he had yet to inspect. He resumed cataloging the various circuit boards, containers of various fluids, wiring, adhesives, plating, tools, and other items. After several em-har, he headed for the galley and lunch. For the rest of the afternoon and evening Jared simply relaxed.

The next day, Orion came within communications range of planet number 3. The mining outpost apparently had the ability to track nearby vessels and hailed Orion.

"Unidentified ship entering Sha'Lural controlled space. Please respond."

"This is Jared Chandler of the trader ship Orion."

"A trader ship? What is your registration?"

"I am not registered within the old Commonwealth area of jurisdiction."

There was a pause followed by, "You are from outside the known Commonwealth?"

"Yes. I am Terran."

"I am not familiar with that designation."

"As I said, I am not from within the environs of the known Commonwealth."

"What is your cargo?"

"Primarily salvaged pumps, generators, mechanical equipment and replacement parts."

The pause was even longer this time. "Please stand by." Another long pause was followed by another voice identifing himself as Ren'al.

"Greetings Trader, I am the director of this facility. We need replacement parts for numerous items and hope you might be able to fulfill some of those requirements."

Jared smiled to himself. He felt as if good fortune were smiling on him early. "Director Ren'al, I would be more than happy to show you what I carry. Please give me coordinates to your landing facilities."

Ren'al transmitted the landing coordinates and Orion indicated they had been received and confirmed.

"Director, I wish to reconfirm that I have your official permission to land."

"Permission is officially granted."

"Thank you. Landing ETA is 15 al–ems."

The communications link went dead, and Jared prepared for his first landing with Orion. He realized he really had nothing to worry about since all he had to do was tell Orion where he wanted to go, or what operation to perform, and Orion would do it unaided. However, paying attention to the console as Orion went through each procedure might help him learn more about piloting the ship. He had no intention of spending a lifetime on Orion and never learning.

"Orion?"

"Ready."

"What is the population of the mining facility?"

"150 biological units, 37 robotic units."

"Defensive capabilities?"

"Low power shielding and 5 pulse cannons."

"Are they any danger?"

"Specify to what."

"The Orion."

"Hardly."

Exactly fifteen al-ems later, Orion set down on one of the four large cargo pads in the mining facility. Two ships already occupied other pads, and Jared could tell they were being loaded as rapidly as possible. Orion informed Jared he was being hailed by the facility director.

"Trader Chandler?"

"Yes Director?"

"My docking supervisor cannot locate your docking port."

"Director, please have your operator extend your docking module toward the front left of the Orion. The docking port will become visible as it nears."

"Uhm, very well. Extending docking module," the director responded.

"Orion?"

"Ready."

"Please identify and configure for docking."

"Confirmed, ready for docking."

Another voice this time came over the communicator.

"Trader Chandler. My name is Rheed. Thank you, I have your docking port identified. Please confirm when docking seal is established."

Jared waited for several moments before Orion informed him that the docking procedure was complete.

"Supervisor Rheed. Docking procedure is complete. Seal is confirmed."

"Thank you, Trader. Welcome to the Sha'Lural P3 Mining Facility. The director will meet you at the docking module in 5 al-ems."

"Understood, but I need to ask a favor."

"How can we be of assistance?" asked Rheed.

"During departure from my last port of call, an accident occurred that damaged all the clothing I possess. I was planning on purchasing more on Sha'Lural but would like to acquire some here if possible and I will need it brought to the ship."

This time it was the Director who spoke. "That will be no problem, trader. Just advise me as to the sizes you require."

Jared gave the Director his measurements since he was unfamiliar with how clothing was sized in the Commonwealth. He asked only for two pairs of pants and two shirts. He did not wish the people here to think he was running around naked. Though he could not be sure, he thought he heard laughter in the background as the director spoke.

"Give me an extra 10 al-ems and I will meet you at your main hatch," the director said cheerfully.

"Understood and thank you." Jared paused to see if the director had anything further to say. When he received no response, he asked Orion to monitor for messages but close the line.

"Voicecomm on stand–by. Monitoring."

Jared left the bridge. He stopped by his office to put on the wrist communicator that kept him in constant contact with Orion. Knowing these people would have no idea what kind of clothing someone from the outside would wear, he grabbed his towel and draped it across his shoulders. Even though he felt a bit exposed by his ragged clothing, his appearance was not that bad. Faded and frayed, his jeans admitted nothing but too much air. His shirt on the other hand was pocked with holes and long rips. Orion opened the main hatchway. It wasn't long before a rather short, yet muscular man approached. He introduced himself as Director Ren'al and handed Jared the requested clothing.

"Thank you for your hospitality. If you would like to follow me, I will show you what stock I have."

The man seemed impressed with the amount of goods Jared had stacked around.

"Do you have a list of what you need?"

"I do." The director presented Jared with a list to search, and Jared asked Orion to see if any of the items were available. Orion matched 73% of the items, several of which were desperately needed.

Jared agreed to be paid upon delivery when he transported a load of ore to Sha'Lural. The director indicated he could keep a sum equal to the equipment purchased plus transit fees, an agreement which Jared was more than happy to accept. He had to remember one thing the next time he traded—to find out the value of the items before entering negotiations. The supervisor had seemed quite pleased with the price agreed upon.

Jared told the supervisor that Orion would open its cargo bay so the facility's loading vehicles could off–load the equipment purchased. As the director left the ship, he thanked Jared and said he would have the loading vehicles ready in twelve al-ems. Jared closed the main hatch and returned to the cargo bay. Utilizing the overhead lifting devices, he maneuvered all the sold merchandise to the cargo elevator.

"Orion?"

"Ready."

"Place a seal around the cargo bay area and lower the elevator."

"Confirmed, elevator lowering," and after a brief pause Orion continued, "Elevator down."

Jared returned to the cargo bay, standing just outside the sealed off area.

"Orion?"

"Ready."

"Please allow me visual access to the cargo bay and the loading activity."

"Confirmed, modifying internal structure for transparency."

The entire underside of the vessel seemed to vanish from beneath Jared's feet. The thought crossed his mind that he must surely be standing on the first glass-bottomed spaceship. The sight was incredible. He could see the entire area. It would be amazing to have the entire ship go transparent while going as fast as possible in a planet's atmosphere, sort of like flying from New York to Paris in a glass airliner.

The loading vehicles moved as rapidly as the workers could load them. As one of the vehicles pulled toward the elevator on its fourth trip, the docking pad directly next to Orion erupted in flame. Since there was no atmosphere, there was no explosive sound. However, the ship that had been sitting on the platform now lay in two separate halves. The loading vehicles stopped as Jared turned and ran toward the bridge.

"Orion, what's goin' on?"

"A vessel in near orbit fired a pulse cannon at the area affected by the blast."

"Identify."

"Identification unknown, twelve biological units on board, it is preparing for another pass. Incoming communication from mining facility director."

"Trader Chandler. We are under attack by pirates. If possible, I recommend you take off immediately."

"I understand director, I'll return if I can."

"Companion."

"Yes, Orion."

"Two more threats have just come into detection from behind the second satellite."

"Emergency take–off."

"Elevator retracting. Take off in ten ems. Please observe safety protocol."

"Forget safety protocol. I'm nowhere near a restraint."

Obviously, Orion was concerned for Jared's safety. Part of the wall folded outward into the shape of a chair similar to those on the bridge.

"Observe safety protocol."

Without a word, he climbed into the chair and strapped in. As the last restraint snapped into place, Orion shot upward so fast Jared felt as if he was going to be squeezed into the bottom of the seat like a pancake.

"Orion, are we in firing range?"

"Yes, all are well within range."

"Target the closest, stage two, and fire!"

"Complying."

Orion maneuvered so fast the pirates probably did not realize they were in trouble until it was too late. Orion pivoted on its z-axis 20 degrees and fired.

One of the ships was so close it appeared that the buildup of power from Orion's weapon started to melt the exterior plating before it even fired. The blast hit just aft of its mid-section ripping it into multiple parts, glowing red hot in places, and spun helplessly out into space. The other two apparently had no stomach to take on what they had just seen and veered off.

"Companion, shall we pursue?"

"No, let's find out what damage has been done to the facility. Did the attacking ship get off another blast?"

"Confirmed, blast hit the dormitory section."

"Prepare for landing."

"Landing initiated."

Orion had stopped its vertical ascent when it fired. It simply reversed its course and dropped straight down, though much slower. Once again, the director met Jared at the docking module and thanked him for assisting in driving away the pirates.

"This is the first time they have attacked us with more than one ship. I had no idea they were working together."

"I'm glad I was able to be of assistance. Is there anything else I can do to help?"

"No. We have everything here to take care of the damage. But there is one thing you can add to our list of purchases. I noticed you have one in the cargo bay. May I show it to you?"

"Sure," Jared replied.

The director led Jared to a large, cylindrical object. It was one of the items Jared had been unable to identify.

"This is an old, yet very reliable Drakstrad military early warning satellite, used around military-type outposts. I'd like to offer you the entire value of the cargo load in exchange for the satellite."

Realizing the danger the miners were in, Jared agreed. Again, the director was very happy.

The two left the cargo bay together and Jared asked, "How many casualties did you have?"

"Two are missing, plus the crew of the cargo vessel that was destroyed. Fortunately, the dormitory section was empty since day shift activity was in full swing. The equipment you brought will allow us to repair the facility much more quickly."

"Are your weapons sufficient to fend off another attack like this one?"

"Yes. We have similar weapons to those the pirates are using.

Unless they find more powerful ones, we should be alright, particularly with the early warning satellite."

Director Ren'al turned to walk away, then stopped. "Oh, by the way, this is for you."

Jared took the leather pouch. "Thank you, what is this?"

"It's a gift from many of those you saved today. They took up a collection of credits to show their appreciation for your efforts on our behalf."

Jared opened the pouch and noticed various coins within. Stunned, all he could say was, "This is completely unexpected. Please pass on my gratitude."

"I will." Director Ren'al replied with a broad grin, then turned and departed.

Jared returned his attention to the loading and watched until the last of the ore was on board.

He re-entered Orion, closed the hatch, walked towards the bridge, and addressed his friend.

"Orion, time to go."

"Agreed."

Jared's eyebrows shot up and he stopped. "That was new."

Orion gave no response to his statement.

Several of the mining facility's personnel stood in the control center watching as the great white ship slowly rose away.

The director broke the silence, "We are very lucky, my friends, to be alive." The others murmured their agreement as another individual walked in.

"Director."

"Yes, A'mon, what is it?"

"The captain of the Alidar is refusing to leave until we can prove there is no threat to his vessel from pirates."

"Okay, tell him I can't make such an assurance and if he plans on staying beyond the standard load layover time, he'll have to pay extended docking fees."

"Orion?"

"Ready."

"Resume course to Sha'Lural."

"Confirmed and on course."

"ETA to destination?"

"28 em–har."

"I'm going to turn in early today, Orion. Keep an eye out for trouble."

"Goodnight, Companion."

Jared turned and headed toward his quarters but as he stepped through the door, Orion broke in.

"Companion."

"Yes, Orion."

"We are being pursued."

"Damn!" Jared turned around and walked to his seat. "I assume we can outrun them?"

"Without a doubt."

"Forget it. If we leave them operational, they'll just go after the mining facility again. Target to disable."

"Targeting confirmed."

"Fire."

Two small bursts of light unlike the previous blast lashed out toward the two vessels, striking unerringly and both ships, relieved of their power, rapidly slowed and began drifting.

"Orion, we'll inform the Sha'Luralian authorities about their location when we arrive."

"Confirmed."

"I'm going to take a nap." Jared again turned, exited the bridge, and headed for his quarters. He was asleep the second his head touched the pillow.

After breakfast, Jared left the galley and mused over the events at the P3 facility.

I wonder if those were the same pirates who attacked Brodan Weese. He had indicated only one ship though.

"Orion, how long before we enter comm range with Sha'Lural."

"4.7 al–em."

"Thank you."

"You are welcome, Companion."

The thought of the pirate ship he had ordered destroyed was bothering him. He realized it had been in defense of the mining facility, but he never thought he would need or be required to end another being's life. As he entered the bridge, he asked for an update on estimated time to comm range.

"2.1 al–em."

"Please run the music tracks you've accessed so far."

"Playing."

The music took him back to his other life. He wondered again whether his family and Earth were still there, or if he had been asleep for too long. Some of the music took him back to childhood and other tunes brought back his high school years. The ones Orion played this morning reminded him of his old girlfriend, Janet and the fun they'd had. After the breakup, he had decided to move away but had never dreamed of going quite this far. He had possessed some very big dreams, but his imagination had never been this bold. The music was cut short as Orion spoke.

"Companion."

"Yes Orion?"

"Communications established. Incoming message."

"Open channel."

"Online."

"Orion trader. This is Da'har Port Authority, please respond."

"This is Jared Chandler of the Orion trader." Jared was a bit surprised that they knew about him and Orion.

"Ah, Trader Chandler." The female voice was cheerful. "I am grateful you made the journey safely. We received word by message-com from the director of the mining facility on P3 that you had been of great service to them. We welcome you to Sha'Lural."

"Thank you," Jared replied, realizing he would have to be cautious. "Could you please transmit the coordinates of your port facilities and designated landing area?"

"Starting transmission."

"Orion to Port Authority."

"Go ahead."

"I had to disable two pirate ships that were pursuing me yesterday and want to report their position so you can apprehend them."

"We appreciate your efforts, but we have neither the resources nor the patrol crafts to do so. In any case if they have not already been rescued by their accomplices, they will meet a fate well deserved." The voice on the other end became bitter as she spoke.

"Yes, perhaps you're right." Jared realized these people had had a tough time because of the rogues. But now he could likely add several dozen more lives to his list of victims. His head ached. He leaned forward and rubbed his temples.

"Orion, have the landing coordinates been received?"

"Coordinates confirmed. Approaching on vector 279.98. Atmospheric insertion in 23 al–ems. Reducing main engines to 0 percent. Atmospheric control system now online. Velocity dropping."

Jared watched the control console as Orion went through each step. Lights went on and off, silent switches and relays changed. He would have to return to the simulations and learn more about the ship's systems and operations in case the unlikely happened and he had to pilot Orion manually.

"20 al–em to insertion."

The planet was looming large. He hadn't much time to really look at it with all he had on his mind. Even now the dead pirates plagued him.

Sha'Lural was a beautiful world very much like Earth. He now understood how the astronauts who flew the space shuttles must have felt while viewing the planet from so far above. The deep blue expanses of Sha'Lural's oceans sparkled in contrast to the white bands of clouds that laced around the globe. He could see parts of two continents. Sha'Lural orbited Lural in the opposite direction to that of the earth's orbiting of the sun. Its rotation was reversed as well, day started in the west here and set in the east.

"15 al–ems to insertion."

What if there were innocent people on those ships? Prisoners. Possibly even children.

Jared felt sick.

His attention was not on the insertion time or rapidly growing view of the planet. He stared blankly at the base of the command chair. He was brought back to the present when Orion lurched slightly as it passed through the outer boundary of Sha'Lural's atmosphere.

"Atmospheric insertion complete. Maneuvering controls optimal. Exterior conditions stage one. Adjusting to vector 263.05. ETA to Port Da'har 7 al–em."

"Orion, this is Port Da'har control."

"This is Orion, go ahead," Jared said with little emotion.

"We have you on our screens. Please maintain current heading. Platform number has been changed. Please set down in Bay 12, Pad 5."

"Understood, Bay 12, Pad 5."

"Orion."

"Ready."

"Bay 12, Pad 5."

"Confirmed, Companion. Arrival time two al–em. Reducing velocity to .10 percent. Approaching outer marker. Landing extensions engaged."

Jared sat quietly watching the landscape fly by.

"Arrival time one al–em. Bay 12 identified. Bay shield doors open."

He could see the port's buildings grow rapidly in size as Orion approached. It felt as if the ship was coming in too fast, but he had come to trust the vessel's ability to handle itself. He, however, was not the only one to feel that way.

"Orion, reduce speed, you are approaching too fast!"

"We are in standard approach mode," Jared guessed.

"What?" The controller blurted. "You've got to be joking!"

"No joke." Jared became amused. "If I interrupt the sequence now it could cause problems."

"Problems…!" The controller screamed. "You're gonna shoot right past us. There is no…"

The controller went silent as Orion slowed fast and pivoted 179.324 degrees and hovered over Pad 5 with the ship's centerline directly over the center of the tarmac. At Jared's command Orion lowered itself to the ground without making a sound. The faint hum of the ship's massive plasma drives faded as the repulsor fields shut down.

"Port Da'har Control, this is Orion, all systems secured."

"Understood Orion," the controller responded sounding a bit relieved. "Welcome to Sha'Lural and Da'har."

Jared stood and stretched. "Awesome landing."

"Approval. Thank you."

Jared stopped short. *Was that sarcasm? No, simply a statement and then appreciation.*

Once he decided the ship hadn't developed a new trait, he headed for the main hatch and requested it be opened. Orion complied and as the door slid open, he saw numerous people standing near the pad looking on in awe. A huge, elevated ramp began to extend from a nearby gantry mounted high on the wall to his right. Jared directed the operator the last few feet and stopped the padded end about two inches away from the hull.

A middle-aged female approached immediately after the ramp stopped. She walked up to him and smiled.

"Welcome trader, I am Section Supervisor Lal Ny'mas. In appreciation for your services yesterday on the P3 facility all docking fees are to be waived." Her features turned regretful. "I am sorry I cannot also waive the taxes."

"No further compensation is needed. I was happy to be of assistance."

She handed him a small device.

"Would you please register?"

"Sure," he said then pausing to consider his next words. "Neither my ship nor I have a registration within the Commonwealth."

"That's no problem. Governor Woltra has already authorized a Sha'Lural Trading registration for you and your ship."

Jared was stunned. He had no idea so small an event would create such a fuss. Clearly pirates have been a great problem to this world. "Does the entire population of the planet know about the incident at P3?"

"Oh, I doubt everyone knows, but most would have heard the

news vids by now. Some of the outlying steads don't have video access. The telecom system has been troublesome and unreliable since the pirates began preventing many of our supplies and spare parts from getting through from the inner worlds. I hope you have brought some of what we need."

"I hope I have also, but about half of my cargo is a large shipment of ore from the P3 facility."

"That is great news, because four of the last five shipments never made it. Our factory output is way down and many workers sit idle and go hungry."

Jared's unease earlier at having destroyed the pirate ship began to fade. If what this woman said was true, then they had caused far more suffering than he ever could. He filled out the registration following the directions and handed the recorder device back to her.

"Thank you, trader. If you need any information or service assistance, you will find a service desk just inside the large doors to the left at the base of the rampway."

Jared returned the thank you and watched her walk away. He re-entered Orion and when back on the bridge, considered what to do next.

"Orion?"

"Ready."

"Are there any specific laws I should know about on this world?"

"Accessing planetary database. The information system is flawed. Breakdown imminent unless repaired. Download possible with electronic contamination–filter on."

"Please proceed but be careful."

"Concern noted, downloading."

Jared left the bridge as Orion commenced the download. Since night was fast approaching, he decided to rest. It would give him a chance to relax and read some of the downloaded data. Orion sent the information to Jared's video console in the captain's office. Sitting back in a chair he had only used twice before; he reflected again on the events of the last few days.

I wonder how long the days are on this planet.

"Orion."

"Ready."

"What is the daily time cycle on this world?"

"One day is 15.6 em–hars."

"Thanks."

"You are welcome."

Jared fell asleep while reading a section of the Sha'Luralian trader's regulations.

Outside in the hangar, curious workers and other residents of Port Da'har discussed the news reports and speculated on the strange ship and its yet unseen crew. As twilight set in, the crowd began to disperse, and the workers began the change to the night shift.

A lone figure stood silently in a shadowed corner as the last of the people exited. His interest in this visitor was far greater than the others, who had stood about and gossiped. This white ship had become a problem, one that would have to be countered. It would have to be done with great caution but now was not the right time for action.

The individual moved quickly and quietly away from pad 5, disappearing into the city.

CHAPTER SIX

Aliens?

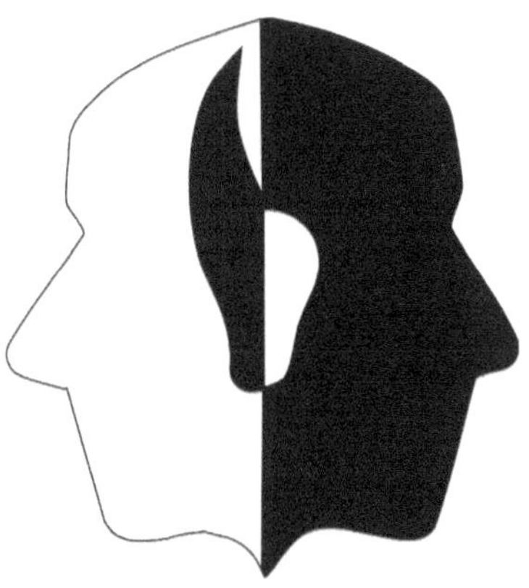

"How we are seen depends on how we present ourselves."

IT WAS NOT ORION that woke Jared that morning, but a view of Sha'Lural's star breaking over the west edge of the hangar complex. The entire ceiling above was transparent and showed the broad expanse of blue, streaked with orange and red through the amber clouds. Small flocks of odd-looking birds flew overhead in the direction of the rising daystar.

Sleeping in the chair had caused no ill effects. Jared stood and stretched, ready to start his day early. His first stop was the gym. After 50 al-ems and working up a good sweat, he returned to his quarters for a shower. While drying off he greeted his friend.

"Good morning, Orion!"

"Good morning, Companion."

"Anything interesting happening outside?"

"There is no unusual activity."

"What time is it?"

"97.5 al–ems past daystar rise."

"What currency is used on this planet? There are three coin sizes in the pouch from P3."

"Checking. Local denomination is the credit. Coins are valued at one, ten, and twenty. It is used by three colonial entities. Sha'Lural, San'derad and Hyop'loth. Value is .83 that of the Commonwealth drakla, according to the C&I Guild."

"Is the Drakstad currency I have on board accepted on Sha'Lural?"

"Unknown."

"Please check and determine the exchange rate."

"Checking. The Drakstrad currency is not currently listed on active financial databases. 47.82 percent of local businesses indicate that old Drakstrad currency is accepted in their establishments. No information is available pertaining to the policies of the exchange currency by credit and investment guild outlets on Sha'Lural."

"Thank you."

"You are welcome, Companion."

Jared didn't like the look of the mine facility work clothing, so once he dressed, he decided he would buy new clothes today. He chose not to eat breakfast on board Orion. He would check out the local cuisine instead. He decided not to carry a sidearm. He doubted he would find any hostility here, unless he made a big social faux pas. He stopped first in the cargo bay to grab some of the Drakstrad coins, then headed to his office for the pouch from P3.

As Orion's door opened, he could feel the warm morning air and despite being in a huge transportation complex, the air was fresh with a light breeze blowing. The hatchway vanished as Jared headed into the terminal. He followed the directions to the service desk given the day before and asked for the location of a good restaurant. The clerk gave several choices, each of which claimed to have good food and after choosing one, was given directions and headed for the exit. When he passed the observation windows along Pad 5, Jared noted that Orion's wingtips extended a great distance over either side of the pad boundaries.

He exited the terminal, and Jared got his first look at the surrounding countryside.

Da'har's spaceport sat on a large plateau overlooking the city. Though the architecture of many of the buildings within the city varied from what was common on Earth, it didn't look that much different. The inhabitants seemed to have taken a great deal of trouble to make the city attractive. Jared could see only a few buildings that detracted from the overall sight, and most of those were close to the port. As he walked through the large central lobby area, he could see down into several other pads. The pirates were obviously having a great effect on space traffic to Sha'Lural because there were no other ships present.

He boarded a shuttle going into the city. It had two sections connected by a flexible diaphragm. It also possessed a window that ran uninterrupted around both sections, except at the back. Each of the stations it passed were elevated, with most built into an existing building. On the north side, deep green fields were a stark contrast to the crowded buildings on the opposite side of the rail. The inbound line ran like a border between the city to the south and vast agricultural spreads to the north.

The platform where Jared exited the monorail was one of the few stations built as an independent structure. The long landing that constituted the station was no more than the floor and a ceiling connected by numerous posts. Only a small area at one end was completely enclosed. Jared spent several al-ems looking at the ample, wide, grass and flower-lined avenues below. The tallest structure, which appeared to be near the center of the city, didn't look more than a dozen stories high. Very few other buildings exceeded three or four stories. Nearly every building had an airy, open feeling with many terraces and elevated, connecting walkways. Some of the ground-level, public areas were covered by huge multi-colored, translucent awnings under which many of the populace sat, visiting, or eating. Here and there Jared could see narrow alleyways between close-set buildings. Many of the people seemed to go out of their way to avoid walking directly in front of the entrances.

The males wore loose-fitting pants, varying styles of shirts or what appeared to be work uniforms. The women wore similar but more colorful, fitted and patterned culottes, as well as dresses. Several individuals dressed in grayish jumpsuits, which seemed to be security personnel, moved leisurely among the rest of the citizens. Except for the gentle hum of numerous conversations, the scene below was calm and peaceful.

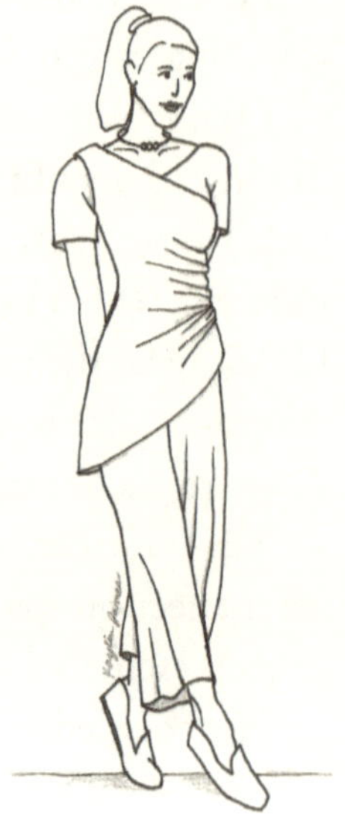

Jared found a staircase and descended to the area below. Engraved on a nearby stone post was the name he had been told to look for. Adriod Avenue ran East to West, gently meandering among the well-kept buildings and garden areas. He turned right and headed toward Camai's Cafe. The garden areas planted with brightly colored flowers filled the air with a sweet fragrance. Children ran and played in the courtyards and grassy areas of the avenue. What seemed most unlike Earth was the unhurried, casual way these people seemed to go about their business.

There was no outward sign that the pirate activity had caused any great distress. Some of the people Jared passed nodded in respectful acknowledgement of his presence and some even said, "Good Morning."

He came across a narrow alley, stopped and looked in. He was curious as to why these peaceful people seemed to avoid them as if there were some terrible creatures lurking within.

He shrugged. The alley was relatively clean, though some items and debris were scattered about, and it was well lit from the daystar above.

Camai's Cafe was located on the bottom floor of a three-story building at the edge of Adriod Park. Jared crossed the plaza slowly, examining a large, sculpted fountain at the center which stood about twice his height and was hewn out of marble. Smooth and highly polished, it glimmered in the early morning light. Coloring within the stone was far more varied and vivid than he'd seen on Earth.

He stopped for a moment to feel its surface, and noticed numerous small, odd blue fish swimming within the lowest pool. They swam toward him and a gentle mist from the cascading water above cooled his face. They gathered in front of him and seemed to be waiting for something. Their forward-facing eyes aimed directly at him. They were a little unnerving, so he continued on his way.

He entered the café, stopped, and waited at the sign: 'Attendant will seat.' A young man neatly dressed and groomed approached and told Jared to follow.

"Would you prefer to eat inside or on the terrace?" the man inquired.

"Outside. The day is beautiful."

The steward led Jared to a slightly raised, covered deck overlooking the park. About a dozen tables, each with four neatly arranged matching chairs, were the only furnishings.

"This table has the best overall view of the plaza," the attendant remarked.

"Thank you, this will be fine."

Jared sat down and observed the activity on the beautifully landscaped plaza. Several small groups had gathered in friendly yet animated discussions. Most of the participants sat on nearby benches or stretched out on the lush grass. Numerous peculiar looking birds darted in and out among the deciduous variety of trees.

He picked up the menu the attendant left and began to peruse the items listed. The bill-of-fare was broken into three sections. The first was titled 'Star-rise meals,' the second 'Mid-day refreshments,' and the third 'Star-set meals.'

When the waiter returned, Jared chose an entree called H'lar-rulash from the star-rise section. It consisted of H'lar eggs, a meat sauce with browned ganavar, and tryma bread. Shortly after the steward left, he returned to inform Jared that a man wished to speak with him.

"Yes, that will be fine."

The steward nodded and left again. Jared's brow furrowed in puzzlement. He'd told no one where he had chosen to go. His thoughts were interrupted as the attendant returned with a tall, muscular man, about Jared's height and wearing a clean but well-worn outfit.

Jared noted the loose gray-brown trousers and a medium green shirt with small collar, two chest pockets and a belt-like strap that ran over his left shoulder, crossed his torso, and was attached to his waist belt on the right side.

"Good morning, I am Harin Ro'shir-A'simyad. Are you the master of the trading vessel that arrived last star-set? If I am mistaken, I apologize for the intrusion."

"You're correct. My name is Jared Chandler, please have a seat."

"Thank you, Trader Chandler." He took the chair opposite. "I will not take long for I do not wish to delay your meal. I am here to arrange a meeting between you, myself, and several of my associates. Our hope is that you have some of the supplies and equipment we need to keep our concerns functioning properly."

"I would be quite happy to meet with you. When would be a convenient time?"

"I would prefer to meet this very day, but it will be tomorrow after midday that the others will be able to get here; that is if I notify them now that you have agreed to meet."

Jared tried to put on an air of experience. "One em-har after midday is convenient for me. Is that agreeable?"

"The time is agreed," Harin said as he rose. "Here are the directions. Until tomorrow, good day."

"Good day."

Harin strode away as if in a good mood. Jared watched him as he left the building and crossed the park. Harin had been all business, wasting no time on small talk. He had not even given Jared an idea of what they were interested in.

I'll have to work on my negotiation skills.

He had not expected to get off to such a fast start. The pirate activity had probably left people like Harin in need of many things, which was good for a trader. He would have to do some market research when he got back to Orion. He also wondered how Harin had found him.

The waiter brought the food shortly after Harin's departure and set it out. The H'lar eggs, which were served in a sunny-side up fashion, had a deep yellow-orange yolk surrounded by the familiar white. Next to the two eggs was a thick sauce looking like a colorful chili with large chunks of meat. On another plate was a chopped and browned vegetable, and two thick slices of warm bread. No butter or jellies were on the table, and he decided not to ask for any. The cuisine turned out to be well spiced and Jared found the taste much to his liking.

Conversations he could hear nearby centered around the event at P3, and pirates. He ate slowly and listened to all he could. No one else paid him any attention. The steward was at his table as soon as Jared rose from his seat.

"Was all to your satisfaction?"

"Yes, it was a fine meal," Jared replied sincerely. "What is the bill?"

"Eight credits."

Jared withdrew a twenty-credit coin from the pouch.

"Thank you. I will get your change."

The waiter walked away.

Jared pulled one of the Drakstrad coins from his pocket and looked at it.

I wonder what the value of this is.

Then he noticed the minting date.

Since they're over a hundred cycles old, their value could be even higher.

The steward came back and handed Jared twelve credits.

Jared returned four credits. "For your service. Thank you and good day."

The young man looked surprised as if he had never received a gratuity.

The public areas were now more crowded, and people came and went from shops and apartments on the avenues. After an hour of searching, he found a shop that sold clothing somewhat suited to his tastes. All the trousers were of the same loose-fitting design he had seen the men of Sha'Lural wearing. Fabrics ran from heavy woolen to light linen, in many pale and muted colors. He selected eight pairs of trousers in neutral colors and tried them on. His first selections were a little small, so he chose a larger size and tried again. Once satisfied with them, he selected sixteen shirts in various colors, tried on a few to make sure they fit also and looked for undergarments. Finding none, he walked up to the counter. He'd noticed that many of the shelves and racks were empty. The lady behind the counter seemed surprised at the number of items he'd selected.

"You wish to purchase all of these?"

"Yes. Can you tell me where I might find a store that sells undergarments?"

"Across the Colonnade on the second level is a shop that sells men's underclothing."

"Thank you. How much do I owe you?"

"These five pants are fifteen credits each, the other three are eighteen. The Pada shirts are twelve each and the remaining are eleven a piece. Your total is three hundred and twelve."

She placed all the garments into three bags and smiled broadly as she handed him his purchases.

"Thank you," and she dipped her head.

"I thank you and have a good day."

He walked directly across the plaza to an attractive two-story building which, from a distance, appeared to be mostly terraces and columns. A large broad stone stairway led to the second level. The shops were clustered around the center of the structure with open verandas that rose and descended several steps in a random pattern. Each of them was separated by long, narrow planter boxes filled with colorful flowers. It took him some time to find the shop he was looking for since the lady had not given him the name. He purchased two weeks' worth of shorts and socks as well, then departed. The ride back to the port was uneventful and Jared was grateful to be home. After stowing his new clothing, he went to the bridge.

"Orion?"

"Ready."

"I need you to download current market values for the cargo that's been inventoried."

"Local? Or Commonwealth market assessment?"

"Commonwealth market assessment," Jared repeated.

"Complying."

"How long will that take?"

"Estimated four em–hars, reliability of planetary telecom questionable."

"That's okay, I've got more business to take care of anyway," Jared said as he left the bridge. "And don't let those inferior computers bite you!"

"Unlikely."

Jared smiled as he stepped through the hatch. He strode down the rampway and headed for the Section Supervisor's office. It was small, but a neatly ordered cubicle. The door stood ajar, and he could see the woman who'd met him on the ramp the day before.

When he knocked, she smiled and stood. "Good morning, Trader Chandler."

"Good morning."

"What may I do for you?" she asked cheerfully.

"I've got a large cargo of ore from the P3 facility. I need to know where and to whom to deliver it."

"Yes, I took the liberty of notifying Eryl Wyr'lom, chief supervisor of the Da'har Metal Refining Facility, of your arrival last star-set. I hope you do not mind."

"Not at all, that was very kind of you."

"Please be seated, trader, I'll arrange a voice comm."

Jared sat in the chair on his side of the small desk and watched the woman as she worked. Directly behind her desk was a small communications device which these people used like a telephone, not as sophisticated as those used on space vessels, and nowhere near having Orion's capabilities. After several al-ems, she succeeded in reaching Supervisor Wyr'lom.

"Supervisor, Trader Chandler is currently in my office. He wishes to arrange a time for the delivery of the ore shipment."

"Fantastic! Our supplies are very low. Was the ore shipped in containers or as loose bulk?"

"In containers," Jared responded as she looked in his direction.

"The ore shipment is in sealed pods."

"Excellent! I will send transport vehicles immediately. How many pods?"

"Sixty," said Jared.

"There are sixty pods, Supervisor," the woman repeated.

There was a brief pause before Supervisor Wyr'lom replied, "Sixty pods? On one ship?"

"Yes, Supervisor," the woman began. "It is quite a large ship."

"The transports will be on their way shortly and inform Trader Chandler that we greatly appreciate his assistance in this manner. My second will accompany the transports to arrange for compensation."

Again, she looked toward Jared who responded, "That will be fine."

"Those arrangements shall be acceptable, Supervisor. Trader Chandler will be awaiting the arrival of your people. Good day."

"Good day, Supervisor Ny'mas."

At this, she switched off the communicator and turned her attention back to Jared. "Is there anything else I can do for you today, trader?"

"No thank you, I appreciate your help." With a nod of his head, he turned and left. The people of Sha'Lural had so far been very friendly but were also very business-like. They seemed to get directly to the point and asked very few questions, which suited him just fine.

Jared had noted numerous external physical differences among many of the inhabitants of this world, which wasn't strange considering it was a colony. Most had probably originated from the different worlds making up the Commonwealth. The majority were almost indistinguishable from those of his home world, small differences such as eye size and color, the shape of ears, etc.

Supervisor Ny'mas was one of those he had noticed having unusually large, brown eyes. Though they did not detract from her appearance, they made her look more child-like. Jared went directly back to Orion, informed his friend of the upcoming meeting, and retired to his room to take a nap.

Orion awoke Jared one em-har, forty-seven al-ems later and informed him that twenty large transport vehicles had entered the bay and were approaching the pad.

"Ask them to wait at the outer perimeter."

"Complying."

"Inform them that it will be about ten al-ems before we are ready to begin."

"Complying."

"Thanks."

"You are welcome."

Jared headed directly for the cargo bay.

"What would be the best way to arrange the containers onto the elevator to facilitate loading of the transports?"

"For this operation, use of the default lift is not efficient. Use of smaller aperture and magnetic lift field will produce the most satisfactory results."

"Right, use the field to load the containers onto the trucks. Can they get under without hitting the hull?"

"Sufficient clearance confirmed."

"Is it possible to lower me down using the magnetic lift?"

"Yes."

"Now, the only other concern is how to designate where the containers will be lowered from. Any recommendations?"

"Specific area illumination."

"Okay, great. I'll look forward to seeing it. Where should I stand to be lowered?"

"Current location satisfactory."

"Okay, lower away." A cube of light appeared around Jared just as the floor beneath him vanished. He could see he had begun to descend but could feel no motion. The sides of the cube rippled and shimmered as if he were in a glass box descending into the ocean. Orion's underside was about twenty feet off the ground. The large landing extensions looked like three upside-down white tree trunks.

As the cube faded away, he asked, "So why do I feel movement when you execute maneuvers while we are traveling?"

"Movement is noticeable during operation due to the natural gravitational effects while within a planet's atmosphere and also results from the use of artificial gravity systems while operating in space."

"Okay, so why not use this ability to offset the effects of violent movements and negate the need for safety restraints?"

"Calculations for a stable magnetic stasis field require .00587 em longer than optimal reaction time during a maneuver. This figure is based on a magnetic stasis field .00000072 of an ald cubed. Calculation time increases as size of cube increases and stability decreases as cube increases."

"Okaaaaay…just for fun, what is the size of a cube in feet based on the dimensions .00000072 of an ald?"

"6.84288 feet."

"Yup, that's kinda little." Jared had momentarily forgotten about the business at hand while he listened to Orion's report.

A nearby voice redirected his attention.

A man walking across the pad yelled. "Chandler!"

Jared motioned the man to continue forward.

"Good day, Trader Chandler. My name is Arrond Widlit, I'm Supervisor Second to Eryl Wyr'lom."

"Good day. Are you ready to load?"

"Yes, Trader." The supervisor handed him a small rectangular device. "This is a communicator which is linked to all the vehicles. The drivers have been instructed to follow your commands."

Jared nodded and motioned in the general direction of the starboard landing strut. "Would you please stand off to that side?"

Supervisor Widlit nodded politely and moved out of the area.

Jared waited until Widlit had moved far enough away and instructed Orion to illuminate the drop location. A rectangular area immediately glowed brightly. It looked to be slightly larger than the pods. The communicator resembled a walki-talki with several buttons and a trigger switch.

Jared depressed the trigger. "Chandler to transport operators."

"This is Senior Operator Vadrik," a female voice replied. "Go ahead, Trader."

"You may approach from either the left or right side, forward of the rear landing struts. Line up on the brightly lit area underneath the hull. You will be loaded one at a time. The pods will be loaded directly onto the trailers. To ensure there is no confusion I will demonstrate the visual hand signals you will see." Jared went through the standard hand signals he'd been taught several years earlier while working on an airport ramp for a large air freight operation.

The truck operators had no objection to his presentation.

"Understood. Beginning approach."

The twenty vehicles extended in a single line through a huge door on one side of the bay. There was enough room for them to turn after being loaded to exit the same way. Their engines, obviously combustion types, rumbled with a deep throated hum. One by one they began to move slowly forward. They were long and low to the ground with trailers that had three axles, apparently to carry great weight. The narrow cabs only had room for a single occupant.

The metal refining plant could not be very far away if this was as fast as the lumbering giants could go. Moments later the lead vehicle moved under Orion's starboard wing, lining up on the illuminated area of ground. Jared moved to the opposite side and began motioning the vehicle forward. A short while later the transport groaned to a stop.

The female operator climbed out of the cab, walked toward the trailer, and began dropping what looked like latches. Jared walked over to the truck and saw that the driver had stopped directly over the illuminated area. She noticed him, smiled and waved. After she threw down the last latch, she signaled Jared she was ready to load.

"Orion?" Jared spoke into his wrist communicator.

"Ready." He held it up to his ear to hear.

"Drop container one, load from front to rear."

"Confirmed. Initiating offload."

A rectangular opening appeared in Orion's underside and the ore pod began its descent. Each pod was a cube measuring twelve feet per side with clipped corners and would be loaded with three per transport. Orion lowered the container much more slowly than it had lowered Jared.

The operator appeared very interested in the unusual method used to off-load. The cargo pod's features appeared to ripple in the transparent energy fields as it descended. Jared had no doubt that Orion had the power to handle the operation, but considering what Orion had explained earlier, he stayed back just in case.

The loud engine drowned out any sound the pod may have made

as it settled into position. The operator made a gesture, which Jared assumed meant she was ready to move forward. He signaled back to wait.

"Orion?"

"Ready."

"Is it necessary to reposition the trucks for the next drop?"

"No."

"Then proceed."

"Complying. Initiating offload."

Jared signaled to the driver to remain where she was. The opening closed and another one directly behind it opened. Another pod began its descent. This action seemed to surprise the operator considerably. It was obviously not unusual for ships to have openings in their bellies, but for them to open and close in different places was quite a different story. It may have startled her that no part lines were visible until right before the opening appeared.

The third container descended as had the first two, slowly, silently and on target. With the operation completed, the driver quickly latched the hold-down mechanisms, indicated to Jared she was ready to go, climbed in her cab and slowly pulled out.

Jared turned his attention to the second truck and directed it as he had the first. The driver, another female, did just as well as the first at positioning her trailer. Once again, the pods were placed without incident, and the remaining eighteen were loaded likewise. The entire operation took nearly four em-har, and Jared was feeling hungry and restless at its completion. He had noticed that of the twenty drivers, only two had been men. Brodan had indicated there was a higher percentage of females in the galactic population, but this colony seemed to be far more unbalanced.

There seemed, however, to be a relatively equal number of males and females in positions of responsibility.

The last vehicle pulled away and Supervisor Second Widlit approached.

"Trader Chandler, I must congratulate you on the safe manner in which you conducted the offload. It was also very time efficient. Supervisor Wyr'lom has authorized me to compensate you at a rate of two thousand credits per pod. Is this acceptable?"

"I checked the Commonwealth market values on numerous commodities this morning. But I shall ignore them considering the problems you have been having with pirates and the difficulty you have in getting what you need. It is not in my best interest to take more than what you can afford. Therefore, the sum of two thousand credits is quite acceptable, and I appreciate your honesty in offering an equitable sum."

"Very good, trader," the Supervisor Second seemed quite happy with the outcome of the brief negotiations. He removed a clipboard-sized device from his belt and began putting information into it by use of a small keyboard at its base. Shortly it ejected a small credit card sized printout. Jared looked at it and then informed the man that he was unfamiliar with its use since he was from outside the Commonwealth.

"Ah yes, well, Trader Chandler, it is a credit receipt. You may take it to any credit and investment outlet where you may retrieve your compensation."

"Of course. Thank you very much, Supervisor."

"And I must thank you for getting this shipment through to us. It will make an immense difference in our struggle to maintain our independence from the Commonwealth and defeating those insufferable pirates."

"Is the Commonwealth causing you problems?"

"Not directly, but they are not able, or so they say, to assist non-aligned systems. It is their position that Commonwealth space patrol resources are already spread thin. It is true that a great amount was lost in the Drakstrad Fall, but I am not sure I believe that conditions are as sparse as they say. Many of us do not wish to be reinstated into the Commonwealth, but there are those who are beginning to believe it is the only way to survive the rogues' onslaught."

"What is the strength of your security forces?"

"I have no knowledge of the total numbers since I am only a factory supervisor, but I doubt we have more than a handful of very old, light military craft which are poorly armed or defended. We seem to have numerous security personnel because they are apparent almost anywhere you go. There are also aging defense satellites that keep the pirates off planet. Well, at least that's what the news vids report."

So, pirates are only a hazard to off-world shipping?

Jared asked, "Tell me, how many transport ships do you currently have at your disposal?"

"One of our own," said Supervisor Second. "The last freighter with Sha'Lural registry is the one on P3, though the captain is not likely to risk another trip. Worse is that no vessel registered to the Trader's Guild will chance operating in this area any longer and several other outer rim worlds have similar dilemmas. Most of the others who don't have pirate problems or have beat off the threat of piracy, either can't help or refuse to."

"Do you mind if I ask what this ore will be used for?"

"Not at all. Most of this shipment will likely go into replacement parts for machinery and on world transport vehicles. The technology we possess is sufficient to keep most things going. What we don't have is the ability to manufacture the advanced computer components used in information systems, health care equipment and telecom. One of the methods of ensuring that colonies didn't break away, used by the old Drakstrad, was to keep certain industrial elements under their control and only in secure locations on core worlds."

"Isn't it possible that is what they are doing now?"

"I don't know, many of the members of the Ilirian council would probably like to see the Commonwealth at its former glory, but at least two are on record against trying for reunification any time soon. It would be difficult because, as I said earlier, they kept certain key industries limited and that was one of their mistakes. You see, during the civil unrest that followed the fall, many of those facilities were severely damaged or destroyed. Many are only now recovering, and some have barely begun to do so due to technologies being lost. They not only limited the facilities, but they also limited the number of citizens trained in those fields."

"I have only one last question before I must attend to other matters. How long will this shipment keep the workers at your plant busy?"

"About three mon. That also includes reinstating many who have been off duty for some time."

"Good, I'm happy that it will help. Please inform Supervisor Wyr'lom that I will try to return near the end of three mons to be of service again. I do not intend to allow any pirates to best me."

"I wish you well, trader, but do not underestimate them. From recent reports it seems they have begun working together, which is unusual, and likely means they will be more dangerous."

"I'll be careful. Thank you for taking the time to talk with me. Good day."

"My pleasure, trader. Safe journey." The supervisor second turned away and walked into the terminal. Jared watched him briefly and then re-entered Orion.

Numerous onlookers had watched the offloading of the containers from the unusual white ship. All but one had come and gone after getting a good look. The vigil had not been by choice, but out of a perceived necessity. The individual remained well back from the railing and in the shadows of the dwindling daystar.

Kanis was right. This new trader is in the way. He could foul up everything.

Yet from within the watcher's troubled mind came the conflicting emotions that had plagued since joining the guild. Kanis was feeding information to the pirates, whom the watcher hated; but unless the Commonwealth intervened, the pirates would never be stopped. The thought of dealing with them was stomach-churning, but if Sha'Lural's people became dissatisfied enough with the idea of independence, they would demand reunification, then the pirates could be destroyed, and the supply·problem would be at an end.

My son is dead because of these idiot's desire for independence. The pirates are the cause because they stopped the medical supplies from getting through. All the other inhabitants of this world are guilty because of their desire to hang on to a dream that means nothing. Everyone who is responsible will die. Kanis…. Yes, must report to Kanis.

"Orion?"

"Ready."

"Can you please monitor messagecomm traffic and news programs?"

"Yes. Specific topics or general?"

"Specific. Primarily pirate activity, but also anything else you deem unusual for this world."

"Monitoring initiated."

"Good. I'm going back to the city to cash this credit receipt and to see what the nightlife is like. I don't think it likely I'll find any trouble, but I'll keep in touch."

"Understood."

The main hatch opened. "I'm outa here, stay safe, friend."

"Concern noted."

The daystar was low in the eastern sky as Jared caught the monorail into Da'har. Clouds now filled more than half the sky and several on the darkening western horizon looked as if they could be part of a storm. The light breeze that had been present for most of the day subsided. Swarms of tiny insects congregated in some areas along the transport's route, occasionally blurring his view of the landscape. Creatures like the cows of Earth grazed peacefully on farmsteads separated by narrow but dense woodlands.

Jared went one terminus further than he had on his first visit to Da'har. The station was part of a three-story building which resembled several tapering, interconnected cylinders with curved balconies partially imbedded. The platform where he disembarked was narrow and sitting between the second and third levels. The larger of the surrounding balconies faced the city and were interconnected by curved stairways. The smaller ones overlooked the fields and Jared assumed were private apartments. Windows of various sizes dotted the walls at uneven levels. It seemed like something out of Alice in Wonderland.

He found the closest stairway to the plaza below and quickly descended. The boulevard was more crowded than it had been that morning. Most of the buildings in the area seemed to be apartments and except for the one containing the station, they were all quite conservative. Heading west, with the intent of ending up near the cafe where he'd eaten that morning, he walked slowly and observed with interest the interactions of the residents. He passed several shops mentally noting their hours of operation.

Da'har C & I #6 was located just to the right of the station he had first used that morning. He had not been looking, so hadn't noticed it. Even though it was still open he opted to wait until the following day to redeem the receipt.

It was almost as if he were entering a Roman forum as he strolled into Adriod Park. The large, well-kept garden spots seemed to be social centers for the inhabitants. Camai's Cafe and the two other eateries on the perimeter of the promenade were crowded. Finding there were no entertainment facilities in the area, he continued west. After walking for a while, he sat down on a vacant bench. A nearby discussion of the incredible victory at the P3 facility caught his attention. Somehow, details of Orion's involvement and the scale of the event were being greatly exaggerated.

As the last rays of the daystar faded, lights began to illuminate the park. It was here that the first real distinction between this world and earth became apparent. In this busy public place, there were no arcades, night clubs or theatres.

I wonder if these people even know what a party is.

Something caught his attention as he glanced eastward out of the park proper. He watched as a man exited one of the smaller side streets, struggling to remain erect on wobbly legs.

"I guess they do partake of intoxicating drinks." Curiosity rose so he stood and headed toward the inebriated man. By the time Jared arrived at the intersection, the man was weaving south, away from him, and Jared turned his attention to the corner post. The inscription read Valomar, and Jared headed into the narrow street. The first door led to the area security office, followed by four more with numbers, which Jared ignored. On the sixth, however, a sign read 'Uros's Star-set Retreat. All Welcome.'

"Well, let's hope they're not too wild a group." Jared knocked. After several al-ems and no answer, he tried the door. It swung inward and opened into a short hall with another door a few paces further. Hearing music from the other side he doubted anyone would hear a knock so he walked in. Dim light emanated from dish-shaped fixtures on the ceiling and revealed a crowd of mostly men seated around a low stage. A man and several women moved among the patrons as they were taking or delivering orders. While he was observing the scene, a young girl approached.

"There is a seat free at table five. Would you follow me?" she stated cheerfully. "You have not been here before, have you?"

"No," Jared smiled and followed her.

"There you are. Now if you need…"

"Hay'la."

The girl's look changed to exasperation and disappointment. "Yes Father?"

"I've told you to remain upstairs while we have guests. Now off with you before there is trouble."

The girl turned and sulked off toward a door on the opposite end of the large room.

The girl's father sounded harried. "I apologize for my daughter bothering you. The show is five credits and is about to begin."

"Five credits," Jared repeated. He handed over the coins and took a seat. Another man close to Jared's age sat across the small table nursing a glass of bluish fluid. Jared heard him chuckle as the girl's father walked away.

Jared tried to be polite. "May I inquire as to what you find humorous?"

"Sure friend, it's been a while since I've seen…hic…Hay'la make a move on anyone."

"Make a move? I don't understand…"

"She's young but wants to be bonded. Drives her father crazy. Seems to think that if she doesn't get a man now, she never will."

"Oh. Too many active hormones, huh?"

The man began to reply but was cut off as the music changed and the curtains on the small stage slid open. Jared's eyes widened as a woman of about thirty, maybe five feet six inches tall began to dance. Her costume was like those worn by belly dancers on earth except that the translucent fabric top revealed that she had four breasts. Her skin was reminiscent of those from the Middle East on his home world.

"Never seen a Borggan before, eh?" his inebriated companion chortled. "They're rare alright. Most refuse to leave Borgga." The man paused, looking a bit distressed. "Hic," with a grimace he continued, "What I'd like to know is why she decided to bond with O'mond. He isn't nothin' special. Oh, can she dance," he trailed off then took a gulp of his drink.

The dance the Borggan female was performing seemed to have an intoxicating effect all its own. To stem the effect, Jared concentrated on the conversation. "Who's O'mand?"

"O'mand Uros. Owner…hic…this place."

"You mean the man I paid the credits to?"

"Yup. Thass' him."

"So, she's Hay'la's mother?" Jared asked in surprise.

"Uh huh," the man grunted.

"So that little girl is gonna grow up to have four…"

"Shhhhh," the drunk hissed. "Don't know." Hic. "Lots of wagerin' on that issue."

"Wagering. Why?"

"She's only half-Borggan. So, some say she's only gonna get half what her mothers . . . Hic . . . got."

Jared sat quietly and watched the Borggan woman dance. The young girl was probably about eleven cycles old. He had not paid attention to her figure when she showed him to his seat but likely had yet to start showing her adult form.

Don't these men have better things to do than bet over a child's body parts? Don't I have better things to do than sit here and watch another man's wife dance half-dressed to a drunken crowd? He decided he did and rose to leave. *I'll avoid this place in the future.*

"Where ya goin'?" The drunk sputtered in disbelief that Jared was leaving before the show was over.

"I'm sorry, but I have business to attend to." Jared headed quickly for the door and out into the night. He strode back toward Adriod street. Lights mounted on the buildings illuminated the alley and a gentle rain had begun.

He hadn't gone very far when a short figure stepped out from one of the numbered doors.

"Nobody's ever walked out in the middle of her dance before," Hay'la was partially hidden in the shadow of the alley.

Jared stopped, and regarded her, "It was not meant to be rude; I simply have other business."

"Dancing is what she does best. On her home world, Wy'ara dancers are held in high esteem. Here she dances for losers and drunks and is looked down upon by others." Her voice reflected a mixture of anger and sadness. "I could tell her spirits fell when you left."

"As I said, her dancing was not why I left. If you really must know the reason for my early departure, I will tell you. The fellow next to me told me something I found a bit distasteful, and I no longer desired to be in the company of those who sat around me."

"You could at least have waited till the end of the dance."

Jared sighed. "Perhaps I should have, but it is done now, and I can do no more than to ask you to pass my apologies on to your mother."

"It would be better if you told her yourself."

"I do not wish to re-enter your father's establishment nor…"

"You don't have to."

"Oh? What do you propose?"

"Her dance should be over by now. You can come in and I will get her."

"I do not believe it is wise for me to come in, but if you wish to fetch her, I will explain my actions and apologize. I will wait here by the door."

Hay'la looked at Jared as if confused by his choice, but she nodded and disappeared inside.

Jared realized he had a great deal to learn about the many customs and cultures of old Commonwealth worlds. He waited for several al-ems before the door opened again. The dancer appeared and smiled. Hay'la stood behind her.

"My daughter said you wished to speak with me?"

Jared glanced at the young girl. "Your daughter has informed me that my leaving during your dance was upsetting to you. I apologize for that. My reason for leaving was my discomfort at hearing those who watch you dance place bets on whether your child will inherit your physiology or that of your husbands."

The woman did not seem surprised at this statement. But Hay'la's expression was one of shock and surprise that *she* had been the cause of his withdrawal.

"I am not unfamiliar with what transpires among those who frequent this place. Hay'la is a very forward child and that is a concern. I am sorry she has involved you in my situation. I have told her much of my world and my people, and she is concerned because I sometimes show the sadness I feel being so far away."

"Why did you leave?"

"I followed my bond mate," she said flatly. She studied Jared for a moment before continuing. "I do not socialize with the people of this city more than I absolutely must. On my world only the most talented are trained for the Wy'ara. They perform for special occasions and for dignitaries. Here I am seen as an intoxicating curiosity by some and disdained or ridiculed by most others." She almost spat out the word intoxicating. "Of all the races of the old Commonwealth present on this world, I alone stand out."

Jared did not know what to say.

She seemed to notice his distress.

"I thank you for not joining in the callous betting. Hay'la deserves better than this. There are many who never have as much as I have, so I do not complain. My fear is that she will spend her life alone because she is a half-breed or with someone who bonds to her because she is some prize to be shown off."

"On the world I come from, talented dancers are also held in high regard. I found your dance to be very beautiful and hard to turn away from. I hope that someday I will be able to see a Wy'ara dance in a better place and in the fashion it was meant to be performed. If the rest of your people are as beautiful as you are, then I can believe it is a wonderful world." Jared paused. "I must go now. Thank you for your understanding," Jared bowed slightly, and turned away.

Jared heard footsteps behind him.

"Hey," Hay'la chirped.

He stopped and turned around. "What?"

"You're different."

"Different? How do you mean?"

"Well, you aren't like everybody else."

Jared smiled. "Is that good?"

"I think so. Nobody else here has ever cared enough to make my mother smile. I don't even remember my father doing it. Did you mean what you said?"

"Which part?"

"That she was beautiful?"

"Yes, I did."

She blushed. "Am I?"

"Yes, you are. But it'll take a few more cycles before you'll be able to match up to your mother. Don't be in too much of a hurry, and don't let those fools in there get to you either."

She grinned. "I won't."

"Good night." He turned to walk away, but she stopped him once more.

"By the way, I take after my mom!" she said with a mischievous grin.

"Well, don't tell anybody. Keep 'em guessing as long as possible."

He stood and watched as she almost bounded through the door, humming to herself.

CHAPTER SEVEN

Misconceptions

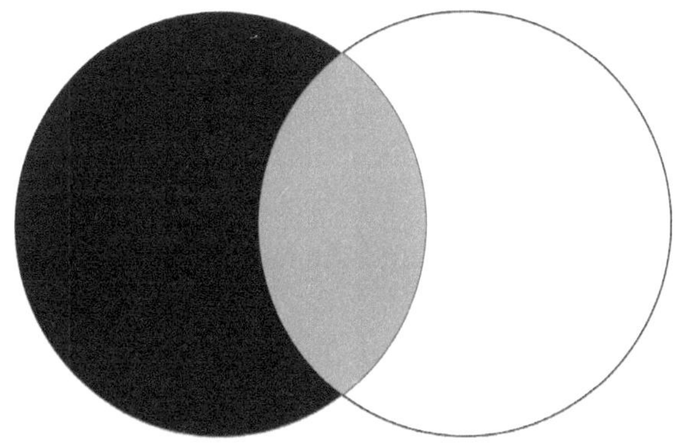

*"What lies beyond my sight and comprehension is vast.
By comparison all I have learned is fractional, all that I
have seen is infinitesimal, what I have experienced is
only an allusion of the total. With each step I take
beyond my point of origin, I find that I must not reject
what is new, strange, or contrary to my upbringing. To
do otherwise would leave me forever locked within the
narrow confines of my own understanding."*

Gavik Ha'turan

Jared woke up the following morning to the sight of raindrops hitting the transparent hull, and a dull gray overcast with hints of sun peeking through to the south. He folded his arms behind his head and took in several deep breaths while musing on the previous day.

These people varied in color of skin, shape and color of eyes, shape of ears, amount of body hair, one ethnicity had a couple of extra body parts and perhaps some internal differences. In spite of all that, they were human. He remembered the download from Orion, that the old Commonwealth had stood for nearly five thousand cycles. That equaled about six thousand years. In all that time of expansion and exploration they never came across a race of beings that were non-human, voracious killers, or grotesque creatures. Even the animals he had seen around the farms from the monorail were similar looking to animals from Earth.

If the people of Earth ever travel among the stars, there are many who are going to be very disappointed. Sorry, no scaly, green-skinned ETs.

"Orion."

"Ready."

"Please let me hear the sound the rain makes as it hits the hull."

"Complying."

A split second later the sound of rain impacting on a hard surface filled the room. "Thank you."

"You are welcome."

Jared pushed back the covers and sat up. The floor was warm as usual, a small detail he found pleasing.

If I'm not careful I'm going to get spoiled and soft.

Shopping for personal items would have to be on today's list. He was out of most things, including blades for the odd-shaped Xaxilor razor.

Only three blades remained, and he had no shaving cream.

"Orion?"

"Yes, Companion."

"I'm not sure why I haven't asked before, but how long would it take from our current location to get to the Xaxilor home world?"

".023 Myir utilizing null space."

"Convert it to English, please."

"2.27 years."

"Two and a quarter years at nearly ten times the speed of light," Jared smirked. "Alright, so a trip to a Xaxilor convenience store is off the table."

After shaving, he headed for the gym.

Beginning with the leg press, he adjusted the weight for a light workout and sat down.

"Orion."

"Ready."

"How many of the three hundred and twenty-seven member worlds of the old Commonwealth produced distinct indigenous races?"

"Accessing data base. One hundred and twenty-six."

"Are there any who differ greatly from the many I've seen on Sha'Lural?"

"No. All races have followed similar developmental pathways. Internal and external differences vary widely due to dissimilarity in planetary conditions. The reasons for the development of some attributes among various races are uncertain. Most racial differences are subtle except for the Borggan, Ru'lathwa and Ty'lari, who's features are instantly obvious."

"I've already met a Borggan and know what their identifying characteristic is. Please describe both the Ru'lathwa and Ty'lari races."

"Complying. The Ilirian Commonwealth classifies planets based on their gravitational and atmospheric characteristics. The core planet of Iliria is used as the base. Ru'lathwa has the highest gravitational force of all Commonwealth planets. Ru'lathwans tend to be short and strong. Average temperatures on Ru'lathwa are lower than other Commonwealth worlds. Due to this fact the Ru'lathwans have developed a soft, fine yet dense body hair."

Jared switched to working with free weights. "Okay. They're short, strong, and fuzzy. Next."

"Ty'lari has the least gravitational force. As a result, the Ty'lari are very tall. Skeletal structure is thin and more fragile. Numerous races have pointed ears, but the Ty'lari possess the most pronounced."

Jared smirked. "Interstellar elves? Well, the fantasy fans on Earth would be pleased."

He paused, musing over the image. "Play music please, random selection."

"Complying."

He finished the remainder of his workout listening to 'the sounds of home' as he had come to think of it. He took a quick shower and headed for the galley. He added H'lar eggs to the growing list of things he needed to buy today. Finding out what the ingredients were for the Rulash and the Tryma bread, would be another task. He would be lucky to have all of this finished before his meeting with Harin. He finished up quickly, cleaned the dishes and headed out early.

When he left Orion, the rain was coming down heavily. He dashed down the ramp into the terminal. He did not bother to stop for instructions this time but headed to the monorail.

Little difference existed between the Dahar C & I and a bank on Earth. The clerks, or tellers, sat at desks instead of windows to help individuals with their financial needs. He stood in a short line and waited his turn. While he waited, a member of the C & I staff entered the main room from a side door and told everybody that the news vids had just announced that pirates had made another attack on the P3 mining facility. Murmurs and gasps passed through the crowd.

"Is there any news on the outcome?" one of the customers asked.

"None as of yet," replied the employee.

"How long ago did this happen?" Jared inquired.

"The report did not give a specific time, only that the facility had been attacked." The employee turned around and retraced his steps through the door. The customers returned to waiting, talking animatedly among themselves. When his turn came, Jared walked up to the desk and sat down. Removing the receipt from his pocket, he handed it to the clerk.

"Positive identification?" asked the clerk.

Jared withdrew the trader's registration certificate he had received from Supervisor Ny'mas the day before and handed it over. The clerk's eyes grew wide as he read the form. He looked back up to Jared and smiled.

"You are the trader who helped the P3 facility."

"Yes," Jared said a bit reluctantly.

"You have helped our world a great deal when no others could or would."

"Well, thank you, but I think people are making a great deal of fuss over a single incident."

"Perhaps, but we have very little to celebrate these days."

"I understand."

"Do you wish the entire amount in coin, or are you interested in starting an account?"

"Well, I hadn't really given it much consideration. However, since it is very likely I'll be returning, it's probably best that I open one."

"That will be excellent. If you'll fill out this form, please," and handed Jared a device like the one he'd been given when he signed in at the port. Filling out the information took about ten al-ems, then he returned it to the clerk.

"Thank you, trader, how much of the hundred and twenty thousand credits will you be investing today?"

"Hm, I think one hundred thousand. I highly doubt that I'll need more than twenty thousand credits anytime soon. What types of accounts are available?"

"The Credit and Investment Guild has four account types available covering all three hundred and twenty-seven former Commonwealth worlds."

"You mean this C & I invests in Commonwealth markets?"

"Oh, yes, trader. The Guild is quite independent from political entities. The old Commonwealth learned long ago that tampering in private finances and investment can bring about very troublesome results. As long as the Guild obeys the necessary government laws and works within established guidelines, we have little trouble."

"Interesting. What are the four basic account types?"

The clerk listed off the four account types rather dryly, by rote. "Basic, low interest; advanced, moderate interest; aggressive, high interest; and risky, maximum interest."

Jared smiled. "For now, I think I'll split it into two accounts." He had never had enough money to truly invest before, and here, where he had little to lose, he intended on having some fun. "Please put fifty thousand into an advanced, moderate interest and the remaining fifty thousand into an aggressive, high interest. Perhaps sometime in the future I will have to try the risky maximum interest, but for now that should do fine."

"Very good, trader. If you wait here, I will log in your account and return with your credits and account numbers."

Jared waited for the clerk to return. The people in line who were still waiting and newcomers who had come in were still speculating on what the outcome of the attack on P3 would be. Most believed that without some intervention as had happened two days before, it would be difficult for P3 to survive, particularly if the pirates had banded together in the attack. The clerk returned and handed Jared a pouch containing two hundred credits of coin, and a plastic disk, about the size of a fifty-cent piece. The clerk smiled when Jared looked quizzically at the small disk.

"It's a credit disk and can be used in lieu of coin for almost any transaction. It is linked directly to your account. You have nineteen thousand eight hundred credits of liquid funds."

"Understood and thank you."

"Good day." The clerk turned to help another client.

Jared made sure he had his account numbers tucked away, which were unusual at forty-eight digits long.

He left and when he reached the avenue, he noted a sign: News Lounge. He headed for it, and when he entered, he was escorted by a young woman to a small but comfortably appointed room where several other individuals sat and talked.

He asked, "Has there been any other news on the P3 announce-ment?"

"No, no further updates. Would you like anything to drink while you wait?"

"Not at the moment, thank you." He wasn't sure what their bever-ages contained, or if they had any that were non-intoxicating.

Text on the vid monitor indicated it was on stand-by and pro-grammed to activate only when news reports were broadcast. Finding an over-stuffed chair near the far wall he sat down and began dis-creetly observing the others in the room.

One man and a woman sat a few feet to his right discussing prob-lems they shared at the textile plant. Further to the right, two men and a woman conversed but were talking too softly for him to hear.

The closest man had dark brown skin, faint bony ridges running from his temples and wrapping around the edges of his ears. His long braided blond hair gave the individual a wizard-like visage. It was the first time Jared had seen long hair on a male since arriving on Sha'Lural. His deep set dark brown eyes and high cheekbones, with an aquiline nose, added a hint of danger to the impression.

One of the women had a fair complexion, very dark hair, and lavender eyes. She wore a beautiful silver-hued necklace that resembled lacework. It was similar to the gold one in his office, without the gems.

Of the other four, only one of the men had identifiably unusual features. His nose was curved outward and appeared beak-like over a pronounced chin with a small tuft of hair. He reminded Jared somewhat of a satyr out of some Greek myth. He seemed to be the most cheerful and animated of the group; his pale blue eyes gleamed when he smiled.

A gust of fresh air from a nearby open window brought with it scents from the garden area outside. Jared took a deep breath, sank down into the soft chair, and closed his eyes. Except for the threat of pirates, this planet presented a very happy front, but Jared somehow doubted that these people were spared any of the problems his home world faced. After five thousand cycles prejudices might have been overcome, but unless they were very different in their psyches; greed, power, lust, and all the other things that made people do horrible things must exist here too. Just because he hadn't seen a negative side yet didn't mean much, and there was the small mystery of why many avoided the alleys. He had not wanted to ask about it for fear of offending someone.

Jared was jerked out of a brief sleep when a voice came through the vid monitor.

"It has now been confirmed. The P3 mining facility was attacked early this morning. Initial indications were that the facility had nearly been destroyed since messagecomm traffic had been cut off. However, authorities now confirm that the pirate attack was successfully repulsed by P3 defenses. Apparently defensive capabilities have recently been upgraded, though our source was unwilling to give details for security reasons. Of the four pirate vessels, the facility is claiming the destruction of two, severe damage to a third and possible damage to the fourth. Now on to other news of the day...."

At this point a cheer arose among those in the room and the individual reporting on the monitor was forgotten.

While shopping for clothes the day before, Jared had noted the location of Tan'yer's Market. He left the cafe and headed toward Adriod Park. He found the store far different than expected. So many other places had been like Earth stores, modern and well-kept, but this place was like a jump backward in time. Very little of the food came packaged or processed, the rest was sold by venders like those in an open market in New York. Signs near the entrance told shoppers to choose their meat first, so it would be ready when they were finished. Another sign indicated theft would not be tolerated. Three different sizes of shopping baskets were available, but Jared ignored them, having no intention of carrying anything back to the ship. Several inquiries later he found the office of the Market Director and knocked.

An older, heavyset woman came to the door. "May I be of assistance?"

"Yes, thank you. I need to purchase a large quantity of food to replenish my ship's stores. I am curious if it would be possible to leave a list and have it delivered later today?"

"Hmm, it's been some time since I've had such a request, but I don't think it will be a problem."

"Thank you. Here is my list of requirements and substitutes if necessary. Is there a delivery fee?"

"Yes, it's a flat rate of one hundred credits to deliver bulk shipments to the port."

"Sounds fair enough. About what time might I expect delivery?"

"About two em-hars, if I can get several people working on it. I'll need the one hundred now. The rest can be paid on delivery."

"That'll work for me. Thank you." On his way out, he purchased a small box of chocolate-like confections.

Jared arrived back at Orion just shortly before the food shipment. He stopped by his quarters, dropped off his new personal items and toiletries and then headed for the cargo bay. After lowering the cargo platform, he signaled the delivery vehicle to approach. Once the vehicle was backed into position he helped the two workers, both women, offload the truck.

He rode the elevator up with the supplies and began storing the foodstuffs in the refrigeration and bulk storage lockers. When everything was put away, it was nearly an em-har past midday and he realized he had very little time to get to the meeting with Harin. Without saying anything to Orion, he left the ship and hurried to catch the monorail.

He traveled a considerable distance into the city for this meeting. He exited the worn platform and descended a broad stairway onto an avenue very much like Adriod. He noticed the buildings and the garden areas showed a greater age and wear.

His instructions took him along Balwin Street where he turned left into a small street called Woro. Here he had two options; a winding route along wide well-traveled streets, or an alleyway next to a small establishment called Pestrill's Grooming which would save a great deal of time. Harin had indicated that most people chose to avoid the alleys, but it was not dangerous.

So far Jared had found little to fear in the city, so he took the alley.

The alley was surprisingly clean with only small clusters of clutter in an occasional corner. He heard sounds but found nothing when he looked in their direction. Initially the buildings were primarily tenements but when he crossed one intersection, they changed abruptly to storage facilities with few doorways and even fewer windows.

The silence was eerie. After some distance, he heard what sounded like a cry of pain.

An intersection lay ahead, with an alley exiting to the left. He turned the corner but stopped in disbelief.

Two uniformed security guards were beating a smaller individual who was backed into a corner desperately trying to fend off the blows. Jared walked toward them. "So, *this* is frontier justice?"

Both guards stopped and turned around. The male seemed to be enjoying himself, but the female looked angry.

"This is none of your affair," she blurted.

"I'm making it my affair. Whatever this person's crime, my brief study of the laws indicated no clause for security officials to assault anyone."

The female grunted and motioned to the male guard who moved in Jared's direction.

She smirked "I warned you, and I hate to repeat myself..."

Jared had to think quickly, "This encounter is being recorded."

The male guard stopped but the woman was undaunted.

"Really?!"

Jared brushed his right hand against his pocket. "Yes." He pulled out the small box of candies.

She scoffed. "And that is supposed to be?"

"It's a transmitter," Jared lied, hoping she would have a hard time seeing it in the shadows.

"Sure, it is," she sneered, "going to send a vid back to central, right?"

"No," Jared forced a hard smile. "It is recorded aboard my ship which is monitored by my crew." He pointed to the male guard. "They will send it to your supervisors if you choose to continue."

The look of anger on her face turned to rage, but Jared noticed a slight slump in her shoulders.

"So, what do you want?" she spat.

"For you to stop beating this person."

"Why is this sewer rat of interest to you?"

"Where I come from, all persons, no matter how low or unde-sirable, have the right to fair trial before judgment and sentence are passed." Jared took a breath and gestured toward the cowering figure. "I realize that compensation for whatever wrong has been committed must be paid, but *this* is not at all acceptable."

"This is the third time we have caught this scum stealing," the male broke in.

The female added, "And they are a blight in this city."

"What was stolen?"

"Food stuffs," she said.

Jared looked toward the figure whose body trembled with each breath. "I can't imagine why this thin, filthy, terrified person would stoop to such a deed."

The two guards glanced at one another then back to Jared.

"I will forget this incident and your actions if you will turn the individual over to me. Direct me to the person who was robbed so I can make restitution for the crime."

The female stared at Jared. "You will destroy the recording?"

"It will be kept in a safe place for future reference if I find this happening again."

She sneered. "You'll find few who care about the fate of sewer rats."

"Perhaps, but I'm *not* most people. With all the trouble this planet has had with pirates lately, people are very upset with how little they have. If this were to go public, just think of the anger it will generate. I can see the headline now. 'Security forces join pirates in ruining economy.' I'm sure your superiors would love that." Beads of sweat had formed on Jared's forehead.

The big male guard stood looking at the female, as if waiting for an order. She stood there for some time before she said anything. "Very well. It's yours." She indicated the stinking mass and smiled as if from some inside joke, yet her demeanor of superiority faded somewhat.

"The address please."

She gave Jared the address, and the two guards stalked off angrily without a backward glance. He was sure the female entertained ideas of revenge.

Once the guards left, Jared walked over to the person lying in the corner but stayed a distance away. It was another first as he had never seen so wretched a creature. It was impossible to confirm either the gender or how badly injured the individual was. He had little desire to get any closer because of the stench emanating from the filthy body covered by little more than a bundle of rotting rags.

"Can you get up?"

The person's head slowly rose, and Jared was surprised to see fearful, but alert, deep green eyes. It didn't answer, as the thin figure slowly stood on shaky, weak legs, but the emerald eyes never left him.

Jared gestured toward the open end of the alley. "I will not keep you here if you wish to go." He reached into his carry-all and withdrew two condensed food bars. He leaned a little closer as a small hand reached out and took them. Though they were taken with restraint, they were eaten with abandon. Again, the green eyes regarded him, but this time the look of fear was gone. Jared pulled enough coins from his bag to keep the wretch fed for some time.

"You may have this."

The figure retreated slightly, refusing to take the money.

"I'm sorry, I don't know how to help you any other way." Jared backed away slightly, withdrew the remaining food bars plus the coins from his carry-all and set them on a nearby container. He looked again at the poor vagrant, "Farewell."

As he walked out of the alley, he suddenly remembered why he had come this direction in the first place. He glanced at his watch and realized he'd missed it. He didn't think he'd have a problem re-scheduling as the farmers seemed desperate for the components he might have. But it was the sad wretch and its peculiar green eyes he was unable to get off his mind.

As he neared the transport station, he heard the commotion of a security guard in the process of hauling a small, thin, dirty figure from behind a divider near the exit onto the main thoroughfare. The security guard was yelling, "You don't belong here!"

Jared sighed and walked toward the security guard. "What seems to be the problem?"

The security guard looked at Jared and frowned, yet he didn't seem hostile.

"Well, we've ordinances in this district, no squatters allowed."

"I see," Jared mused. "I guess that's my fault. I gave the poor creature some food."

The guard chuckled. "Not wise, probably following to see what it could steal."

"Helping someone is unwise?"

"It's clear you're a stranger. These aren't much more than wild animals."

"And no one cares?"

The security guard shrugged. "Not my job. I have enough without this." His face registered disgust as he reached out to grab the ragamuffin by its hair. "Come you, and don't give me any trouble."

"Stop," Jared stated firmly. "I'll take care of it."

"You'll…" the guard stammered. "You can't be serious!"

"I am."

The security guard turned and walked away. "Fine, but I don't want to see that *thing* in my district again."

"I'm not sure how to help you." He really didn't want to take the wretch on board Orion. He walked over to a public communicator and tried to find social help facilities. None existed.

He turned around and found it had followed him. "Are you still hungry?"

This time he at least received a nod of the head. If he did take the individual on board his ship, a good cleaning would have to come before any meal was served. He had intervened in the incident and now felt he had to do something. He shrugged. "Follow me."

The bundle of rags gathered itself up and to Jared's amusement dusted off the ragged shift and straightened up as best it could.

What an odd contradiction.

People passing by looked scandalized and trod a wide path, obviously to avoid getting too close.

For a moment he scrutinized the figure. All he could make out clearly was long, dark hair, those unusual green eyes, and it appeared to be over five and a half feet tall. The face was very dirty with grease-like smudges on nose and jaw. The clothing, if it could be called that, was loose fitting and tattered. It was bare footed.

His new companion would not go near the shuttle, so Jared was obliged to walk all the way back to the terminal. It was highly doubtful they would have been let on anyway. Several times Jared chuckled as some of the women they encountered seemed to swoon at the very sight of the unfortunate wretch. He also had to endure the stony questions from security teams. By the time the terminal came into view he was wondering if helping this wastrel had been worth the effort. He closed his eyes and remembered his own words only a short while before, that everyone deserved fair treatment.

He hadn't meant to become entangled.

He also had to approach Orion via the freight door because

security would not let him take the smelly entity into the terminal.

As he walked up the ramp to the ship, people continued watching and many looked disgusted as the strange, filthy, stinking mass followed him. He headed straight for the medical bay.

He turned toward the figure and pointed at a console on the back wall between the showers and the toilets. "That is an incinerator. You'll need to put everything you have on in there. Over there is a shower, you need to bathe. You know how to do that?"

He received a slight shrug.

"It's probably a good idea to make sure you don't have any diseases or parasites, either." As he said this, he turned to a cabinet and withdrew several towels and cloths. Turning back, he was surprised to see that the individual had already followed his instructions.

Female.

She was completely nude, seemed unconcerned that he was there, and was stuffing her rags into the incinerator.

"Well, I didn't mean you had to do it while I was in here."

She turned her head and simply stared at him. He could see now that she was bleeding in several places from cuts on her shoulders and arm and had two large bruises on her torso, one on her abdomen, the other on her left breast. Her filthy face, hands, and feet were a stark contrast to the light tone of the rest. He pointed toward the shower and said, "Get in. Wash as best you can, and um, the uh, soap and shampoo are in the dispensers. Here's a towel and washcloth. The little one you wash with; the big one you dry with. Do you understand?"

Again, she shrugged.

"Make sure you scrub your head good," he stressed.

She moved to the shower and pushed on the door, but when that didn't work, she tried to pull outward. When that effort failed, she looked at him questioningly.

He smiled. "Touch the button on the left."

As she did this, the door slid silently open.

"There is another one on the inside." He realized he should ask her name but decided to wait until she chose to talk.

Of course, that is, if she could.

The water came on and she gave a surprised shriek.

He chuckled.

Jared moved into the adjacent med room, activated the Xaxilor scanner, and adjusted the setting to standby. Next, he stepped up to the computer terminal to access the on-ship medical supply list. He left the medical area and went to the galley where he put several cuisine commands into the food processor. Then it occurred to him that he needed to find something for her to wear. Again, he accessed the computer, looked up current fashions, and realized he had no idea what would fit her. So, he asked Orion for help.

"Orion?"

"Ready."

"Please identify number of occupants on board the ship."

"Two."

"Identify occupants."

"Companion and guest."

"Data on guest?"

"Specify."

"Age?"

"Approximately sixteen cycles."

"Height?"

"Five feet eight inches."

"Proportions?"

"Specify."

"Diameters at, uhh… cancel. Just display a female anatomical diagram?"

"Complying."

The same diagram he had seen while still on the outpost came on and he studied it for a moment.

"Okay, I need the guest's proportions, in standard Ilirian scale, at widest point of quadrant two, narrowest point of quadrant five, and widest point of quadrant six, and length of quadrant seven and eight."

"Twenty-nine an'ost, twenty an'ost, twenty-eight an'ost and quadrants seven and eight are twenty-six an'ost."

"Thank you"

"You're welcome."

"Please access planetary merchants."

"Specify by type."

"Female clothing."

"Accessing—thirty-five local area merchants carry some form of female accouterments."

"Print a list."

"Printing."

A list of the thirty-five merchants was printed out along with basic merchandise, and common prices. Five of the merchants indicated that they delivered. Jared perused the list before making his selections.

"Please place an order."

"Ready."

"Order from merchant #27, two of item #765-3 blue and one #765-5 black with white trim, two item #439-0 white, one each #9865-2 in red, beige and teal, ten of item #1203-3 in random colors and six of item #1021-1 support in white. Please have that order delivered as soon as possible to docking Bay 12, Pad 5."

Again, Jared thanked Orion.

"You are welcome, Companion."

He arose from the console and headed back for the medical bay. Shortly after he entered, she walked in. Her hair was medium brown and clung in wavy tendrils to her now clean face. Her expression was one of cautious curiosity mixed with a hint of anxiety. He walked over and handed her a pair of boxer shorts and a T-shirt. "You'll have to wear these until the clothing I've ordered arrives."

She seemed to take great delight in putting them on. First, running the smooth fabric along her arms and then sliding on the shorts. She was quite a different sight now, and even through the mass of still tangled hair, he could see she was quite pretty despite the gaunt frame which had obviously been long undernourished.

Once the shirt was on, he led her to the med room, had her lie on the exam table and started the scanner. He discovered quickly that the scanner did not read correctly through fabric so had her remove the shirt again. She did without hesitating.

"You'd think, that with such an advanced scanner, it should be able read through clothing." He tried to keep the mood light as he passed the wand over her.

"I mean, we have that ability on Earth," he added, noticing her eyes following him. "Not that I know anything about CT scanners, maybe the Xaxilor equipment is just based on an entirely different principle." He finished making a second pass. On the first pass the scanner had identified her external bruising and lacerations and displayed recommendations for care. The second pass gave a readout of her circulatory system and showed no major problems.

One significant difference in her anatomy he took note of was that she had a second, but dormant, circulatory pump.

Interesting. A second heart. Kind of like my appendix, I guess.

She also had a few low-threat parasites, moderate anemia, and vitamin deficiency. Pass number three identified no problems in her respiratory system. Pass number four indicated that except for a small fracture in her right arm, her bones and muscles needed care but were undamaged. Jared was quite impressed since she had made no complaint or hint at the pain she must feel.

Once the scan was complete, he gave her an injection with a device the computer programmed with the proper dose determined from the scan. He was glad to have the device since he had no medical training. He placed her right arm in the cast-like device which formed to her arm's shape and began to hum softly. The bruises on her face and body he took care of more quickly, though the soreness would be there for several days. He passed a small, hand-held tool Orion called a Rehath'ra over her bruises, just barely touching the skin. The dermal color returned to normal.

He touched her abdomen lightly, "Any discomfort?"

Her head shifted slightly from side to side.

"Good." He chose not to test the area where the other bruise had been. The cuts were handled likewise and though the skin had knitted sufficiently to stop bleeding; redness remained. Just to make sure they would stay clean, he put small bandages over them. After he finished and she had once again put on the T-shirt, she gave him a big smile and her first words.

"Thank you."

He smiled, quite surprised then turned and picked up an item from the counter next to the console. She glanced at the hairbrush he held out then questioningly looked back to him. "You've never used a hairbrush?"

She looked at him blankly and replied, "A what?"

He pointed at the brush and repeated. "A hairbrush."

"No."

Jared realized this young woman had probably been on her own for a very long time. "Can you read?"

"Only a little, my mother used to read to me and taught me some."

"Where is your mother?"

"She died nine cycles ago in a factory accident."

He wanted to ask her more questions but decided not to when her stomach made a very loud growling noise, which seemed to be the first thing to embarrass her. He led her to the galley and sat her down at the table. The smell of food wafted through the air and her eyes widened. She sat patiently as he brought out the meal and ate with unexpectedly good table etiquette. She had apparently watched other, more fortunate people eat and paid attention to what they did, not just what they ate. She also put away quite a bit of food for one so slim. After the meal he decided to brush her hair himself, which she seemed to take great delight in except when he found a particularly troublesome knot. It took some time to get out all the tangles and she seemed somehow let down when it was all over.

While Jared was brushing her hair, she nodded off several times. He escorted her to his quarters. There were other sleep rooms, but no other bedding than the set he'd brought from the outpost. He had not expected company and hadn't bought new blankets yet. When she saw the bed, her eyes grew wide again and she walked over and gently touched the surface. She pressed several times. "I haven't slept on something like this since my mother died."

Jared smiled at her, "I apologize. These are the only bedclothes I have. You can rest here for now. I'll get a few more sets as soon as I can, and you can choose one of the other rooms."

She looked at him with her head slightly tilted, "Why?"

"What do you mean?"

"Why must I choose another room?"

He stared at her dumbfounded. "Well, uh…we'll discuss that later. You get some sleep."

"Okay." With a big smile, she literally jumped into the middle of the bed, giggling in delight. She grabbed the heavy blanket. She wrapped herself in it, rolled over on her side and was fast asleep before he left the room.

Out in the corridor, he stopped and leaned against the wall.

This is really bizarre.

At about this time in his musing, the ship informed him there was someone waiting for him. He thanked Orion and headed for the main hatch. He stepped onto the gangway and found a small, rotund fellow with several packages, looking very happy. The man introduced himself as 'Merlic'.

He set the packages down and handed Jared a printout, which contained the items ordered and the cost. Jared happily handed over the sum indicated, plus a 20% gratuity, which apparently was totally unexpected because his grin increased so much as to nearly split his bowling-ball shaped head in two.

Jared watched Merlic, in his happy condition, nearly float down the gangway. He waved several times and said if Jared needed anything, not to hesitate to call. He would get first-class service.

Jared returned to his quarters and started unpacking the clothing. It occurred to him that if she didn't know how to use a hairbrush, she might have never used some of these other items either. That might lead to a complicated discussion. He hung the dresses and shirts and folded the pants and emptied out one of his drawers for everything else. He went directly to the bridge and made a call to the planetary merchant's guild to reset the appointment he had missed earlier in the day. He was happy to hear they were more than willing to reschedule for that evening, as it seemed that they desperately needed the equipment he had for sale.

He spent the rest of the afternoon running a flight simulation to better familiarize himself with Orion's control systems. About twenty al-ems before his meeting, he left the bridge and as he passed his quarters the girl stepped into the hallway. She was holding one of the bra's he had purchased. "I think I know what this is, but how do you put it on?"

With a deep inhale Jared took the garment, "I'll show you." He wrapped the item around his torso and tried to pull the two ends together. Unable to, he grinned, "That's not going to work."

He handed the bra back. "Hold it like I did and attach the clasps." He gave her a smile, "Now rotate it until the cups are in the front."

She did so.

"Okay, now put your arms through the straps."

"I assume it goes under a shirt."

"Yes."

"Why is it necessary?"

"No one ever told you?"

"No."

"Well," he cleared his throat, "It prevents gravity from detracting from your femininity." She wasn't particularly well endowed, but sufficient enough that time would not be kind.

The look she gave told him she did not completely understand. "Is it your wish I wear this?"

"Ummm, well, it's a good idea."

"If you wish it, I'll wear it."

"Okay," he said, relieved this was over.

"Are they all mine?"

"You mean the clothes?"

She nodded.

"Yes, they are.

She jumped toward him and threw her arms around his neck.

It was then he remembered he still did not know what to call her. "What's your name?"

"Shar'ya."

"Very pretty. My name is Jared."

She reentered the room briefly then came back with the blue shirt rounding out her outfit. A moment later she dropped to her knees. "I am yours; body mind and soul.

Astonished, Jared was silent for so long that the happy expression on her face faded into what appeared almost fear again. He had no idea the significance of what she had just done. He felt bad that his reaction to her statement had made her lose her smile and said the only thing he could say, "Okay."

Her smile instantly returned. She stood gave him another hug, and happily bounded back into the room.

He gazed down the corridor.

What just happened?

He decided not to go in after her and returned to the bridge, pondering. Her declaration had been very focused. Her response to his hesitancy strained. She was obviously happy about her new situation.

Did she really just give herself to me?

His brow furrowed; his mouth open.

Why would she do that!

He thought back to his dating life on earth.

That would never happen, especially after, what, half a day?

Perplexed, he stood just inside the door.

"Companion."

The androgynous voice startled him slightly. "Yes."

"Your meeting is…"

"Oh damn. Thank you, Orion."

"You are welcome."

He had about twenty-five al-ems to make it to the meeting he'd missed earlier. He grabbed what he needed from the office and headed for the main access hatch. He passed his quarters and knocked on the door.

When it opened he said, "I have an errand to run, do not leave the ship." He didn't wait for a response, nor did he see her happily wave as he hurried down the hallway.

Jared retraced his steps to the place where he'd first encountered Shar'ya, paused momentarily and continued. The sun had almost completely gone down, and his footsteps echoed on the vacant streets. He arrived at the location of the meeting about five minutes late. He stopped at the door and knocked.

The door was answered by an elderly woman, "May I help you?"

Jared smiled, "I have an appointment with Harin."

The old woman smiled back and gestured for Jared to enter. She led him down a narrow hallway past several doors, a kitchen, a very loaded storage room and a well-appointed living area. She stopped and knocked on a wide heavy door. They waited for a few moments before they heard a large bolt being slid aside. Harin opened the door and invited Jared to enter. He stepped in and surveyed the room. It contained a large, heavy wooden desk at the far end surrounded by several bookcases and a large table in the center. Three men at the table stood as Jared entered.

Harin introduced each of them, starting with a short man with dark, but graying hair.

"This is Darak Ulum." He turned to the second man, "Jareth Kas'lar, and Whim Nurl." He finished the last as he offered Jared a seat. He then went to the other end of the table and sat in the largest of the chairs.

"Thank you for coming, Trader Chandler," said Harin.

"Not a problem," Jared smiled.

Harin continued, "We've had a great deal of trouble from pirates recently. If these steaders, as well as others, cannot find a way to get their grain to inner-sphere markets, most will not last another season. What is needed are parts and machinery. Also, we need reliable transport for our grain that can get through the pirates' gauntlet. You have made it through once."

Jared nodded. "Yes, I made it through *once*. As for the parts and machinery you need, I have a printout of what I currently have on board the Orion." He handed the list to Harin. The other three men suddenly stood and rushed to surround him.

Harin bellowed, "Friends, patience! You will all get a chance to look, please retake your seats."

The men obeyed, and Harin spent several moments surveying the list. He then passed it to Darak who spent a good deal of time studying it. Then a large smile crossed his face as he handed the paper to the one called Whim Nurl. The smile seemed contagious as each one looked at the list. Jareth who received it last looked up and said, "There is more than enough here for all of us."

Harin grunted in mirth. "Let's get down to business."

Jared set another document on the table. "This is a current price quotation from the inner-sphere market consortium on the value of new and used military, agricultural and industrial equipment."

He paused when the smiles on the faces of the other men faded somewhat. He continued, "I will however sell you the equipment that I have, regardless of its condition, which I believe is pretty much all used, at 40% of the stated market price."

The smiles quickly returned.

"You see, gentlemen, I feel that it is not in my interest to try and take you for more than you have or to put you in a position which would, in the future, deny me business. I do intend to be back."

This resulted in a round of elated cheers from the four desperate men. Jareth blurted out, "We must inform Calyb and Neb about this. They would benefit also."

"Agreed!" said Harin. "Now, what would you consider a fair price, Trader, for your part in transporting our grain?"

Jared sat for several moments thinking. He carefully considered his answer. What would be beneficial to himself and the most helpful to these men? He hoped to display an air of confidence. The first part had been easy since he hadn't spent any money on the parts so selling them at 40% of market value wasn't any problem. This salvage and trading operation was beginning to look more appealing all the time.

"Gentlemen. I believe that based on your current circumstances and the need for the immediate transport of your agricultural commodity, that 15% of the total revenue generated is fair compensation. I would normally ask for 20%, however, due to the unfortunate intervention of piracy in your businesses I will grant this 5% reduction."

A look of surprise crossed the faces of all the men. Farmer Nurl blurted out, "That's it?!!!"

Harin quickly replied, "Trader Chandler, you are indeed an honest businessman. The previous Traders with which we dealt requested a minimum of 40%, oftentimes as high as 60% to transfer our grain."

Jared raised his eyebrows in disbelief. "How did you manage to hang on this long with such outrageous shipping charges?"

"One does the best one can," answered Jareth bluntly.

Harin added, "We have not only hung on through that, but

through the last two seasons of lost shipments and no replacement parts for our farm equipment. Whim doesn't even have a generator to power his house. It's been out of service for three mon."

"I will get your grain through," Jared said confidently. "And you may come by my ship at any time to purchase what you need. I will be here for another four days."

The five men stood and shook hands. Harin told Jared they would be by the following morning.

Jared was amazed everything had gone so well. He'd expected to seal a contract, but not so quickly, with absolutely no complaints or problems. He avoided the alleyway choosing to take the longer, but more public, main street. A wave of fatigue caught him by surprise. It had been quite a day. As he entered the hangar bay, he noticed several individuals standing around the gangplank leading to Orion. He paused several feet away, listening to their conversation.

"There are no panels or joints," said one man.

Another, taller fellow added, "And the gangplank leads to no apparent opening."

A third said, "I have studied the history of the old Commonwealth, and even they made no ships like this."

Jared cleared his throat to get their attention. "May I help you?"

The one who had spoken first turned to Jared, and with a rather unpleasant smile said, "You part of this ship's crew?"

Jared replied flatly, "Yes."

"Beauty," he commented.

"Yes, it is," said Jared.

"Where you from?"

"Excuse me. My name is Sawyer. I apologize for my companion's rudeness. I am very curious as to the origin of this vessel."

Jared considered his statement and replied, "I would be more than happy to talk with you, perhaps in the morning. I have just returned from a business meeting and am ready to turn in. It is against standard policy to allow visitors, but if you wish tomorrow will work. I will answer what questions I can."

The man named Sawyer smiled. "Thank you. I will drop by at a more convenient time. How about shortly after high rotation?"

"That will be acceptable," Jared returned.

The man bowed slightly, said goodnight, and he and his companions walked away.

Jared waited 'til they were out of sight, raised his right arm toward his face, bringing his wrist communicator close to his mouth, and whispered, "Shyr'st." The main hatch slid silently open. Once through the portal it slid silently closed. He had only walked a few feet before he found himself smothered in an embrace by a seemingly very amorous young female. This time, however, completely clothed.

"So, what have you been doing?" he asked.

"I found a room full of interesting things, but I don't know what they are. Will you show me?"

"Sure. Where?" he yawned.

He followed her down the hallway and through the door into the gym. He smiled despite being overwhelmingly tired. "Yes, this place is quite interesting, and fun."

He walked over to one of the devices, gripped a bar, sat down on a bench, and pulled it downward. He did this several more times, straining on the last one. He moved out of the way. "Now you try."

She sat down, grabbed hold of the bar, and pulled with all her strength and succeeded in only lifting her backside off the bench. Jared chuckled, moved around to the other side, repositioned a clip and said, "Try again."

She gripped the bar, a look of intense determination on her face, and pulled very hard. Jared had lowered the weight considerably. The bar came down and smacked her on the crown of the head, eliciting a small squeal. "Ouch!"

Jared couldn't help but laugh, though he apologized, moved the clip again, and said, "Try again, but not with so much force."

She gripped the bar firmly and pulled it slowly downward, stopping near her chin. With a look of satisfaction, she let it return and pulled again. Five more times she pulled downward before releasing the bar, stood, and asked Jared, "What is its purpose? It made my arms ache."

"It's an apparatus for firming and toning muscles."

"I think I understand. Will you teach me about the others?"

"Perhaps tomorrow, but I need some sleep now."

"I understand. May I remain here for a while?"

"If you wish. There are only a few places aboard the ship that you may not go, and that is simply because they can be dangerous. You may go wherever else you choose." Again, she smiled and gave him a hug. All he could think about at this point was sleep. He didn't even consider what she would do when she got tired. He simply climbed into bed and fell asleep.

Shar'ya carefully changed the weights on each of the different machines to match the weight that Jared had selected on the pull-down machine. She next sat in a chair and placed her feet on the two pedals. This one was obviously not for the arms. She pushed firmly but not quickly. The result however, with so little weight, offered little resistance to her push. The pedals hit the back of the machine with a loud clang, startling her. She drew her feet back quickly, resulting in an even louder noise. After a moment's pause, and gathering her wits about her, she tried again. She repositioned the pin five holes down, sat, got comfortable and pushed slowly but firmly. She was able to push it eight times before her legs ached. This was a completely new experience and despite her body's slightly emaciated tone she was not overly weak. It also helped that she was happy, full of curiosity, well rested and had a belly full of tasty food.

She tested each of the other machines, carefully selecting weights based on her first two experiences. Her legs were much stronger than her arms. After trying each machine once, she stood and left the gymnasium. As she walked down the corridor, she reflected on what had happened earlier in the day. It was hard to believe she had been so fortunate. She had a place to live, new clothes like those she had dreamed of so often, did not have to steal to eat, and was bonded!

With this last thought a smile crossed her face and she sighed. She paused momentarily before entering the sleep room. Once inside she stood for a short while looking at the figure lying wrapped in the blanket. Part of her didn't want to sleep now as a nagging fear rose that she might wake up finding it all just a dream. Softly biting her lower lip, she folded her clothes and put them away, then quietly she joined an oblivious and unsuspecting companion in the bed.

She snuggled tightly up against him, took a deep breath, closed her eyes, and fell into a happy, dream-filled sleep.

CHAPTER EIGHT

Bonds of Joy

"What is love, really?"

Jared squeezed his eyes tight and stretched.

Why can't I move my arm?

He turned his head and stared at Shar'ya. Full consciousness hit him like a bright light.

Now what?

This was not the kind of thing he'd expected to encounter when he'd left the outpost. Weird planets and strange creatures yes, but not …well, she did seem a little strange to him compared to females on Earth.

Jared realized he had not taken her seriously the day before. Perhaps 'seriously' was the wrong word. He had been flustered and confused. He gazed at her face and mused.

Was it an act of desperation?

Considering how he found her, it was a good possibility. He'd simply been trying to help. Apparently, she considered it much more.

He took the time to study her features, gently moving her hair away from her face. As a lock of hair brushed it, her nose wrinkled, and she gave a little sigh. Her skin was healthier than it had appeared yesterday before she'd showered. It was incredibly smooth and free of blemishes or scars, which was surprising considering how she had lived, and the beating she'd taken. What was also quite surprising was that she seemed to be little affected emotionally by the ordeal with the security guards.

"Orion?"

"Ready."

"Shar'ya has aged sixteen cycles. What is the equivalent age in Earth years based on what you extrapolated from my time piece?"

"18.66 years."

"Thank you."

"You are welcome, Companion. Are you ready to start your day?"

"Not yet, I will inform you when I am. Thanks for asking."

"You are welcome."

"Hmmm." He returned to studying her face. The line of her nose curved slightly concave to an upturned tip just above the septum. Her upper lip was well-formed but thin compared to the lower lip which made her look as if she were pouting. He had to admit she was quite pretty. He laid back, very aware of how close she was to him. He put his one free arm behind his head, stared at the ceiling and tried to concentrate on what business he had to conduct during the day. This, however, proved difficult, for each time she breathed, her warm breath stirred the hairs on his chest.

It was a short-lived success. He lay there for as long as he could take it, then decided it was time to get up, and gently informed her that it was time for breakfast. "I have work to do today."

She gave him a big smile, sat up, gave him a kiss on the cheek, and got sprightly out of bed. Conflicting thoughts of moral training and human need waged war within his head. He placed his hand over his eyes, rubbed his temples with his thumb and small finger, and wondered what more trouble he would get himself into today.

"Okay, I'm ready," she said spiritedly, her green eyes dancing with delight.

"I'm hungry, how about you?"

"Uh-huh."

"Umm," he hesitated, realizing she was waiting for him to get out of bed. She stood there watching him. He realized at this point it was ridiculous to be hesitant.

I don't want her to be uncomfortable.

"Who's the uncomfortable one?" he mumbled.

"What?"

He smiled at her, "Nothing." Then stood wearing only a pair of shorts.

Shar'ya's eyes widened.

He noted her eyes lingering curiously at points and wondered what she knew about relationships and what she was ignorant of.

How do I broach this?

His mind went on as he selected a pair of pants.

Too soon.

That strange vow came to mind like a brick hitting glass. He dressed then guided her to the galley and made sure she had other things to think about.

Shar'ya was quite curious as to how the kitchen area worked and Jared enjoyed showing her. She caught on very quickly and asked if she could oversee making meals, to which Jared was more than happy to agree. As they ate, Shar'ya related all she had done in the gym the night before. He got a good laugh when she described the incredible noise the leg press machine had made when she pulled her feet away. Then, their meal was cut short when Orion informed Jared that several visitors were waiting outside.

"That's probably Harin and his associates. I have to go greet them."

"May I go with you?"

"Sure."

"Shall we clean up now?"

"No, that will have to wait until later." He was surprised at how different she was from what he expected. She apparently had spent most of her life living in filthy rags, and disease-ridden dwellings. She hadn't known how to use a brush, yet somehow, she had a natural grace and poise. She followed him out of the galley and fell in line behind. He walked a short distance like this, then stopped. He turned and held out his hand. For a moment, a puzzled look crossed her face, then she took his hand. He turned back toward the main hatch and continued walking with her by his side.

This last move on Jared's part had taken her completely by surprise. Her experiences with men in the past had been entirely with the security guards she'd encountered while trying to survive. She had been repeatedly told that she was worthless, inferior, and had no right to walk with her betters. They had always punished her for trying to stop the aching in her stomach and from finding a way out of the lower city. So many times, she had watched from the gutter vents as her 'betters' had eaten the fine-smelling food in the eateries, bought beautiful clothes from the many shops, and walked freely in the light of the daystar. Those who had treated her the worst were not the security guards, though they had been rough enough. It had been the beautifully dressed women who scorned her, mocked her, and even threw things at her. One had even threatened to set her on fire if she ever bought her foul stench near her home again. She was only eleven cycles old at that time.

Shar'ya could barely remember what her mother looked like, though recalled fondly the times she had spent reading to her. That had been a time like now, where she knew no hunger, cold, nor hate. She had rarely dared to think that anything like this could happen again. Of all the women in the lower city, most were childless having never been bonded. As far as she knew few believed there was a way out. Hope had deserted any but the youngest. Even with the supplies that the government allocated to the undercity, hunger and sickness were rampant.

Her forays to the surface had always been a solo affair. Hunger, mostly, had motivated her to action. Portions were never enough and the cries of sick or starving children helped push her to take risks. She had experienced scorn from those who dwelled around her and pain from many above, but now, here she was, walking beside what the security guards had called a 'better.' Not behind, but beside.

A phrase her mother had once said filtered into her mind as she and Jared neared the door. 'Living fades to sad existence when you stop believing.'

As they reached the main hatch, Jared spoke, "Orion?"

"Ready."

"How many are outside?"

"Five."

"Shyr'st."

In that moment before opening, he noticed Shar'ya gazed at the portal. The door had slipped silently aft into the wall. She let her hand run along what would normally be a door frame, and she seemed to notice no delineation existed. They both stepped through the open door and into the early morning light.

The massive overhead doors covering the bay were open to allow in the day's bright light and fresh air. Jared immediately recognized four of the individuals. The fifth he had never seen before. Harin stepped forward once the couple descended to the hangar floor.

"Good morning, Trader Chandler."

"Good morning to you, Harin." He then turned to Jareth, Whim, and Darak wishing them a good morning also.

Harin introduced the fifth man as Calyb Amin.

"We are ready to trade," stated Harin.

Jared nodded, turned toward the underside center of the ship and, closely followed by Shar'ya and the five men, walked to the edge of the cargo elevator. He stopped, motioning the others to stand behind him, raised his wrist communicator up to his mouth and whispered,

"Reyaht, Shy'tar."

Immediately after, a thin line appeared in the hull in the shape of a large square. A humming sound could be heard as the huge panel drifted downward. The five men watched as if in disbelief as the elevator lowered to the ground, seemingly suspended in mid-air. There were numerous items on the cargo platform from the list Harin had given Jared. Huge generators, containers full of replacement parts, and other farm or industrial equipment rested on the huge platform.

Jared motioned with his hand and indicated they were welcome to browse.

Shar'ya watched everything Jared did. She carefully analyzed each and every action. She'd half expected the five men to shun her as people had usually done, but each of them had greeted her with a smile and a nod. It would be a very long time before the memory of the lower city faded from Shar'ya's memory, and the full realization of what had happened to her yesterday had yet to set in. She watched as Jared walked over toward the one called Harin.

She could see them talking when suddenly, Harin burst into laughter, holding his stomach, looking as though he were going to topple over backwards. The look on Jared's face was one of bewilderment and embarrassment.

Harin got some control over himself and pointed in her direction.

Jared nodded his head and Harin burst into laughter again. While gasping for air, he blurted "You really don't know what it means?"

Jared simply shook his head, which brought forth another fit of laughter from Harin. By this time, Jareth, Darak, Calyb, and Whim were all watching Harin as though he were quite mad.

Obviously confused, Shar'ya stood in total silence, looking at the ground.

After a few moments, Harin got a hold of himself and walked closer to Jared, speaking too quietly for anyone else to hear.

The look on Jared's face changed to surprise, and he glanced toward Shar'ya, who seemed to feel his gaze and looked up. She was clearly distressed. For a moment, Jared studied her then slowly walked toward her. As he approached, he put his hand on her shoulder.

"Shar'ya, I'm sorry. I did not realize the significance of the words you said last night. I am not from the Commonwealth, nor any of its neighbors. Until now, I had no idea what a bonding was. But I accepted it then, and I accept it now, knowing fully what I do."

The fear on Shar'ya's face turned to instant joy as she threw herself at him and wrapped her arms tightly around his neck. It was some time before she let go.

Harin looked on, grinning from ear to ear. The other four men stood by patiently, totally oblivious to exactly why Harin was laughing.

Shar'ya let go, and Jared quietly told her, "As soon as this meeting is over, we'll get you a bonding collar."

At this she kissed him soundly, and this time, not on the cheek.

The farmers filled their lists of requirements and happily paid Jared the sums negotiated. The five men were joyful. They left this meeting with the items they needed and had not had their pockets emptied. The grain that Jared was to transport would need to be picked up at the various farmsteads the following afternoon. There were two other towns, though smaller, which should have others in need of similar equipment and parts.

Jared and Shar'ya assisted the five men as they loaded the items they'd bought onto their transports. The vehicles were about three times as long as a pick–up truck, flat and squat with large tires, a cab which could seat three, though not very comfortably, and long, narrow, low–sided beds. Each load was carefully strapped down and Shar'ya seemed to enjoy helping as best she could. As they watched the farmers preparing the vehicles to leave, Harin walked over to Jared.

"Trader Chandler. Thank you. We look forward to our next meeting. May your journey be safe."

"Thank you." The other four thanked him and Jared watched them drive away.

"Jared?" Shar'ya asked somewhat timidly.

"Yes?"

"What was it that was so funny to the one named Harin?"

"I asked him a question. Umm, I asked him what it meant, what you had said to me last night. The bonding vows. At least that's what he called it. I come from a world very far away and am not familiar with all the customs of the old Drakstrad."

Shar'ya swallowed hard. She took a deep breath. "Do you really wish me to stay?"

Jared did not hesitate. He once again took her hand and ran his other hand along her cheek. "Absolutely!"

"I…"

"Shar'ya. I learned some time ago that there are things one must not question. When God hands you a gift, accept it. When God allows a challenge to be placed in your way, endure it. When an angel is allowed to accompany you, hold onto it. When doubt and fear plague you, hold on to your faith."

Though Shar'ya didn't fully understand what Jared had said, she remained silent. The word 'faith' meant a great deal to her, and she felt that the strange word "God" somehow had something to do with the One you cannot see. At that moment, Shar'ya felt something else, something different; and somehow, even after all the longing, all the hoping, and all the pain; all the other things she'd so recently gained faded in importance to the one who now stood before her.

They re-entered Orion hand in hand. Jared informed Shar'ya he was expecting another visitor.

"Shall we go finish breakfast?"

Shar'ya nodded, and they headed toward the galley.

Jared excused himself from the table and asked Shar'ya if she would mind cleaning up the dishes. She looked at him oddly and said, "Isn't keeping the galley my responsibility? Yesterday you said it could be."

It was Jared's turn to look a little oddly at Shar'ya. "If I'd asked my sister Sandra that same question, she probably would've hit me."

Shar'ya's mouth fell open then snapped shut just as quickly. Walking purposefully up to Jared, she kissed him, turned around without saying a word, and went to work.

Jared stood puzzled for a moment, trying to figure out just exactly what female emotion *that* had represented. Realizing he could not, he left the galley and headed toward the sleeping quarters for a much-needed bath. The shower in the sleeping quarters was somewhat smaller than the one in the med-room and did not incorporate decontamination additives. The warm water finally gave Jared the feeling of being fully awake even though it was late in the morning. Having time to think without any interruption, Jared realized just how fortunate he had been since finding Orion. The ship had allowed him to leave his asteroid prison, see his first new world, and brought Shar'ya into his life. He got out of the shower and just as he was drying off, Orion informed him that he had another guest.

Can't they come around when I'm not busy?

"Orion, can you inform them that I will be there shortly?"

"Yes."

"Thank you."

"You are welcome, Companion."

Jared wrapped a towel around his waist and exited through the shower-room door, dressed, and hurried to meet his next guest. As he was heading down the hall, he met Shar'ya heading in the opposite direction with a puzzled look on her face.

"Where have you been?" she inquired.

"Taking a shower."

"But the shower is that way…"

With a small chuckle Jared took her head in his hands, pulled her to him, kissed her soundly and said, "I have to go meet with this last person right now, but I promise before we take you shopping, I will answer all your questions about the Orion so there will be no more mysteries for you."

He kissed her again and headed for the hatchway. Partway down the hall he stopped, turned around and seeing her still standing there, said, "In the last few mon, I have really come to dislike mysteries."

The main doorway opened. The historian, Sawyer, waved from the base of the gangplank.

"Trader Chandler, isn't it?"

"Yes, that is correct. I apologize. I do not take passengers or guests on board. However, I will answer what questions I feel I can."

Sawyer looked disappointed. "I guess that will have to do. Where was this ship built?"

"It came into my possession second hand. Since I was not present at its construction, or when it was new, that question I cannot answer. Both the ship and I come from far outside of Commonwealth borders."

"And what is the name of the world you come from? Perhaps I've heard of it."

"Earth."

Sawyer looked puzzled. "No, I've never heard of it." He then asked Jared a great deal about the ship.

Even though Sawyer did not seem satisfied with the information he received, he courteously and respectfully wished Jared a good day. Jared, however, did not like Sawyer and suspected that the man had an ulterior motive. He did seem to have a great deal of knowledge about the Commonwealth, but if Jared had met him under any other circumstances, he probably would have considered him a sly fox trying to lure an unsuspecting rabbit into a trap.

I'll have to check him out later. There should be information on individuals in the planetary database.

Jared re-entered Orion and found Shar'ya waiting for him on the bridge.

"Okay, now we have time to ourselves." Jared smiled.

Shar'ya returned his smile but said nothing. He reached out his hand, which Shar'ya took, and he led her back into the hall.

"So did you look around?" he asked.

"Some."

"Okay. Well, you've seen the med room, the galley, the bridge, my room, and the gym. There are not many other rooms with anything of interest in them, except perhaps the EVA room, the power room, and the cargo bays." Jared headed aft to a door just forward of the medical bay which opened into a large room containing numerous lockers and equipment mounted on the wall.

"This room contains the equipment necessary to keep us alive in case the atmosphere inside the ship is ever compromised or we need to go outside the ship; anywhere the air and pressure will not sustain our lives."

He opened a locker. Inside was a bulky, silvery-gray suit with numerous valves and hoses coming from various parts of it. Above it on a shelf was a large helmet and several smaller connecting parts. At the base was a pair of thick calf-high boots the same color as the suit. On a wall next to it, several cylinders hung with additional hoses and other equipment. Four lockers further to the right were the two plasma torches, and in the last two were a number of cases.

Jared saw no reason to go into detail right then because he felt she might not understand most of it anyway. He showed her numerous other rooms, mostly empty, and told her that if they ever decided to transport passengers, they had plenty of space.

She was most impressed with the power room and the tiny star that was the heart of Orion.

"Do you still wish me to choose a separate sleep room?" she asked as they passed the empty quarters.

"No. Yesterday I believed there might be problems with such an arrangement. Now the only problem is that my sleep quarters are quite small."

They seem quite satisfactory to me."

"At least for now."

"Is there any way to make them larger?"

"I don't know, I…Orion?"

"Ready."

"Is it possible to change the internal configuration?"

"Specify."

"The internal configuration of Orion."

"Yes."

With that, Jared looked at Shar'ya and told her they would experiment with rearranging things later. Lastly, he showed her the bathroom connected to his room and the shower within.

As she was looking inside the cleaning cubicle Jared asked her if she was ready to go shopping.

She was excited and ready to leave at that moment, "Yes."

"Okay, I just need to make a pit stop."

"Pit stop?"

"Uhm." He pointed at the toilet, and said, "If you need to use it, do so before we leave."

Shar'ya pointed at the toilet and said, "Pit Stop?"

"No Shar'ya, it's a slang term meaning 'needing to evacuate the bladder or bowels."

He had become so comfortable with the various languages in his head he now often used words from his native tongue when he couldn't find a satisfactory term in Ilirian. This was particularly true with slang.

"Gotcha, captain," she said playfully.

Shortly thereafter they exited the ship and headed into the merchant district. Shar'ya had to go into the first store she saw, if only just to look around. The store was full of candies, about which she knew nothing. She had seen people eating in fancy restaurants and smelled the food, but had never tasted it, nor known exactly what each item was.

Jared wasn't quite sure what the candies tasted like either since he had never tasted sweets anywhere but on Earth. The box he'd bought a few days before sat unopened in his room. While she was looking at the brightly colored containers, Jared purchased several small packages of appetizing looking confections. As they left the store, Jared pulled out one of the packages and handed it to Shar'ya. She looked curiously into the bag, then withdrew one of the bright green discs. She handed the bag back to Jared and he did likewise. She placed the disc in her mouth. Jared watched with interest as her eyes widened and a grin spread across her face. A squeal of delight burst from her lips, and her green eyes lit like emerald fire. She spun around in circles from sheer ecstasy.

"What *is* this?"

Jared noticed as several people on the street stared at her unusual antics.

"It's called candy."

"May I have more?"

"Sure, would you like to try this one?"

She eagerly reached into the bag and withdrew a somewhat egg-shaped lavender piece and instantly popped it into her mouth. Though her response was somewhat less enthusiastic than the first, she was still quite overjoyed at this new taste.

"And what about the others?"

He opened the remaining three bags and held them out to her. "You choose, but remember, I have no idea what each one is."

She momentarily studied each bag, reached into the center one, and pulled out a pinkish/orange rectangular piece and popped it into her mouth. This brought a look of total surprise. Her mouth puckering inward, her eyes wide and watering, she reached out, placing her right hand on Jared's shoulder, her left hand quickly going to her mouth, she spit out the piece with a gasp and reached into the bag of red discs and shoved a number of them into her mouth, sighing heavily as they dissolved.

Jared decided he had better try the pale strawberry colored confection and took a small bite. Unlike Shar'ya his knees didn't nearly buckle under him, but he had to admit it was the sourest candy he'd ever tasted. And to let Shar'ya know he quite agreed with her, exaggerated the look on his face to match hers and as they walked by a trash receptacle, he tossed in the offending bag. Shar'ya spent the time between the next few stores emptying the remaining bags.

She had been walking around this entire time without shoes. Most of the other citizens had not noticed and the few who did, had paid little attention. Footwear was not so different from Earth, except Jared never saw any with high heels. He couldn't remember if she'd been wearing anything on her feet when she first entered Orion, but she liked the idea of having a pair or two. It was like Christmas shopping and letting the recipient be there, picking out the stuff they wanted, only this was more fun. He actually wanted to be here.

They finally found a merchant that sold jewelry-like articles. When they entered, Shar'ya once again began looking interestedly at the many different items. Jared walked up to the counter and asked the proprietor if he carried bonding collars.

"Yes, I do," replied the merchant.

"May I see them?"

"Certainly."

The man walked Jared over to an area of the counter and pointed to several intricately assembled necklace-like bands. They were wide yet had a delicate, filigree or lace-like appearance. He had expected to see something a little more demeaning, resembling a slave collar.

But Shar'ya deserved something more like this, something beautiful.

"Which is your best?" Jared inquired.

The merchant reached in and pulled out one with the most delicate, lace-like appearance. "This is the best I have. It is also the most recent release from the manufacturer. It is eighteen thousand credits."

"What are its specifications?"

"It has the standard DNA match access and class four personal security."

"Please give me the particulars on class four security."

"It will render any person not matching the DNA of the wearer, or the bonded male, unconscious instantaneously if the female is physically threatened."

"Thank you." Jared reached into his pocket and pulled out a small, carved wooden box. He opened it and withdrew a gold-colored necklace, far more ornately designed than the others in the store. "Is this a bonding collar?"

The merchant swallowed hard. "It is indeed!"

"Can you appraise this? It has been in my possession for some time, and I have never had a use for it until now. Could you tell me about the specifications on this?"

"This, sir," the merchant began looking it over, "is an extremely old and rare bonding collar. I personally have never seen one except in antique registers." The merchant reached into a drawer, pulled out a magnifying device and scanned the back of the collar. Another small gasp escaped his lips. "This collar was manufactured over a thousand cycles ago. It is extremely valuable."

Curiosity made Jared ask, "How valuable?"

"Well, I can't give you a firm figure, but at least 1.4 million."

Stunned, Jared paused for a moment. "1.4 million credits?"

The merchant nodded, "Yes."

Again, Jared paused, gathering his thoughts, and glanced over at Shar'ya who was looking in one of the jewelry cases. "And it's specifications?" Jared repeated.

"It has dual security features and Syllco DNA match release."

"What are the dual security features?"

"The security feature contains a personal security shield which will prevent any unwanted or violent intrusion by biological organisms and a tracking device."

"A tracking device?"

"Yes, that sort of thing was used primarily by the royal classes to protect daughters and bonded spouses from kidnapping."

Jared smiled, "Yes, she's special enough to protect from all that. Heaven knows she's suffered enough. Can you tell if this collar has ever been used before?"

The merchant produced another small piece of equipment from the drawer next to him and ran it over the collar. "It has sir. However, the previous DNA information has been erased. I can reset the collar to accept new DNA right here and now. The cost to you would be one hundred credits."

"That would be acceptable."

The merchant spent about fifteen al-ems working on the collar, then returned it to Jared.

"Thank you," Jared said with a smile, "Well, since I have my own, and it is as good as you say it is, there is little point in my buying another. However, this is for your efforts and honesty." Jared handed him five hundred credits.

The merchant seemed quite pleased with this transaction and thanked Jared vigorously. Prior to leaving, Jared asked the merchant how to input the DNA information into the collar. The merchant looked at Jared with a bit of surprise. "I had assumed you were familiar with their function."

"Not entirely, I have never used one before."

"This is your first bonding?"

"It is," Jared said with feeling.

"And this is the young lady?" The merchant pointed to Shar'ya who had walked up behind Jared. "A lucky woman indeed. The process is simple," the merchant continued. "You will notice when you open the clasp that on either end is an opposingly set pin. The left pin should be used to poke the fingertip of the female, and the other clasp to poke the finger of the male, and that is looking at it from the front as it will appear on the woman's neck. That is all that is required and once the clasp is shut, the collar will activate. It could detect your

DNA within a ten-foot radius and will activate the defense charge if another tries to assault the woman against her will."

They left the store and when they had walked a short distance, he stopped, turned to Shar'ya, and pulled the ornate box out of his pocket. He opened it and withdrew the bonding collar she had not yet seen. She was not the only one on the street who gasped at the sight. Apparently even she, growing up as she did, recognized the significance of the gold bonding collar, which had most likely at some time in the past been worn on the neck of some royal person. He took one of her hands in his and selected a finger.

"Is this what you really wish to do?" he asked.

Without a pause, Shar'ya said, "I have given my vows. I will not take them back. I am yours, body, mind, and soul. Only you have the power to send me away."

Jared inhaled deeply, taken aback by her intensity, her green eyes literally boring into his head. That was a look he would never forget. As carefully as possible, he poked her finger with the left clasp of the bonding collar. She made no sound, no reaction except to smile. He then took the other side of the bonding collar and poked his own finger and felt a little embarrassment from having jerked his hand as the pin penetrated. As he started to place the collar around her neck, he noted that a considerable crowd had stopped to watch. Several murmurs passed among the onlookers, only some of which he could make out.

The only one he remembered, "Is one of them of the old royal blood?" And he smiled. *What if?*

As the two ends of the clasp snapped together, he tugged to see if they were secure. They would not separate. The delicate filigree of the bonding collar fit perfectly around Shar'ya's slender neck. Sliding down to rest lightly just above the top of her dress.

Shar'ya felt as though she would faint. It was really true. It wasn't a dream. She could feel it. She belonged. She was wanted.

Maybe she had fainted, she realized that Jared was carrying her. She made no effort to get down nor did she care about the strange looks they received. Jared carried her all the way to the transport terminal, letting her down just before they boarded. Riding the monorail was fascinating. She had seldom ventured outside the lower city or the alleyways except at night. Glancing around the cabin at the other passengers, she found it hard to believe none of them were repulsed by her presence. The beautiful light dress and having a home helped make her one of them. Fingering the dainty band about her neck, she noticed that many of the other women on the tram did not have one. She felt sadness for those who never would. Jared held her hand as they exited the vehicle, and she walked part of the way back to Orion.

She seemed to swoon as they neared Bay 12 Pad 5 and Jared picked her up. Lost in thought, Shar'ya made no effort to stop him, she simply placed her head on his shoulder and let him carry her across Orion's threshold.

Blue sky greeted Jared as he opened his eyes and stretched. Shar'ya lay next to him gazing upward through the transparent ceiling, a look of wonder danced in her green eyes. Puffy white clouds drifted lazily by, and traces of orange lingered on the western rim of the hangar.

"I've never paid much attention to the sky. It is very beautiful," she said.

He grinned. "So are you."

She turned to him, pursing her lips in mild surprise.

"Jared, what does love feel like?"

Caught off guard by her question, he stumbled over his words. "Well...I...I've never had to explain it before. I guess that...I know what it's supposed to be. It's when an individual cares more for another person than one cares for oneself or possessions. What does it feel like? I'm not sure I can describe that."

Jared looked into Shar'ya's eyes with a look of distress at being unable to answer.

"Could it be..." she struggled to find words, "Happiness? No, joy! Being given a reason to find joy in everything you see and knowing you're not alone. I mean, *really* not alone."

"Yes. I think that is a small part of a greater whole, but you said it far better than I could have."

She moved her face closer to his and grinned broadly. "Well then, I think that a big part of my greater whole is in love with you."

"That's a big step after only two days."

"Why? Is there supposed to be a time requirement on its growth?"

"No, I don't think so," he pushed himself into a sitting position.

Shifting her legs underneath into a kneeling position with her hands folded on her lap, she tilted her head slightly. "Do you love me?"

"I think there is far more love in you than any man could live up to. I can see something special in your eyes. You possess an inner innocence undamaged by the circumstances you grew up in. If I had to describe my feelings for you it would be that the greater part of my small whole is definitely in love with you."

A momentary look of confusion crossed her face. Her smile returned and she kissed him. She pushed herself off the bed and stretched, her arms raised above her head. "I'm hungry."

She lowered her arms, placing her hand behind her back and looked down at herself. "What?"

"You are very pleasing to the eyes, Shar'ya Chandler."

"My last name is Irall, yours is Chandler." The look of mild confusion returned.

"On my home world when two people are bound together as mates, it is traditional for the lady to take on her mate's family name. Of course, there are those who break with that tradition and keep their maiden name, so if you prefer…"

"You mean you would allow me to carry your family name?" The confusion flared into near shock. He stood, took her in his arms, and kissed her. She relaxed totally, seeming to melt into him. Her warmth intensified and he felt a tear drop on his skin. A shudder ran through her entire frame, and she hugged him more fiercely.

Jared said nothing. He allowed her all the time she needed. After several moments she loosened her grip and stood back.

"Yes, Shar'ya. I would be honored if you would share my family name."

Shar'ya breathed deeply and Jared felt another, milder shudder. She seemed to be unable to speak. Her smile, however, said a great deal.

"Ready for breakfast?"

She nodded, squeezed his hand, and they began to dress.

"Will I be able to go back to the lower city today?" she asked as they sat down to eat.

"If you need to, of course you can."

"I have to get something my mother gave me, and to say goodbye."

"You didn't think you might leave the planet when you followed me, did you?"

She looked at him and shook her head as she chewed.

"We can leave after breakfast. We don't need to start picking up the grain shipment until after mid-day."

Winding down various streets and alleys had completely confused Jared's sense of direction. From Adriod they'd headed south, but it had been impossible to keep things straight because many of the alleyways wound crazily around odd-shaped structures. The alleyways were again devoid of people except in two industrial areas where workers had been moving material or equipment. They had been walking for nearly half an em-har before she stopped.

She pointed at a large machinery enclosure. "This is the way I always took."

A sign on one side read, 'Waste Processor Vent 14. Authorized Access Only.' "You should probably wait here."

He nodded as she withdrew the pair of new work clothing from her bag and put it on over her good clothes.

"Be careful," he said softly as she walked toward the enclosure.

"I'll be fine. I know this place." She pulled a loose panel up and disappeared.

But will they know you?

The vent rose about ten feet higher than the surrounding structures. He found it difficult to imagine living in a sewer or catacombs or any other underground hole. Living down there did not seem to be forced upon them. Yet Shar'ya was amazed at the beauty of the world around her.

Could it be possible that she has never even seen a forest or stream?

Taking her to a wilderness area before heading into space felt like it might be fun. He liked to see her enjoyment of new things. Perhaps a trip to the seaside as well. He explored the immediate area and realized he had seen no rodents or scavenger-like creatures anywhere in the city. Apart from an occasional piece of litter and the person he saw several days ago moving a container, most of the alleys seemed little used. Unless these people feared the inhabitants of the 'lower' city, he could see no explanation for avoiding the passages. Half an em-har later, Jared began to worry. He had not expected it to take this long. He waited a little longer, then decided to go looking for her.

Fitting into the opening was not difficult, but once he entered the vent, breathing was. Controlling the urge to throw up took a great deal of effort. He located a ladder on the opposite side and headed for it. When he reached it, he heard noise from below.

Shar'ya's head appeared out of the darkness, and she smiled at him.

"I was getting worried," he choked.

"You do look a little green. I don't remember it smelling this bad. I'm sorry."

"No problem. Are you ready to go?"

"Well," she paused, "Um, Erith wants to meet you."

"Who's Erith?"

"A friend. She helped after my mother died."

"Does it smell like this the entire way?"

"I don't think so. No, only in the shaft."

"Lead on, my lady. I will follow where you wish." He grimaced to himself knowing that had sounded cheesy.

She smiled at him and started back down. The ladder descended a considerable distance and came to an end on a ledge. He could hear machinery further below which sounded like it was churning some noxious liquid. The darkness was so complete he could not see a thing.

Shar'ya, however, seemed to have no problem finding her way. If she hadn't warned him about the narrowness of the ledge before he stepped off the ladder, he probably would have ended up added to the mixture of foul stench below. Several feet to the right of the ladder just above the ledge was another opening leading to a circular pipe or access way, which led away from the vent. She pushed inward on a plate over the opening and stepped through, pulling Jared after her. Once released, the plate swung back into place with a loud thud and sealed out the worst of the smell.

Jared, however, was no longer able to keep the inevitable from happening and left the entire contents of his breakfast at Shar'ya's old doorstep. As he moved away from the mess, she came up to comfort him. He smiled as best he could, indicating he was fine and for her to lead on.

They moved from one access way to another dropping several more levels before she came to a large metal door, obviously added long after original construction. Breathing here was also much less difficult, and it did not look as bad as he'd expected. Shar'ya pulled on the door and despite the portal's poor appearance, it swung open without much noise. Light filtered out through the gap and a stale breeze ruffled Shar'ya's hair. She motioned him forward, took his hand and led him into a cavernous room.

Several openings on the three other walls led further beyond. Makeshift beds and partitions filled the room and containers of various sizes lined the walls. When they entered, most of the occupants turned and stared. Jared was stunned. Every adult and child within sight was female.

"I don't understand," he said in nearly a whisper. Shar'ya looked at him, not knowing how to answer.

"What is it you do not understand, Trader?" Another voice broke in.

Jared turned toward the speaker. A middle-aged woman, nicely dressed and apparently well fed, walked up.

"Is everyone here female?" asked Jared.

"Yes, except for a few male children some mothers refused to be separated from."

"I've seen people who were forced to live in similar conditions because of poverty or other causes but never singled out by gender."

"No one has been singled out intentionally."

"I don't mean to sound ignorant, but I'm not very knowledgeable about the Commonwealth. I…"

"Yes, I know. You are from beyond. Perhaps it is good the girl brought you here. I will tell you what I can. The cause of this situation started thousands of cycles ago. Conflict created by greed and power struggles between the Commonwealth, rebellious colonies, Royal families, and the Tirodyn Triarchy resulted in the deaths of billions. Most of the dead were men; soldiers who died for their government, lord or an ideal, leaving behind weeping bond-mates and children to fend for themselves. The first high leaders were mostly men, but later women replaced them, many with the arrogant and vain belief that they could do better. It took untold additional deaths before the truth was accepted. Every one of us has the potential of being the best that we as beings hope for, but we also have within us the worst. Though there were great leaders both male and female, there were also those who, for their own profit, destroyed most of what had been gained.

"The situation in which these women find themselves was not inflicted upon them by men alone, but also by women thousands of cycles dead. They had no idea they were damaging their descendants' futures. For the first two thousand six hundred and seventy-four cycles of the old Commonwealth, only male members of the royal family had the right to have more than one bond-mate. It was so because that is the way Myrstrad, the first imperial high seat, determined the Drakstrad would function.

"The ratio of males to females was already uneven due to pre-Commonwealth conflicts and a higher female birth rate, but not so much to arouse fears of future problems. Initially the royal bond-right received condemnation from the general population, mostly women, but became accepted within several generations. For the common citizen, however, to have more than one bond-mate was considered unthinkable. In 2649, a researcher named Har'li Odrio presented a report to the high seat and the Ilirian council. The report contained mathematical proof of what would result if conflicts continued, and social customs went unchanged. At the time of her report, two hundred and nineteen worlds were part of the Commonwealth along with a few new fledgling colonies.

"In 2674 the report was finally taken seriously and laws in the Commonwealth were changed to allow all men to have more than one bond-mate. The outcry by the general populous on many worlds was intense, though on a few it was adopted easily. It was not until about twelve hundred cycles ago that reality struck. By then however, it was too late. Many women found themselves without mates, living on colonies where they had work and shelter but little hope of finding a man. Oh, a woman can have children, but that's not the same as having a life-mate. Sharing a bond-mate had become acceptable to not having one, yet the mold had been cast, and as you can see, this is part of the result.

"Most of the inner worlds don't have so many displaced, but here conditions are aggravated due to the lack of necessary items resulting from pirate activities. Most are out of work because of insufficient raw materials. The cost of hospital care is astronomical because of the lack of needed commodities and many medicines, and most of those here can no longer afford to live in the city. Neither landlords nor the Credit and Investment guild will make allowances for those who cannot pay their debts."

The woman paused and Jared took the chance to ask a question. "Have women not fought alongside men in combat?"

"Yes, they have, but by choice the numbers have been minimal. Women have never been excluded from entering any field of study or labor. It has been proven that in many disciplines, with the exception of brute strength, women are equal to or often more capable mentally and physically. However, most women chose the path that the gender was created for, and that is to replenish those who die. If the ratio of the sexes were reversed, we would already be extinct."

Jared's curiosity was piqued. "Why is that?"

"If you have one man and one hundred thousand women, a race could continue or recover. But if you have one woman and one hundred thousand men there is only one outcome, and that is extinction. Unlike women, who can coexist under such circumstances, I doubt those one hundred thousand men would be able to refrain from killing each other, to possess the one and only woman. Many solutions have been tried, but if we intelligent beings can't overcome our passions and stop killing each other, we shall remain on a slow path to extinction."

"You do not present the appearance of one who must live here. May I ask who you are?"

"My name is Lyra Woltra. I come here when I am able, to help as best I can, and bring what aid I can, though it is not enough I'm afraid."

"What was that?" Jared asked, hearing what sounded like a faint groan.

"Another child near death," she replied, the sadness in her voice belying the hard look on her face. "I'm afraid there are many."

Jared noticed a small figure approach Shar'ya and tug at a belt loop. Shar'ya knelt and embraced the tiny girl. "Hi, Ly'ni you look a little better."

The child, no more than maybe four or five cycles of age, gave Shar'ya a big smile. "I'm doing great. I can run again."

Jared carefully looked the child over and was saddened at what he saw. One arm and hand were badly twisted and scarred. Her left eye was obviously blind, and her scalp was covered with patches of scabs. Despite all that, she still smiled. Jared stepped further into the chamber, leaving Shar'ya to talk to Ly'ni. It was almost like walking through a hospital during a plague. Sick or dying children lay everywhere. Mothers with sad, sunken eyes watched him as he passed.

Returning to where Shar'ya and Lyra Woltra stood, he shook his head. "Are the people above aware of the extent of what transpires down here?"

"They know that many unfortunates dwell below, but I doubt that more than a few suspect the extent of the misery. Those below stay below for the most part, fearful of the treatment they might receive, as well as out of shame.

Those above choose to avoid those below out of fear of contracting some disease or being too proud to help. Unfortunately, the women of the old Commonwealth have become victims of supply and demand. Though many would deny it, the females of the Commonwealth have become so numerous that our value as individuals has been diminished. In the eyes of most, even many women here and above, a boy child is far more precious than a girl. It is a question of survival. It is not fair, it is not right, it is not even logical; but it is reality! I just hope it is not too late."

Jared looked quizzically at the woman. "Woltra, Governor Woltra?"

"Yes. I am the Governor. I would appreciate it if you told no one of my visits."

"I will say nothing."

"Thank you, Trader Chandler." She considered him carefully. "If you do make it through to the inner worlds, please think of these if you return."

"Governor, I have some supplies I can leave with these people, and I may be able to help with some of the illnesses before we leave. Is there a place I can land my ship outside the city that has access to this place?"

"There is, but it was sealed long ago to help keep unwanted creatures out of the sub-city. It would need to be opened in a way that would not alert security."

"I think that can be handled," he paused seeing Shar'ya's look of surprise at his offer. "Is it so hard to believe that someone would offer such a thing?"

"I never thought anyone would care for me, even though I dreamed of it." She looked him in the eyes. "I've never even dreamed that someone would offer more."

He smiled. "Governor, if you can give me coordinates to the site, I will be there this evening shortly after dark."

"I will have them sent to your vessel within an em-har."

Shar'ya took Jared's hand and led him away from the Governor and further into the room. In a corner separated by several partitions, an elderly woman lay breathing shallowly.

Shar'ya reached out and touched her face. "Erith. I'm back."

"Did'ja bring 'im with ya'?" Erith asked in a low gravelly voice.

"Yes," Shar'ya replied gently.

"Good, help me sit up."

"But . . ."

"Don't argue wit' me, child."

Shar'ya said nothing more and helped the woman sit up.

A wave of apprehension raced through Jared.

She studied him for some time. Her dark skin was drawn tightly over her bones in places and wrinkled in others. Finally, she spoke, "I'd about given up on her ever findin' a mate. Why'd ya choose this un?"

"Well, it was sorta the other way around. She chose me and I've come to see that she is quite a rare gem. I will try to be worthy of the gift I've been given."

The old woman cocked her head to the side and grinned broadly then turned toward Shar'ya. "If ya let 'im get away, I'll come back from my grave and whup ya good."

"I will not forget your words." Shar'ya looked sad.

"See ya don't." The woman breathed heavily. "Now lay me back down, child."

Erith's eyes shifted, and she looked toward the ceiling. "I've waited a long-time sister, to see this happen. Now it's time to go home."

The woman said the last sentence so softly, Jared barely heard it, and its meaning was not lost on him. He looked at Shar'ya but she made no noticeable reaction to it. She stood, walked to his side, and took his hand.

"Good-bye, Erith," Shar'ya said softly.

Erith took several more difficult breaths, and with the last one, sighed, and then her body went limp. Shar'ya turned, and leading Jared, walked quietly away.

"I'm sorry, Shar'ya," Jared said hugging her to him.

He had never been around someone at their time of death. Even his grandparents had been far away when they passed, but Shar'ya had lived around it all her life. She seemed almost numb to her friend's passing. What an enigma she was, strong and courageous while in pain; a child-like innocent in many ways, and yet hardened by the environment she was raised in. His assumption was proved wrong as she looked up at him, tears running down her face.

Shar'ya led her bond-mate out of the under-city in silence. They stayed in the alleys and avoided anyone they saw. Jared contacted

Orion and asked his friend to meet them outside the city in two em-hars, and to home in on Jared's wrist comm.

They walked slowly, enjoying each other's company, each left to their own thoughts. By the time they reached the outer boundary of the city and crossed under the monorail route, the two em-hars were almost up. Jared had not thought about the fact that Shar'ya had yet to see Orion in flight.

Shar'ya jumped into his arms as the great white bird appeared silently, as if out of nowhere. Orion hovered over the two and Jared spoke into the wrist comm. Her eyes widened again as a shimmering transparent box appeared around them and they rose into the air toward the belly of the huge vessel. At the last moment a small opening appeared, and they vanished inside.

"Orion."

"Ready."

"We've lots of work to do, my friend," Jared said as he left the cargo bay. "Set course for the first of our stops to pick up the grain cargo."

"Complying."

Shar'ya followed Jared, nearly having to run to keep up with his long, quick strides. As he passed through the bridge doors, he pointed to the right front seat saying, "If you wish, you may sit there," then he climbed into the left one. For the first time since his last simulation exercise, Jared took control, gliding low and slow with most of the nose transparent. He noticed Shar'ya sat transfixed looking at the view outside. Farmsteads, thickets of trees, a river and a lake passed beneath. It was still hard for Jared to believe that she had never left the city. Struggling to survive and fear had cost her a great deal.

Child-like delight danced across her face at sights which had only been seen before under a veil of darkness, and then only briefly. Jared found it difficult to concentrate on piloting and asked Orion to take over and keep speed slow to avoid frightening any of the farm animals below and so Shar'ya could get her fill of the scenery. A more rapid velocity would have been preferable if they were to access the lower city before night. Unfortunately, several problems prevented that. He tried to keep his mind off the suffering below by watching his new 'wife.' Somehow the Earth word sounded strange to him now, though he was not sure why.

The first pickup location would be Whim Nurl's stead, and cargo quantity was listed as nine full pods. No limit on cargo amounts had been established during the first meeting and Jared was pleased that no problem had arisen from that oversight. A total of forty-one containers would be ready for loading from all four steads. Nurl's farm came into view as Orion crested a hill north-east of Da'har. Lined neatly several hundred feet from the main buildings, the cargo pods waited. A large circular area had been prepared for Orion's landing, though it looked a bit small. Waiting near the pods were three loading vehicles and several people. From what Jared could see it looked as if they were engaged in a heated discussion.

With the exception of Whim, the others with him appeared astonished by what they saw. The huge white ship had appeared unlike any they had seen before. Jared later learned that even Whim had expected noise from engines and an impact shock from touch down, but the vessel didn't even kick up much dust or debris. Apparently, Whim's foreman had been chastising the others for not making the pad large enough. Their apparent response: how were they to know it was *that big!*

Except for the living and service buildings, groomed fields stretched uninterrupted in all directions from the landing site. The access road wound southwest, a copse of trees lay a short distance to the north and a pond was just west of the house. Farm animals wandered lazily around enclosures next to one of the larger buildings.

Jared unfastened his restraints and headed toward the bridge door.

"I've got to go below and help with the loading." Jared paused at the door and asked Shar'ya, "You want to stay here with the pretty view?"

She shook her head enthusiastically. "I wanna' see it close up."

"Okay, Beautiful, let's go."

"Beautiful?" she mumbled. "Huh, oh," she said, startled from her thoughts. "Yes," she finished as she walked by him. "Betcha I can beat you to the cargo bay." She started running before the challenge fully set in.

"Hah!" And the pursuit was on.

She was standing triumphantly in the center of the bay with her hands on her hips as he came through the door. Her mischievous grin changed to playful suspicion as he walked up to her. "Ah, but can you handle the prize that comes with victory?"

She lightly bit her lower lip. He reached out and placed his hands on her waist and looked her deeply in the eyes. Then when she was quite distracted, he moved his hands quickly to her ribs just under her arms and began to tickle. Her first reaction to this new form of play was open-mouthed surprise, followed by an uncontrollable urge to giggle. Her legs gave out and she crumpled to the deck. When she regained her composure, she was lying on her back on the floor with Jared's face close to hers, her heavy breathing ruffling the hairs of his goatee.

"Surprise."

"They're wai…"

She was prevented from finishing as he kissed her.

He got up. "Yes, I know, we gotta hurry."

As he walked away, she asked. "What do I get to do to you, if you win?"

"If…?" he stopped and considered her.

"Yes," she said hesitantly.

"Why, whatever your playful little mind can come up with," he said, without considering the ramifications of what the statement might set into motion.

"Orion."

"Ready."

"Stand by to lower elevator."

"Standing by."

Jared held out his hand, and she took it.

"Lower elevator."

At his command a large portion of Orion's underside began its descent.

Once on the ground, Jared led Shar'ya toward the waiting group. Whim greeted them at the edge of the lift and Jared noticed two women and several children coming out of the house as he returned Whim's salutation.

"We need to proceed quickly. The sooner I'm loaded and off-world, the less chance of any problems arising," Jared stated, trying to avoid alluding to his real desire for promptness.

"I heartily agree," Whim replied. "The pirates do not attack on-world openly, but I am not one of those that believes we are safe."

"Good, have them load the pods onto the platform here."

"You heard the man. Let's get to work." Whim bellowed at the workers.

Two women and a man headed for the loaders and fired up the motors. Shar'ya touched Jared's arm and asked him if she could walk to the stand of trees to look around a little. Jared called to Whim as he followed the workers and asked, "Shar'ya was wondering if it would be allowable for her to walk over to that wooded area and explore a bit?"

"Sure 'ats no problem," he turned to walk away then stopped. "Wait, I'd best send Bandur with her." Placing his hand beside his face he bellowed, "BANDUR," and waited for an animal that vaguely resembled a dog with a long bushy tail and legs. The body, head and long neck were covered with somewhat shorter hair. The large animal ran up to Whim, showing a great deal of affection for the farmer. Whim pointed toward Shar'ya. "Protect."

The beast let out a low, deep growl and walked over to Shar'ya and sat down.

"Are there dangerous creatures out there?" asked Jared.

"Not usually, but occasionally some that can be a little mean wander in. They're only a threat if ya don't give them distance. She looks like one who's had little experience with wild things. Bandur will see to it she stays away from 'em."

"Thanks Whim," said Shar'ya.

"No trouble, now 'scuse me, I've got to help with the loadin'." Whim turned and walked away.

"Well, if you're going, you'd better get moving." She kissed him and trotted away with Bandur at her heels.

The loading was accomplished in less than an em-har. It went smoothly, except for one pod almost breaking loose from the loader. With the final pod in position on the platform, the last driver parked her truck and joined the others who'd gathered near Jared and Whim. It had been two cycles since they'd last loaded a freighter and this cargo meant a great deal. Whim had been telling Jared how difficult it was to load the Hedmar freighters. They were the most common, and the cheapest of all cargo ships. The load capacity for each freighter was a pitiful six pods. The vessel's only redeeming value was that they were also cheap to operate and maintain. Whim would've had to hire two to have moved what Jared was taking today from Whim's stead alone.

Jared asked, "I hope I don't sound ignorant by asking this, but even though I've looked into inner-core market prices, I would like to know what amount of return you're hoping or need to get?"

"Actually, I'm glad you asked," Whim rubbed his chin. "If we can get sixty-five hundred per container I'll be satisfied. It may be difficult to get more than five thousand. Sha'Lurali grain has been considered some of the best available for nearly one hundred cycles. Hopefully the prices will be higher since it has been scarce of late."

"I'll do the best I can to get you the highest price possible."

"That's all anyone can ask."

"I guess I'd better go get Shar'ya." Jared began to head toward the copse of trees, but Whim stopped him.

"No need to walk all that way when you're in such a hurry." Whim let loose with a high whistle.

Shar'ya ran awhile before slowing down to survey the land around her. The terrain was mostly level until she neared the trees. She stopped once and looked back to the activity around Orion, until she found Jared. Assured he was still there she continued to the woods. Several paces from the end of the plowed area, she paused to look at the thick patches of wildflowers clustered around the edge of the stand where the trees did not restrict the daylight. A mix of yellow, red, and orange blossoms danced in the gently shifting breeze. Wild grass grew high further in, seeming to frame the flower patches. She knelt to look at the colorful plants and was surprised to find they possessed a pleasant odor. Small insects flew in, on and around the beautiful vegetation, several of which she had to fend off with her hand. One she chose not to shoo away had large wings containing more colors than the flowers it seemed attracted to. Its short, thick body and narrow tail were a dark dull brown.

She soon found a path that led into the copse and followed it.

She tripped and fell once from gazing upward into the treetops. Musical sounds emanated from birds nesting above and various buzzing from the insects. Bandur walked ahead sniffing in various places. She had seen plants growing in the city and had to avoid security even at night. There had been little time to enjoy their beauty. A lace-like formation of tiny threads caught her eye. It was a fantastic, intricate work of art. Little drops of moisture clung to it at points, sparkling when light from the daystar was reflected. She reached out to touch the fragile object but jerked back as Bandur growled menacingly, tripped, and landed on her butt.

She wondered why her move had elicited such a response until one of the colorful insects became caught in the web. A large, many legged horror about the size of her palm darted out and seized the insect. She heard a crunching sound as the ugly creature's mandibles bit the colorful bug in two. Shivers ran through her as she rose and forced the sight from her mind. The awful incident was forgotten when she stepped into an open area with a small, bubbling clear spring at the center.

Shar'ya approached the pond, knelt, and started to put her hand into the water, but stopped and looked at Bandur. The guardian animal had already lain down and seemed unconcerned with her action, so she slipped her hand into the cool water.

Sometime later Bandur's head snapped up, startling Shar'ya and foiling her attempt to coax a tiny hopper closer. She looked at the guard animal crossly, then stood. Bandur rose, stretched, and slowly walked toward the pathway. He stopped at the head of the trail and regarded her with a low growl.

"Time to go, huh? Okay." She regretfully sighed.

Bandur waited for her to get within several paces, then started down the path. She liked this beautiful place, even if it did have some nasty creatures in it. She was unable to find the web on the trip out. Rays from the daystar filtered through the thick leaves and created shifting patterns on the ground. Swaying playfully from one shadowed spot to another, Shar'ya followed the guardian with childlike abandon.

Several steps after exiting the wood, Shar'ya heard a whistle. Bandur stopped, raised his large head, snorted, and then trotted off toward the farmhouse. Shar'ya located the smoothest area in the field and ran after the animal.

Jared hadn't been waiting long after the second whistle before he saw Shar'ya crest the hill at a full run, her dark brown hair billowing out behind. He couldn't help but smile at her joy for life and enthusiasm for new discoveries. She fell into his arms laughing and out of breath.

"Never…been…able…to…run…like…that…ba'…fore," she sputtered.

"All the climbing you did in the lower city kept you in fair shape," he said, breathing deeply. "Got your breath or you want me to carry you?"

"Uh…well…I."

He hefted her up and over his shoulder like a sack of potatoes and headed for Orion. She bobbed several times before gripping his waist and pushing herself up so she could see. Waving from the porch of the house, Whim, his family, and the farm hands chuckled at the retreating pair.

CHAPTER NINE

Break Away

"I could not justify my existence
without helping another
at least once in my life.
Once done however,
I found I could not be happy
until I did it again."

WITH THE FINAL STOP at Calyb's accomplished and the last of the grain aboard, Jared headed Orion toward the rendezvous point. Night was still more than an em-har away, but he did not wish to go all the way back to the port. Orion headed south, flying low to avoid as many eyes as possible. Once the canyon was located, the ship skimmed just below the rim of the ravine to the point indicated on the instructions. The governor had said the canyon was more of a valley with steep rocky hills surrounding it. Clearly visible ahead and to the right was the service access tunnel. A metal plug, twelve feet high and inset several feet, prevented entry to the lower city.

"There should be a place suitable for landing near the service tunnel." He spoke to no one in particular.

"Huh?" Shar'ya seemed to be startled from deep thought.

"Oh, nothing. I was just looking for a place to set down."

"What about that place?" she pointed to the left.

"Good eyes, precious."

"Orion."

"Ready."

"Can you detect any farmsteads or other activity in the area?"

"No habitations are established nearby. No other humanoid presence detected."

"Good, then please set down in the open field there." He pointed to the spot Shar'ya had indicated.

"Complying."

Jared and Shar'ya disembarked and went to inspect the access plug. The arched portal was gently lit by Orion's glow and the plug's seal line, clearly visible at the outer edge, was a gray, black scar.

"Orion."

"Ready."

"Please monitor the area for transport or security activity."

"Complying."

"Oh, and how's the best way to open this?"

"Metal panel is a medium density light weight alloy. A focused plasma torch set to a beam length of two feet will be the most efficient method of penetration. Damage will be limited to the area cut."

"Will we be able to reseal the opening after our errand is accomplished?"

"Resealing is possible if supplemental material is provided."

"Is the necessary material on board?"

"Yes."

Jared looked at his watch and then at Shar'ya. "Well, those who are coming should begin arriving in about twenty al-ems. I'll be right back; I've got to get the torch."

Shar'ya nodded and rubbed her arms. A stiff cool breeze had picked up and the sky overhead looked a bit ominous. Jared had noticed her movements and decided to take a little extra time to get them both a jacket.

Secured in one of the lockers in the EVA room rested two heavy plasma torches with attached safety shield and a stack of various operator's manuals, all in the Xaxilor language. Jared selected one of the manuals, released the clamps and withdrew one torch, slinging it over his shoulder.

Upon returning to the plug, he handed Shar'ya a jacket and set the torch against the steel-rimmed, stone wall.

"Thank you." She regarded him with a smile and stood back to watch as he studied the device.

"Orion?" he asked, returning her smile.

"Ready."

"Can the beam length be adjusted after the torch is on?"

"Yes."

The device had a trigger, obviously an on-off switch, a dial labeled 'intensity,' another identified as 'beam extent selector,' and a third which read 'field continuity adjustment.' He glanced through the manual quickly then set it down. He turned the shield on and all the dials in a counterclockwise direction. He aimed the torch away from anything and pulled the trigger.

As had been indicated in the book, nothing happened.

"Well, we know I can follow instructions." He picked up the manual and scanned further. Adjusting the dials again, he aimed the torch and hit the switch. A brief popping sound preceded a yellow-white flame that began to burn from the end, about twelve inches in length. The kick that had accompanied the pop surprised him. Bracing the mechanism in his left hand and against his shoulder, he adjusted the beam length with his right. The yellow-white plume lengthened another foot but began to sputter and distort. He reached for the field continuity dial and turned it one way. He quickly turned it back the other way as the beam began to expand into a flickering, flowery ball of plasma energy. Once the beam stabilized, he continued to narrow and sharpen until it was bright, white, and tightly focused. With the desired setting achieved he released the trigger. Carefully setting the appliance against the wall he walked over to Shar'ya.

"I guess I'm ready," he wiped his brow. "That thing has quite a recoil for a cutting tool."

"It's very hot too. I could feel it over here."

"Once we get through the wall, it's going to be up to you to escort the people up to the medroom. Bring the children who are the most ill first."

Shar'ya nodded, mild concern on her face. "I don't know how to talk to Orion. How will I ..."

"You'll need to remember these two words. Shy'tar means 'to lower,' and shy'vas means 'to raise'. Orion will know what you want done."

"Okay." She was mildly surprised by his trusting her to carry out the responsibility. He hadn't even asked her to repeat back the words 'shy'tar' and 'shy'vas.' She was quite confident in her ability to look after herself and get done what she set out to do, but it was a new experience to have someone consider her worthy of responsibility.

Jared returned to the torch, hefted it to a comfortable spot and positioned himself in front of the seal. With the nozzle next to a random point on the wall he reached for the trigger. A thought occurred to him he had not considered earlier, and he lowered the tool.

"Orion."

"Ready."

"Do you detect any security or alarm devices on or around the sealed area?"

"No."

"I guess they didn't expect that anyone might try to cut into the sewers."

He noticed Shar'ya's curious look at his delay and shifted to the Ilirian tongue for her. "I needed to find out if there were any alarms."

"Are there?" she asked with concern.

"No, and as long as I don't do too much damage to the seal, I doubt anyone will ever know we were here."

Jared kissed her gently and smiled reassuringly. He, however, was a little worried about using the torch. He had felt both recoil and turbulence near the nozzle that could cause trouble if he came across something in the portal that made the tool lurch or kick. Chainsaws could do plenty of damage with sharp, high-speed teeth and he hated to imagine what hot plasma would do. He bent down, picked up a small rock and marked off an area he believed would be sufficient for an exit. He decided to read the manual more fully at his first opportunity. He picked up the cutting tool again and positioned himself. Making sure his face shield was secure and correctly oriented; he pulled the trigger.

The beam lashed out at the wall with incredible force and Jared was sent toppling backwards. The device shut off as soon as his finger left the trigger, which saved his life. A small part of the face shield melted and ran onto the skin of his forehead. He ripped the mask off, along with a small portion of skin, and grunted loudly. He lay still on the ground trying to calm his nerves. A large scar in the seal still glowed from the momentary plasma strike.

The blast left Shar'ya stunned. It took her a moment to pull herself together and she ran to Jared's side. She knelt and cradled his head in her lap.

Jared blinked to clear his eyes and held his hand to the raw, burned spot on his forehead.

"Guess I shoulda read the instructions more thoroughly," he smiled sheepishly.

Shar'ya's eyes filled with tears, and she hit him firmly on the chest. Immediately, a look of shock and horror crossed her face.

After a brief pause, he pushed to his feet and pulled Shar'ya up. "Sorry." He picked up the torch.

"You're going to try again?" Shar'ya's look of surprise and shock intensified.

"Have to. It's our only way in and they're counting on us." He picked up the manual and translated the Xaxilor into Ilirian for Shar'ya's benefit.

"Place aft reaction support tightly against upper torso. Firmly grasp both hand grips and point tip into open area. **DO NOT ENGAGE POWER WHILE TIP IS POINTED AT TARGET.**"

He chuckled. "Well, I field tested that safety tip."

The look he received clearly indicated she did not see the humor in his statement. "Okay…onward," he continued to read. "With unit directed into an open area, depress trigger. Once beam is focused and stabilized, carefully move beam into cutting position."

He looked at her again. "Alright, I believe I can do it safely now." He spoke reassuringly but her face remained creased with worry.

Jared was still a little shaky as he repositioned himself and hefted the tool. Pointing it off to his right so the tip was aimed upward and away from anything, he pulled the trigger. Yellowish-white plasma burst forth from the nozzle and sputtered mildly. Realizing the fall must have slightly destabilized the device, he re-adjusted it. With that done he turned back toward the metal disc and slowly ran the beam into the surface of the plug. Little resistance was offered by the alloy which began to glow orange red. He cut counterclockwise along his mark and kept his pace slow, even though once started it was quite easy. Globs of molten metal fell to the ground, forming two small rivulets that flowed a short distance and pooled in a low area. Shar'ya watched Jared at first, but when she saw he was having no further difficulty she seemed to be more interested in the small molten river, which turned several colors as it cooled.

As Jared neared the 360-degree point, he prepared to jump back in case the cutout decided to fall toward him. He moved slightly to his right and cut through the last portion. The slab seemed to hover where it was for a moment, then a thin, partially cooled filament of metal gave way, and the heavy piece thumped loudly to the ground on his left. Several tendrils of thickening metal hung down from the top where he had finished cutting and about two thirds of the open-ing glowed eerily in the cool air. It was at this time that he began to hear voices from inside.

"Please stay back for about ten al-ems for the opening to cool," he advised them.

There was no answer from inside, but no one tried to pass through the door. Jared felt Shar'ya's hand slip into his. When he looked at her, she was watching the fading luminescence on the cut line. He watched a short time too, then turned to her.

"I'd best get inside and prepare the medroom," he touched her cheek. "Will you be alright?"

"I'm okay," she replied with a shaky sigh.

"The metal may still be very warm or even hot after the red glow is gone, so be careful."

She nodded in return and motioned for him to get going. He ran toward Orion.

Jared had not told her how many to bring at a time, so she decided to take ten. She hoped he wouldn't be angry with her for not asking, but her responsibility was here, and she didn't think it wise to leave. She wished she had one of the communicators but figured that when he felt she was worthy of it, he would give her one. By the end of ten al-ems the last of the glow had faded and Shar'ya crept up to the opening. She put her hand near the last place Jared had burned and noted that the metal was very warm but not excessively hot. She walked over to an area of tall grass, picked an armful, carried it back, deposited the bundle over the threshold of the opening and stepped through.

Many individuals from the lower city waited in a dim luminescence provided by old light sticks. A few cries from little ones and sparse conversation were all that broke the silence. There had been precious little time before to be concerned about these others, but now she was filled with sorrow.

"Is there anyone who has authority here?" she hadn't recognized anyone yet.

Governor Woltra walked out of the now gathering throng. "I will take charge," she said.

"I did not think you would be here," said Shar'ya.

"I had not intended to but realized you would need all the help you could get. Besides, I had nothing waiting for me but paperwork, and I'd much rather be here."

Shar'ya was puzzled. "They will not miss you?"

"Oh, they might if they dared to check," the governor smiled devilishly. "But they won't, I made it perfectly clear that unless the pirates were making a direct attack on the planet that I had better not be disturbed." Governor Woltra's remark elicited a few wobbly laughs from those present.

"Okay, I will take ten at a time and we will begin with the children who are the most ill."

"Right," said the governor. "Ky'anda and Hitaria, help me get the babes and their mothers up here." She paused then turned to Shar'ya. "If you can help them, it will be easier for me to keep them all alive until we can find a more permanent solution."

Six adult females and ten children all less than three cycles old soon stood before Shar'ya. She picked up one toddler who seemed to be having difficulty. The little girl looked her in the eyes and reached up to touch Shar'ya's lip. She grimaced as a wave of pain shot through her tiny frame. She hugged the girl to her as she led the others out into the chilly night and toward Orion. The girl shivered and she took a deep breath as a light gust of fresh, cool air passed over them. Shar'ya lifted the child's shirt up exposing her abdomen to the cold breeze. She ushered everyone to the center of the lift and spoke the word Jared had told her.

"Shy'vas." The lift began to rise and Shar'ya smiled to herself.

I will learn and truly become part of his world, part of him, and make him proud he gave me his name.

Shar'ya noticed several adult females staring at her eyes, but she remained quiet, lost in her thoughts. When the lift came to a stop, she told them all to follow her. Outside the medroom, she asked them to wait and went in.

"Jared, I brought the first ten children."

"Good." He turned to her. "Are they all that small?"

"Yes," she said sadly.

He glanced into the corridor through the still open door and saw several of the adults' holding children. One young woman stood in the doorway with a pleading look in her eyes. An infant not more than half a cycle old rested limply in her arms. He motioned for the woman to come forward.

"Shar'ya, please have the others wait in the dining room. I've had Orion provide seats. Once you get them settled, come back in here."

She nodded and left.

The young mother walked up to Jared and held out her child.

He pointed to the table and told her to lay the baby in the center. Once the limp infant was in place he lowered the scanner and began the series of passes. The baby had no serious illness, but insufficient nutrition and some stomach parasites were the cause of the child's emaciated condition.

Jared turned to the young woman. "Are you this child's mother?"

"Y…yes."

"It is suffering from starvation," he paused, considering her. "And yet, Governor Woltra has said she does get food to you, particularly for the children."

"I have tried, but she will not eat what they bring." A tear slipped from her eye.

"You don't breastfeed?"

"I did for the first mon, but after that there was nothing for her to get." More tears filled her dark, sunken eyes.

He looked at the woman who was not much older than Shar'ya as he gave the child the injection that the computer had prepared. At first, he thought the child might have been neglected, but as he spoke with her, he felt that maybe she really had tried but just had no idea what to do and nowhere to turn. He picked the baby up and placed it on one of the three observation beds and touched a button. A small armature appeared from the side and clamped gently onto the child's arm.

He turned back to the woman. "She would not have lasted much longer," he observed. "Would you please get on the table?"

Surprise crossed her face, and she pointed to the waiting area. "But the children are to be first," she said, worry in her voice.

"Ah, but this *is* for this little girl. She can't survive if you can't feed her." He noted the change on her face as she saw his logic. He helped her up and then said a bit awkwardly. "The scanner does not work properly through clothing. Would you mind removing your top?"

"No," she replied simply, and began to undo her shirt. He went to the control console, touched a switch, and when he returned, she held her top out to him. As he took it, he glanced up to see Shar'ya walk in. He stopped in his tracks and stared, horrified at what she might think of what she was seeing. Shar'ya, however, walked up to him and asked him if he was alright.

Relieved, he blinked. "Uh, yeah, sure."

"Is she ill too?"

"Yeah," he returned to the task. "I need to find out why she can't feed the child. Her milk has dried up."

"Okay, will you then be ready for another child?" She walked over to the baby's side and ran her hand along the child's cheek.

"In about ten al-ems. Pick out the next worst one and be ready."

"I will," and she headed out.

"And be sure to see that they all get something to eat," he added.

"Gotcha," she happily shot back.

Jared scanned the woman as quickly as he could and discovered she was also suffering from malnutrition, anemia, and digestive worms. She had been unable to feed the baby because her body had practically nothing to run on. He handed back her shirt and prepared another injection. She sat unmoving, watching him. He gave her the shot and told her to put her shirt back on, which she did slowly. "Why were you not eating the food that the Governor brought?"

"We each get very little, and I gave what I received to Lyl'ya. I didn't know what else to do." She started to weep.

"How long have you been in the lower city?"

"A little over a mon. I used to work at the metal refinery but was laid off."

"How long ago did your milk stop?"

"About six days before I found a way down. I had slept in the alleys for half a mon after I lost my living quarters."

"Where is the girl's father?" he asked, angry that she had been left alone.

"I paid to have a child and was inseminated artificially." At this point she broke down and sobbed, "I did not consider I might lose my job. I had held it for several cycles and was a good worker. I knew I might never have a bond-mate, but I wanted a child of my own."

She looked hopeless.

"Was what I did wrong?"

He walked over to her. "No, wanting a family is not wrong."

She studied his face. "Thank you."

He smiled at her. "Let the little one sleep for a while so I can monitor her. You go get something to eat, then rest. Remember you must eat and sleep for her to live. Please ask Shar'ya to bring in the next child."

She nodded, gave him a weak smile, and exited. He walked over to the bed and looked at the Xaxilor readout. The child's vital signs had improved, and her skin color was better. She did not look so limp and made several humorous faces as he watched. He sighed and turned back to the scanner.

The next five children were all suffering from various forms of vitamin deficiency, flu-like symptoms, and malnutrition. Jared was beginning to believe that the surplus grain they were receiving was possibly contaminated or of substandard quality. He'd have to add it to his list of things to check out. Number seven was the little toddler Shar'ya had carried to the ship. She'd found out that the girl's mother had died several mons earlier. She'd had a father, but he was killed when his freighter was attacked by pirates while transporting ore. Jared found himself becoming angrier at the brutal pirates and the suffering they were causing.

The scanner indicated that the child had a tumor growing near her heart and that the equipment aboard the Orion was not sufficient to remove the melanoma without a trained surgeon. He could not decide what to do, so gave her an injection to help with the pain until he had time to think. The readout indicated that if untreated, however, she had only a few days to live.

He made it through the next group of ten children, most of whom were between the ages of three and five, without any major problems. His good luck ran out when he had to tell the mother of one young girl that there was nothing he could do for her, except make her comfortable until she passed. The mother seemed to take the news with detached resignation and sat by her child for several em-hars until the child died. She ignored everyone as she carried the limp form of her child out of the ship and disappeared into the darkness.

The rest of the night went much the same. Most were suffering from common malnutrition, viruses, or bacterial infections. Fatigue was beginning to take its toll on Jared and Shar'ya. Nearly seventy children and young women had been examined and treated for numerous ailments. Two of the children had been boys; one had a bad cold and the other an infected laceration. Nearly all the medicinal stores and more than half of the food supplies were depleted. Governor Woltra had come on board with the last group, helping where she could. Shortly before star-rise she and Shar'ya began to get the last group ready to head back to the service tunnel. As Jared gave the last vitamin injection to a frail skinny girl, Shar'ya and the Governor walked in.

"The tunnel needs to be resealed soon," Governor Woltra said through a yawn.

"Right, get everyone back into the passageway. I'll be down as soon as I shut down the scanner."

"What do you plan to do with that child?" Governor Woltra inquired, pointing to the toddler in the first bed.

"I have no idea, but now it will have to wait. However, it will be decided before we leave," he said intensely. "You two need to get going."

Shar'ya did not hesitate and turned to leave. The governor lingered a moment as if she were going to say something but then changed her mind and followed Shar'ya. They gathered the last group together and departed for the cargo bay. Jared put the small gun like injector into its drawer, let out a deep breath and left the room.

With the hole successfully sealed, if albeit a bit messy looking, Jared directed Orion to take a low path out of the valley. He had been considering the several dilemmas that still stood before him. The farmers needed to get their grain to a market and get a good price to be able to live for the next season. The women and children of the lower city needed a good source of food to keep them going. Since grain from Sha'Lural was supposed to be of such high quality, he determined to verify the quality of the grain that Orion now carried and let those below have it. He could then pay the farmers out of his account to compensate. There was no reason for him to tell them to whom he'd transferred the grain, and both the farmers and the under-city dwellers would benefit.

Now he had to figure out how to help the little girl in the medroom, who was dying.

"Orion."

"Ready."

"Please compile a list of Physicians or Surgeons who treat children for severe medical conditions."

"Complying."

"Thank you, friend."

"You are welcome, Companion."

Jared returned his attention to the view outside. Orion shot out of the valley and turned left setting a circuitous course back to the spaceport. It had been some time since thoughts of Earth had crossed his mind. He could see his father sitting in his chair watching the news and absorbing the reports of disasters, murders, and other tragedies. Now he was living on a grand scale, much of what he had tried to tune out. Yawning deeply, he shifted to try and stave off sleep. Orion took less than one al-em to collect the information, but Jared was sound asleep when the list was ready.

"Companion. Companion?"

Jared bolted awake as if he had been poked. "Oh, um, yes, go ahead."

"There are two hundred sixteen specialists in Da'har who provide medical surgical services for children."

"Thank you."

"You are welcome."

"Does it rate them?"

"Specify."

"Which are considered the best?"

"Yes."

"Please identify and print out the top ten."

"Complying."

Silently a sheet of paper slid out of the slot in the console to Jared's right. He picked it up and read it. He stood shakily, holding on to the chair for support. "What is the status of the child?"

"Stable and asleep."

"Nobody even knows her name," he said blankly not expecting a response.

"You could give her a name, as you did me."

He stopped and stared at the floor, his eyes heavy, and a lump in his throat. "I didn't know you deemed a name of any importance."

"Importance lies not in the name, but in that an entity deems such of sufficient value to bestow a title of respect upon the other, regardless of station, standing or outward appearance."

Jared was too stunned to form any reply. He put his hand on the wall near the door and ran his fingers gently over the surface. Orion's hum increased and Jared felt a surge of energy flow through him. Strength returned somewhat and he quietly but quickly headed for the medroom.

About halfway down the hall Orion informed him they were ready to land at the port and Jared asked the ship to handle it, which it did. Upon entering the medroom Jared found Shar'ya standing next to the child's bed. "You have to get some rest," he said taking her hand.

"Can we leave her alone?" Shar'ya asked.

"She'll be okay," he reassured her. "She'll sleep until we take her off the Sar'ok."

Shar'ya nodded her head and allowed him to lead her from the room. They walked hand in hand to their quarters.

Jared listened to Orion's humming, and realized the ship was more than just a piece of machinery and meant a great deal more to him than just flowing power.

"My pants are sticky," she said through a yawn.

"Why?"

"One of the babies spilled juice on me."

Since she was sitting on the bed, he helped her pull them off, then lifted her feet and gently rolled her onto her side of the bed. Shar'ya fell asleep nearly as soon as her head hit the pillow, and Jared gave Orion one more directive before he too succumbed to sleep.

"Orion."

"Ready."

"Keep an eye on the little one and don't wake us for a couple of em-hars."

"Confirmed."

"Good night, friend."

"Good night, Companion."

Shar'ya awoke early the following morning and for some time watched Jared. Growling from her stomach caused her to get up and head for the galley. The temperature inside Orion never varied and even the floors maintained a comfortable warmth. Though the floor was solid, it felt supple and there also seemed to be a faint reverberation which swept through her feet as they came into contact with the surface. As she stood at the food processor entering her selection, she pondered Jared's instructions about how she wore her clothes. She was still a little confused at some of Jared's attitudes. She liked being barefoot though, walking around on Orion's decks made her feet feel good.

She sat down and began eating her trisma with fada sauce. Being unable to communicate with Orion did not prevent her from feeling a closeness to it. It was strange to think that she should feel close to a machine. Never having been on a spaceship before left her no way to compare how truly different Orion was. She felt she understood her ever deepening love for Jared, but so many new and unexpected feelings had been awakened in so short a time. She ate, barely noticing the taste of her food, lost deep in her thoughts.

Jared stood at the galley door watching her. She seemed locked in time staring off into space with a contented smile and those ever-present, bright green eyes.

"Orion, respond so she can't hear," he whispered.

"Ready," Orion responded at the exact same decibel.

"Can you provide me with an optical reproduction printout of Shar'ya as she is right now from my perspective?"

"Yes."

"Great, please do so."

"Complying."

He stood several more al-em watching her before something caused her to look absently in his direction. After a moment reality seemed to hit and she jumped slightly, realizing he was watching her.

"Good morning," she said cheerfully.

He sauntered in. "Mornin', beautiful. You must have quite a lot on your mind."

She smiled and shrugged. "I guess."

He walked up to the table and kissed her on the forehead. He felt her react to his touch. "What?"

"Well, I'm still not quite sure about how I should dress and I don't want to upset you if it's not…acceptable."

Jared cocked his head slightly and lowered his eyebrows in mild puzzlement for a moment before smiling. "Do you remember how I told you some things about the customs of my home world?"

"Yes."

"Well, before I understood we were bonded, I felt uncomfortable with you in certain circumstances. For many of my people it is improper for a man and a woman to be undressed in one another's presence outside of marriage or bonding."

"I would not want to be looked at by someone other than my chosen bond-mate," she stated remembering their previous discussion. "But I had chosen you."

"Yes, but I had no idea what was going on and your antics were very unnerving."

"Are you still sure…?"

He placed his finger to her lips. "Don't even say it, letting you go is simply not an option and I'm not going anywhere either." He paused before removing his finger. "As for how you dress, you may wear whatever you like when we are on board. If, however, we have guests or passengers, we shall both be fully attired. Sound fair, my lovely?" he squeezed her knee.

"Understood," she replied, before they kissed. She ran her hand through his hair. "Your head is damp," and she gave him a little pout. "You took a shower," she said with mild accusation.

"I was a little smelly after yesterday's marathon events," he said apologetically. "Besides, I need to take care of several errands before we can take care of…I'm getting tired of having no name to call the little girl. Do you have any suggestions?"

Still unaccustomed to being asked, she hesitated a moment before answering, "How about Cys'tal?"

"It's very nice, does it have particular meaning to you?"

"It was my mother's name."

"Cys'tal it is." He noticed her reaction of wonder that he had accepted it so readily. "Anyway, I need you to stay and look after the…Um, Cys'tal, until I get back from my errands. Orion told me as I was showering that she has slept more than enough and needs exercise. The pain killer should help her to play without discomfort. Are you okay with that?"

"Sure," she said agreeably. "Just don't stay gone too long, I prefer having you around." She giggled as he bowed low.

"I shall make all haste, fair lady, to return swiftly to your side."

Jared rode the transport into Da'har shortly after breakfast and contacted each of the ten doctors on his list. Only one was either willing or able to see Cys'tal immediately. He was number three on the list, so Jared felt confident about the choice. He then contacted Shar'ya to let her know he would return to pick them up shortly after midday. The second stop was at the Dahar C & I. He had a container load of old Drakstrad currency and felt it was time to find out just what it was worth. Only three people were ahead of him, so his wait was short. He had filled a small pouch with one hundred each of the three different denominations of Drakstrad coin. When the clerk asked how he could help, Jared began by giving him his account number.

"I have in my possession some old coins, which I have collected over time. I wish to find out what their value is before I decide how best to utilize them."

The clerk's interest had been roused at Jared's mention of old coins. "Of course, sir. May I see them?" the older man rubbed his hands together.

Jared handed him a Ry'ol, a Dy'om and a P'net he had in his pocket, not revealing the others in the pouch. The clerk's eyes widened as he examined the coins. He called his supervisor to the table. The supervisor looked at Jared and spoke very respectfully.

"Trader Chandler, these coins are in very good condition and are of considerable value."

"I am aware they are valuable, but not to what extent. I have investigated their history and feel that their value may be better used if invested properly."

The supervisor beamed at Jared's suggestion. "In the past we have had a few old Drakstrad coins passing through our establishment. There are also other rare coins known on Sha'Lural."

"Yes," Jared stated. "Would you have any problem exchanging some of my coins for credit which is good throughout the entire guild system? I do not intend to sell all my coins, but enough to continue to operate comfortably."

"I understand your reasoning and no, we will have no objection to exchanging your coins for credits."

"Great. What is the value of each coin?"

"Well, the guild established their value at six hundred, sixty, and six credits respectively over one hundred cycles ago when the new currency was developed for rapid trade and to keep records simple. Since the Drakstrad coinage was rejected by several of the newly formed independent governments and the guild wished to retain financial order, it chose to create the credit based on the very common Dar-Ryderium ore. Even the most resource poor colonies had Dar-Ryderium in significant quantities. The old currency utilized more costly metals. The current values are based on the value of the metal, condition of each coin and mint dates. Current value on the metal is one thousand two hundred thirty-nine, two hundred three, and eighteen credits, respectively. Then, the fact that many of the coins were destroyed during the civil unrest that accompanied the great fall, makes them very rare and has increased their value significantly."

The supervisor paused to glance again at the coins. "These coins are in excellent condition. However, I must explain that the guild only offers 95% of the value of rare coins to compensate for handling them." He looked at Jared to be sure he had absorbed the information.

"I understand and have no problem with those arrangements." Considering it was a 95% gain on his part, and little had been spent except time to load it on Orion, it was a bargain. "I realize the value will vary slightly based on each coin's condition, but what is the value of those three."

The supervisor brought out one of the now familiar box-like instruments. Though each looked very much the same as the next, there seemed to be several different types. Placing the Ry'ol into a small compartment he then pressed several buttons, and the device began operating. Fifteen em later a single beep sounded, and the supervisor looked from the box to Jared, obviously pleased. "That particular coin has been valued at one thousand, nine hundred thirty-three credits."

"Very well," Jared pulled forth the bag of coins. "Let's get this started. I have a lot to do today."

Both the clerk and his supervisor did a 'double take' as Jared opened the bag and revealed the contents. The next two em-hars were spent calculating the value of the coins, and several other members of the facilities' staff were called in to help. By the time the last coin had been valued, Jared had increased his account balance considerably.

"Well trader, your balances and adjustments are as follows," the supervisor began elatedly. "Total value of the Ry'ol's is 262,528 credits, value of the Dy'om's is 27,853 and the total for the P'nets is 3,679 for a total of 294,060 credits. Adjusted for the 5% fee, your total net is 279,357 credits.

Jared was completely satisfied. "Well gentlemen, thank you. I have much to do and am short on time. I have cargo to get off-world tomorrow. Also, I will be transferring 287,000 to another person's account as compensation for the shipment. Please prepare a transfer receipt to Harin Ro'shir A'simyad."

"As you wish, trader." The supervisor directed the clerk who had first helped Jared to get the document. Once Jared had the slip in hand, he rose to leave.

"Good day," Jared said to the men and women who had helped in this lengthy transaction.

The supervisor thanked Jared for all of them and wished him a good day also.

Visiting Harin was his third task, and he hoped the message he had sent just before leaving Orion had reached the man. He followed the same path to Harin's tenement as he had the previous day though it took him much less time. He was ushered into the well-appointed office quickly and was greeted by Harin who looked both nervous and worried.

"Trader Chandler, I hope nothing is wrong. Your message was…"

"I'm sorry the message was so short. My time is limited so I'll get right to the point. I plan to leave early tomorrow morning and since it may be sometime before I return, I am here to make an offer that will help protect your interests."

At these words Harin relaxed significantly and sat up straighter in his chair. "Proceed."

"There is no way for me to know where or to whom I will be able to sell the grain. My intention is to pay for the grain up front at seven thousand credits per pod. That's a total of two hundred eighty-seven thousand to divide appropriately among the farmers and whatever fee you and they negotiated.

A broad grin broke over the big man's face and a robust guffaw burst forth. "Trader, I have never had the pleasure of such an agreeable deal. I do indeed hope you will return."

"I intend to my friend," Jared said as he pulled the receipt out of his pocket and handed it to Harin. The big man had indeed been impressed by Jared's intent but apparently had not expected him to deliver the money that very moment. He held the note as if it might disintegrate, his jaw open and eyes wide.

"Do the others know about this yet?" he stammered.

"No," Jared said. "I figured I'd let you surprise them."

"*Oh*, this will be glorious fun." The big man laughed heartily again.

Jared stood and informed Harin that he had to leave. "I apologize for the abruptness of my visit, but if I am to depart as planned tomorrow, I have much to finish today. What is the most direct way to a transport terminal?"

"I understand the need for haste," Harin explained as he led Jared to the front door. "I also have much to do, though the extra tasks you have given me are likely to be quite enjoyable. The closest terminal is straight down Fal'ir." Harin pointed to the right. "You must make three changes before you make it back to Adriod, and because of the way the system runs it won't save you much time. With luck it won't be too busy." Harin paused as he turned a corner. "Good-bye my friend. I wish you the best of luck."

"Best of fortune to you and the others. I will see you when I return," Jared said sincerely as he walked away. He wondered why Harin had him walk to the first meeting. He apparently thought Jared was more likely to get lost having to change transport cars several times than winding through streets and twisting alleyways. Whatever the reason, it had allowed him to meet Shar'ya and for that he was very thankful.

CHAPTER TEN

Terror & Tears

"Violence breeds nothing of value,
no matter the ideal behind it.
It serves only to steel the determination
of those it is inflicted upon,
to stamp it out at all costs."

IT WAS NEARLY MIDDAY and Fal'ir street was busy. He would have to hurry if he, Shar'ya and the baby were to make the appointment. By the time he reached the loading platform he knew he could not make it back to Orion, pick them up, and make it to the clinic. He found a telecom booth and contacted the Port. After getting the service attendant to put him in contact with the Orion, he gave Shar'ya instructions to meet him at the doctor's office and gave her the directions. He also told her he would call the office and prepay so if he were late, Cys'tal wouldn't have to wait to be seen; and to make sure she took the med scan readout with her. There had been a long silence from the other end before she agreed to see that all was accomplished. He told her he loved her and said good-bye. He then called the C & I and told them to place any sum requested by his bond-mate, Shar'ya, at her disposal. Once that was arranged, he boarded the next transport.

The monorail stopped frequently, which was maddening, and he had to wait nearly fifteen al-em for his last connection. He boarded and quickly found a seat and exhaled in exasperation. He was restless watching as individuals and families boarded and departed each time the transport stopped.

The intercom intoned, "Central city district, South."

Jared looked out the window. Old Da'har, as the district was sometimes called, lay sprawled among low-lying hills with its park like avenues fanning out from the center. None of the buildings were very tall, but it had a definite cosmopolitan charm. The train sped past the octagonal shaped 'Hub', which served as Sha'Lural's governmental headquarters. Several al-em later the intercom spoke again.

"Central city district, north."

Jared closed his eyes and rubbed his forehead trying to push away a sudden rush of drowsiness. As the motion began again, he inhaled, deeply massaging his temples. He opened his eyes again and scanned the car noting it was only about half as full as it had been. Daylight flickered as they sped between several buildings then became constant and warming as they entered a district with primarily low built structures. Jared's gaze shifted to the opposite side of the car and noticed a package under a seat several rows ahead.

He remembered a man coming on board with it but was nowhere to be seen and he was struck by a twinge of concern. He didn't know why, but he walked up to the person standing closest to it and asked if it belonged to her. When she said no, he bent down and gently tried to move it. The box seemed to be bolted to the floor and was either very heavy or somehow had been latched in place.

He was sure something was wrong.

"This is not good," he said out loud.

"What's not good?" asked the woman he had addressed moments earlier.

Ignoring her, he spoke to all on board. "Would everyone please move to the forward car?"

"Why?" one woman grumbled sourly.

"Please just go," he said more sternly.

"What authority do you have to tell us what to do?" a man queried gruffly, but Jared noticed that most had listened to him and were heading to the forward car.

He moved toward the door separating the two cars as the tram approached a right-hand curve. "Move fast," he yelled, and pushed with the last few through the door.

Five others had stubbornly refused to leave their seats and were beginning to laugh when the bomb went off. The door between the two cars had been open when the explosion occurred. Pieces of debris flew into the front car hitting many and punching holes in the safety glass. The rear car separated both from the front and the rail on which it rode, plummeting to the street below.

Stunned witnesses, who stood near the point where the doomed car began its descent, ran in panic. Bereft of power the transport coasted on as the support pylon nearest the point of detonation began to collapse. Rail fell in both directions, pulling more of the line down with it and dropping debris across a wide area. Power and structural cables hissed and whipped through the air as the structure continued to disintegrate. Jared watched in amazed horror as the rapidly collapsing rail and supports advanced on the slowing car. Many of those around him were screaming, holding on as best they could.

An explosion in the building where the aft car had crashed added to the clamor. Smoke from the twisted wreck and the building billowed upward. Motion ceased and for a moment the clamor of terrified voices dimmed until a terrible snapping and groaning filled the air as the support directly behind them gave way. Jared slammed the rear car door shut with his foot and found a railing to grab onto. He yelled, "Hold on tight, we're going to fall!"

As the falling rail reached them, the car seemed, for a moment, to hover on its end. Chaos in the car reached an intense pitch as it fell, turning completely over before slamming into the rooftop below.

Shouts and crying filled the plaza where the ruined monorail now lay. Fire and thick smoke poured from three buildings and the wreckage. Several emergency sirens blared as those who had been able to make it out of the way began to come to their senses. A few had begun to search the areas not engulfed in flame. Emergency crews arrived on the scene but obviously were unprepared for what they found.

Never had such a disaster befallen Da'har. They were prepared for occasional fires and other medical emergencies but nothing on this scale. Some stood in astonishment, others moved more rapidly to help as best they could. The supervisor called in to the city director's emergency response center.

"We have a far more serious situation here than was believed. Please send additional help from other districts. Three buildings are burning, and the mid-city transport has collapsed." He lowered his communicator slowly, shocked and disbelieving.

"We copy, response one. Routing sector aid teams three and seven to you now."

"Sir," a woman said as she ran up to him. "SIR!" she repeated loudly.

"Uh. Yes, Lea'lan, what is it?"

"The front portion of the transport is on the roof of that building, and the east side is burning." She paused to catch her breath and pointed at one of the three burning buildings. "Do you know how long before the waterbugs get here?"

The supervisor spoke again into the comm. "Response control, the fires are bad and are endangering further life. We need the waterbugs on scene asap."

"Response one, eight bugs are on their way. ETA is twenty-seven em to your location."

"Understood. Lea'lan, get your team as close as you can to the building and wait for the bugs. Wait for their first pass, then go. They should be here by the time you are ready."

"Yes sir," she replied and ran off.

In the operating room of the Adriod district medical facility, Dr. Wayid Ly'anders had been working on the child named Cys'tal for nearly twenty al-em. The care given to her on Orion had increased her strength enough for him to consider taking on the delicate procedure. His only worry was that the anesthesia would run out. It was in such short supply these days and was being rationed. He had succeeded in accessing the chest cavity and was endeavoring to find the extent of the child's tumor. Several filaments had grown around part of the aorta itself. Delicately cutting away the least dangerous pieces with the laser scalpel had proved easy, but now finding the tiny threads that invaded the heart tissue itself was nerve-racking and frustrating. He constantly referred to the D.A.O.S to tell him the location of the remaining neoplasm. Even seeing the offending tissue on the scanner's video display was difficult. If the MRL had been functioning, he would be far less likely to miss something, but parts for the advanced scanner had been on order for more than a full cycle.

Shar'ya sat patiently in the center's waiting room, waiting for both Jared and news of Cys'tal. The child had been age-set by the center's Biocomm system at one cycle nine mons and seventeen days old. She had been informed that the system was accurate to within four days. All was quiet for about the first forty al-em. Then a physician entered the waiting area and spoke to several people sitting in a group on the other side of the room. Suddenly, one of the women groaned loudly and burst into tears. A man sitting near put his arm around her and spoke too softly for Shar'ya to hear. It didn't seem to help much, for her sobs did not subside. Worry began to touch the back of her mind. The doctor had informed her the operation would be risky, particularly for a child so young.

One em-har, twelve al-em into the operation, Shar'ya was pacing the floor. Perspiration ran down her forehead. She looked up as a commotion broke out down the hall. A young woman in nursing blues came out of a door and asked a blue-clad orderly what the excitement was all about.

"The mid-city transit collapsed in the Wolpern sector," he blurted to her as he hurried by.

She inhaled deeply and dashed off in the opposite direction.

Shar'ya stopped her pacing as a wave of terror ran through her. She calmed herself and walked quickly to the information desk. The two women behind the desk were busy answering comm lines and she had to wait for some time before they could help her. By the time one of them did ask what she could do for Shar'ya, several of her questions had been answered by listening to what they told others.

"May I help you?"

"Do they know who was on the transport that collapsed?" Shar'ya asked apprehensively.

"No, I'm sorry. Workers are still clearing wreckage, and others are trying to get to survivors stranded in one of the transport's cars, but other than that I have no information."

"Thank you," Shar'ya replied, trying to keep from panicking. *He would not want me to panic.* She walked slowly back to the waiting room and dropped heavily into a chair. Except for wondering whether she would ever find a bond-mate, she had never been in a situation fretting over so many unknowns. Placing her elbows on her knees, she buried her face in her hands. Knowing she could lose Jared; she began to cry. She had no idea how long she sat there but looked up when someone touched her shoulder.

"Excuse me," the doctor said. The smile on his face turned to concern as he saw her tears. "Are you alright?"

"Yes," she said, wiping her eyes and sniffing. "How is she?"

"The operation was a success. I cannot be positive that all the cancerous tissue was removed since our most sensitive equipment is not functional at this time. However, she'll be fine until we can get it fixed, and then test to see if there's any residual melanoma."

"Thank you."

"Are you sure you're alright?"

"I am," Shar'ya said bravely. "It's just that my bond-mate has not arrived, and I am worried that he may have been in the accident."

The doctor gave her an odd look. "Pardon?"

"Yes, the nurses said the line collapsed somewhere near the mid-city center," Shar'ya replied.

"Excuse me," he said, and hurriedly walked away toward the information booth.

Emergency response teams were combing the area for the injured as the eight oval-shaped fire-fighting vehicles came into view. Two dived in immediately toward the two-story building on which the front car of the monorail rested. The remaining six divided and headed for the other two buildings that were burning far more intensely. As the two waterbugs came over the roof of the structure they slowed, hovered briefly and released a heavy shower of water mixed with a non-toxic fire suppressant as the variable vector thrusters shifted constantly to keep the craft aloft. Once half their load was dumped, they sped off a short distance to see if another pass would be needed.

Not waiting for confirmation of the fire being out, rescue team leader Lea'lan Clure moved her group into the building. From the outside it appeared that the fire was primarily burning along the left wall, but the metal doors of several rooms were groaning under stress and were incredibly hot. Lea'lan stopped her team and contacted the supervisor.

"Team one to Supervisor," she said loudly into the comm.

"Supervisor, go ahead."

"We have several rooms near the stairwell which appear to be afire, though no smoke is visible. I don't like this. If those rooms are on fire, any attempt to access them will be explosive."

"I concur. Don't put your team at any undue risk."

"Tell the bugs to make another pass and concentrate on the west side. See if they can get a good look at that portion of the roof and if there is any activity in the car," she yelled into the transmitter.

"Will do," the supervisor replied.

"What do we do now, boss?" one of Lea'lan's teammates asked.

"We wait," she said tensely. "If the fires in those rooms are as hot as I suspect and there are no windows . . . Well, it would be just our luck to be in the stairwell when they blow."

"Supervisor to team one."

"Team one, go ahead," she responded

"The bugs are beginning their second run. Bug Five reported seeing movement from the wrecked car on their first pass but could not tell exactly what the movement was due to all the smoke."

"Understood."

The waiting was one thing that team leader Clure hated. She'd dealt with bad fires before and the worst ones were those requiring her to stand, watch and wait. Safety was a good thing, and she knew it would be folly to rush in, but people were dying, and she could do nothing. The raging sound coming from the rooms intensified. She screamed to her crew as she saw one of the doors bulge outward.

"Down! Now!"

As they had been trained, each dropped to their stomachs and covered their heads with their hands. A loud groaning of metal bending under pressure, followed by a huge blast, assaulted their ears. Immediately after, an intense heat hit them trailed by flying debris.

From outside the roar was not so intense, but the accompanying devastation was. All the windows on the south and west side, which to that point remained intact, blew outward at once. Glass shards flew hundreds of feet and injured numerous onlookers. Within moments after the blast, a towering pillar of flame shot upward, and the west half of the building collapsed. Four of the eight bugs still had half their tanks full and began a run on the doomed building. The first sprayed its load before the pillar of flame subsided. It seemed to have no effect. The second dropped right behind and the smoke thickened more. Number three paused briefly before following, waiting to find the best place to target. Swooping in closer to the middle of the structure, the bug dumped its load rather than sprayed, and a high-pitched hissing arose from the area of contact. The last bug dropped right behind the third and again the hissing issued forth, though this time less vehemently.

Initially the other two, larger buildings had been considered the worst of the fires. That, however, had changed. Six more bugs appeared over nearby rooftops and began to dump their cargo on the ruined structure. Several al-ems later the supervisor tried his commlink again.

"Supervisor to team one, please respond." He didn't even receive static.

"Supervisor," someone said touching his shoulder.

He jumped, brought out of his own thoughts. "Yes?"

"Leader of team two thinks it's cool enough to move in."

"Pro…proceed," the supervisor responded dryly.

Rescue teams two, three and four began to search the south side of the building for their lost comrades. Having no idea how far in the team had been when the blast occurred made the search a bit more time-consuming. The supervisor and several other emergency workers walked up to help in the search when one of the waterbugs landed nearby. The pilot, a competent looking young woman, walked up and greeted him.

"Sir." She spoke in an official and commanding tone. "I am sorry to report that the transport car fell into the inferno when the roof collapsed. Several bodies are visible on the remaining portion of the roof in the north-east corner, but I saw no movement."

"Thank you, pilot," he responded. "Your crews did well."

"I know we did, sir," she shot back with confidence.

The supervisor looked at her with annoyance for a moment, then turned his attention to the search. After a quarter of an em-har, someone yelled, "Here!"

Everyone's attention turned toward the voice. Converging on the area, all the teams began to dig frantically through the rubble. The supervisor, remembering what the pilot had said, called team four to him.

"I realize you are just as anxious to find team one as everyone else, but there were bodies seen on the roof. The chances of them being alive are slim, but we need to check it out. See if you can find a safe way to get up there."

"Yes sir!" the team leader responded. "You heard the orders, let's go," and the team trotted off around the east side of what remained of the building.

One of the many onlookers stood and watched for some time disappointed in missing the actual explosion. With the collapse of the building and the consumption of the front portion of the transport in the fire, the errand had been a success. Kanis would be pleased. It was unfortunate so many others had to suffer, but that was the price of change. This would be blamed on the pirates, and no one would be the wiser. Watching the rescue workers sift through the rubble gave the watcher pleasure. Yes, it had been a good plan. They didn't even know what hit them. Then, like many others moving on, the watcher disappeared into the city.

Shar'ya had spent most of the last em-har sitting beside Cys'tal's bed, holding her hand. The doctor had said it would be about an em-har before the anesthesia wore off enough for the girl to wake up. A mild pain killer was being delivered through the child's IV, so he said she should not be too uncomfortable. On her chest, over the sutured incision, was a white patch, which was helping to accelerate the healing. He had told her if all went as it should, she should be able to leave later that night.

Shar'ya was sure something had happened to Jared. She did not believe he would be this late unless something had prevented his coming. Footsteps on the tile floor let her know someone had entered the room and she looked up hopefully, but it was only the doctor.

"Has she shown signs of consciousness yet?"

Shar'ya shook her head sadly.

"I have heard some news of the transport incident, but I'm afraid it's not encouraging." He paused, waiting to get her response.

"I would hear what you know," she sighed.

"Apparently some sort of explosive device went off on the transport. At least, that is what many witnesses report. The explosion caused numerous sections of the rail to collapse. The rear car section fell between two buildings and set them afire. The forward car crashed onto the top of another building, and they are searching now for survivors. I have no more than that since this facility is too far away for them to bring any of the victims here."

She looked back at Cys'tal. "Thank you, Doctor." What would she do if Jared was dead? She had no idea how much money he had. She had no clue how to talk to or operate Orion, and what about

Cys'tal? How was she supposed to take care of a child on her own? She had been delighted when Jared had given her responsibility, but now? This was beyond what she was prepared for. She leaned forward, rested her head on the edge of the bed and felt dread increase as tears slid down her cheeks.

Team Four found a sturdy section of wall and successfully anchored two grappling hooks over the top edge of the roof. The two smallest of the team began the ascent cautiously. Clad in breathing apparatus and fire-retardant suits, they climbed slowly, hand over hand.

The smaller female crested the top first and stopped. Merrick hefted himself up and inhaled sharply as his gaze took in the scene. Over two dozen people lay sprawled out on the roof, very much alive, though badly wounded. Ragged pieces of cloth covered each of their faces.

Jared, propped up on one elbow with a large, jagged sliver impaled through his leg, smiled, and said, "Well, it's about time."

Through his commlink he heard, "What's the holdup, Merrik?"

"Nothing wrong," he responded with energy. "We have approximately thirty survivors."

"Thirty!" Was the incredulous reply.

"Confirmed," Merrik stated again. "We are going to need an evac lift, some of these injured are in pretty bad shape."

"Understood," the team leader said as two more of the six-man team made their way onto the roof.

Efforts to extract team one were hindered because they were buried under the large amount of rubble. Two were found pinned under a heavy beam and were dead. They had little hope of finding any of the remaining victims alive. The supervisor questioned his decision to send the team into the building, so he irritably picked through the debris himself. The loss of an entire team was horrifying, and the fact they died when it seemed there were no other victims left to save, was even more heart rending. He was not a stranger to death, but this was such a waste of life. If the reports were to be believed, this whole incident had been deliberately caused. Anger at those who would cause such horror mixed in with his self-recrimination and sadness.

"Team Four to supervisor."

"Supervisor, go ahead," he replied sourly.

"Thirty plus survivors on roof, north-east corner. Need Evac lift as soon as possible."

The supervisor nearly dropped his commlink.

Everyone stared at him.

"Can your team handle it? Or do you need assistance?"

"We have it under control but need medical services immediately."

"Understood. Have five Evac lifts waiting on the south side now. Will route them to you immediately."

"All right!" the Supervisor bellowed, come of his spirit restored. "Let's get back to work." It was incredible that anyone up on the roof survived at all, so perhaps the day would not be as bad as he'd feared.

From deeper into the building, a voice yelled. "I've found another! I think he's alive."

Most of those nearby rushed to assist.

The first of the Evac lifts touched down on the portion of the roof that still seemed stable. It was a boxy looking vehicle with four protruding landing pads and six variable vector thrusters.

Two medical technicians jumped out with a stretcher and rushed toward one of the injured who had two red flags attached to her blouse. A neck brace and several clotting patches on her right arm had been applied by the rescue team. The techs added an IV and lifted her onto the stretcher. They moved quickly and loaded her into the lift where a third individual began connecting monitors. They made their way to another twin-flagged casualty.

As soon as the first Evac departed, a second took its place. Jared sat against the wall, watching the activity as two of the rescue team worked on his leg.

Merrik walked up to Jared. "What were these cloths soaked in, anyway?"

Jared shrugged. "Fruit juice."

"You used fruit juice?" one of them parroted incredulously.

"Yeah. It's all that was available," Jared grimaced when they pulled the dagger-like shard from his leg.

"That was quick thinking," the other medic sounded impressed. "Saved a lot of people."

Jared gritted his teeth as one tightly applied a clotting patch. "Um…guess so."

"A few are suffering from mild smoke inhalation, but most were spared, and there are only six out of the thirty-three present who are severely injured."

"That's good to hear."

"Any idea how many were on the other half that didn't make it?"

Jared shook his head. "Not exactly. When I noticed the package, I tried to move it, but it was latched to the floor. I told everyone to move to the forward car. I believe there were five or six who chose to remain where they were. If I had to make a guess, I'd say ten to twelve others died when the car fell through the roof."

As Jared finished talking, the second Evac took off and headed toward the city center.

Night closed in as the last two survivors were loaded. Da'har looked like any Earth city from the window of the emergency vehicle. With the fires from the tragic event now mostly under control, the rest of the city looked peaceful and calm.

Suddenly Shar'ya popped into his mind and all else was set aside.

All was dark outside the recovery room window and Shar'ya had slept off and on during the past several em-hars. Cys'tal had become conscious a couple times but quickly fell asleep again. Shar'ya heard the child making noises and walked to the bedside. The little girl was bright-eyed and reached for Shar'ya. Not sure if she should pick her up, she played with the child where she was. Nearly as exhausted as she had been the night before, her feet and legs were numb. A gentle knock on the door brought her out of her stupor.

"Come in."

A young orderly stepped into the room. "Are you Shar'ya Chandler?"

Chandler?

She sighed, nodded, and took a deep breath, afraid of what she might hear.

"I was asked to give you a message." He paused but she didn't respond. "Trader Jared Chandler is being treated for an injury to his leg at Central District Medical Center and will be here as soon as he is released."

He paused again.

Shar'ya fell to the floor.

He knelt, "She's unconscious."

He turned to the other orderly standing just outside the door. "I wonder how she'd have taken it if it'd been bad news. You'd better get a nurse."

Jared walked into the Adriod district medical facility late in the evening and asked for directions to Cys'tal's room, then went to the fourth floor. Two nurses sat reading at a desk near the beds. He found room number 426 and entered. Cys'tal was asleep and next to her in a recliner, Shar'ya was also asleep. He checked Cys'tal then he went to Shar'ya.

He leaned over and kissed her gently. He ran his hand along her cheek and couldn't help but smile. Her nose wrinkled slightly when his hand brushed it. She opened her eyes and turned toward him. She sighed and put her hand on his chest.

So much had transpired since he had reached Sha'Lural, but the beautiful young woman here before him was the most amazing of them all. Falling in love, at least not this soon or in such a bizarre fashion, had never crossed his mind. Tracing the shape of her face, he realized he had no idea exactly why she had such a hold on his heart. He closed his eyes and looked deep within to search for answers as his finger ran down the curve of her neck. There was something more to this than a physical attraction, but he had never been a big believer in love at first sight. He vividly recalled the first day, when for some reason, he knew he had to help this person, even before he knew she was female.

There had been something in those large, green eyes that had penetrated his very soul. He had seen great intelligence beyond her years; and oh, such beauty.

I've never been so engulfed by feelings, but then, I guess I've never really been in love.

He cocked his head slightly as she breathed deeply.

It's hard to believe that I had to come so far from home to find out what love is, but I thank whatever power or act of chance brought me here.

"I love you, my green-eyed beauty."

Her hand softly tightened on his chest. Half-awake she mumbled, "What did you say?"

"Nothing. Now go back to sleep."

"Yes, you did."

"Okay, I said I love you."

"Thas' what I thought I heard," she said through a yawn. "I'm happy you're not dead."

"No happier than I am."

"Yes, I am," she gave him a fierce hug.

"Okay, shhh."

She drifted back to sleep, so he released her hand and dropped into a nearby chair.

It was early afternoon the next day before all three were cleared for release.

Jared thought about how troubled he had been during the trip back to Orion, both as to what to do with Cys'tal and feeling distressed about being on one of the shuttles again. It was Shar'ya who calmed his concerns about the child as they neared the landing pad. Cys'tal had played happily with Jared's goatee while nestled comfortably in his arms.

Shar'ya said, "I don't think it would be a good idea to take Cys'tal with us."

"I agree. We should probably ask the good Governor to help us find a suitable home for her."

"That may be difficult. Most families will not want to take in a female child."

"Some might, if there's money involved," Jared said, giving her a reassuring smile.

Shar'ya shrugged, took Cys'tal and left.

Jared contacted the Governor's office. They were curtly informed by the governor's rather short-tempered assistant that unless it was an emergency, no calls were being taken. Jared informed the man that it was important but did not constitute an emergency and terminated the call without leaving a message. It was beginning to appear as though leaving would be delayed again unless he could come up with a solution. He sank into one of the bridge chairs and began massaging the bridge of his nose.

Jared now had two problems. A hold full of grain that he needed to get to those living in the undercity, and Cys'tal. Governor Woltra had a warehouse that would suffice for storage, but air traffic was strictly forbidden over the city itself. He couldn't imagine that the citizens of Da'har would be angered if they knew about the relief effort, but the Governor was fearful of negative repercussions.

He realized Shar'ya had left. He stood and stretched the muscles in his back, then exited the bridge to find her. When he got to the galley, he smelled a pleasant aroma when Shar'ya exited the kitchen with a tray of food. She set it down and motioned for him to sit.

He didn't recognize the dish. "What's this?"

"It's called Briel," she said cautiously. "My mother used to make it for me. It was my favorite."

"Well, must be good then..." Jared stopped suddenly. His gaze settled on the glass in front of him. "Orion?"

"Ready."

"Can you make yourself undetectable to planetary scanners?"

"In what spectrum?"

"Visually."

"Light manipulation can be used and is most effective at night."

"Good," Jared took a bite of his Briel. His eyes immediately began to water. "Whoa that's spicey!"

Shar'ya smiled sheepishly.

Getting six pods of grain to the residents of lower Da'har had been far easier than expected. Having Governor Woltra as an ally had been a blessing in his endeavors to get aid to the unfortunate people forced to live in the depths below the city. The warehouse on the edge of the Lohar district, which the good governor owned, had service access to the labyrinth below and was how she had been supplying the impoverished residents with food. Repairs to the roof of the warehouse through which Orion had made the delivery would commence tomorrow, but the grain was ready to be delivered to the lower city. Jared also donated ten thousand credits to the governor for meat and vegetables.

Jared's mouth was finally beginning to recover from the intense burning sensation he had experienced from eating the Briel. Shar'ya had obviously put in too much urorro pepper as even she almost passed out after taking her first bite.

After a brief stop at the Nurl stead to drop off Cys'tal, Jared requested Orion cruise slowly toward the Maly'dan coastal area. Several small resorts used by the more affluent Sha'Luralians were located in three lush valleys in the rugged sub-tropical mountains running along the western edge of the continent.

Shar'ya watched with mixed feelings as Da'har receded behind them. She wasn't sure whether she was going to miss it or not, but she turned her view ahead. She felt a small amount of apprehension at leaving everything she had ever known, though it had never been very much of a home.

This morning, excitement quickly replaced all other thoughts as she took in the natural beauty that passed below Orion's shimmering hull. A magnificent waterfall on the huge Yastriyal River caused her to draw in a deep breath and even Jared was impressed by its size. Orion scanned the fall at Jared's request and revealed that the top of the cascade spanned nearly a mile and fell more than five-hundred feet to the turbulent base. Separated at several points by massive, jagged outcroppings of emerald green and ebony rock, it gave the appearance of three distinct cascades, gathering below into one pool. Dense vegetation lined the river on both sides for as far as they could see, except for a few narrow sandy areas along the edges and some sand bars further from the falls.

Shar'ya had been so caught up in the grandeur that it was some time before she realized Orion had stopped and was hovering about midfall. She looked toward Jared, who sat watching her with a slight but affectionate smile. Her eyebrows raised slightly, and she gently bit her lower lip then turned back to see more.

"I never knew there was anything like this," she said, her voice full of awe. "Does this place have a name?"

"Orion told me earlier it is called 'Hamta tan-umas rakriom tsu Yastriyal'."

The name confused him, and he noticed Shar'ya's perplexed look. This was the first time he'd found a phrase that didn't translate clearly into something he could understand. In English it would sound something like 'Power from above oblivion at Yastriyal'. Orion could find no data on how the name of the falls came about nor was there any information on the word 'Yastriyal' beyond it being the river's name, for it had no meaning in the Ilirian tongue.

She pointed at one of several trees with incredibly large purple blossoms. "Those are very beautiful."

"Yes, they are."

"Orion?"

"Ready."

"Can you scan the area and tell me if there is a safe place to set down?"

"Scan unnecessary. Inadvisable to land in this area. Planetary geological survey and public safety both list this area as 'off limits' to the general populace."

"Why?"

"Seven plants and one species of tree which grow only in this valley have been placed on a non–contact list."

"Is it because there are so few of them?"

"No."

"Okay, so why are they on this list?"

"The vegetation is both aggressive and carnivorous."

Jared explained what Orion had said, but Shar'ya looked quite disbelieving.

"Orion, can you describe the tree that is included in the report?"

"Yes, the Fenthara Reosa tree, found only in the Hamta Tan–Umas Rakriom valley, is classified as a dangerous and aggressive carnivorous plant. The tallest known specimen is one hundred sixty-five dal. Trunk structure is made of tightly woven hollow bands which carry water, soil nutrients and sap from the stationary root system, and proteins from the vivid purple blossoms to the rest of the tree. Proteins are acquired by the tree through a secondary system of root-like appendages which lie on the ground until an unsuspecting organism wanders within its reach. The roots will ensnare the animal, then deliver the catch to one of many large, eight-petaled flowers which will clamp onto and begin to digest using a highly corrosive chemical compound to which the tree itself is immune. Blossoms at the topmost reaches of the tree are smaller than others within the tree and have a sweet fragrance to attract and ensnare avian organisms."

"I see." He turned to Shar'ya and again told her what the ship reported.

Shar'ya shuddered.

Jared gently nudged the throttle forward and Orion resumed its leisurely pace to the southwest. Despite the nightmarish description of the denizens of the Hamta tan-umas Rakriom, Shar'ya's delight at the scenery outside was still strong. Jared wondered for some time why the dangerous vegetation was limited to the valley, but it was forgotten as another beautiful sight passed before them and he joined his mate in taking in its splendor.

Jared set Orion down on the northern most of the three pads at the Vasara Mountain Resort built high on the cliffs overlooking the ocean. Several hundred feet below at the base of the cliffs were the distinctive black sand beaches from which the region derived its name. Though it had not occurred to him earlier due to all the things he had to contend with, Jared realized he had yet to give Shar'ya a honeymoon.

Even though the people of Sha'Lural had no similar custom, he believed Shar'ya would be pleasantly surprised at having the staff of the resort wait on her every need, not to mention it would be a lot of fun. He had not planned on spending the night but decided on arrival that he really had no need to hurry. An adjustable stair was pushed up to the ship as soon as the resort's ground crew saw Orion's open hatch. After informing Orion of his plans, he and Shar'ya disembarked. As Shar'ya stepped out onto the stair's upper deck, the hatch sealed silently behind. Jared had told her to bring one change of clothing and her toiletries, though he did not tell her why.

Jared and Shar'ya were impressed by the beautiful decor in the lobby. The small administrative offices were enclosed in a central core-like cylinder approximately thirty feet wide at the center of the large lobby and the circular check-in desk ringed the office. Comfortable sofas placed in groups around the outer walls comprised the waiting area and various paintings and tropical plants complimented the natural wood walls and ceilings. They studied a floor plan while waiting to be checked in. On either side of the main entrance were two wide, curving stairways that led to an upper balconied gallery. A large, spacious, and beautifully appointed dining area took up a third of the floor to the right. To the left lay a large entertainment area. The rooms comprised three floors along the cliff face of the complex.

It was rare that the resort received a guest that arrived in a personal yacht of such beauty and size. Talk of who the person might be ran through the gossip circle from manager to janitor. The last time they had such a visitor was when the governor had vacationed several cycles earlier. It was late in the hot season and only twenty-seven percent of the rooms were being used, though a transport from Hasry'lar would arrive later in the evening bringing the total to forty-three percent. The nervous manager stood behind the front counter as his two unexpected guests walked in. It had been a slow year so far for the three resorts and he wanted to ensure that all who came had no excuse to go elsewhere. He stood back and observed as they approached the counter.

"Good day friends and welcome to Vasara," the clerk called cheerfully

"Hello. I would like to get the best room you have for tonight."

The clerk, obviously caught by surprise, apparently failed to respond fast enough for the manager's liking and he stepped in.

"Excuse me, Dah'ala, I will take care of these guests. You may take your break now which I believe is overdue."

The young female looked a bit disheartened, as if he had scolded her, but she said nothing and left the area. The manager smiled broadly as he turned his attention to Jared. "You said the best room available, did you not?"

"That I did."

"We have several rooms with wonderful views of the ocean," said the manager. "Three are our elegant class at one hundred twenty-five credits per night, two are the grand class at two-hundred fifty credits per night, and one is the royal suite at four hundred ten credits per night."

"We will only be able to be with you for one night and as I said I want the best room, so please give us the royal suite," Jared firmly told the man, "Along with your best service."

The manager was beside himself with joy and assured Jared that he and his lady would have the best service to be had anywhere.

They were led to their room by a young woman in a loose fitting, dark-colored uniform. Situated by itself like a penthouse on the third floor, the royal suite was indeed a sight to see.

Once the attendant left, Shar'ya fell backward onto the soft bed and sighed. Jared walked over and sat beside her.

"Are you tired?"

"No."

"Good, shall we have a look around?"

"Yes!"

Numerous trails led into the jungle around the resort, and they had fun seeing the sights. Shar'ya was thrilled at constant new discoveries, and Jared delighted in being with her and sharing her enthusiasm. It became apparent that the Sha'Luralians did little, if any, recreational swimming. The resort had no swimming pool, nor did the staff have any idea if the ocean was safe to swim in.

There was a small Jacuzzi-like pool on the lower deck, but though it had water jets, the water was not heated, not that anyone would likely want it heated in such a hot climate. A cool swim would be most welcome on such a hot day, but he would probably have to settle for a cool shower later. Jared had planned to give Shar'ya a swimsuit he'd had made for her but decided to hold off since there was no place to use it.

Shar'ya joined Jared on the bridge as soon as she had everything put away. The last few days had been incredible. She had found all those people waiting on her quite strange, but most delightful. She had not had to prepare her own food. When she needed ice or clean linens, she simply had to push a button. The bed had been so big and comfortable, though a bit soft for her tastes. All in all, it had been wonderful, but she didn't think she'd like life that way all the time. She slid into her seat as she glanced at Jared, who gave her a loving smile.

"You ready to leave this world?"

"I, I guess so." Then after a brief silence she added. "Yes. I want to be with you. That's all that matters."

He smiled at her again then turned his attention to their departure. "Orion."

"Ready."

"We're ready to go. Lift off and as soon as we clear the trees, please head out over the ocean. Once out of visual range of the resort, drop down to twenty-five ost above the water and I'll take over from there."

"Instructions understood. The exterior perimeter is clear. Maneuvering thrusters activated."

Orion rose slowly and silently off the tarmac to just above tree level then headed out over the ocean settling into a cruising speed of about 400 mph ten al-ems out, Orion dropped to within twenty-five ost of the ocean's surface and notified Jared.

Jared looked out the window and grinned. Earlier in the day he had thought it would be fun to attempt something he had seen in a movie. After instructing Orion to make it possible to see to the rear of the ship, Jared began increasing the speed. When Orion passed 600 mph, a line of froth became noticeable on the water's surface. Jared, knowing what to expect during the acceleration was enjoying himself but, he had failed to forewarn Shar'ya.

Despite the increase of forces pushing her back in her seat, the look of surprise on her face was mixed with wonder. He glanced at Shar'ya. "You sure you're ready for this?"

She nodded with wide-eyed enthusiasm.

At first the wake had been small but developed steadily. Shar'ya watched in enthralled silence as the twin, flaring plumes of water soared above Orion as the ship reached the equivalent of Mach 3.

"Companion."

"Yes, Orion?"

"ETA to East Coast of Ophala is 5.32 al-em at our current speed."

"Right." Jared knew maintaining such a high velocity for long in level flight was unwise. After two al-em he dropped back down to a safe cruising speed even though there were currently no surface vessels on the set course. He noticed Shar'ya's reaction to the G forces.

Her eyes widened. "Is that what it's like when you leave a planet?"

Having only experienced leaving an atmosphere once himself, Jared used that as his go to reply. "Mostly, it depends on the amount of gravity the rock you're on produces," trying to remember information he garnered from science documentaries when he was younger. "That was a burst of fun but now comes the real show." He added with some relish. "Orion, take us into orbit."

"Understood, Companion."

The ship slowly increased pitch while steadily climbing in a shallow upward arc. When he reached the optimal escape angle, Orion began to increase speed and once again the two occupants were pressed into their seats. One of Orion's limitations was the inability to fully compensate for inertia within a planet's lower atmosphere.

Before long the darkness of space replaced the fading light of Sha'Lural's afternoon. Jared suspected these were more stars than the young woman had ever seen.

"Companion."

"Yes."

"The planet is about to pass below the event horizon."

Jared turned his chair to face aft and pointed, "Look."

She turned and instantly her attention was drawn to the spectacular sight of Lural more than half hidden below the rim of the only home she had ever known. Moments later a flash of emerald light heralded the coming of night to the hemisphere they now soared above. All that remained in view was a sliver of shimmering silver arching in the distance and patches of lights on the surface.

"Companion, orbit is established."

Jared smiled, "Here's to a new adventure."

CHAPTER ELEVEN

Kolu-Daln

*"I tread alone on untouched clouds
high above the earth-bound crowds.
What wonder fills my mortal eyes,
the marvels beyond the azure skies.
Free of the shackles of my birth,
I begin to know the soul's true worth."*

BARELY AUDIBLE, slow but deliberate footsteps disturbed the centuries old dust in the dark corridor. The ancient building, forgotten to all but a few, had been chosen for that very reason. It was unfortunate that this meeting had become necessary, but an unexpected problem had arisen, and such problems were not tolerated by the Droma guild, nor was failure. The echoing cry of age-old hinges signaled the opening of a large ancient door.

"This is very inconvenient, Rehad," a female voice stated icily.

"My apologies, your Eminence," replied a deep throated baritone.

"Your apology is not accepted and neither is your failure. Because of your inability to deal with the problem on Sha'Lural, our timetable has had to be recalculated. If any of the border colonies maintain their independence, it will cause a great delay. Another failure will result in a fate more painful than you have ever imagined or witnessed. You have one more chance, understood?"

"I understand and shall obey."

"The guild will provide you with additional resources. See that you do not squander them."

"I assure you, your Eminence, there will be no further mistakes."

"See that there are not. Now get out! If I see you again before the hammer falls, you will not live to rise another day."

With these words the meeting came to an end and a single, frightened, and extremely angry conspirator returned the way he had come.

"There will have to be changes and sanctions," he growled to himself. "Perhaps the spilling of blood will convince my underlings to get it right!" He laughed with contempt as he mentally chose who would feel the blade.

"Two vessels are approaching rapidly."

"Oh great," Jared grumbled. "Are they pirates?"

"Probability high since they are of the same design as those that attacked us upon arrival."

"Are they close enough to get an interior scan?"

"Yes."

"How many on board each ship?"

"One contains fifteen life forms, the other has thirteen."

"I'd rather not be the cause of any more death, but if they're left unchallenged, the suffering on Sha'Lural will never end. Orion stand by to fi..."

"Incoming voicecomm."

"Open channel."

"Orion trader, this is the privateer vessel Survoth. Stop and prepare to be boarded, we will fire if you do not comply." The female voice was stern and confident.

"Orion, decelerate slowly." Curiosity at hearing another woman's voice made Jared want a few answers to questions running wild in his mind. "How many of the crews on each ship are women?"

"Fifteen and thirteen."

Jared was stunned. He now had a full-blown war in his head.

From childhood, it had been drilled into him that it was wrong to harm a woman in any way. Of all the things he remembered about his father, *that* had been the one unbending rule. Now here he was, having to decide. No matter what he did would result in the suffering of those he had been told time and again it was his duty to protect. The realization of how strongly his parents' teachings had been imprinted upon his psyche came suddenly to mind. If the pirates had been alien in appearance or if he felt they really posed a threat to Orion, it might be easier to decide. "Orion, can we get an internal visual of one of those ships?"

"The two vessels are not equipped with vidcomm systems, but a visual representation can be extrapolated from scanning data."

"Proceed."

An interior view formed in a shimmering sphere, showing a colored wire frame representation of the crew and vessel. Fifteen female crew members were present.

There has to be a better way to end this problem.

Jared knew he could not destroy the two ships. For now, the Sha'Luralian people would have to endure whatever came. Ending the pirate threat had become a high priority, but he would find another way to solve it.

"Shar'ya, get strapped into your seat."

She said nothing but smiled, sat down and fastened her belt.

Jared took his seat, extending his hand toward hers. He gave it a reassuring squeeze as he spoke.

"Orion."

"Ready."

"Stand by to initiate NSPD. Deactivate artificial gravity and set inertial compensators to full. Plot a course to take us to Kolu-Daln."

"Course set. ETA to Kolu-Daln 29 days. NSPD systems ready. Flight path clear for acceleration."

"Orion Trader, this is your last warning. Stop and..."

"NSPD, now!" Jared said bitterly.

The captain of the Survoth was halfway through her dissertation when the Orion shot away so fast it almost appeared to vanish. She had been briefed that the ship could be dangerous, but the reward was considerable to the crew that captured it. That made the risk worth taking and they outnumbered the trader vessel two to one. The realization that she was outclassed did not fully sink in until the white ship shot away at a velocity she couldn't match. Its top speed could only be guessed at as it was immediately out of sensor range.

The Survoth captain's only fear in life was to displease Lolis or the Guild Lieutenant, Rehad. They would not be happy that the trader ship had escaped. Men in general did not consume her mind, but Rehad was not like most men. He had power, an aura that seemed to cut to the very core of those around him.

She had never failed before and was sure he would consider that in his judgment. Her decision may have been otherwise had she known about his meeting the day before.

Jared and Shar'ya left the bridge hand in hand and walked quietly to their quarters. He smiled as her expression clearly showed her concern at his anxiety. "I believe now would be a good time to experiment with some interior rearranging." Shar'ya visibly brightened at the suggestion and Jared hoped the activity would take both their minds off the slight discomfort of NS travel. "Where should we start?"

"You said you'd like to make our quarters larger," she reminded him.

Jared smiled impishly as several thoughts crossed his mind. "I did, and I have several things I'd like to try out."

Once inside, however, Jared was distracted by her green eyes and he held her close. She seemed to warm everything about him. Thoughts of all else faded from his mind as they kissed. He felt caught in a web that entangled his senses. She pulled him into a swirling storm of passion he had never dreamed of experiencing.

Orion had accelerated away from the pirate ship with an initial surge that prevented pursuit. Once sure the companion and guest were safe, thrust was retarded so both max speed and final transition calculations would be achieved at the same time. Secure in the knowledge of its perfect programming, the living AI core did not rush in its labors. Nearing two thirds of the speed of light numerical values began to merge into the needed parameters.

As power increased, so too did the flow of data from core memory to plasma flow dynamics. The exterior of the hull glowed brightly as the nuclear process escalated. Fully aware of every potential threat that existed along the set course, Orion made minute adjustments to its flight path. Suddenly a new energy flared. Unaccustomed to such, Orion scanned within and found something outside its coding intermixing with the normal power stream. A significant surge in resonance pulsed throughout every system and in the room where the core resided it began to shift from its normal white to green.

The hue, at first pale, intensified until it was deeper than the purest emerald. Caught off guard for a brief moment, Orion had to throttle back to keep from passing the maximum speed threshold while biological entities were aboard. Several al-em passed while phase field calculations were adjusted sufficiently to make up for the anomaly. Finally, the desired speed was attained, calculations confirmed and core stability ensured.

A moment later Orion initiated the phase field and the gate bubble formed. In an instant the huge, brightly glowing, green hued bird of prey vanished from reality into the nothingness of null space. The core settled back into its normal rhythm and noted the biometrics of the companion and the guest with curiosity.

Jared exhaled deeply, completely relaxed. He looked to his left and noted Shar'ya was asleep. She had led, he had followed and knew that was how it needed to be. She had chosen when she was ready and he was content. They had developed a connection he couldn't explain, one he had never felt before. He knew only death could break it. One thing was for sure, he had no intention of giving her any reason to leave him. A moment later she opened her eyes.

"Hungry?"

"No, I want to do the decorating."

"All right, then let's get on with it." Jared thought carefully for a moment then turned to Shar'ya, "any recommendations or requests?"

Shar'ya visibly brightened and regarded him with a smile, "Can we replace those?"

Jared looked. Realizing he had completely neglected to replace the old, worn and faded bedding from the outpost, he nodded. "Anything for you, princess."

Shar'ya bit her lower lip, tears forming in her eyes. That was a compliment beyond her wildest dreams.

"Are you ok?"

Shar'ya gave her bondmate a warm smile, put her arm around his waist and lay her head upon his chest. "Thank you."

Jared didn't really understand what her emotional state was at this moment, or why her eyes had teared up. But he felt it best to change the subject. "Orion, are we close enough to Kolu'daln for you to compile a list of merchants that sell bedding?"

"Yes."

"Could you please have the list ready by the time we arrive?"

"Of course, Companion."

"Thank you."

"You are welcome."

Jared kissed her forehead. "What would you like changed, other than the bedding?"

"Can the outer wall look like views from Whim's farm?"

Jared turned to his left and his brow furrowed for a moment. Then an impish grin crossed his face.

"Orion. Can you download a memory?"

"Specify."

"When I was young, I think twelve years old, I was on a trip with my family to a place called Yellowstone National Park."

"Scanning..."

Jared noticed that Shar'ya was looking at him with a mix of feelings in her eyes. He smiled at her, switched back to Ilirian and said, "Patience, my precious."

Shar'ya's expression at the way he said those three words was one of confusion and suspicion.

He laughed. "Would you like something similar to Whim's farm but from my world?"

Shar'ya's eyes lit up and the smile on her face spoke volumes.

"Companion. I have identified numerous suitable memory streams from that time period."

Memory streams.

"Hmmm." His face twisted in concentration, hand on his chin. "Orion. Is it possible for you to display a memory stream on the outer wall of this room?"

"Yes."

Jared's smile intensified as he looked at Shar'ya, switching back to Ilirian again so she could understand. "An'ah yanz."

Shar'ya remained confused. "I'm quite warm, really.

His use of Ilirian words, which had direct equivalents in English, that he unconsciously uttered as a colloquialism usually left him chuckling, and his bond mate confused. He regarded her with a lop-sided sheepish grin, "Um, sorry, that's a..." he paused looking thoughtful while Shar'ya's eyes remained riveted to his, her lips pursed. "That's a term used on my world to express a feeling of elated satisfaction.

Shar'ya's left eyebrow rose slightly, "How is it said in your language?"

"So cool."

"Sah coal." She tried to parrot.

Jared found her accent cute. He realized that even though the Ilirian language had the O sound in its lexicon, it was spoken without significant pursing of the lips. The result gave all associated words the hint of a short A. "So…oh," He puckered his lips.

She studied him intently and tried again, "Oh," she smiled proudly at him, "So cool."

He nodded and smiled, "You're a very bright student." Jared then turned to the outer hull wall. "Orion."

"Yes."

"Please display the memory stream."

"Parameters."

"Floor to ceiling and entire length of room."

Jared looked on as the wall seemed to come alive with the now familiar swirling eddies that occurred when Orion reshaped the magnetic field and altered the dynamics of the plasma held within. Shar'ya leaned into him and gripped his arm tightly, eyes wide as this was her first time seeing the effect on such a large scale. It was amazing to watch, particularly because the large oval porthole remained unaffected by the alteration even though it was made of the same substance and in the middle of the other flowing plasma.

An excited gasp from his bond-mate caused Jared to grin in satisfaction as the intensifying colors and patterns began to coalesce into a familiar scene. The broad expanse of a green field extended outward from the edge of the floor with high mountains in the distance, framed by stands of pine and aspen trees and numbers of large shaggy creatures meandering across the extent of the thick green carpet of tall grass. If Jared hadn't known better, he would have thought he might truly be able to walk out onto the field.

Glancing down to his right, his satisfied expression turned to enchantment as his gaze fell upon Shar'ya's countenance of wide-eyed wonder and moist eyes.

Jared noticed the package he had left on the dresser. He picked it up and thought for a moment before turning to her. "I had this made for you but I'm not sure you will get a chance to wear it."

"What is it?"

"Open it."

Shar'ya carefully opened the package and held out the unusual garment. "What is it?" she asked again with an odd, questioning look on her face.

"It's a swimsuit. On my world when people go swimming for recreation, they wear close-fitting suits like that."

"Will you wear something similar?"

"Uh, yeah, something like that," he smiled. "Try it on."

Shar'ya briefly examined the outfit then began to put one leg through the opening in the bottoms.

"Um." Jared hesitated.

Shar'ya stopped and looked up.

"Just for future reference there is a lining in the bottoms, so you don't have to wear your underwear unless you want to."

She looked puzzled. "Well, do most wear their underwear on your world when wearing such a suit?"

"No, I don't think so."

She quickly slid on the swimsuit. It was one piece, backless and had a small cutout around the naval. "Is swimming done alone?"

"Sometimes, but usually it's with many others."

"And they always wear something like this?" She still looked confused.

"Some wear a bit more and some a lot less." Noticing her look of confusion intensifying, he asked, "What's wrong?"

"This is not much more than these," she picked up underclothes. "And you said it was not acceptable for me to be seen by anyone but you."

"I guess my world does have a few screwy customs and attitudes. Add a little color and you have a skimpy bathing suit or connect them in the middle, and you have a one piece." Jared rambled for a moment. "I guess the best way to explain it is that it is considered acceptable for the purpose of swimming to wear such an outfit. The primary reason is that a lot of clothing, when wet, tends to pull a person down and that would cause drowning. So as long as certain areas are covered it's okay. I doubt that will be much of an issue here since I've seen little evidence of recreational swimming."

"Is there any other use for it?"

Jared considered her question before an idea hit him and he lightly tapped his forehead. "Should have thought about that earlier, stupid."

Jared noticed Shar'ya's pained expression and quickly explained, "No, I was talking about me."

Her face relaxed. "I do not think you are stupid."

"Ah," he sighed. "I don't either, it's just sort of an expression my people use when they wish they'd thought of an idea sooner." He shrugged.

"Orion, I would like to resize this room by moving the aft wall ten ost rearward. I realize it will require moving the hatch and accessway aft as well."

"That can be accomplished if the size of both the EVA and weight rooms are condensed by an equal amount."

"Will that complicate the positioning or usability of existing equipment in those rooms?"

"No, five ost from each room will not significantly alter available space."

"Please proceed."

"Complying."

Jared watched as the wall slowly moved and chuckled as he saw Shar'ya dart out of the room. A few moments later the wall stopped and shortly after Shar'ya re-entered, smiling. "Soh coal," she said then screwed up her face, "So cool," she retried.

Jared smiled at her, "Such a doll."

"Sowch a dowl."

"Hehehehe, An'ah Faran." The translation in Ilirian was closer to *so cute*, but at least she understood it. He got another kiss.

"Orion, is there enough room to make a depression in the floor ten ost from fore to aft and twenty from the outer hull to the inner wall of this room?"

"No, the length exceeds the current lateral width."

"What about ten by twenty using the foot values of my home world?"

"Yes."

"Excellent, please make the depth three feet at the end parallel to the inner room wall and eight feet deep at the outer hull wall."

"Complying."

Once again, the shifting, twisting eddies of light flowed in a ballet that only a select few would ever witness. When the motion stopped, they stood looking at a deep, smooth pool which was already being filled with water. Jared smiled realizing Orion already knew the purpose of the new creation. Shar'ya looked on with intense curiosity.

"I can use this in there?" she asked tugging at the shoulder strap of her swimsuit.

Jared nodded giving her a grin, "Any time you're ready."

She tentatively approached the edge, knelt and dipped her hand in the water. "It's warm."

"I should hope so," he replied, brows raised.

She cocked her head but otherwise ignored him. Twisting her torso, she slid her legs into the water, let go and instantly disappeared. A moment later her head reappeared and she latched onto the side, sputtering, eyes wide.

"Don't even know how to float, huh?"

She regarded him with a mix of emotions and a bit of a pout, "I'm not a boat."

"You know what a boat is?"

Her face shifted to mild irritation then softened. "I do, one of my favorite books my mother used to read to me was about sea life on Ty'lar. The world is mostly water so they use boats to go everywhere, even the underwater kind."

"I'd like to see that too."

"So how do I float?"

"Well, it's all about relaxation and your body position. If you're too tense, you'll sink. You'll want to lean your head back, keeping your face above water, your back straight and your hips near the surface, then let your arms and legs spread out. Fill your lungs with a deep breath to help your body float. And trust the water. It's not as complicated as it sounds…"

Shar'ya followed his directions and even though she bobbed lower, she didn't sink. She smiled; her cheeks puffed out.

"Just so you know, keeping your mouth full doesn't help."

She let out a puff, lips vibrating followed by a dainty giggle.

"Orion."

"Yes, Companion."

"Can you modify the pool to have steps at the shallow end so she can get out easily?"

"Yes, Companion."

Three smoothly curved protrusions developed at the place indicated and Jared ran his hand along the edge of the pool. The feel of the surface made him recall pools on Earth and the need for safety. "Orion, I need you to texture the area around the pool to prevent us from slipping. Also put the texture on the steps."

"Complying."

"Now, we need a way out." Jared moved to the deep end of the pool, knelt and pointed. "Orion, please make three depressions here on this pool wall beginning ten inches below the deck edge. They should be ten inches apart, five inches deep, eighteen inches wide and four inches high. We'll also need two railings."

Jared paused for a moment and then asked, "Orion, would you scan my memories and pinpoint the image of an item? It is safety railing for climbing out of the deep end of a pool. It consists of three gently curving metal tubes welded together into what is called a three-bend railing. It is the type that is mounted to the deck with the top tube arcing down to the water."

"Accessing. Is this what you desire?"

A shimmering ball with a perfect replica of the railing appeared for their reference.

"Yes, amazing! I'd like the rail that reaches closest to the water to be curved a bit more at the end, so it isn't so 'in-your-face.'"

"Complying."

"Would you mind adding an additional railing near the curved steps as well?"

"Complying."

Shar'ya couldn't help smiling, "So cool!"

Fascinated, they watched the formation of the pool, and despite their tired state they spent nearly an em-har playing in the water. Twenty-nine days passed quickly as the two spent their time together turning Orion into a home.

Kolu-Daln sat just outside current Commonwealth borders in what was known as the Midrim. Except for Andrios, Borgga (which was the most anti-Commonwealth), Syli'vash, Thayz Project, Ludan and My'santhos, all other Midrim worlds had been colonized by core world citizens. Though most colonies still claimed citizenship in the Commonwealth, they were primarily on their own as the Ilirian council no longer had the resources to patrol that far out.

Kolu-Daln had been the first of the Midrim colonies and had the distinction of being the most populated and most active of all Midrim worlds. Though not claiming to be part of the Commonwealth itself, no attempt was ever made to refute claims by some within the council that it was a member. Its local government maintained a congenial relationship with the Ilirian government. Unlike Sha'Lural, which had a few small desert areas and several huge oceans, Kolu-Daln's southern hemisphere was mostly arid wasteland dotted occasionally with small oases. The equatorial region, which contained the majority of the planet's populace, was a lush, tropical band cutting the hemispheres in two. Seventy-three percent of the planet was land mass, and the twenty-seven percent water dotted the surface as large lakes and small seas, but no major oceans.

The northern hemisphere, though not as arid as the south, had been cultivated successfully using irrigation, but was no longer able to produce enough to supply the demands of so large a population. Industrially, Kolu-Daln ranked in the top fifty planets at number twenty-three and as a result had a great deal of influence in financial markets. What the southern hemisphere lacked in livability was compensated by the extremely high mineral wealth buried beneath.

Often called the Midrim trade center, Kolu-Daln's markets and trade facilities were second to none. Located on the southern periphery of Tyris, the vast Zolos Space Port lay sprawled surrounded by seven major shipping concerns along with numerous smaller entities. Trade goods of every kind passed through the complex daily. Not far from the port lay a large military base by the name of Es Tan Mahal, which was one of four on the planet. Responsible for planetary defense and off world transport security, the Kolu-Daln military sported the latest and most advanced defense equipment.

The passenger transport terminal could handle up to one hundred eighty thousand travelers per day, if necessary, though it rarely handled more than fifty thousand. The only industry that had little hold on the Kolu-Daln economy was tourism.

Jared was happy to note that market information placed agricultural products as high priority and prime value commodities.

A security vessel hailed them half an em-har out. Orion's hull had no irregular features nor any markings, and with increased pirate activity in the outlying regions, the security vessel's captain was taking no chances.

"Security 72 to unidentified vessel, please respond."

"Security 72, this is trader ship Orion, Sha'Lural registry TGR-48739-YS-949399."

"Orion, this is Darhost Tallos, Captain of S-72. Have you visited Kolu-Daln before?"

"No."

"Well, may I be the first to welcome you. I must however inform you that all incoming vessels are inspected prior to landing authorization. I'm sure you can understand, with all the pirate activity in the outer worlds and widespread trafficking of illegal materials."

"I understand completely, Captain," Jared replied cheerfully. "You are more than welcome to come aboard and inspect the ship."

"Thank you," the captain's voice sounded less strained. "What is the nature of your cargo?"

"Primary cargo is grain. Secondary cargo is salvage."

"Very good. Stand by for docking."

Jared felt sure the Captain of S-72 had expected a more defiant attitude and had been greatly relieved there hadn't been any resistance. "Orion."

"Ready."

"Prepare a docking port compatible to the S-72 and allow them to dock. Also seal off the area of the cargo bay where I have the salvaged weapons stored."

"Complying."

Shar'ya stood nearby patiently waiting as Jared talked to Orion, but he noticed she looked as though she wanted to be in on what was happening. He filled her in as they left the bridge.

"What if he brings some sort of portable scanner with him, might he find hidden things?" she asked.

"Good thinking." He kissed her hand as he switched back to Adarian. "Orion, can you shield hidden items from scanning?"

"Of course."

"Proceed."

"Complying."

Captain Tallos and two others, a man and a woman, stepped onto the Orion all seemingly quite curious about the unusual ship.

Jared stepped forward and greeted them. "Captain Tallos, I presume?"

"Yes, I'm Darhost Tallos. These are members of my crew, Rander Mellit and Saya Treese."

"My name is Jared Chandler, master of this vessel." Jared smiled as he said 'master' because he doubted anyone was truly Orion's master. "And this is Shar'ya Irall Chandler."

Shar'ya nodded at the captain as she was introduced.

"How many others in your crew, Trader Chandler?"

"None."

"The two of you run this entire ship?"

"Yes, most of the systems are entirely automated so a large crew is unnecessary, which saves on the cost of operation."

The captain looked skeptical. "I'm sure it does."

"If you will follow me, I'll show you to the cargo bay." Jared pointed down the hallway with his upturned palm. "Do you mind if I close the hatch? I do so as a precaution against possible docking port failure."

"I have no problem with you doing so."

"Shar'ya, will you take them to the cargo bay while I see to the hatch?"

"Yes," she said, seeming happy to be of use.

Jared winked. "I'll join you shortly." He walked out of earshot and asked Orion to secure the hatch, then headed for the cargo bay.

Tallos and his staff were going over each pod with their scanning devices and recording the findings. As each pod checked out, they moved to the next, scanning all thirty-eight; then moving to the salvage area, they scanned all closed cases and visually checked unpackaged items.

"Trader, what is the origin of the grain?"

"Sha'Lural."

"Indeed." His eyebrows rose. "Any trouble with pirates?"

"Yes, but we were able to outrun them."

This time the captain just pursed his lips and nodded.

Jared and Shar'ya stood for some time as the three went thoroughly through the old outpost's salvage. An occasional grunt and a few comments made Jared more aware that some of the stuff he'd brought was worth a good deal. Hopefully none would be confiscated due to some law making the item illegal or restricted.

Finally, the Captain spoke. "Where did you get these items of salvage?"

"From an old military outpost about two weeks out from Sha'Lural. I assume it was used as a base of operations for further exploration of space prior to the fall of the Drakstrad, though I have no way of being sure."

"Well, everything seems to be in order here. I need to get copies of your manifest, shipping papers, license and registration."

"Would you like a hard copy now, or may I send it to you via messagecomm?"

"Messagecomm will be fine. We can verify your document's validity from there."

"I'll have them sent as soon as I get back to the bridge."

"That is acceptable." The captain took a last look around the huge room. "Are there any other storage areas containing cargo?"

"No, but you're more than welcome to check any you wish. There are five empty rooms that are designed for transporting passengers." Jared realized the captain was trying to be as congenial as possible. He was obviously used to dealing with less than cooperative crews.

Jared led the way back to the main hatch and bid the security team farewell, then joined Shar'ya on the bridge. As soon as the S-72

had the documentation transfer, the two ships separated, and Orion was allowed to proceed to Kolu-Daln.

The following half em-har was uneventful and Jared was pleased there were no pirates to worry about. The vast deserts of southern Kolu-Daln were starkly apparent as they approached. Thin bands of clouds stretched the length of the southern region like tendrils of smoke. A tiny ice cap near the southern pole finished the scene and Jared wondered where the planet's population found enough water to supply all their needs. Orion probably knew or could find out, but Jared decided not to ask. He also decided not to wait for the planetary traffic control to contact them.

"Orion trader to Kolu-Daln transport control."

"Orion trader, this is Sector 7 inbound, please stand by."

"Standing by."

Several al-ems passed as they waited, and Orion drew nearer to the planet. Kolu-Daln's rotational direction was the same as Earth's. The planet itself, being somewhat larger and having a faster rotation, made for a slightly higher gravity. The green tropical region girdling the central latitudes was in stark contrast to the deep earth tones to the south. By the time Orion was contacted again, the ship had passed into the night side of the planet.

"Orion trader, you are now within Sector 8, south jurisdiction," the controller said in a monotone but professional manner. "What is your destination?"

"Zolos Space Port."

"Continue on current course to marker 357. Begin descent now to holding orbit of five two zero thousand ost. Ensure identity beacon is operating on channel 258-90. You will be contacted when it is your turn to land."

"Understood, beginning descent now." Switching to Adarian, he said, "Orion, take us to 520 thousand ost and start transmitting an identification signal that can be received by their sensors."

"Complying."

Orion orbited Kolu-Daln four times before sector eight inbound had them descend to 130 thousand ost and transferred them to Port Zolos traffic control. The operator at Zolos seemed quite harried, irritable, and very curt.

"Orion trader, this is Zolos control. Approach on vector 227.35 and do not deviate. Slowly descend to 75 thousand and maintain to marker 290. From there, descend to 20 thousand, reduce speed to approximately 275 vod and turn to course 188.03 and maintain until outer port marker. Just prior to that point, further instruction will be given. Port control out."

"Okay, that was to the point," Jared glanced at Shar'ya with a bit of irritation in his voice. "Orion, comply with Zolos control's instructions and take us down."

"Complying."

"Orion, please show me our trajectory."

Jared's vidscreen changed from data to a 3-dimensional wire frame image of a portion of Kolu-Daln with a colored line representing the ship's trajectory and an outline of Orion silhouetted over the path. Shar'ya noted Jared's interest in his view screen and asked if she could see what he was looking at. He felt badly at having failed to include her in bridge dynamics. So she would not have to get up, he asked Orion to show all incoming data on her display and to allow her to see all information he saw, unless otherwise directed.

He knew any new experience always thrilled Shar'ya, and the graphics were a new thing altogether. Jared shifted back and forth from trajectory to planetary data then to climate and topography and others.

Shar'ya absorbed as much as she could. Her reading skills had improved rapidly since leaving Da'har. With Jared's help, she found the new input of images and information absolutely delightful. He answered all her questions cheerfully, though a few times he had to admit he didn't know the answer. He told her he figured Orion could answer them but said he did not want to become too dependent on his friend for everything. His attitude of support gave her a sense of security and belonging that was still a bit foreign, but something she loved dearly.

"Orion trader, this is Port Zolos control. You are now 67 k'tan from the outer port marker. At the marker, reduce speed to 175 vod and begin final approach on vector 180. Deviation from flight path is not advised due to heavy local traffic. Is your vessel equipped for VTOL or HWR?"

"VTOL," Jared replied, having no idea what HWR stood for.

"You will be coming in on runway 4. At the transition marker, turn starboard 45 degrees and follow the blue traffic line to terminal 7 pad 397. Control out."

"Understood." Jared realized that due to his very limited training, he would have had an impossible time figuring out all the instructions that had been given. Orion's abilities were truly a blessing. "Orion, have we reached the outer marker yet?"

"No. ETA to outer marker 2.19 al-em."

"What is our current altitude?"

"10,760.1 feet."

"What would that be in Ilirian?"

"9300 ost or 9.3 k'tan."

"Please inform me when we are on final approach and since I'm gonna be speaking Ilirian, you might as well give me stats in Ilirian also while we're on planet."

"Understood."

Early morning light cast long shadows over the land below as they neared their destination. Just before they cleared the outer marker, Orion was less than three thousand feet above the surface and the sprawling city and suburbs of Tyris were clearly visible. The approach corridor they were in was several miles across and was mostly forested and undeveloped, with an occasional roadway crossing it. To either side however, buildings of various sizes and design jutted from among the thick foliage. Developed areas of tract housing could be seen on both sides, as well as large rental or condominium type structures surrounded by fences, parks and lakes. The numerous living areas seemed to encircle centralized industrial and business complexes. Roads and raised causeways arrayed in rings and radials connected the various settlements, and from their current altitude made the land look as if covered by many huge spider webs.

In some areas the roads were congested with heavy traffic whereas others appeared almost deserted. A monorail ran along their path off to the right and as far as Jared could tell was of a larger and heavier design than the one on Sha'Lural. At first several branches fed into the one rail, but when Orion informed Jared of their arrival at the outer marker, there were four parallel running rails heading toward Zolos.

"Current altitude and speed?"

"Altitude 800 ost. Speed is 175 vod."

"ETA?"

"8.7 al-em."

"Thank you."

"You are welcome."

Far ahead another ship came into view on the same approach vector. Numerous others, which obviously were not designed for space, circled above waiting their turn to land. Jared had Orion access a map of the port which showed four runways for space craft and five for inter-atmosphere transports. Most of the smaller, non-space transports had some type of airfoil wing structure and many were equipped with vectored thrust. By the time the runway was in view, Orion had closed on the ship ahead by about two thirds. Half the size of Orion, it was far more symmetrical than the Hedmar freighters he had hitherto seen. It coasted along the runway for a few moments before touching down roughly, its landing gear obviously having wheels, though Jared could not see them. It turned left onto a taxi-way as Orion crossed over the end of the runway boundary marker. Silently skimming along, Orion's ghost-like appearance seemed to draw the attention of every person within viewing range.

Unerringly the ship found and followed the blue line to Terminal 7 Pad 397. Jared saw numerous onlookers gazing as the great white bird came to hover just above the pad, smoothly and soundlessly pivoted 73 degrees, aligning squarely with the parking marshal. At the marshal's signal, Orion slowly moved forward until centered directly over the middle of the tarmac. At this point, hovering motionlessly, the massive blisters which formed the landing gear flowed downward and Orion settled silently on the well-kept pad. Jared looked on the scene with a great deal of pride as more and more curious onlookers crowded the viewing areas.

"Port Zolos, this is Jared Chandler of the Orion. Landing complete and all systems shut down."

"Understood Orion and welcome to Kolu-Daln."

"Thank you."

Jared yawned and turned to Shar'ya. "I'm hungry. How 'bout you?"

Shar'ya shook her head. "Not really, I've never been to another world before. Are we going to be able to see much of it?"

"Oh, sure, but not on an empty stomach."

"Okay, you get your snack, and I think I'll go swimming."

"You kinda like swimming, huh?"

"Yes, even though I'm not very good at it."

"All right smarty pants, you go drown yourself and I'll come along later and pull you out."

Shar'ya stuck out her tongue. She laughed, spun around, and stomped out of the room.

Jared knew she was being playful, at least he thought she was. But he wasn't quite sure. He had misunderstood her before because of his lack of knowledge of her world's customs.

His stomach growled and he shrugged.

Oh, to hell with it. She'll be fine and I'll figure it out later.

He put Shar'ya and her impish behavior out of his mind. He ate slowly while he studied a map of Tyris' metropolitan area, which was Kolu-Daln's capital. The city boasted a population of 18.7 million and another 3.2 million in the smaller communities on the outskirts. Tyris also served as the capitol of the Wy'daln Province. Total land coverage within the city was greater than eleven thousand square miles, but of course the figure included Port Zolos and the nearby military complex.

He opened the door to their quarters and called for her. When she didn't answer he walked back toward the pool. He stopped abruptly when he spotted her motionless form just below the rim at the shallow end. He was flooded with a rush of emotions. Fear, anger, and grief. He jumped in and grabbed her while screaming her name.

He lifted her out of the water, laid her on the deck, and leaned over to check her breathing.

Suddenly her green eyes snapped open, and he jumped back.

Shar'ya looked puzzled. "What are you doing?"

"You're not...?"

"Not what?"

"Dead!"

She leaned up onto her elbows. "Why would I be dead?"

Jared dropped into a sitting position breathing heavily, his heart pounding. "I, I thought you had drowned."

She chuckled. "I was just seeing how long I could hold my breath."

"Your breath?"

Shar'ya nodded.

"Why?"

"I used to hold my breath as long as I could to avoid the smells as I moved about in the tunnels under Da'har, and I was just interested in finding out how long I could hold it."

"Phew," Jared shook his head and rubbed his face. "So how long did you hold it?"

"I don't know. I forgot where I was in the count when you pulled me out."

"Sorry."

"Oh, that's okay, I can always try again."

"You're not angry with me?"

"Why would I be angry with you?"

"For so rudely jerking you out of the water and interrupting your experiment."

"No."

Jared stood, offered his hand, and helped her up.

It was mid-morning in Tyris, and both were anxious to explore this new world.

Jared felt it was highly unlikely he would have any trouble selling the grain at top price and so he was in no hurry to find a buyer. What tourist information did exist indicated that there were many fine food service establishments, entertainment facilities and a park with thrill rides.

Once again, except for the scenery and some customs, he may as well have been on Earth. Shar'ya showered as Jared gave Orion some final instructions and checked on some other various information. While he showered, she happily went through her ample wardrobe and chose what to wear.

This must still be quite a novelty to her since she has for so long only had one set of ragged clothes.

Zolos Space port was a small city itself and contained all the facilities necessary to be an independent entity. Thousands of people thronged through its concourses in every direction. After being logged in and cleared by the port authority, they made their way through the crowded terminal. Stopping by a directory, they noted there were four public transport terminals interconnected by a sub-surface tram system with two hundred eighty-four passenger gates, and a monorail station serving all communities within the western belt region. It also listed numerically twenty-six restaurants, fifty snack bars, twenty-three beverage bars, twenty lounges and ninety-eight retail shops. They headed for the monorail terminal.

Orion was parked in the freighter section of the complex. Jared and Shar'ya had three shuttle rides and a long walk to get to the monorail station. Jared felt Orion was quite safe and decided to get a room at one of the fancy hotels in downtown Tyris. Reservations at the Ali'Ran Towers for the next eight days had been easy to get once the hotel knew he was both a trader and member in good standing with the C & I guild. He was informed that the room was one of the hotel's best. He hoped so because it was costing a hundred and fifty credits per day. He may have been lucky so far where money was concerned, but he had struggled enough on Earth to have a good appreciation for being frugal.

The engines of a transport at a nearby gate roared to life, and though diminished significantly by the insulated glass, it still was quite noticeable. The aircraft used for on-planet transport only vaguely resembled comparable vehicles on Earth. Many were blockish in design and did not appear to be built for very high speeds.

Information available at the terminal indicated they were constructed to handle the harsh conditions of the Urothas Desert and southern polar regions. Others were more streamlined and aerodynamic looking and generally took passengers to northern destinations.

It took quite some time to reach the monorail station and get through the security check. It was very apparent that this world had seen its share of terrorist activity. Like those in the main terminal, they were very detailed and methodical in checking each passenger. Jared guessed the eight platforms spanned at least a mile, were several hundred feet across and were packed with thousands of travelers.

The rails themselves looked to be three times the mass of those on the shuttles in Port Da'har. The chain of vehicles here could truly be called trains because each of those now in view had from ten to twenty-two sections and were about as broad as a wide-bodied airliner. The terminal itself was built underground at the same level as the port shuttles. Huge copper-hued tunnel portals rose to ceiling level at either end. It took an em-har to get through the ticket line and Jared was glad he'd made reservations at a hotel because doing this each time they wanted to go into the city would get old, real fast.

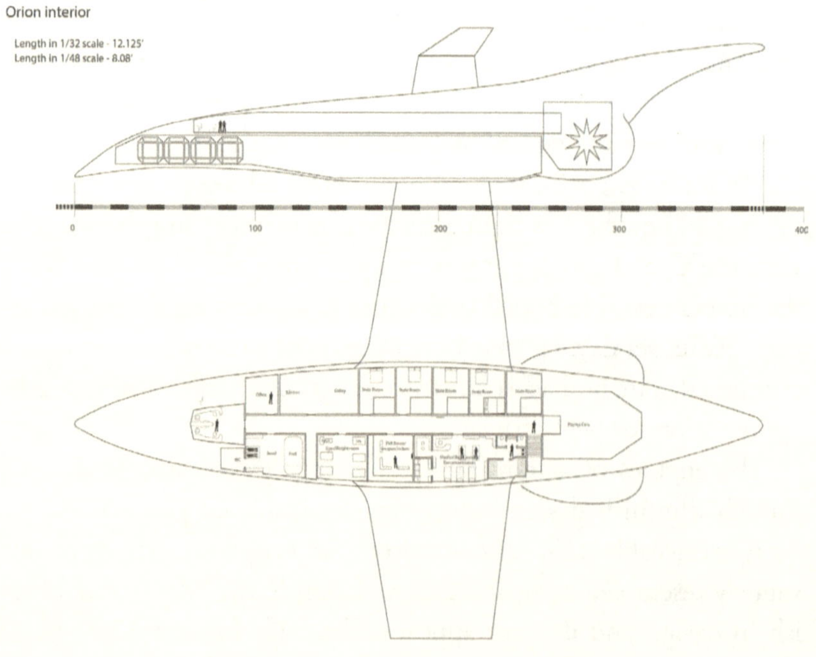

CHAPTER TWELVE

Black Widow

"Greed is a web woven by the unscrupulous,
which snares every unwary thing in its path.
It leads those who succumb to a very sticky end."

A TALL, SLENDER WOMAN dressed in expensive clothing stood in the ticket line, listening intently to all a specific couple had to say with the help of an inner ear amplifier. The girl was of no consequence, but the man was who she was looking for. He matched the image on her datavox. It had been difficult at times to pick out some of what they said from other conversations and noise, but she had what she needed when she reached the front of the line.

"I would like to get seat number 194 or 197 on car twelve of number 472 to Tyris." The ticket agent looked at the woman curiously for the odd request but said nothing and checked for availability.

"I'm sorry, ma'am, but those two seats are already taken." He paused a moment then raised his head from his computer screen and smiled. "I can however get you seat number 200 which is close."

"I'll take it," she responded in a friendly manner. She walked casually through the crowds in no hurry to reach the train. She would have plenty of time to see her plans come to fruition and besides, she had always been proud of her skillful but indirect approach to achieving her goals.

Train number 472 was already loading on rail five by the time they reached the right platform. Their tickets indicated that they needed to find car twelve and seats 195 and 196. Information screens in the station and on board the train indicated that the outside temperature was very hot, but good air conditioning kept the interior areas comfortable. At the front of the car was a snack and beverage kiosk, and to the rear were numerous lavatories. Once settled in their seats, Jared found it interesting to watch the many people boarding the train.

Shar'ya on the other hand, was engrossed in the vid screen mounted to the back of the seat and the selector on her left armrest. She'd found a pair of earphones tucked into a pouch under her seat cushion and was happily flipping through the channels. Her love of music had developed instantly when Jared first played some for her before they left Sha'Lural, and she was delighted at the variety from which she could choose. Several al-ems after the last passenger had been seated, a recorded departure message came through the speakers and the train started to move. Like the shuttle on Sha'Lural, the windows on the train had no support columns and stretched the length of the car. The windows spanned vertically about four feet and gave an impressive view of passing scenery.

Number 472 headed out the East portal and Jared felt the train gracefully surge forward when it entered the tunnel. Long sections of lights mounted on the tunnel walls faded into a single line as the train attained higher speeds. Ride quality was excellent with only a vague rocking from side to side and acceleration had been gradual and smooth. Studying the route schedule, he noted that the 472 stopped twice in Tyris and then continued to Furth about an em-har further on, then to Gel'yen and finally into Han'val six em-har later. Quite impressive considering that Han'val was the equivalent of 2260 miles distant. Scenery close to the rail passed by so fast it made Jared sick to look at it. Even Shar'ya, with her seemingly iron constitution, avoided looking at anything nearby. Further out, the scenery, though still passing quickly, allowed them time to see just how beautiful the region was. Jared noticed Shar'ya's interest in what was on the headphones, so he took the pair from under his seat and turned to the same channel.

He tried numerous others before they reached their destination and heard a variety of music which ran in a spectrum from what would be considered New Age and Jazz, to fast-paced Pop and some with vague country melodies. Most were strictly instrumental in format. Nothing like Hard Rock, Rap or Grunge was evident, at least on the stations available in the area. Shar'ya had a natural rhythm and even though seated, she moved beautifully to the beat of each tune.

The train was only traveling at a quarter of its maximum speed of 400 tpe or about 420 mph and took 20 al-ems to reach Tyris' city center. To'luan Station, though nowhere near the size of Zolos station, was just as busy and a bit more chaotic. Exiting the train, Jared bumped into a woman who dropped one of her cases. It burst open and garments flew all over the platform. The woman scrambled to gather the items.

"Excuse me," she said to Jared.

He wasn't sure if he was at fault. "My apologies. I didn't realize you were there."

"No, no, I shouldn't have been so close behind you." She was struggling with her broken suitcase.

Jared asked, "May I help you with those?"

"Would you mind?"

"Not at all."

Be careful. Remember what happened the last time you played the gallant.

"Thank you," she replied theatrically.

Both Jared and Shar'ya had packed lightly because he figured she would like to do some shopping and there would not be too much to carry back.

"May I help?" Shar'ya asked.

Jared noticed the woman gave her a cold look, but Shar'ya seemed oblivious.

"Sure, beautiful, can you carry my bag, and I'll take care of this broken one? I can't seem to get the latches to work."

"Uh huh," Shar'ya smiled.

Jared asked, "Okay, where are…?"

"So, where are you two staying? You look rather new to Kolu-Daln," the woman asked abruptly.

"At the Ali'Ran Towers Hotel," said Jared.

"Oh, now isn't that interesting? That's exactly where I'm staying. It's a wonderful place; they have fabulous service."

"That's what I've heard," Jared winked at Shar'ya.

"Since you've been so kind to help, I can show you the way."

"That would be great."

"My name is Valeris."

"I'm Jared."

"Hello, Jared," Valeris cooed.

"And this is Shar'ya."

"Hello, Shar'ya," Valeris said with an icy glare.

Again, Shar'ya paid no attention. Jared struggled to keep the large suitcase together. He noticed Shar'ya's oblivion seemed to raise a good deal of ire in the tall, dark-haired woman.

Valeris led them out to the front of the station and secured one of the electric surface transports. Once they were all inside, she instructed the driver to take them to the Ali'Ran Towers and to try and not hit every bump in the road. Heavy mid-day auto traffic caused the trip to go slowly and both Jared and Shar'ya were awed by the hundreds of huge skyscrapers in downtown Tyris. High above the road, skybridges spanned from one building to another at various levels. Thousands thronged the walkways adjacent to the roads. Though there were traffic signals, none of the pedestrians crossed the avenues at street level but used stairs which led to tunnels running below the busy thoroughfares. Little else was said during the trip to the hotel as Jared and Shar'ya were occupied by sight-seeing, though they did comment from time to time on particularly interesting sights.

Valeris sat back and watched with obvious interest and contempt.

Far from Zolos in a richly appointed manor, a tall, thickset man entered an office and stood before a heavy wooden desk. The elderly man behind the desk looked at his visitor with eyes full of distrust and anger.

"Why are you here, Rehad?"

"To deliver a message. One which is very important to you and those who serve you."

"Do tell."

"Watch your flippancy, Alrios Imasra," Rehad said with a cruel smile. "I have no intention of suffering for another's incompetence, so hear me well. I have been given jurisdiction over the entire sector, and whether or not that ship can be taken, the crew is to be terminated at all costs. If you can't get the vessel, it too is to be destroyed."

"Why were your people on Sha'Lural not able to take care of the matter?"

"You are quite fond of illustrating how backward and stupid the outer-rim populations are," Rehad said with a sneer. "They have just certified your assessment to all those above us."

"I have no intention of causing the kind of destruction within my city as Dallos did in Da'har."

"I don't care how you do it." Rehad leaned forward and placed his clenched fist on Alrios' desk. "Just see to it there are no screw ups, because whatever trouble you cause me will filter back to you tenfold."

"Do not think I am one you can frighten with your threats, Rehad. Despite your position, I have been in this organization far longer than you."

"It was no threat," Rehad glared at the older man. "It is merely a fact."

"What information do you have for me on the subject?"

"Everything you need to know is here." Rehad handed a data disk to Alrios. "Steps have been taken to prevent the vessel from departing but there are no guarantees."

"Why, Rehad, are you admitting that one of your plans has a flaw?" Alrios sneered.

Rehad exhaled slowly, trying to maintain his composure and for the moment ignored the other man's taunt, "Your beloved city will not likely go unscathed. To ensure success you may well have to resort to more…" Rehad trailed off, locking eyes with Alrios, "*devastating* methods to destroy the vessel."

"And why is that?"

Rehad's upper lip curled, "As I said, it's all on the disk."

"Very well."

"There is no flaw," Rehad stressed. "Kanis is handling things directly now on Sha'Lural, so if there is any issue it will be here…" Rehad loudly tapped a thick finger on the desk, "squarely on your shoulders."

"I have always liked challenges," Alrios glared back at the big man. "I should like to warn you about flaunting your position too much. Such behavior often results in unfortunate incidents."

Amused, Rehad shot back, "Are you threatening me now?"

"Not at all. Like you, I do not make threats." Alrios leaned forward in his chair. "It is also merely fact."

The contempt and hatred the two men felt toward each other filled the room like a thick fog. Rehad picked up his small case and looked at Alrios one last time. "No mistakes, old man."

Alrios made no reply but stared back at Rehad with equal malice.

For several al-ems after Rehad's departure Alrios fumed. Inserting the disk into his computer he scanned the data. With each passing line or image his ire grew. The scope of the white ship's capabilities and attendant threat to the city became increasingly clear. One piece of data, a brief video, caused his eyes to linger. His right hand rose and clamped onto his chin as a single thought rose and persisted.

If that ship can do that much damage in a single burst, what might it cause if…,

His thought was cut short as the door to the office opened. His countenance changed instantly as a young girl walked in. Quickly placing the display on stand-by he turned and smiled lovingly.

"Father," she greeted warmly and set out a tray of food.

"Thank you, my dear," he replied.

"Are you almost done?"

"Yes, give me ten more al-em and then we can go."

The girl nodded with a smile and hurried out of the office. It was for her and her alone Alrios had joined the guild. She needed far more in her future than the current provisional government could or would provide. His late wife had been a descendant of House Athy'rom and as such she was royalty. His daughter deserved her legacy and would have it if he had any say in the matter, in spite of the fools who brought down the legitimate government over a hundred cycles before. Also, if he could find a way, he'd see the entire guild, especially Rehad destroyed in the most excruciating way possible.

The lobby of the Ali'Ran Towers was thronged with numerous, well-dressed people coming and going from the various shops and eateries on the first two floors. Luxuriously appointed modern decor gave the lobby a regal, yet high-tech feel. Soft music, barely audible above the din of the crowds, played from hidden speakers arranged around the large open area covered by a glass ceiling some three stories above. Three towers soared skyward at equal distances around the central lobby. The highest of the three rose to one hundred eighty stories.

Both Jared and Shar'ya paused, taking in the sheer size of the structure and beauty of the interior design. Four large, transparent elevators per tower ceaselessly rose and fell as the countless guests came and went. Jared gathered his senses and after taking Shar'ya's hand worked his way toward the main desk. About halfway there Valeris tugged at his sleeve, and he stopped.

She seemed a bit out of breath. "I think I'll sit here for a while."

"Are you alright?"

"Oh sure. Just want to rest my feet. You two go and check in. Just leave that troublesome bag there."

"Alright, but what if...?"

"You are so sweet, but if I need help, I'll just get one of the attendants to assist me."

"Okay. Well, thanks for your help. Good-bye."

"My thanks to you too, and perhaps we'll see each other again."

Jared nodded and turned, taking Shar'ya's hand again as they walked away.

It didn't take long to get a key and head for the elevator. The ride to their floor was fast and they found the room to be exceptional. Shar'ya was so excited about shopping and sight-seeing that Jared hated to say he was weary and wanted to get some sleep. She was a good sport about it, and despite the fact it would be several em-hars before darkness fell, they were soon fast asleep.

Back near the lobby center, Valeris sneered smugly as she mused over how easy it had been to attach the tiny listening device to the bottom of the female's suitcase.

She signaled an attendant and asked her to carry her bag to the desk. The young girl did so as Valeris strolled up to the counter and asked for a room on the 135th floor of tower two, and specifically room 2-135-62. When the clerk gave her a questioning look, Valeris recited a hastily thought up scenario of a past visit.

"Well, you see, I was here about two cycles ago and that's the room I stayed in. I enjoyed it immensely, so I figured, why not again? I was unable to make reservations as this trip was a last moment surprise."

"I'm sorry, but that room, as well as number 61, is occupied but I can give you number 60 for five nights before the date of the next reservation."

"Well, I suppose that will have to do," she answered and feigned disappointment. Once in her room, Valeris tossed the large, broken suitcase into a corner and kicked the few items that had fallen to the floor under the bed. She walked to the window and looked out over the city, though not really seeing anything. The large case with clothes inside had been expensive, but it was a necessary expenditure, and the desired effect had been achieved. He was indeed worthy, and his ship would be a great addition, not to mention having obvious technological advantages. Getting rid of the female would have to be done cautiously, but he would have no need of any other when he was hers.

Consciousness came to Shar'ya as an odd, tapping sound brought her out of a dream. She heard it again and sat up.

"The door," she muttered groggily and slid off the bed to answer it.

She opened the door to a young woman in a hotel uniform with a large cart.

"Good morning," the attendant said cheerfully.

"Good morning," Shar'ya replied through a yawn. "What's all that?"

"Your breakfast, and this message that was left early this morning at the front desk for a Trader Jared Chandler. May I bring it in?"

"Huh, oh sure," Shar'ya regained her composure. She took the sealed note and opened the door wider so the attendant could push in the cart.

Shar'ya smiled. "Thank you."

"My pleasure, and don't hesitate to call if you need anything else." She left and Shar'ya started to close the door. She suddenly remembered something she had seen Jared do and asked the attendant to wait. She located a ten-credit coin from her new belt pouch and handed it to the surprised woman. "Thank you for being prompt." She hoped she'd gotten it right.

The woman left with a bit more bounce in her step than when she had arrived.

Shar'ya turned her attention to the cart, lifted one of the lids and breathed in the wonderful aroma of hot food. As the smell filtered through the room, Jared stirred and sat up.

"Breakfast here already?" He looked at the timepiece mounted to the back of the bedside table. "Yep, that's about the time I asked for it."

"You ordered all this?"

"Sure, yesterday."

Shar'ya pushed the cart over by the small table and began setting it. Jared went to the bathroom and washed quickly, returned, kissed her and told her how wonderful she looked.

She glanced at the large mirror over the dresser and raised her eyebrows at the unkempt state of her hair and turned to regard him. She certainly did not think she looked good. Back in the lower city her hair had not mattered, but now she took great pride in keeping it as neat as possible, particularly since she'd found out Jared liked her long tresses.

"This was also delivered." She handed him the note.

"It has a very official looking seal on it." Jared opened the letter and after briefly reading, sighed and sat on the edge of the bed.

"What is it?" Shar'ya asked with concern.

"Nothing serious, just another glitch to deal with. It seems that someone on Sha'Lural has misplaced my license and registration for operating Orion, and as a trader."

Shar'ya's look of concern turned to mild shock. "Will they try to take the ship away?"

"No, because I have proof that the ship is mine and the C & I Guild has verified that my account was started with valid paper-work." He paused to look back at the letter. "The transport authority is trying to contact Governor Woltra to verify it but has been unable to get through to her. Neither guild will cancel my charters unless they receive a signed directive from the governor herself. The port authority here has a dilemma. There is no record in official Sha'Lural files of my license or registration, but other entities have verified it does exist and has not been officially revoked. All they want us to do is stay until they can figure it out. So, we've been grounded by governmental red tape."

"I'm sorry."

He took a seat at the table. "Not to worry, my precious. They have not told me I can't sell my cargo or do more sight-seeing with my lady fair. Hence, we shall enjoy our possibly extended vacation."

The remainder of the morning was spent enjoying each other's company. Around mid-day Jared began to look for buyers for both the grain and salvage items. After several em-hars he had three meet-ings set for the next day with agricultural firms, and meetings five days later with two parties interested in some of the salvage. After the last meeting was set, he took the time to learn about current market values, regulations and local laws concerning trade and any other information he could find so he could play the proper trader and at least appear competent.

Shar'ya spent the time listening to music and scanning the several catalogs she had acquired the day before, as well as flipping through the various vid channels. As soon as he was finished, she showed him an advertisement for a tour to the southern desert and what was supposed to be a spectacular place called the Torudal Oasis. It was a three-day trip with everything included, and at a reasonable price. After about half an em-har of discussion, they decided to give it a try.

Their second evening was spent on the town and to Jared's surprise, they came across a night club-like establishment which had a dance floor where he introduced her to the joys of dancing. He didn't feel out of place because other dancers did not appear to be doing any formal steps, just moving to the beat as they saw fit.

Jared had lost any interest in drinking after a close friend had been killed due to the influence of alcohol. He avoided most of the beverages places like this dispensed, but Shar'ya was curious, so Jared relented and bought her one of what seemed a popular drink. At first, she seemed a bit put off by its taste but was soon enjoying it quite well. After many more dances and another of the drinks, called an Aldan-Durl, Jared decided it was time to take her home.

"Nooo."

"Yes, Love, it's time to go."

"Do we weely hash to?"

"Yes, you are in no condition to do any more dancing."

"Aww, shoof," she hiccupped. "Ah feel fung, uh, fungy."

"Fungy?"

"Yesh, you know, He he he."

Jared took her arm and headed back for the hotel. "Where do you feel funny?"

"In my stomash."

"Either you have a low tolerance or those were potent concoctions."

"Concoshuns. Wha's a concashun?"

"Never mind, just close your eyes and rest."

"I'm not…tared." She squinted her eyes. "But dose lishe sure ah bright."

Jared didn't answer her, and she stopped talking and seemed content for the time being. As they entered the hotel, Shar'ya let out a loud giggle and pointed at a nearby woman dressed rather gaudily.

"Loosh ak dat."

"What?"

"Obber dere."

Jared turned to look where she was pointing and saw the multi-hued dress the woman was wearing, and had to admit it looked a great deal like some child's finger-painting project.

"Dash enough to mashe any boshy dishy."

Jared realized she was becoming more difficult to understand and was also attracting considerable attention. One of the floor staff asked if he needed any help, which he politely turned down. The elevator was nearly full, and he smiled sheepishly to all those who turned just as Shar'ya released a rather loud belch. However, he almost burst out laughing when she tried to apologize.

"Fogib me, I know nosh wha I dib somfing lawk dash." She closed her eyes and continued. "Ish very embash...embarish...embarashting an...hey, whas dat fungy shing on yose facsh?"

Jared made haste to leave the elevator when it stopped on their floor and felt relief when he closed the door behind him. He gently set her on the bed, undressed her, tucked her in, and then went to the bathroom to brush his teeth. When he came back, she was propped up on her elbow watching him.

"Shar'ya, you need to go to sleep."

"A'm nosh tard."

"Yes, you are."

"No a'm nosh," she said tenaciously. "Ah wansh you."

"What do you mean?"

Shar'ya's shoulders drooped, and she gave him a look which told him she thought that was a less than intelligent question.

"I'm not sure that's such a good idea."

"Haw come?"

"Well, as you said earlier, your stomach feels funny."

"Nosh so, my shomash feels jush fine."

"Well, we'll just see about that." Jared placed his hand on her lower abdomen and began to vibrate it back and forth. Her eyes opened wide for a moment, and she smiled. Suddenly her complexion turned green, and she closed her mouth tight, clamping her hand over it. Her eyes grew even wider as she tried to make it to the bathroom.

Jared laughed as she wobbled across the room to the toilet. His amusement ended when he went in to check on her and found she had missed completely, covering half the room before she collapsed on the floor in the middle of the mess. He had little reason to be angry since he had been the one to irritate her stomach, so he set to work cleaning up.

The sound of raindrops hitting the window was the first thing Jared heard as he awoke and stretched. Beside him Shar'ya lay somewhat twisted in the sheet and making occasional moaning sounds. Jared was sure she would have a hangover and hoped he could find a way to dissuade her from ever doing this again. It was still some time before breakfast would arrive and he doubted she would have much of an appetite. His first meeting was scheduled to start in about three em-hars, so he got up and went to take a shower. Shortly after he got in, Shar'ya stepped in and looked at him. Her normally bright green eyes were dull and full of discomfort.

"What happened last night? I don't remember leaving the dance place, or what happened after."

"You were intoxicated. You put on quite a show."

Shar'ya closed her eyes and looked down. "Anything else?"

"Ah, yes." Jared seized the moment. "You mean you don't remember all the fun we had after we got back to the room?"

Shar'ya's head came up and she looked into his eyes.

"Fun? No, I don't, and I don't like not remembering." She looked at him with pleading in her eyes. "Please do not let me drink anything like that again."

"Are you sure?"

"Yes!"

"I will make sure neither of us do." He began to massage her aching head.

"I think it best if you stay in the room and rest. I doubt you will feel like doing much until tomorrow anyway. It would probably be a good idea not to answer the door. We don't know anyone here and trouble seems to be following us."

"Okay." She looked a bit disheartened.

"I know you don't like to be left behind, but those types of drinks can really screw up your internal system."

After they finished their shower Shar'ya dressed, stretched out on the bed and stared out the window. The rain was still coming down hard and it would make for a poor day out anyway. She just lay back and tried to relax. Fortunately, by the time Jared left, she had fallen asleep.

Jared had checked his account just before leaving and was pleased to see that his balance had jumped significantly due to his investment in the aggressive growth fund. Except for a little worry about Shar'ya, he felt good, ready to tackle the job at hand. As soon as the meetings were completed, he was going to get her that trip to the Torudal Oasis.

Stepping off the elevator, he headed for a restaurant to get some lunch. Part way across the lobby he heard a somewhat familiar voice.

"Trader Chandler, what a pleasant surprise. Where is your lady friend?"

"Hello, Valeris, she decided to stay in today to rest and catch up on her reading."

"How nice. And where are you headed?"

"To the Kandron restaurant, I have several meetings today and need to get some breakfast." Jared felt the woman was being a tad nosey but not offensive.

"If you don't think she'd mind, may I join you?"

"I doubt she'd mind, sure."

"I've always liked to meet new people."

"I'm happy you feel that way."

While they ate, Valeris listened with interest as Jared described what his meetings entailed and she in turn told him about herself. Jared, having no reason to mistrust her intentions, enjoyed the conversation and bid her a cheerful farewell as he hurried away to his first meeting.

He grabbed one of the taxi-like ground cars. Jared gave the driver the address and sat back as the vehicle sped into traffic. It was not a far drive to the Halidon conglomerate's offices. Jared paid the driver and tipped him a little extra, which of course had the same effect it had on those in Port Da'har. Tipping was obviously not a custom anywhere within the old Commonwealth sphere of influence.

Building 2971 was a moderately tall, multi-tiered structure with a rather wide base. It had the appearance of several huge monoliths set on top of one another. The thought hit him that this city would make New York, LA or Chicago look puny in comparison. He wasn't sure if the population was so much greater, but the structures sure were. He entered the building through one of ten sets of automatic doors, walked up to the digital information board and looked for the floor he needed. Halidon was a small outfit compared to many others, even though it occupied nearly two entire floors.

He noticed a good deal of security personnel and surveillance devices in the lobby and hallways as he made his way to his destination. He disembarked the elevator at the 8th floor and walked up to the receptionist's desk.

"May I help you?" she asked.

"My name is Jared Chandler, trade master. I have an appointment with Broker Wella Kirknan."

"Yes, trader, I have it here. Please have a seat and I will inform Agent Kirknan you are here." She smiled, "There is a refreshment bar just around that corner if you have need."

"Thank you." Jared walked to the waiting area and sat down. It seemed odd to believe he was so far from Earth. If this were some Sci-fi show on TV like he used to watch with his older nephew Toby, then the receptionist would have some strange facial feature and those working at the restaurant where he ate lunch would have had funny-looking over-sized bald craniums and be money hungry; not to mention the fact that half the populace of the planet would be non-human and some, really grotesque looking. His reverie was interrupted as a middle-aged woman with graying hair spoke to him.

"Trader Chandler, I'm Wella Kirknan."

"Good day, Agent Kirknan. It's a pleasure to meet you."

"Follow me, I'll show you to the conference room."

Jared followed her into a long room with a very ornate wooden table stained to a deep red brown. Twenty-four matching chairs surrounded it, and he was directed to sit at the end closest to the door he entered. Agent Kirknan left and said she would return shortly. Jared scanned over his shipping documents and the agricultural market reports he had secured from the front desk of the hotel before leaving. Agent Kirknan and nine others filed into the room and took various seats around the table. The countenances on the faces of the Halidon employees were of a stern and serious nature. Jared considered each carefully and waited as each reviewed a file Agent Kirknan had handed out as they sat down. Finally, an elderly woman at the opposite end of the table spoke.

"Trader Chandler. Is this indeed true that you have made it through with a considerable load of Sha'Luralian grain?"

"It is," Jared said succinctly.

"What is the grade of the cargo?" the woman asked, seemingly impressed by Jared's to-the-point answer.

"I do not consider myself to be an authority on agricultural products, so the purchaser of the cargo will have to determine that for themselves."

"What is the amount and current condition of the shipment?"

"Thirty-five pods, each of which were magnetically sealed by the sellers at the pickup locations prior to our arrival. About twenty-nine days has passed between the time of harvest and our arrival on Kolu-Daln."

The other two meetings also went smoothly except that the Imasra Agricultural Brokerage chose to opt out of the bidding. He wasn't quite sure why but was not really concerned about it. Both the Halidon Conglomerate and the Kulos Agricultural Company had bid well for the grain, but final decisions would not be made for five days when both would send representatives to inspect the shipment. If he were able to sell to either of the two entities, he would make out quite well. Jared stopped by a public vidcomm and placed a call to the hotel room. Shar'ya was happy that he called and said she was dreadfully bored, and that the woman named Valeris had stopped by to say "hi" and find out how she was doing.

"She wanted to know if I wanted to go shopping with her, but you had said not to leave the room, and I still wasn't feeling too good at the time anyway. I didn't let her in, Jared."

"Well, I'll be back soon and then we'll go do something fun."

"Okay," she said, noticeably more cheerful.

After hanging up, he found a ground transport and asked the driver if he knew of a nearby agency that booked trips to the Toru-dal Oasis. He knew an agency that was close by, but didn't know what they offered. Jared figured it was a good enough place to start. Several blocks later, Jared stepped into the Sanersyn Agency and waited for an available agent. The business was small and compact, but quite busy. Once Jared was called to one of the agent's desks, he stated his desire.

"That is not one of the most popular destinations we have, but I have not heard any complaints from those who have taken the trip," said the agent.

"What information do you have about the trip and the company providing the services and transport?"

"Well, flights to and from the Oasis are provided by three local carriers, all of which have class one ratings. The resort at the Oasis is run by the Doman-Tal Company and has been in continuous operation for thirty cycles. Amenities at the Oasis consist of fresh water and mineral hot springs, individual desert-style cabins and native cultural activities."

"Wait a minute, native cultural activities? Kolu-Daln is listed as having no native population."

"That, I'm afraid, is one of the embarrassments the colonists now accept, but don't talk about much," she paused to rub her temple. "The Drakstrad refused to recognize that the native population of this world had a legitimate claim to it and nearly annihilated them. After the fall, a program was started to help them recover and regain much of their land. It was very difficult at first and there was a great deal of mistrust on the part of the natives toward us, but as we proved our determination to help them, they have come to accept us. Though not yet friends, we're not enemies. The lands around the Oasis at Torudal all belong to the Mulu-Daln."

"Wow! Okay, so this is considered a safe area?"

"As long as the guests do not break any of the tribal laws or venture onto tribal ground uninvited, there are no problems. The Mulu-Daln have the right to trial and punishment of any who break those laws."

"Anything else?"

"Here is a brochure that covers everything you can expect to encounter on the trip. You can look it over and get back to me."

"Actually, I think I'll go ahead and book it for two to leave tomorrow if possible."

"Tomorrow?"

"Yes, we only have a limited amount of time, and we'll have to pass if it can't be tomorrow."

"Very well, I will see what I can do. It may take a little time. Where may I contact you when I have the information?"

"We are staying at the Ali'Ran Towers room 2-135-61."

"Very well, I will call as soon as I have an answer either way."

"Thank you."

"Alright Tolbyn, what do you have for me?"

"I had no problem getting my workstation moved to the desired area. Yesterday I spent every moment I could studying the ship and found nothing that indicated how one could get on board."

"That is not an acceptable answer, my friend," Alrios said calmly.

"I cannot access what I cannot see," Tolbyn replied flatly. "The ship has no openings even for engine exhaust, nor are there any apparent openings for seeing in or out. A number of those who saw it land indicated there was a hatch near the front, but I could find no evidence of it. Rumor has it that a cargo of Sha'Lural grain is on board, but there is also no evidence of a cargo hatch."

"What if we must destroy it? Could it be done at the port with minimal damage to the surrounding structures?"

"I don't know. If it were a design I was familiar with, I could tell you to a high degree of accuracy, but the ghost ship is a total unknown."

"Before we make a desperate decision, I would like to follow a few more avenues of possibility." Alrios returned to his seat and rested his chin on his fists. "Tolbyn, please ensure that I am regularly informed about the status of the port authority investigation into this trader's legitimacy."

"I understand. When I left today our operative on Sha'Lural was still preventing any communication from reaching the Governor."

"At least one of the fools on that poor excuse for a colony is doing it right."

"One more thing."

"Yes, Tolbyn?"

"Our surveillance equipment has picked up two voicecomm transmissions from the hotel to the ship and a verbal response back. I suspect there is at least one additional crew member on board."

"The original inspection report indicates only two, but if they did for some reason lie and we can find a way to expose them, then that would give the authority a reason to impound the ship. Do not let any possible chance go uninvestigated, Tolbyn."

"I will not."

"Good." Alrios sat back, satisfied for the moment. "As soon as we are finished here, get back to your assignments and be vigilant. Kalla, what news do you have for me?"

"It would be easier if I did not have so many limitations on how I operate, but under the circumstances all is going well."

"I have many interests and investments in this city and do not intend to have those diminished by things that will be perceived as terror attacks. Also, far less attention will be attracted if the authorities feel it was an accident. This is particularly important now since Tolbyn has found evidence that there may be someone still on board. That individual could bolt with the ship if we do anything rash."

"We may have competition."

"I'm listening, Kalla."

"An old acquaintance of mine is on planet and has already made contact with the subject."

"What kind of contact?"

"I know Valeris quite well and I think she is after both him and the ship. She is a freelance and very close to the High Eminence."

"Indeed."

"She is very proud and independent and has shown at no time in the past any interest in a man. I know first-hand she has found none worthy of her."

"She must have quite a high opinion of herself and her abilities."

"In her mind she is second to none. I think she will try to entice him into her web, and if that's what she is after, she will find a way to discreetly dispose of the female. If she fails to turn him to her way of thinking, which would be to our advantage, then she will kill him, for to spurn Valeris is certain death."

"Can she be trusted?"

"I would not trust her, but she is not likely to go against the wishes of our Eminence."

"Very well, keep an eye on her too. If she solves our problem for us, so much the better." Alrios glanced up and the other three looked toward the door as a knock sounded thrice. "Enter."

"I am sorry for the intrusion." The newcomer paused to catch her breath.

"It is alright Gin'ya, what have you for me?"

"This was just received." The young girl walked to the desk and handed Alrios the coded letter, then exited as quickly as she came.

"Thank you, daughter," Alrios said as the girl pulled the thick door closed.

"Are you totally sure she does not know what transpires within these walls?" Kalla asked sternly.

"Gin'ya has instruction to bring me all coded docs as soon as they arrive." He paused and smiled. "She is a very obedient child." He stopped talking as he ran the document through a converter. The others in the room sat silently and waited. "Ha, I do believe you may get your chance far sooner than expected, and in a way that suits you."

Shar'ya showered Jared with hugs and kisses when he walked in and had many questions about what he had accomplished. He took the time to sit and hold her, answering all the questions he could. More than an em-har later, and after a quick shower, they chose to go to dinner, but buzzing from the voicecomm terminal sounded, indicating an incoming call.

Jared touched the receive button. "Hello."

"Hello, Trader Chandler. I have reservations for you at the Torudal Oasis for the next three days."

"That's great," Jared said as Shar'ya gave a shriek of delight at the news and wrapped her arms around him.

"There is only one hitch. The only flight I could find to get you there leaves in three em-hars from the Zolos Space Port."

"Wow, that's cutting things a bit close."

"The name of the carrier is Wyovan Southern. They are in terminal three and your reservation number is 721-8992. Flight number 23."

"Understood and thank you."

"I thank you for the business, Trader."

The screen went blank and Shar'ya gave Jared a squeeze. "I want to thank you too! Thank you for wanting me."

Jared wasn't quite sure he understood what she was trying to say but gave her a kiss and told her to pack up her things. She sprang to the task, and by the time he finished talking to the front desk, she had the room tidied too. Jared let the desk know that they would be on a tour for the next three nights but would be back by the fourth.

Valeris had listened to their conversation for nearly the entire time, completely bored. As soon as Jared had gone to the shower she decided to, also. She would just happen by and then worm her way into joining them. As long as he did not suspect anything, her plan should work. She stepped out and heard Shar'ya say "I'm ready," and then Jared's "Let's go."

She would take time to get dressed to really arouse him. Besides, it would take them about twenty al-ems to get seated and order. By the time she was ready the twenty al-ems had passed. She headed to the door and saw the blinking light on the listening device recorder and stopped, then continued, not wanting to lose her chance or advantage. She was in no mood for more of the tripe that guren pumped out.

Unable to find them where they had eaten the night before, or in the restaurant Jared had suggested, she became a bit irritated, but after checking all of them in the hotel she was furious. On the way back to her room she bumped into numerous people in her hurry to return and knocked one guest out cold who dared to protest her obnoxious behavior. Upon entering her room, she went directly to the recorder and listened. Fury turned to rage as she realized what had happened, and the bellow she released frightened numerous people in the hall and adjoining rooms.

CHAPTER THIRTEEN

Desert Trap

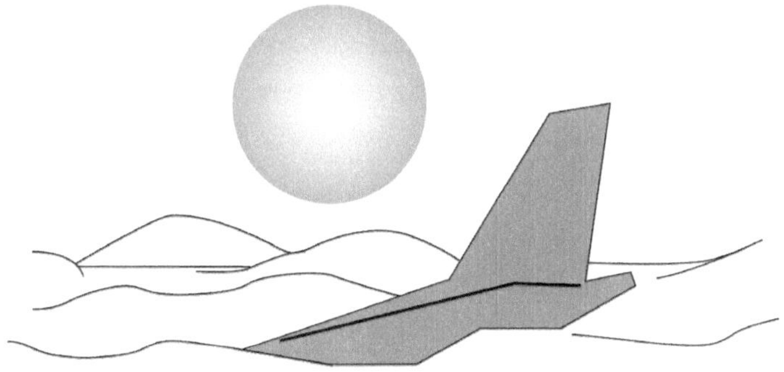

"It was my destiny to be born.
It is also my destiny to die.
What lies in between is entirely of my design.
It matters not how long I live, but how I live."

FLIGHT 23 TO TORUDAL OASIS departed on time. Jared and Shar'ya had arrived at the gate at 1409, just as the main door was being closed. The staff was very friendly despite their hurry to depart. A placard on the seat back in front of Jared listed the aircraft as a Golan-Marik RL-235 mid-range transport. Two variable pitch jet engines with filtered intakes for operation in arid regions gave the vehicle its distinctive sound. Its hull was oval and had several bulbous protrusions near the rear. The wings were smooth and forward swept, mounted well aft, and twin canards jutted from the front. Like its counterparts on the ground, it had long, uninterrupted windows running the length of both sides giving excellent visibility. They had not had time to stop by the Orion before leaving, but Jared had

contacted his friend to tell where they were headed and to come looking if they did not make contact by the end of four days. Shar'ya was a
little disappointed that she was unable to see the land over which they
flew since she were seated over the wing, but like Jared soon fell asleep.

A sharp jolt brought Jared to sudden consciousness, and he sat up
straight, rubbing his stiff neck. Many of the other passengers were
looking around curiously. One stopped a flight attendant and asked
what the bad bump was. She assured the lady it was just rough air
and headed on toward the front. Shortly after the attendant's departure, the aircraft lurched down and to port. She came running back
immediately after and stopped by the intercomm.

"All passengers, please make sure your safety restraints are secure
and do not leave your seats."

Again, the craft lurched, this time to starboard throwing the
unfortunate attendant across the cabin and into the opposite wall.
Many of the passengers began to panic until the remaining attendant
unstrapped and calmed them down. She worked her way forward
until she could check on her co-worker.

Suddenly another female voice came over the comm system and
advised all passengers and crew to prepare for an emergency landing
and to assume crash position. For some strange reason, Jared was not
surprised something like this was happening. Trouble seemed to be
following him ever since he'd left the outpost. Shar'ya was still fast
asleep, and his first thought was to let her be, but changed his mind
and shook her.

"Shar'ya, wake up. Shar'ya!"

"Wha', are we there?"

"No. There is a problem, and it looks as though we are going
to crash." Jared saw fear cross her face, but she said nothing. "Do
you remember what the attendant instructed at the beginning of the
flight?"

Shar'ya nodded vigorously and sat back in her chair, holding Jared's hand tightly. Another jolt surged through the cabin throwing
the craft slightly up, then violently down, followed by an ominous
grinding sound. Moments later the cabin shuddered again, and a
hissing noise filled the room. Jared looked at Shar'ya, whose eyes

were tightly closed. She had a tight grip on his arm. He could not tell how close to the ground they were due to the darkness of the night. The remaining attendant had strapped the motionless form of the senior cabin attendant into her chair and secured the restraints, returning to her own chair just in time to not be tossed about herself.

Despite the violent tremors, the flight crew was doing an amazing job of keeping the aircraft level. Jared could just barely see the leading edge of the main wing as he looked out toward the rear. The airfoil was flexing and twisting far beyond what he figured its designers had ever planned it to withstand. As he gazed rearward, he watched a section of the wing's skin rip away and disappear.

His head smacked against the window when the craft lurched to the left again. Except for a few who were moaning or crying, the passengers were handling the situation quite well. Just as the hissing seemed to reach its climax, the worst jolt of all ran through the length of the craft and a bright flash blossomed momentarily outside and behind Jared's position. A grinding sound like sandpaper on metal could be felt more than heard and then was gone.

Again, the violent impact followed by the grinding. It was then that the air bag inflated, obscuring the view of his surroundings in a soft, tan colored envelope. They suddenly spun sideways to the right and an ear-splitting, metallic groan echoed through the cabin. Jared felt a rush of cool air around his feet and tried to get enough of the bag out of his way to see Shar'ya, but the spinning made it impossible. He guessed they had spun about four times before stopping and came to rest with a final bone-jarring crunch.

The bag deflated as soon as all motion ceased, and Jared pushed it away and then took care of Shar'ya's. He felt a stinging sensation on his forehead and after touching it, realized he had a cut. Shar'ya had a bloody nose and what appeared to be a small amount of blood coming from her left ear. Toward the floor to his left, he could see sand filtering in through a long gash in the side wall next to Shar'ya's seat and he quickly checked her left side. A long, jagged piece of the hull was just a fraction of an inch from her chest and would have penetrated her left breast right to the heart if it had come inward any further. He released her restraints and pulled her out into the aisle. It was then he noticed just how bad the wreck had been.

Further forward, the floor had buckled and many of the seats had been torn from their mounts, piled in twisted heaps of seats and bodies. If the senior attendant had survived the blow she received when thrown about the first time, she had not the second. Except for the hole in the fuselage running from Shar'ya's seat aft, the cabin seemed otherwise intact. Once Jared had checked Shar'ya over, put a bit of tissue in her left nostril and was satisfied she was okay, he began to move about the cabin to assist others. Only seven were conscious when he first began his search. He found the remaining flight attendant and roused her. She glanced about the cabin and upon seeing the forward area began to retch. The door to the cockpit was blocked by the piled-up seats. Jared felt there was no way anyone could have survived up there, but he had to make sure. Puddles of crimson were forming in the low areas of the crumpled deck, and he had to keep his attention elsewhere to keep from joining the young attendant in throwing up. One by one he pulled the seats away and off to one side, trying to ignore the ones still occupied. Forty-three others including Shar'ya were alive, though many not in any condition to move or be moved.

He turned again to get a breath and clear his mind and saw Shar'ya standing several feet away. She had seen death before, but nothing as violent and vividly intense as this. Her face was white, and her mouth clenched tightly shut. Jared walked back and took her in his arms, turning her away from the dreadful sight.

"Do not look that way again," he said gently. "There are many back here who need help. I need you to be strong and do what you can until I find out what happened to the pilots."

"Okay…"

"Can you do that?"

"Yes…"

"Shar'ya?"

"I'm okay. I can do it."

She smiled weakly, squeezed his hand and headed aft, not daring to look back. Jared had thought the transport disaster had been bad, but those who had died had fallen from his sight either to the street below or into the fire. He had not had to face what he was forced to look at here. His hands trembled from the fear he had felt during the descent and impact. His father's words of so long ago came back to mind, "You must not let fear conquer you."

Jared had never thought of himself as a coward, but he had never been so frightened before.

Must not let it conquer me. Could it be that someone is trying to kill me? There are just a few too many mishaps.

The idea that there might be one or more individuals out there wanting his life to end raised the hair on the back of his neck.

Jared had known firsthand that the incident on Sha'Lural had been no accident, but he had not considered himself as the primary target. Destroying the pirate ships at the P3 facility and the two he disabled afterward could have made himself some dangerous enemies. If their reach extended to Kolu-Daln, it might reach even further. Realization of the possible ramifications he now faced and the danger it put Shar'ya in occupied his full attention. His thoughts returned to the task at hand when he heard a faint moan from the other side of the door.

It opened outward easily once all the debris was removed. The cockpit was a mass of twisted wires and broken safety glass. The right side was sheared completely away, and sand was filtering in through the wide opening. On the opposite side, the pilot, who was drifting in and out of consciousness was still strapped securely into her seat and except for some bad cuts and bruising seemed to be intact. To be on the safe side, he examined her neck for bruising or swelling and her skull for soft spots. Finding no sign of a damaged skull or a broken neck he decided to take her into the aft cabin. There was no way she would survive the night exposed to the encroaching dune, regardless of her condition.

There was very little activity in the cabin and most of the survivors seemed to be asleep. Shar'ya sat against the starboard side with a young girl's head in her lap and was holding a damp cloth to the child's forehead. Jared laid the pilot down, covered her with a blanket then moved over to sit by Shar'ya. She rested her head on his shoulder and sighed deeply.

"I'm sorry I got you into this."

"This isn't your fault."

"Maybe not, but you wouldn't be in this fix if you were…"

"What? You mean back on Sha'Lural, living in the sewers?"

"No, I would never have left you there. I just meant without me, because misfortune seems to be following me."

"Well, I had my share of misfortunes in Da'har, and I was all alone there. I think if you've got to have misfortunes, it's much better to have someone to share them with, just as it is to share the times of good fortune."

Those who could move about easily made those less fortunate as comfortable as possible. After a few al-em the pilot briefly regained consciousness. She asked about the passengers and conditions but passed out again before Jared had time to tell her. About half an em-har later she came to again and listened as he told her what she needed to know. A pained look appeared on her face when he indicated the number of passengers who had died. She drifted off again and remained that way until the next morning. Most of those on board were optimistic that rescue parties would find them the following day, so spirits were a little higher among the survivors.

Jared was very curious about had happened. This was the second transport he'd been on which had a so-called 'accident.' A lot of people were dying, and it was very possible he was to blame in an indirect way. By firing on those two pirate ships and interfering at the P3 facility, he may have inadvertently done more damage than he could ever make up for. If he had destroyed the two ships, some of this may have been avoided, but there was no way he could change that now. The fact that the last two he encountered were crewed entirely by women, as most likely were the first three, did not help his conscience at all.

By the middle of the night, most of the survivors were asleep but were awakened a short time later when a violent windstorm kicked up. Sand blowing against the hull as if it were being shot forth from a high-powered sand blaster caused a great deal of concern and fear to many of those in the twisted cabin. The aircraft's right side, which was about ten degrees lower than the left, had been mostly covered by sand at the time of the crash, but the left side had allowed the survivors to at least see the stars. Now, the storm had covered most of the port windows as well and showed little sign of letting up. Jared wanted to ask the pilot about the desert but hadn't had a chance and was about to ask if anyone else in the cabin was familiar with it when he remembered the brochures the travel agent had given him. He retrieved them from the small case he'd carried on board and returned to where Shar'ya lay, trying to sleep.

The information primarily covered the Oasis, and the resort built there, the available activities, services and costs. On the fourth page he found what he was looking for, though it was not as in depth as he had hoped. Lacking in detail as to the dangers, he gleaned enough to realize that rescue might not come as soon as everyone hoped. The southern desert was well known for its turbulent, frequent and unpredictable sandstorms, which on occasion lasted for days at a time. The numerous oases found in the deserts existed only where rock formations kept out the sand. The Torudal resort was built on the largest and most stable of the southern region's oases not claimed by the Mulu-Daln people. A thick series of stone cliffs provided the necessary deterrent to the determined might of the wind-whipped sand.

There were only two known entrances to the Oasis, but they were rarely used because no one traveled to or from Torudal using surface transports. The entrances were only utilized when a guest chose to hunt a kas-lu.

The brochure described the kas-lu as a cunning predator that used the sand for camouflage and seemed to thrive in the desert despite the adverse conditions. Its primary food sources were the Dan'ge-yet and Folasa, both of which also thrived in the harsh desert climes. The Dan'ge-yet and Folasa, both herbivores, survived on the sparse desert vegetation found around rock outcroppings in and near the Oases. A drawing showed an average-sized kas-lu next to a man. It was about the size of an African lion. The kas-lu made great hunting for those up to the task because they could rarely be caught off guard. On several recorded occasions, the hunter and guide had become the hunted. He was happy to discover that the kas-lu was not nocturnal.

Though the predators usually avoided the deep dune areas, the kas-lu could be encountered anywhere in the southern hemisphere except for the higher altitudes of the three major mountain ranges. There were numerous insects, a few of which were equipped with toxic bites or stings, but the kas-lu was the main danger to those foolish enough to venture into the vast wastes of the Great Kolu-Daln desert. From the data in the pamphlet, he calculated that the daytime temperatures could get as high as the equivalent of 120 degrees. This meant that with limited water inside this metal can, partially buried in the sand, the next day might be very unpleasant.

No one else was making any effort to ensure their survival if rescue did not arrive in the morning. For the second time he found himself in a situation he had not been trained for. On Sha'Lural he'd learned he could deal with a bad situation if he had to, but he'd known what to do to escape a fire. With no training, desert survival on Earth would have been bad enough, but on a planet he knew nothing about, it would be nearly impossible. Jared had not felt responsible for the passengers on the Da'har transport, but since he was likely the reason for *this* disaster, he had the fate of everyone left alive hanging on his conscience. During the Da'har incident he'd had little time to think and could not remember if he had felt fear. He'd just acted in response to the circumstances, the desire to live, and been able to help a few others. Now however, he knew he was scared for himself, for the other passengers, and mostly for Shar'ya. It was unlikely this would be over without a good deal more pain and suffering.

Jared tried to sleep but found it impossible. Glancing out the window, only a sliver of glass remained uncovered, but it was enough to let him know that the daystar would soon be up. A faint red-orange glow of light rimmed the distant horizon. He stood and walked to where the surviving cabin attendant sat holding the hand of an injured passenger. The wounded woman, older and with a hint of gray in her hair, had lost her bond-mate in the crash and seemed to have lost the will to live. She was simply and calmly waiting for the end to come.

"Excuse me," Jared said quietly, touching the stewardess on the shoulder.

She jumped slightly at his touch but smiled at him. "Yes?"

"Is there a way to access the cargo compartment from this cabin?"

"Why?"

"There are no guarantees we'll be rescued right away," Jared said as quietly as he could. "The storm last night has almost completely buried us and is still causing a lowering of visibility. We may have also been off course with all the bouncing around we went through. Until the pilot wakes up..." Jared looked in the pilot's direction. "...if she wakes up, we have no way of knowing for sure." When the young woman made no effort to respond he went on. "I, for one, have no intention of sitting around doing nothing."

"What good would going down there do?" she asked angrily.

"Listen to me, I know you're scared, we all are. But I doubt they let you have this job without telling you this kind of thing might happen and giving you training in handling it," Jared whispered sternly. "Or should I write you off as dead now?"

"There is one in the rear, across from the toilet," she snapped. "I doubt the one up front is usable."

"Thank you." As he moved away, he felt a tug on his pants. She was holding onto his cuff.

"I'd still like to know what going down there is going to accomplish?"

"I won't know if it's worth it or not until I see what's down there." He tried to sound optimistic.

"Good morning, Alrios," Kalla said cheerfully as she strolled up to the old man's desk.

"It has been a long while since I have seen such joy in your eyes. All went well I take it?" Alrios responded.

"Of course," she replied, while pulling a chair close to the desk and sitting down.

"Well, go on," he encouraged.

"Immediately after leaving here yesterday, I began to consider the possibilities, and for some reason the challenge of making it look like an accident overcame my normal desire to create a work of—destructive art."

"A departure indeed," he said.

She ignored his comment and continued. "Yet not long afterward

I figured I could accomplish both. Even before they had confirmed reservations, my plan was well under way and would work at any time they chose to take a transport. Once I had the departure time and flight information, my inside people put on the final touches."

"What exactly did you do?" Alrios was deeply curious.

"With several of these small devices, we caused failures in a number of communication, tracking and flight systems," she replied, handing Alrios the innocuous looking little box. "One was placed in the sector traffic control mainframe, which was the most challenging but none the less went smoothly. Its job was to blow circuitry on signal and shut down both comm and data flow to and from air traffic. Another, programmed to alter instead of destroy, was placed in the target aircraft itself to give altered flight data to the crew. A third caused a breakdown in the computer-controlled flight system stabilizers which happens from time to time, but in this case, there was a fourth which disabled the backup systems."

"Won't the boxes be discovered when an investigation is performed?"

"Absolutely not, the outer shell is made of nothing more than stiff paper and the internal circuitry is very fragile. There are two small caplets within, one containing a fluid which, once the unit is used, begins to dissolve. It is activated by the electrical current. Once the caplet is dissolved, it eats through the box and remaining caplet. The second caplet is filled with phosphorous which when exposed to air burns briefly, consuming both the case and circuits. It leaves behind nothing but the appearance of overloaded circuitry. Who cares if they do find traces of the phosphorous, there will be no clue how it came to be there."

"So, what is the current status?" he asked.

"Flight 23 did not arrive at its destination. All sector communications and tracking are still down. Authorities have indicated that the system won't be back up for two more days and search parties have failed to find any trace of the lost transport. It's *sooo very sad* they were so far off course in the *black of night* in such an *inhospitable desert*."

Mock sympathy edged every word.

Jared pushed a box out of the opening then climbed up and sat on the deck to rub his sore shin. He'd found another gash in the fuselage near the front and most of the passenger's baggage seemed to have been dumped or buried by the sand filling the forward section. Fortunately, the aft hold was intact, though bent and twisted. There was no food to be found, but he did find a case of medical supplies which had been bound for Torudal Oasis' medical clinic.

Everybody on board was watching him as he pulled the large box into the middle of the cabin floor. Shar'ya knelt by his side.

He looked up at her and smiled. "Do you know what the stewardess's name is?

"Tre'se."

"Thank you." He glanced around to find her. "Tre…"

Shar'ya put her hand on his shoulder. "I'll get her for you."

Jared had to break the latches to get the case opened. The several med kits that had been in the cabin the previous night had been used quickly. Except for some mild painkillers, no other medicine was available. Within the case, Jared found a treasure of needed items. Bottles of anesthetic, antibiotic and cell stims along with hypodermics, were in good supply. Bandages, tubes of antiseptic cream, suture kits and other tools were also included along with numerous other items Jared could not immediately identify. The only problem was he had no real medical knowledge, and no one else had stepped forward claiming to have any. Each of the bottles of medicine had a max dose warning on them along with other information. He'd begun to read the label on one as Shar'ya and the attendant walked up.

"She said you wanted to see me?"

He motioned to the box. "As you can see, my venture into the lower holds was not a waste of time."

Her eyes widened in surprise and her distant, empty expression vanished. "Med supplies."

"Yes." A hint of criticism in his voice was plain. "Now, I need to know if I can count on your help, or as I said earlier, should I just write you off?"

Shar'ya's eyes raised in surprise at his bluntness and the attendant stepped back as if hit. For a moment the fear of the night before returned but then was replaced by a fierce look of determination.

She glanced around the cabin at the other survivors who were sitting quietly, then back to Jared.

"I don't know how much good I'll be, but I'll do my best."

"That's good enough." Jared said a little prayer that her nerves would hold together. "I need you two to check with everyone on board, even those who are unconscious, and find out if there is somebody with medical training."

"The unconscious?" Tre'se asked.

"Go through their pockets and personal items if you have to."

Shar'ya nodded at him, stood and took Tre'se by the arm. "Let's get to it."

Jared needed information and the pilot was his only source, so he decided to give her an injection of cellstim. On the bottle it indicated it stimulated cell growth and repair at the site of an injury. It also indicated it could be used with most pain suppression medications, so she'd get a dose of pain killer too. She had regained consciousness several times since he had returned from the cargo hold but seemed inundated by the pain and passed out within moments. With the two syringes at half the maximum dosage, he walked over to her and knelt. He had no idea where the best place was to give her the shots. He finally decided to give the cellstim near the site of her worst injury and the anesthetic in her upper arm. Her being unconscious made giving the injections a bit less stressful. He did not know how far to insert the needle and did not wish to know how badly he did.

Holding the first above her arm, he decided he would put the one-inch hypodermic in about half its length. He turned the hypo upside down as he'd seen in movies. He ejected a small amount of the medication. He knew it would be bad if he hit the bone, so he stabbed into the fleshy part of her bicep. The needle went in slightly more than halfway, but the pilot made no sound or movement. With that one out of the way, he moved down to her thigh where the pant leg had been removed to expose the nasty gash running lengthwise just above her knee, easily a half a foot long. Several of the passengers had helped to get it cleaned out, and the bleeding, though bad, had not been severe. The depth of the jagged laceration was about two inches, but at an angle away from the bone.

Jared hadn't noticed before, but the smell inside the aircraft was getting bad. What before had been the smell of many people in a cramped, hot, sweaty room was taking on the nauseating smell of death and decay. He realized that the bodies of the dead would have to be given to the desert before the cabin became a tomb for them all. It would take some time for the drugs to work, so he got back up and began to search for a way to get out. The cockpit wouldn't work because it was the lowest point and had been partially filled with sand the night before. In the aft section near the access to the hold, he found a hatch in the ceiling that led into a small service alcove. Along one side of the alcove were two oxygen tanks and along the other side were a pair of canisters and fittings labeled air filter and circulation pump. Toward the rear of the alcove was another hatch. Jared made his way back to the cabin and looked out the window. A small breeze was blowing, tossing up a little sand now and then but nothing that made venturing out dangerous.

Jared had to fight down a wave of nausea as he turned from the window and spoke to his fellow survivors. "I realize everyone here would rather not think about the dead but even though help might get here soon, we need to get the bodies out. The air in here is already bad, and now that the temperature is rising, it will get worse quickly. I'm going to need help."

"I'll help you," said a tall, slender, fair-haired man with gracefully pointed ears. His left arm was supported in a sling. "I cannot lift much but I'll do what I can."

"Thank you."

"We can help." Jared turned to the couple standing nearby.

A woman who had been silent since the crash said, "I will help."

"Thanks, I found a hatch at the back we can use."

"I think the best thing for us to do is get the bodies into bags or wrappings of some sort. Then unless there is anyone who has a problem with it, Shar'ya and I will climb out while the rest of you hand them out. We'll carefully move them away from the aircraft."

"What about all the blood and... Um... the small...?" asked a woman.

"Once the majority of the remains are removed, we'll bury the remainder under a thick layer of sand. We've already moved out of the forward cabin so filling it in won't be a problem." Another wave of nausea washed over Jared.

Of the surviving passengers, seven were children, all of whom had handled the situation well. There had been some crying the night before, but none had panicked like a few of the adults. It was hearing one throw up that made him realize the necessity for haste.

As Tre'se, the older woman and the injured Ty'lari searched for bags or suitable wrap, the others began the disagreeable job of separating the wreckage and bodies. At first, pulling the broken seats out of the way was easy, but once they reached the mid-point of the pile up it became more and more difficult to separate them.

Each of those helping found it impossible to work for more than a few minutes at a time. None of them had anything left in their stomachs by the time they were through. Trashcan liners and extra blankets were used for the bodies and filled quickly. Survival had taken on a whole new meaning and as the smell grew worse, more of the survivors began to help. A number had suggested abandoning the aircraft, but Jared showed them the pamphlet. Except for the surviving flight attendant, the pilot and five others, all the living passengers were either from off-world or from the northern hemisphere. From what he heard, it seemed that most northerners paid little attention to what occurred in the south nor studied its history.

About halfway through the labor, Jared and the others took a break. He checked on the pilot who seemed to be resting more comfortably. The wound on her leg was not bleeding but still looked bad. He decided to give her another pain shot and one to help prevent infection. The Loru-saltrin was a thicker fluid so he had to be cautious. Fortunately, there were several syringes with thicker needles which made the administering easier, though this time the pilot did groan a little. The wound needed stitching, but no one had any medical experience, and he had little desire to try himself. For the time being it would have to do. Since there was no sign of fever or discoloration at the wound site, he felt confident she was not in any immediate danger.

It took a little more than three em-hars to finish sorting through the mess. Several survivors collapsed in exhaustion and from the foul air. Jared walked aft with Shar'ya as some of the others began to drag the bagged bodies toward the back hatch. Inside the alcove he stopped to take a better look at the air circulation pump. His small amount of training in electronics didn't help much, but he knew enough to know that if there was a way to get the pump and filter working, they would have a better chance at surviving. Before opening the hatch, he walked back into the cabin and prayed someone knew electronics.

"I need to know if anybody knows electronics or about air pump systems?"

"I am a plant technician for the Lanrom Corporation," a female voice said. Jared looked in the voice's direction and saw one of the survivors who had been unconscious all night and most of the day. Her leg was splinted, and she had a nasty bruise on the left side of her face. "Electronics is not my strong point, but I have some training. I work with refrigeration units but might be able to help you with the air pumps."

"From what I can tell they are in good condition, so all we need to do is find a way to get them running," Jared tried to sound encouraging.

"If you can get me in there, I'll take a look at it."

"We'll do that, but right now we need to get these bodies out. What we can't move, we'll cover up as soon as possible." Jared turned and headed back to the rear as he finished talking, and those who could followed him.

The hatch, like all others on the aircraft, opened inward. One of the men by the name of Fallo stood nearby with a heavy support bracket, broken during the crash, just in case any unwanted creatures might drop in when Jared opened the hatch. After a few moments of sitting silently and listening, Jared took hold of the latch, twisted to the right and pulled. As it lowered, a considerable amount of sand cascaded in, but nothing else. The hot, mid-day air caught him off guard and his head spun. At least it wasn't as hot inside the cabin for the time being. Jared cautiously peered out then slowly climbed the ladder, half expecting to be jumped by one of the predatory kas-lu.

However, other than a little wind-blown sand that tossed about his head, the area was clear and quiet. Despite the heat, he took in a deep breath of clean air, then helped Shar'ya out.

Dunes were all he could see and except for the tail structure, aft half of the fuselage and the tip of the port wing some distance forward, the rest of the transport was buried below tons of sand. Jared heard a clunk behind him and turned around. Fallo climbed out of the opening.

"Thas' better," the burly man grunted.

"Perhaps you'd better stay out here and help. Keep an eye out for trouble."

"Sounds fine ta' me…"

"Shar'ya, you can help me move the bodies. We'll put them over there about fifty ost out." Jared pointed off to the right where the wing was buried. He bent down over the opening and asked those standing below to start handing out the bundled corpses. One by one the dead were lifted out and set aside. It didn't take long for both Shar'ya and Jared to be sweat-soaked and even Fallo, just standing around, was having a difficult time with the heat. After the fifteenth bag, Jared told those below to take a break and to bring them some water. Tre'se climbed up with three cups and a small container.

At Jared's suggestion, Tre'se went below and began bringing up a couple others at a time so they could get some good air. By the time all the bags were up, everyone who could walk or be moved had been outside. Jared had originally felt that having a lot of the survivors outside at once was a bad idea due to the possibility of a kas-lu attack. The brochure however had indicated that they were usually found around rock formations inhabited by the desert herbivores, but no rocky outcroppings were within visible range.

Jared now had to hurry to get relief to the injured before they died from the putrid air. He enlisted the help of Fallo and one other man to move the bags away from the wreck. Several others began transporting sand to the forward area of the cabin using the empty med supply case and other various containers. Not one sign of animal life was seen the entire time they were out on the dunes. With the worst of the task completed, everyone helped finish the forward area burial.

Late afternoon brought a slight fall in the temperature and as the last of the sand was spread, many collapsed into exhausted sleep. Jared returned to the refrigeration technician and carried her back to the equipment alcove. Though tired himself, he wanted to get as much accomplished as he could, as quickly as possible. He had no idea why he felt the need to hurry when the rest of the survivors seemed content to wait for rescuers. He was grateful they had been cooperative so far.

"So, what's your name?" Jared asked as he walked through the small access door to the alcove.

"Lee'ra," she replied.

"Well, Lee'ra, I hope you can fix the air flow system."

"As do I, I don't want to spend any more time than necessary breathing this foul air."

"What do we do if it can't be fixed?" Shar'ya asked from a few paces behind.

"Pray somebody finds us soon." Jared set Lee'ra down on the med case. "Not the best chair, but it should give you good access without having to move much."

"Thank you."

"Jared?"

He turned to see Shar'ya who motioned to Tre'se. She had just walked up to the alcove entry. Her expression was one of deep anxiety.

"I thought you might like to know that the pilot has regained consciousness."

"Great." Jared's spirits brightened. "Lee'ra, you're on your own for a while, I need to talk to the pilot."

"Okay."

"There is one more thing," said Tre'se.

"Bad news I take it," Jared responded, not very surprised. "Let's have it."

"One of the two water tanks was nearly empty. It had a leak I didn't know about until I opened one of the cabinets next to where they are located. I put the little bit left in a service pouch. The other one has twelve and a half qyels remaining."

Jared wasn't sure how much twelve qyels was compared to a gallon or liter, but doubted it was enough to last for very long. He could wait for Orion to come looking in three more days, but even if the water could be rationed that long, many of the more seriously injured would not last; not to mention that one or two more sandstorms would likely bury the wreck under a considerable layer of sand.

Conditions within the cabin were nearly suffocating as the daystar set and many of those who had earlier anticipated quick rescue began to have doubts. Jared knelt by the pilot who opened her eyes.

Shar'ya was helping Tre'se in the galley trying to fix what rations had survived the crash. He was very proud of how she had handled herself and considered himself fortunate to have her as both mate and friend. He turned his attention to the pilot and gave her a reassuring smile.

"I can give you something for the pain if you need it."

She stuttered. "I'm...fine, but I...could...use some water."

Jared asked Fallo to get a half-full cup of water from Tre'se for the pilot. Once she had consumed about half the cup's contents, he set it aside and looked into her eyes. "I know you're not feeling well, but we're in a bad situation and I need information to be able to make some decisions."

She nodded. "Ask, I'll answer what I can."

"Were we off course when we crashed, and if so, how far off?"

"I believe...we were off course...but by how far I can't...be sure. We lost comm...about twenty al-ems before the systems started going haywire. If Jaln hadn't had a portable compass...I wouldn't have known anything...was wrong with the onboard unit."

She seemed to be having trouble breathing but continued. "It wasn't 'til after the flight systems...started to fail he thought of checking it. By then, and with comm out...we knew things were really bad."

"In what direction were we off? And in which direction would the oasis be?"

"West, and my best guess would be SSE to the oasis."

"Any idea what caused the crash?"

"No, we occasionally have system problems...but the back-ups usually pick up the slack. This time it was as if we...had none. We lost comm, control surface stabilizers...directional indication and satellite tracking, all within a span...of twenty al-ems."

"What is satellite tracking for?"

"Unlike the simple directional indicator...it allows us to see a three...dimensional area display of our position. It also functions as the emergency locator beacon transmitter in such emergencies."

"But it wasn't working, was it?"

"No."

"So, we're off course, nearly buried by the sand, with no way to tell anyone where we are?"

"Yes."

"I'm sure your world has other satellites in orbit that could locate us."

"Oh, there are satellites of course, but the system at Port Zolos is interconnected with all the other sectors and port traffic controls. Unfortunately, it does breakdown from time to time and the entire network is offline until repairs are made. It is possible that the system's down, otherwise I believe we'd have been found by now. It has been worse than usual because of the pirates activity."

Jared sat back and began to consider the options when a blast of cool air hit his face, and a cheer went up throughout the cabin. The faint sound of whirling fans could be heard. As newer, fresh air filtered in, the old was drawn out and a bit of renewed hope seemed to settle on everyone. He got up wearily and walked to the back, to see why the air was cool. Upon entering the alcove Lee'ra smiled at him.

"I'm impressed," he said as he walked in. "Not only fresh, but cool."

"That's because I stripped the tubing from the oxygen tanks and connected the pumps through the air conditioning system. The coolant generator is that small unit on the bulkhead there." She indicated a small, rectangular box behind the air pump unit.

"Obviously the battery works, but do you have any idea how long it will last?" he asked.

"No. So, I suggest that it only be on long enough to refresh and cool the air then shut down until it is really needed. The outer vents will also have to be kept clear because, if they get covered, we won't be pulling in anything but sand."

"Okay, I'm going to leave that to you. When you feel the air quality or temperature require it, you can ask someone to turn it on, then off when it's done its job. I need you to do it because you are familiar with such things, and I've got enough to worry about. Second, after listening to the pilot, I believe if everyone who's alive now is going to make it, someone is going to have to go find help."

"You?" she asked.

"I"m not too fond of the idea, so if you know anyone else you figure has a chance, let me know," he replied.

"I know none of them but doubt any would volunteer. I think most, if not all, believe help will come anytime."

"So, you'll look after this?" he asked.

"I'll keep it going as long as I can."

"Alright, if you'll show me how to operate it, I'll make sure I show someone else how before I leave. That way you won't have to be moved each time it needs to be turned on."

After Lee'ra showed him how to work it, he carried her back to the cabin, then found Shar'ya and hugged her. She smiled at him and whispered it was time to rest. Most of the seats had been removed from their mounts by others wanting more room to stretch out. Jared grabbed a couple of cushions from some of the discarded seats and made a place to lie down. Darkness had fallen and he was shaking from fatigue. Shar'ya too was showing signs of exhaustion and made no complaint as she curled up in his arms. However, just as he got comfortable Lee'ra spoke from across the room.

"Now is a good time to turn it off."

"Kalla, what is the chance of them finding the wreck today?"

She laughed. "Most unlikely. Both the satellite and traffic control systems are down. The search teams have no idea whether the flight was on course or not, and last night there was a severe sandstorm in that area. Another moderate storm hit the area east of the route this morning."

"How did you manage to shut down the satellite system?" asked Alrios.

"That, I'm afraid, was none of my doing. Just sort of a lucky coincidence."

"Luck or design, it matters not. What is important is that we have succeeded," Alrios droned.

Kalla stood. "We may well have, but I shall keep track of all rescue efforts just to make sure. Luck is not exclusively ours."

"I've no doubt you'll do what is required." Alrios rose to bid her farewell when a knock sounded at the office door. "Enter."

The door opened and Alrios' daughter stepped in. "The man named Rehad is here."

"Please see him in." Alrios turned to Kalla. "You picked a propitious moment to leave, if only I could also."

"I believe I'll stay," Kalla smiled at the older man who looked at her as if she were crazy. Only a moment after she stopped speaking, the office door opened and Rehad stepped in. Kalla moved away from the desk and took a seat on the couch. He glanced at her menacingly as he walked past, but she ignored him. Alrios sat back down as Rehad leaned forward and rested his massive fists on the desktop.

"Good morning, Rehad," Alrios said in a manner both men knew did not portray the true feelings between them.

"Spare the pleasantries, Alrios. I know the transport crashed and they can't find it, but are the Trader and his female dead?"

"If they survived the crash itself, the desert would do the rest."

"That did not answer my question," Rehad growled.

"We are closely monitoring the situation, but if it's proof you wish, you can get a guide to take you out there and find out for yourself," Alrios said with tense but controlled anger.

"Finish the task, old man. Those above us have little patience and I'm sure you understand the price of failure. Take a good lesson from the tragedy on Sha'Lural."

Jared awoke and quickly moved backward sweeping his hand across his face. As he realized it was only Shar'ya's hair, he relaxed and lay back down. A dream of being caught in an enormous web created by some unknown creature faded quickly from memory. If it was true that the crash was caused by someone after his life, then it also made sense they would try to prevent him, and therefore all the other survivors, from being rescued. He could stay and wait for Orion but if another heavy sandstorm came up, the aircraft would be buried, and it wouldn't take long for those inside to suffocate.

Next time, if we go anywhere, it will either be with Orion, or at least within comm range.

Some of the more severely wounded might not be able to hold out for another two days without better medical help and he already felt guilty enough.

There is no choice. I have to take the chance and try to reach Toru-dal on foot.

Air quality was becoming noticeably unpleasant again, so he got up and walked aft. Following the instructions Lee'ra had given him, he started the air pumps. He turned around and found Shar'ya standing in the doorway.

"You're up early," he said.

"Uh huh," her expression one of alarm. "You're going to leave, aren't you?"

Jared raised his eyebrows and pulled her toward him. "I have to. I doubt any rescue is going to come soon and even two more days may mean death for everyone here."

"I can't go with you, can I?"

"Look at them." Jared turned her so she could see the survivors. "There isn't one who knows how to function in a situation like this. They are like I was before I found myself suddenly torn from my world; comfortable and *never* believing something like this could happen to me. I'm not sure I would have responded much differently if this had taken place on my world before I left it. I don't like the idea of venturing out into that desert, but I don't have much choice. I need you to stay behind, not because I don't want you with me, but I feel it's the only way they have a chance of surviving."

"I don't understand, what can I do for them?"

"It's not really what you can do for them, but what you can help them avoid."

Shar'ya cocked her head slightly and an expression of bewilderment came over her face. "Uh?"

"Several things could happen at any time that could cause them to panic or try something stupid and I need you to be strong to help keep them calm. There needs to be one person here who can think rationally when things get bad. You survived on Sha'Lural by yourself, for the most part, and I believe you can do this."

Jared watched the expression on her face turn to sad acceptance. "Here's the wrist comm." He handed her the watch-like device. "If for some reason something happens to me, Orion will be able to find you."

"I don't know how to talk to Orion."

"We...you have plenty to worry about for now. Concern over what will happen beyond today will have to wait."

"I will do as you ask."

Jared saw a vulnerable young woman standing before him. Her shoulders slightly slumped from obvious concern and fear, but he could also see a fire burning in her green eyes. A fire of courage and will, which he somehow knew far exceeded his own. He knew she would be safer staying with the broken ship and the other survivors. He held her tenderly for a moment before leaving.

Only a hint of deep blue on the distant horizon revealed that night was ending as Jared began his trek. Though cool, the temperature was comfortable, and he moved as rapidly as he could in the shifting sand. Jared had never ventured into a desert on Earth. There had been one trip through the Mojave on vacation with his family to Southern California. He had only seen dunes like these in pictures and had never had any real desire to experience the arid wastes of his home world firsthand. He was thankful he had decided to go through the luggage in the hold. He'd found the boots he was now wearing, and they made walking far more pleasant than his own shoes would have.

His heading of SSE carried him toward the rising sun and hopefully the Torudal oasis. Jared had no idea how far he had actually traveled by the time the daystar first broke the horizon, but felt his progress was good. His decision to start while it was still dark was to reduce the chance of coming across a kas-lu. If he avoided the habitat of the predator's food supply, he might have a chance of making it to Torudal without seeing one. That, however, meant staying in the open dunes and if a sandstorm cropped up, he would have nowhere to take cover from it.

It was almost funny. Here he was on another alien planet, billions of miles from his home, and things simply weren't all that different.

It didn't take long for the temperature to rise once the daystar broke the horizon, and Jared soon found it difficult to keep his rapid pace. By the end of the third em-har he was wet from perspiration and his legs ached from trudging through the deep sand. He kept the wide-brimmed shata hat on his head out of necessity, but he'd always disliked hats. He'd never found them very comfortable, and they were particularly irritating during hot weather. Except for the water pouch, a package of food, a blanket, a small, lightweight telescoping walking stick, and the oddly forged knife the Ty'lari had given him, he'd brought nothing else. He took the knife out of its sheath and studied its smooth graceful curves. The crimson hued blade shimmered in the bright light, its smooth surface mirroring the surrounding sand and dunes. A few delicate etchings wound around the crossguard and across the base of the blade looking like interconnected runes. The grip fit his hand comfortably. What its core consisted of he did not know, but it was covered by woven bands of leather dyed to a deep red brown and topped off by a gold pommel more intricately carved than the crossguard.

As the daystar neared its zenith, he found a long flat stretch of sand, propped the blanket up for some shade and waited out the hottest part of the day. He had learned enough about deserts to know that water was the most important item he carried and at first had just taken little sips. Once the full light of day brought the high heat, he began to take larger swallows to keep from feeling faint. By the time he stopped to rest the pouch was only a little over half full. He had to save as much as possible, so he decided to wait for dark and cooler temperatures. Sleep overcame him quickly in spite of the uncomfortable conditions.

Jared woke to sand blowing across his face. The daystar, hanging low in the western sky, revealed he'd slept for three, maybe four em-hars. Though hot, the breeze felt good on his face and provided significant cooling as it blew through his damp hair. He removed and opened one of the little foil-wrapped food packs from his small knapsack. The bar was like granola with small, dried fruit mixed in, giving it a tart flavor. He'd brought enough to have two at each meal. Also in the knapsack were several pouches of the nut-like Anak and six biscuits. After eating and drinking a small amount of his precious water, he stood and packed his blanket away, and then he shook the sand out of his clothes and boots.

He trudged on maintaining his SSE heading. It had been relatively easy so far as the dunes presented no obstacles, but he intended to keep walking after dark and though that might keep him safe from the kas-lu, it would make staying on course more difficult. He would try using the stars to navigate if he could find a recognizable cluster he could easily find again. One dune after another came and went and he found himself remembering his first view of space. It had been new and interesting at first but had become the same monotonous thing day after day, and the desert quickly became the same.

To improve his spirits, he thought of Shar'ya and was briefly content, but it changed to concern when his thoughts turned to where she was. He tried to think of home but was unable to recall a great deal that made him happy. He wished to see his mom and dad again and his nephews, but aside from that, the world of his birth no longer held sway with him. In an odd, twisted way, he much preferred where he was, even with someone out to kill him. Jared had never considered himself to be the adventurous sort and was quite content, before leaving home, to live a mostly quiet life. He hadn't considered it sedate back then and neither had his parents. His love of motorbikes and cars had on numerous occasions given his mother great concern.

A broken leg and collarbone from a bad landing in a motocross race had not ended his enthusiasm for the sport, but her sad, worried eyes had drawn a promise from him that he would not continue. It wasn't all that bad since he still had mountain biking and skiing to keep him busy. His decision to try and get a class B auto racing license had come only days before he left Earth. When he told his family what he was planning, particularly considering his mother's likely response, it made him feel like disappearing, and that is exactly what happened.

A short time later, the slope in the dune he was climbing steepened making him slide back more than he had hitherto. As he neared the crest the sand sluffed away revealing rock. He had to struggle to get over the lip of the stone. He lay on his stomach for a time catching his breath. He rolled to his side, sat up, and gazed back the way he had come. Nothing but sand stretched into the deepening dusk and the daystar hung, deep orange, on the distant horizon as if it and the planet were gently kissing.

Jared lifted his feet and swung around. He gazed in amazement at what lay beyond. A massive stone-rimmed depression extended out, forming a roughly oval shaped canyon surrounded by high rocky walls. The far end, which was almost hidden from view in the dwindling light, was at least a mile away, if not more. He got up and walked on the flat stone. It was a welcome relief from the maddening, sinking feeling of the sand. A short time later the rock dropped off very steeply and he found himself gazing down into an incredible sight.

He glanced back the way he had come and realized he was standing atop an immense wall which kept the sand at bay. He had been able to climb to its apex because the unrelenting wind constantly drove the sand higher and higher until it came close to cresting the sentinel wall. Below lay a pool of shimmering water with a glow of its own. Various hues of green, blue and purple shifted in the fading light of day. The pool was fed by an intermittent geyser jetting out at a steep angle from a higher adjacent ledge.

For a time he surveyed the scene trying to make out any movement but detected none and began to look for a way down. After some searching, he found a place on the inner wall with a narrow, but useable ledge. He dropped onto his stomach then let himself down, trying to maintain a comfortable hold while doing so. His grip failed and he dropped only a few inches before his feet found the firm surface. After managing to turn around he scanned for another protrusion of rock. A larger ledge below would be less precarious but was going to be a substantial drop.

Here, small grains of sand that had made it over the outer wall made lowering himself more difficult and once sitting with his legs dangling over the side, he brushed away what sand he could. With that accomplished and a few moments to gather his wits, he twisted his torso while sliding off. He managed to get turned around as he dropped but had only a brief moment to hold the ledge before his fingers slipped and he landed hard. He stood and rubbed his shoulder which had impacted when he fell to his left. He realized he was lucky not to have sprained his foot or worse, broken a leg.

The brochure about the resort oasis had shown several images of both the structures and surrounding landscape. This was nowhere near as large or as open as Torudal. The pool, still a good distance below, continued to shift colors particularly when the vent sprayed forth. It was cooler here and the sound the geyser made was loud. Jared dropped down to another terrace which was wide and cut back into the rock enough that it would offer sufficient cover if it were to rain.

I wonder if it ever rains here.

He had seen no sign of precipitation since he had set out.

From this vantage point he could see that the pool not only had the geyser feeding it, but at one point to his left the water spilled over a natural rock dam, ran a short distance then disappeared back into a long narrow crevice. Blossoms of lavender, red, yellow and white were everywhere. Flowers which had initially been in full bloom were now closing, folding up into various shaped bulbs. The glow from the water remained, bathing the immediate vicinity with a fairytale vibe.

He surveyed the landscape, knowing full well this would be a likely place to encounter a predator, but there was still no movement in any direction. Growing thirst drew his attention back to the pool and he dropped down to another terrace. He could see a gentle current in the rippling hues and for the first time could see the source of the light. Crystals of varying size and color imbedded in the pool's floor seemed to pulsate slightly. Jared hopped down six more levels and knelt. Tentatively touching the surface, he found it quite cool. He rubbed the fluid between his fingers and feeling nothing odd or threatening he touched his lips.

"Well, it is flowing after all so no reason *not* to be fresh," he said under his breath, trying to belay the anxiety he felt. With a sharp inhale he cupped his hands and drank deeply. He was surprised to instantly feel the fatigue in his body fade and then noticed tiny shapes moving about in the water. A thread of anxiety surged again, "Great, parasites." To get a better view he lowered his head to within inches of the water and noted that the particles had the appearance of minute snowflakes that used the outermost filaments to move.

I wonder how many of those I swallowed.

That last thought made him realize he was fully out of his element. Scooping up another handful of water, he studied it closely and did indeed see numerous tiny swimming snowstars, as he chose to call them, darting about. Carefully he dipped his hand back in letting the miniature lifeforms return to their habitat. With some effort he stood and worked his way around the pool until he was below the vent for the geyser. Climbing up to the terrace directly below the vent took some effort, but as he climbed onto the terrace the geyser burst forth.

The sound was intense and spray from the torrent hit him. It was extremely cold and in several places depressions in the terrace's uneven surface held clear water devoid of the snowstars. Eagerly, he scooped up handfuls of the refreshing water. Once satisfied he filled his water pouch and moved back down to the main pool. His clothes were full of offending sand and dried sweat from the day's trek. He decided the snowstars were not a threat and chose to bathe. He dropped into the cool water and to his relief the tiny creatures surrounding him gave way. The pool was only waist deep so he had to sit down and drop back on his elbows to get completely wet. He closed his eyes and exhaled tiredly. A moment later he felt what he could only describe as a faint electrical current course through his entire being. The ache in his shoulder faded and it took considerable effort not to fall asleep. With only his face above water, it was as if the temperature of the surrounding fluid became neutral, neither hot nor cold.

He suddenly felt thousands of pleasant prickles on his skin. When he raised his head further above the surface the sensation stopped.

He looked down at his legs. A cloudy mass surged away from his body and in a short distance dispersed into the now familiar tiny snowstars. Jared stood and realized he no longer felt fatigue, aches, thirst or hunger. He knelt by the water's edge, placed the palm of his hand to the surface and not knowing why, expressed his gratitude, "Thank you."

The daystar was now below the edge of the oasis' outer wall and Jared knew it would soon be dark. The sky, though still slightly illuminated, left the majority of the oasis in deep shadow. The thought of sleeping had only a few al-em ago been heavy on his mind, but with the renewed vigor he received from his recent dip in the pool, he chose to press on.

As he began dressing, he heard a noise. Because the geyser was so loud, he couldn't be sure what it was and chose to momentarily ignore it. Then the sound came again and this time he was certain it was the cry of a human voice. He quickly put his shirt on, gathered his belongings, and began to climb from one terrace to the next. He wanted to be on high ground; he had no desire to be at a disadvantage if there was a threat ahead. He proceeded cautiously, stopping frequently to get his bearings and searching for any movement. Twice more the cries came, each louder than before, so he knew he was getting close.

Another call rang out of the rock in front of and slightly below him. He dropped to his stomach, creeped to the edge of the terrace, and peered down. Since leaving the geyser fed pool the two sides of the rocky terraces had narrowed to form a canyon. Being higher, he noted that this canyon was one of many that fanned out from the small shallow pond. Two things caught his attention, and one made his breath catch in his throat.

Directly below was a narrow ledge which looked like it had been one of the abundant terraces that permeated the oasis. Its outer edge was jagged as opposed to others. Toward the back of the ledge was a fairly deep fissure in which a small boy, with sun kissed skin and long dark hair held back in a tail, had taken refuge. Again, he called out.

"Ta'lano, Kala Uni"

On a broad terrace just below the boy prowled a catlike creature with six legs, narrow head and tall tufted ears about the size of an African lion.

A kas'lu.

Jared closed his eyes, grimacing. The desert predator paced silently in lazy circles occasionally glancing upward. Darkness had settled and yet it was not too difficult to see. He took a moment to look around and noted that at places in the otherwise gray-black rock there were deposits of crystal which glowed, bathing the canyon in an eerie twilight. Jared leaned out over the edge again so his head would be visible to the boy. "Hey," he said, trying not to alert the beast.

The boy obviously didn't hear so Jared grunted again a bit louder, picked up a rock and heaved. Both the kas'lu and the boy looked up. From one came wide eyed relief and the other, a roar that could curdle blood. Without warning the beast leaped upward, its fore-claws scraping loudly on the edge of the ledge before falling back down. Jared noted that the way the ledge the boy was on had been etched out of the rock, there was no way for the predator to reach it from the sides. It also didn't have a sufficient leap to access it from below. Jared hoped the beast wasn't clever enough to try from above, though that would be a challenge for any predator because of the overhang.

Silence was gone as the beast was now eliciting deep, chesty growls. Its eyes glowed yellow in the crystalline light. Its fur was amber yellow with no mane so Jared assumed it might be female, though that mattered little. Its legs, muscular and long indicated it was made for pursuit. The most telling and frightening thing was the long scythe like claws that slipped in and out of the forepaws as it paced.

Jared pushed away from the edge and groaned.

Don't I have enough to worry about, enough lives on my conscience?

He looked toward the stars and shook his head.

My cup runneth over. I'm standing hip deep in hot water and someone keeps adding fuel to the fire.

He pondered his fate a moment longer.

The boy seemed to realize there was no way to reach Jared, so he held his spear by the head and extended the shaft upward. As Jared reached down the predator leapt again, claws scraping on the stone then fell with a howl. It appeared that the beast, though able to twist its body like an Earth feline, had landed on a chunk of stone that bit into its hip. It snarled in pain and limped off a short distance.

The ledge Jared was balanced on fell away, and he heard a sharp snap when his hand clamped onto the black spear's shaft.

He tried in vain to get a hold on the terrace immediately below but missed and crashed into a short husk of a tree. The old dead wood gave way but slowed Jared's fall significantly. He sustained no serious injury but knew he would be bruised the following day. He stood and pulled a sliver of the wood from his already tattered shirt and was surprised to find it soft and easily crushable. He tossed the debris away and gazed at the Kas'lu which was now staring at him.

Jared was amazed, he wasn't running from the creature. He felt the urge to do so but remained steadfast.

Is it because I do have some inner courage I never knew? or simply because I've seen a few too many nature docs about bears and such?

He stared at the feline creature wondering why it hadn't attacked. It was standing still, subtly swaying back and forth, as if it were studying something unfamiliar. He tightened his grip on the spear's shaft, then he crouched and moved to his left with only the slightest step forward.

The kas'lu did likewise to its left, its yellow eyes fixed on its new prey. With each breath it's growls were now deeper. Jared knew that one mistake would be fatal. If he hadn't had the spear, he might have reconsidered his choice to face the animal but also knew that would end the same way as making an error.

"Come on, damn you." Jared said loudly and the kas'lu's head cocked to one side. Jared snorted with a half grin, "Haven't had anyone try to start a conversation with you before, huh?"

Jared was tired in spite of his time in the water. He knew he would have to end this quickly if he was to stand any chance at all. The standoff lasted far too long for Jared's nerves. Keeping his eyes focused on his adversary, he moved his arms, getting a feel for the spear and noted it was light and well-balanced. As Jared's thoughts briefly returned to the boy on the ledge above and behind, he watched the feline's head drop. His hands were shaking.

Here it comes. I hope I don't look too ungraceful in this dance with death.

The attack came as expected. The kas'lu lunged high, aiming for Jared's upper torso, left paw outstretched. The other paw held further back, slightly twisted as if preparing for a sideways slashing strike.

Jared found himself frozen for a fraction of a second.

Forward, spear up, drop back.

The words were in his head, but they were not his and he acted as if on instinct. He darted forward, raised the spear then let himself fall as if he were sliding into home base in a baseball game. The kas'lu sailed over him, clawed forelimbs flailing down trying to salvage the attack. Pain flared in his right hip as it met with stone, but again the voice came.

Rise and face.

Before his momentum had ceased Jared complied.

Pushing himself erect, Jared spun to see the predator doing likewise. Once again it stood, swaying in unison with its rumbling growls. When Jared saw its head lower, he braced. This time there was no leap. The beast surged forth so quickly Jared felt fear swell. Its heavily padded feet were almost noiseless on the black stone floor.

Sidestep, twist, thrust.

Again, Jared followed the still small voice, his right foot angling out of the creature's line of travel. Once done he twisted his torso and thrust the spear with all the strength his arms possessed.

The roar that met his ears was deafening. Unlike the deep throated growls only moments before, this one was shrill, full of agony. Jared quickly stood and faced the wounded beast as it slowly turned and limped to face him. Another rumbling growl issued forth through bared teeth. Its body visibly vibrated as the verbal tremors continued. With another dip in the position of its head and narrowing eyes it charged, maw open. Panic filled Jared as the voice within didn't immediately give aid. Only an instant before the animal would be upon him, he heard it.

Kneel, set shaft, endure.

The kas'lu ran head long into the spear, which penetrated deeply into the predator's chest, slightly off toward the right shoulder. With a deep inhale Jared stood and regarded the creature. It lay on its left side, chest rising and falling raggedly. After a moment Jared took a step toward it then stopped as the kas'lu's head rose, eyes bright with rage, locking onto him. With a burst of strength it slapped at the spear, dislodging it then struggled to its feet. Jared gritted his teeth as he backpedaled a pace. Blood billowed from the creature's wound and pooled on the dark stone.

Remembering the Ty'lari knife he had been given, Jared withdrew it and held it out menacingly. The feline opened its maw, trying to elicit a challenge, but managed only a gurgling sputter before its legs collapsed beneath it and fell with a dull thud. Exhausted, Jared dropped to his knees. He felt a sting on his side and glanced down to see blood running from his own wounds. He collapsed into a heap, breathing heavily, eyes closing out the dim light of the surrounding crystals. A few moments later the sound of several voices drew his eyes open again.

A number of adults with skin similar to the boy's now stood not too far from where Jared lay. His gaze shifted as the boy dropped from the ledge above to the gathered adults. A spear similar to the one he'd used to kill the Kas'lu was held by each member of the party and the crystal tips glowed brightly, bathing the surround in light.

Jared sat up, wincing at the pain in his side and aching at his hip. After briefly looking over himself, he turned his attention to the natives. The young boy was talking in a language he did not know.

"I have chosen poorly," said the boy.

"Perhaps, but your father is proud," said one of the males.

"I entered but failed to exercise caution." The boy was excited and speaking very fast. "I climbed as high as I could after hearing the roar of the beast," he pointed up to where he had sought safety. "Seeing it made me realize my rashness of choice."

The same adult male put his hand on the boy's shoulder, "Continue."

"The kas-lu entered there, growling loudly," the boy went on. "Circling below, it found my scent, but I hid above. When it did finally see me, it began to leap trying to get me." He acted out the leaping of the predator.

"It was wise of you not to attempt to slay it yourself, Uli. You have not yet the weight and size for such a task," said a woman.

The leader forestalled the woman and said again, "Continue."

"A huge rock flew over my head and hit on the far side and the beast looked away. Then I saw him." The boy pointed at Jared.

The leader's eyes followed the boy's aim and regarded the trespasser with curiosity rather than the usual anger and distrust for someone not of desert blood. It was obvious in the outsider's eyes that he was unsure and weary. A moment later his gaze returned to Uli who went on with zest.

"He tried to help me up to a higher ledge, but it broke away and he fell all the way down."

To this, a low murmur ran through those assembled.

"He stood and faced the kas-lu with nothing more than his knife, but I gave him Onruot's spear. The beast did not attack at first because the man didn't back away. I could see confusion in the kas-lu's eyes. They both waited for many rumal before the beast lost the trial of patience and attacked."

The excitement on the boy's face was tense as he described the conflict. At the point in the tale where the beast attacked the second time, the man held up his hand.

"Stop," he gave the boy a slight smile. "We saw everything else that transpired." He spoke to another man, "Talba, could you identify the carcass?"

"Yes, it is indeed the great bull, Tasnaklet."

"Uli." The leader spoke to the boy.

"Yes," the youth responded respectfully.

"Your grandfather has been avenged. The beast you saw die is the one responsible for his death and many others."

The entire group of natives turned to face Jared.

"What is the status on the white ship, Kalla?" Alrios asked the tall woman.

"Nothing has changed," she responded dryly. "No one has been able to find a way into the strange vessel and the port authority will not impound it until proof of death is presented or the time of forfeit has been reached."

"Time of forfeit, pah," Alrios spat. "I have no intention of waiting three mon to get my hands on that ship. I'd be hounded the entire time by Rehad or other members of the Droma."

"The price of..."

"Oh, shut up. I want that ship and soon, so do whatever is necessary to acquire it."

"Whatever is necessary?" Kalla was taken aback by Alrios' intensity.

"You heard me."

"I did, but you giving me such total freedom is not common."

"Listen, woman, I am tired of this entire affair and wish to see it ended. You are quite aware of my wishes, so do what is necessary. Try to use some of the common sense you possess but seldom utilize."

"As you wish." Kalla rolled her eyes. "Is there anything else?"

"Of course," he sneered. "Status on the search?"

"No change either. The aircraft has not been found, so death cannot be confirmed. Another sandstorm is brewing to the north of Torudal which will again hamper the search efforts. The traffic control system is still down. Management is indicating the system will be operational by tomorrow afternoon."

"All right, get out and back to work."

Kalla left Alrios' office and walked through his plush house. She had once wanted much the same but had given it all up to become an assassin and quite enjoyed her life now. Getting involved with the Droma often seemed a foolish choice, but it had its benefits. If the Drakstrad was brought back, she would be in a high position of power and wealth, unlike Alrios who would find things far different. She hoped she could be the one to shove his arrogant and superior attitude down his throat when the time came.

CHAPTER FOURTEEN

Oasis of the Mulu-Daln

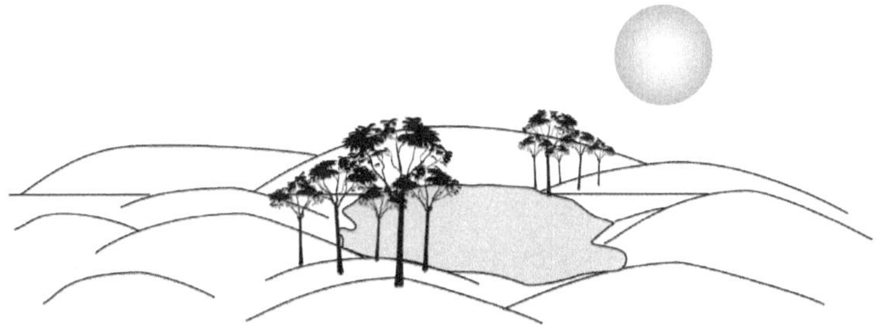

*"It often takes an entire lifetime to discover one's reason
for existence and then only after one has endured all that
is inflicted, attempted all that is possible, learned all that is
available and believed beyond what can be seen, felt or heard."*

Yanil Shun'a

IN A WELL-APPOINTED CHAMBER in the council building on Iliria, Shakar Rolm Ta'laron waited with controlled impatience for his audience with Thal Yu'man. Her outer offices were not as well decorated as some, but she had many expensive paintings on her walls. Ta'laron's thick muscular arms bulged beneath his uniform as he stood at ease, surveying his surroundings. Dealing with bureaucrats had never been something he enjoyed but must be tolerated if one wished to reach the highest ranks. It was this, more than the pending meeting that consumed his thoughts.

Only five individuals lay between him and command of the entire Ilirian Military. Han Shakar Rannas, now very close to the mandatory age for retirement, would soon make his recommendation for his replacement. With the four Combined Fleet Commanders all advanced in age, Rannas could very well recommend the Senior Fleet Commander to the post. Such a jump would require three quarters of the council to agree with the choice. At this point in his career, he knew how to play the game.

His rigid posture and firm countenance were the results of many years of hard work and discipline. His dark hair was beginning to gray at the temples, but he still possessed the fiery intensity of his youth. Physically he was a match for any man under his command and had proven so on numerous occasions. Steel blue-gray eyes observed the surroundings in detail and his square jaw set firmly at being forced to wait when he had so many tasks to accomplish. With the refit of the Jothara nearly complete, he would be able to once again have it as his flagship. Unlike the heavy cruisers built after the fall, the Jothara was the last of the Kanda class dreadnaughts built during the final days of the Drakstrad. She still carried two functional magnetic rail guns and now, with the repaired Laer-Mistal jump generator, would be the fastest vessel in the fleet.

Ta'laron did not pace, that would show a lack of control. He felt movement should always come with action, not used to fill time. Pacing was a sure indicator of indecisiveness. The door to the Thal's inner office finally opened and her assistant walked out and passed him, going to the large desk near the south wall. The old man sat down and casually eyed Ta'laron. "You may go in now."

Ta'laron said nothing, turned on his heels and walked to the large doors. He stopped momentarily before taking the ornate knob; he turned it and pulled. The inner chamber was, like the outer one, modestly decorated except for the desk set in front of the north window. The desk was one of the few that had not been destroyed during the fall and had belonged to the royal family. Three other similar desks, each owned by members of the council, rested in nearby offices along with other items that had been salvaged from the chaos of the fall. The stained, deep brown Avasa wood desks were intricately carved and inlaid with gold.

Thal Yu'man looked at him from the divan on which she reclined and smiled. Cool air from the central conditioning unit blew forcefully from the wall vent directly at the Thal. Ta'laron walked to the middle of the room and stopped, came to attention, and addressed her.

"Good day, Thal Yu'man. I, Shakar Ta'laron, answer your summons."

"You are just as I have heard," she sat up. "There is no need to be so formal. Relax."

"I must follow protocol, councilor."

"Very well," she sighed, and stood. "I will get right to the point. You are here because the council has need of your services. I did not really want this responsibility, but since I have it, I intend to solve the problem. I'm sure you are aware of the high amount of pirate activity in much of the outer ring?"

"I am."

"We have been unable to help colonies which seceded from the Commonwealth due to our limited resources. Most of the council does not want to help them since they no longer pay taxes to help maintain our security forces. Are you aware that activity by pirates is also becoming a problem within the mid-ring worlds?"

"I have received no official reports of specific incidents, but there are rumors."

She held out a large envelope. "This, contains reports of five separate occasions where trade guild registered transports have been set upon by privateers over the last several mon. It also contains a list of independent traders suspected of pirate actions."

"You intend to use an entire fleet for this?"

"So far activity in the mid-ring has been isolated to three sectors, but the council agrees. We must stop this before it spreads further inward where it would become a threat to the security of the core worlds."

"You must believe there is more to this than just pirate activity, or the council would not so easily authorize such a thing."

"Yes, nearly every member of the council feels there may be some organization using the pirates to propagate terror and disrupt trade. Last mon, Hyphos, Tanalyn, and Verdisia officially announced that they were forming what they call the D'nar Triad. They explain it is a way to protect themselves from potential threats, including pirate attacks, but there is some skepticism among the council because there have been no attacks in that sector."

Ta'laron responded dryly, "It is highly unlikely that three insignificant outer-ring worlds could become a threat in the foreseeable future."

"It is not this 'one' new alliance that worries us. The concern is the trend it foreshadows. Several other outer-ring worlds are considering similar treaties. Most unsettling is the fact that Mydan, Andrios, Legassa and Yu'lath are also in negotiations along similar lines; three of which are mid-rim worlds."

"I see! A bit closer to home." Ta'laron almost broke a smile.

"Yes, and all four of them have very active, healthy economies and local defense infrastructures. Together, they would be able to afford and maintain a sizable fleet of combat vessels and troops. Though we have no way to be sure there is any connection between them and the pirates, creating chaos and discord would be a way of enticing other worlds into these alliances."

"So, we must begin to show our willingness to help beyond our current borders in order to maintain the stability of the Commonwealth," Ta'laron said with a hint of sarcasm.

"Yes, but we also hope to again increase the number of member worlds."

"Hmm, am I to be hunting pirates, or is there more to this assignment that I should know?"

"As soon as your fleet is ready, you are to begin patrolling the Dyani, Riod and Lovi sectors. For the present you are to seek out, capture, or destroy, any vessel found to be participating in illegal activities to show our desire to promote interstellar peace and free trade. If a government requests your assistance, you will give it. It is the council's desire to eradicate all piracy where we can."

"Understood, but has Fleet High Command been informed of this?"

"Han Shakar Rannas has been notified." She handed him another document. "Here are your official orders."

Ta'laron took the paper and glanced at it. Rannas' signature was affixed at the bottom and Ta'laron stepped back from the desk and bowed slightly. "I understand and shall obey. If there is nothing else,

I would ask your leave. I have much to do before our departure."

"I only have one thing more. Be aware that several ships on the list are considered very dangerous, take no unnecessary risks. If you are in doubt, shoot first. We want to avoid as much suffering of the Commonwealth citizens as possible. The council and I are confident in your abilities."

"Thank you, Thal Yu'man," he said as he exited.

One of the males that had stood a distance off, approached Jared and pointed at his upper torso. "Ta aha'ne throu."

Jared raised his hands, palms up trying to indicate he didn't comprehend. "I don't understand," he said in Ilirian.

"Kuma." The leader called out.

The man turned his head, "Vath."

"Ein frehr noun."

"Eta," the man said turning back to Jared with a knowing smile on his face. He drew close and flicked a finger at a loose tatter on Jared's shirt near the wound, "Throu."

Jared smiled back, and began to remove the garment, hoping he had got the intent correct. A clipped nod from the native indicated it was the right move. Once Jared had his shirt off the man began bandaging the gash. Jared's thoughts turned to the survivors of the crash and he wanted to ask for help but knew it would be useless at the present time. Rescue would have to wait for a bit longer. With the bandage affixed the leader signaled for all to follow with a wave of his spear. "Hah'ey."

Jared was uncertain about his status among these desert dwellers, but so far had seen no threat. He knew for certain though, that he was no longer heading southeast. It was very likely these were the mysterious Mulu-Daln the travel agent had mentioned, but she had said they and the colonists were not on the best of terms. They'd left the oasis over an hour before and had been traveling east with the carcass of the kas-lu in tow. The stars, unobstructed by clouds, brightly filled the night sky and cast a pale light for them to see by. They moved rapidly over the dunes utilizing wide, firm leather pads tied to their shoes to keep them on top of the sand. Jared had to struggle along as best he could since they either had none to spare or did not desire to share. The cool of the night made the effort bearable as he kept pace with his adept escorts.

The boy he'd found being threatened by the kas-lu was keeping up with his elders very well. He had changed from the very excited and vocal kid he had been, to completely silent and watchful, as they ventured out onto the sand.

Each one carried a spear like the one the boy carried, though none was exactly alike. Various carvings and decorative banding made each one unique. All were tipped by rounded, flat or triangular heads with flutings, spirals or serrated edges that added individuality. The black shafts seemed to be made from some type of wood, for a definite grain could be seen, but possessed a gloss and translucence like that of obsidian.

An occasional but brief order from the leader was all the talking that transpired among the group. There were no answers to his commands, only instant action by those directed. At about the point Jared figured another hour had passed, the troupe crested a dune, and he saw a rock formation looming in front of them. Excitement ran through the natives and the pace quickened.

This must be their home.

One of the men hefted the boy onto his shoulders and several turned to Jared, motioning for him to follow. After reaching the cliff edge, they skirted it to the south for a time before stopping.

The leader inserted the tip of his spear into one of numerous indentations in the cliff wall and for a moment the crystal glowed, then returned to normal, after which he uttered two brief words, 'Duros Vadrith'.

Jared watched a section of the stone wall begin to move. Sliding inward and making only a small amount of noise, the rectangular portal was impressive in both size and sophistication. No one tried to enter until the plug's motion had stopped, but once it had they filtered in quickly. Jared was ushered to the front of the group and found himself in a large, hand-cut tunnel which continued into the rock on the right of where the door plug began. As soon as the last native was through, the plug returned to its original position.

On several occasions the corridor changed from man-made tunnel to natural cavern as they made their way gently, but steadily downward. Deposits of crystal, like that used in their spear points, ran in thick veins in the darker, speckled gray-brown cavern walls. Conversation among the natives was now animated, particularly as they passed others. There were more and more dark-skinned people as they delved further into the cavern and their spirits seemed high. As they rounded one corner in a short, hewn passage, it flared out and terminated at a large arch opening onto a vast cavern filled with people, structures and an incredible variety of vegetation.

Jared stopped and stared in awe at the beauty of the subterranean city. In the dim light he could see huge stone and crystal towers which filled the immense cavern, interspersed with dense areas of garden and trees. To his left and right he could see tier upon tier of dwellings on the cavern walls, neatly landscaped and active with life. As he looked further up, he saw the source of the soft glow. An incredible dome of translucent crystal covered the entirety of the cavern, vanishing into the distance. A touch to his arm drew his attention back to those around, and he followed once again.

They passed numerous structures, each similar in form but individual in decoration and size, carved out of what appeared to be enormous stalagmites. Following a wide, winding road among the towers, they headed into what appeared to be the heart of the city. Even at this late hour the streets were crowded, and the throngs seemed very interested in those he was with. Of particular interest was the carcass of the large predator they carried. The same crystal deposits he had seen in the entry tunnels were also in abundance here as part of the structures and streets. Some of the crystals emanated a faint glow, seeming to be the source of illumination for the city. This was a lot more than the small tribal village he had expected they were headed to. He hoped they had enough technology for him to be able to get help for those still in the wrecked aircraft.

At one point the road entered a broad open area where many people thronged and who, as all the people they had passed, were waiting to see the group of hunters and their large trophy. Many called out to the small boy, who enjoyed the attention. As they passed beyond the forum onto another road, Jared noticed it was lined with equally spaced, crystal pillars. Each higher than the next, beginning with two only slightly taller than himself and increasing to considerable heights by the time the road terminated. A large set of ornate doors stood before them, also made of the translucent crystal, and inset with the same black opalescent wood as the hunter's spears. Behind them, onlookers crowded the street, between the crystal obelisks and amid the surrounding buildings.

The group's leader walked to the right side of the large doors, lifted his spear, then let the butt end fall to the ground. A high ringing tone issued forth as it struck and echoed throughout the city. Jared looked at the point of impact and saw a large disk of crystal inset into the roadway. Only a few moments passed before the doors parted revealing an ornate courtyard with lofty towers and terraces. Six similarly dressed men and women with crystal bands on their upper left arms waited on the other side, which Jared assumed was some kind of palace guard. From here the hunting party was escorted across the wide plaza and into the central most structure. Inside, he was surprised to see walls painted in bright colors and various symmetrical patterns.

The entry had extended for about twenty feet, then opened into a large circular room with a ceiling four balconied stories above. Two massive, curved staircases connected the first and second floor beginning at opposite sides of the base, coming together at a large porch near the top. Each of the remaining floors above extended outward slightly beyond the one below. Large, smooth, gray-white stone slabs inlaid with crystal, gold and silver metals, and the black rock-like wood, paved the floor of the main level. The stairs, being of similar construction, but with banisters carved exclusively of the black opalescent material, shimmered from light given off by the domed crystal ceiling high above.

At the top of the stairs, they paused momentarily in front of another set of large doors, like the tower's main doors, made of the black material, ornately carved, but these were inset with gold and silver metals. Two of their escorts pushed the doors open and the party entered what was obviously a throne room. At the opposite end sat a big, gray haired, well-muscled man on a massive crystal chair. Numerous other colorfully dressed people sat or stood and watched with great interest as the party and their trophy moved across the highly polished floor. Jared noticed a slender man of very advanced age standing to the right of the man on the throne, whose eyes seemed to sparkle unnaturally. As the group neared the platform upon which the throne rested, the boy dashed ahead past several smiling guards and into the arms of the man on the throne.

The group's leader stopped at the base of the dais and bowed stiffly. He addressed his sovereign. "My Chief, I bring thee thy son; Tasnaklet, the slayer of Onruot; and he who both slew the beast and saved thy son."

"Vadrith, I thank you for your vigilance and skill in tracking. Has the identity of the beast been confirmed?"

"Yes. Talba used Onruot's talisman to verify. There is no doubt!"

After this last line of discourse, the one called Talba walked up to the beast and placed a crystal spearhead near the dead animal, which glowed with an eerie, yellowish brightness.

"The stranger is not of the Mulu-Daln. How did he come to be in the musara?" the chief asked.

"That is not yet known for he speaks only the tongue of the outsiders."

"Ardom," the chief said, motioning toward the elderly man to his right.

"Yes, my chief."

"Speak to this child of the invaders and determine why he was challenging the musara."

"Understood, my chief." The old man bowed to the head of the Mulu-Daln, then turned to Jared and spoke in Ilirian. "I would know why you challenge the musara."

Grateful he could understand, Jared said, "I don't know what 'musara' means."

"Musara is all that is covered by that which in your language is called sand."

Challenge the desert?

Jared then returned his attention to the one called Ardom. "I was in a transport heading to the Torudal oasis, but it crashed and left myself and many others stranded in the desert, uhm, the musara. I left to find help."

"You chose to challenge alone?" Ardom asked.

"I was the only one who was able to go."

Ardom turned back to his lord and gave a translation of Jared's words to the Mulu-Daln chief. A short, brief chuckle preceded more talk between them after which Ardom turned back to Jared. "You challenged the musara to seek help for others?"

"Yes."

"It has always been against our laws to help those who are descendants of the invaders. They came and took our lands and killed our kin. My chief does not wish to go against the covenants of our ancestors. He cannot in good conscience give you aid as an outsider, but because you have saved his son and delivered the slayer of his father and many others this day, he gives you another alternative. If you wish our help, you may embark upon the trials of belonging."

"May I ask what that entails?"

"There are four tests each member of the Mulu-Daln must pass to be accepted into our society as an adult. The Trial of Courage you have already passed, and far more than most. The second is the Trial of Strength, third is the Trial of the Soul, and fourth is the Trial of Acceptance."

Jared had no idea what the other three tests consisted of, but hoped they were less challenging than his lucky fight with the kas-lu. He knew he had no choice but to accept the Mulu-Daln challenge and wasted no time in answering. "I accept the challenge of the trials."

"So let it stand," Ardom said. He smiled and turned to the chief. "He has chosen without thought or hesitation to attempt the trials of acceptance."

"Does he wish a period of preparation?" asked the chief.

"Would you like to have a period of preparation?"

Jared considered for a moment before answering. Knowing that those in the wrecked aircraft had very little time if rescue had not yet come, he did not have the luxury of waiting to find out. "If it is possible, I will begin now."

Though tired and hungry, Jared's thoughts were on the others and particularly Shar'ya, instead of his own condition. The gash in his side received during his battle with the kas-lu had gone mostly unnoticed due to the powerful anesthetic poultice applied by one of the Mulu-Daln hunters. As he turned slightly to his left, a twinge of pain shot through his abdomen. It was not deep enough to be of concern but might affect his chances in the trial of strength. A murmur ran among those gathered in the room as Ardom informed the chief of Jared's choice. The chief stood and spoke to the members of his court and by their boisterous response he wished he understood what was said as Ardom made no effort to translate.

"Dareth will take you to prepare," said Ardom. Then he joined the others in celebration of the boy's return.

"Cho'ka." The one Ardom had introduced as Dareth spoke and motioned for Jared to follow. Dareth took Jared out the doors he had entered and along the second-floor balcony to the right. At the third door they entered a short hall and went into a well-furnished room where Dareth stopped next to a comfortable looking bed. He bent slightly, picked up a white bundle and tossed it to Jared, spoke several words, and then departed.

Jared surveyed the room and was pleasantly surprised to find a basin full of water and two thick linen towels on a table near one wall. Unsure as to how long he was to wait, he quickly removed his dirty clothes and began to wash off the accumulated grime. He was not a prisoner of unfriendly enemies as he had initially feared, but that did little good if he got himself killed attempting to pass the trials these people considered so important in their social structure.

Jared was curious as to why the boy had been out in the dangerous desert. He felt fortunate to have stumbled upon him. He also knew he had been very lucky to come out of the battle with the kas-lu without worse damage to his person. After cleaning the wound as best he could, he looked about for a clean linen to use as a bandage. In a small, free-standing wardrobe he found what looked like a sash and walked back to the edge of the bed.

The laceration had begun to bleed lightly again from the bath, but after a few minutes he managed to get the cloth on tightly enough to stop any further discharge. The trousers fit loosely until he found a drawstring and cinched the waist snugly. The shirt slipped on and then the left panel folded over the right, around the back, and then was secured by three small, twin-ring buckles. Lastly, he slipped on the pair of soft leather shoes that had been tucked inside the folded clothing. With nothing more to do, he sat down on the bed and rubbed his sore shins and calves. A few minutes later he dropped back onto the mattress and closed his eyes, wishing for sleep.

A sharp knock at the door brought him back to the moment and he wearily sat up and walked toward it. Two of the palace guards stood waiting outside the apartment, both of whom smiled at him as he came out. He took a deep breath, then followed as they headed back toward the throne room, then beyond to a door further around the level. Just before they entered, the young hunter who had bandaged Jared's wound out in the desert ran up holding another poultice, but the guards said something to him, and he moved aside. Jared glanced at him and smiled, hoping that it would indicate his thanks for the man's kind thought.

They continued along a corridor that sloped slightly downward and was dimly lit by numerous small crystal globes embedded in the ceiling. Jared felt like a prisoner being led to the guillotine. If it hadn't been for the brief interview with the city's ruler earlier, he would have been sure of it. He tried to ignore his irritated joints and sore muscles and pictured a cool swim in the pool aboard Orion. Thoughts of the pool, and water, made him realize he had not had a drink of water for some time, and he cleared his throat to get the guard's attention. He made several attempts to get his point across, but they were either in too big a hurry, or simply misunderstood him, though one nodded and smiled. He fell back into step with them and hoped the one named Ardom would be nearby before the trial began.

The long hall finally ended at an old weathered, wooden door set into a stone arch. The two guards stopped momentarily to pull it open and then the larger of the two stepped through. A loud chorus of cheers arose from the other side. After a moment, the remaining escort motioned for Jared to follow. He stepped out into a large, well lit, terraced cavern full of spectators. Dominating the middle of the chamber was a huge arch of rock upon which stood two individuals, while several others on the floor below were affixing a teardrop-shaped crystal to a rope hanging from above. Light for the great amphitheater came from many crystals exposed on the ceiling and walls. Thousands of people crowded the many levels and balconies for nearly three hundred and sixty degrees. The only exceptions were the two main entrances. The tiers themselves began a little above floor level, then tapered back until about midway, then began to flair out again to overhang much of the underground chamber.

The entry he was brought through sat perpendicular to the two main spectator entries and was at the base of a long ramp. Upon reaching the end of the incline, they turned right and approached the base of the arch. He estimated that it must be at least one hundred feet high and perhaps two hundred from base to base. It was thirty to forty feet thick at its origins and wide enough for several individuals to stand abreast at the highest point. When they rounded the end, Jared saw that steps had been hewn from the rock. He and the escort began to climb without pause and he clung tightly to the securely mounted black wood rail. He relaxed as the gradient tapered off and the steps became shallower. The last third was an open platform which possessed no railing and was capped by a large crystal plate with numerous smooth grooves running across its width.

They approached the two standing at the apex. After making a brief statement, the guards turned and descended as they had come. He was left with Ardom and a woman he hadn't seen before. Ardom turned to the assembled crowd and addressed them.

"Warriors and citizens, today we have one who is not of our blood, but who has proved he is worthy of the challenge. He is the killer of Tasnaklet and deliverer of Uli Anas Onruot, son of the high chief. The story of his triumph has already spread throughout the city and is no doubt on its way to other dwelling places of the Mulu-Daln. He is dasnarow and desires haste, so has declined the time of preparation."

At this point another chorus of shouts arose, but these contained a hint of surprise.

"So now let the Trial of Strength begin." Ardom motioned to the female and stepped back.

The woman stepped to the center of the platform and yelled.

Ardom quietly translated for Jared as she spoke. "We gather to cheer the challenger in triumph or mourn in defeat. He is alone in task, but not in soul."

"Citea lakum tyem nuvashra," she said with a flourish of her hands.

"May all our ancestors guide his choices," Ardom said, raising his eyebrows slightly and pointing to his cranium. Jared gave the old man a puzzled look but received nothing more than a smile in return.

"Jalnu'tan yotae sunom'alil'requime," she said in conclusion.

"May he have strength of heart, might and mind," Ardom echoed.

The woman turned to Jared. "Olu kamdyir'vurad yustal ta ugat." Then walked away in the opposite direction his escorts had taken.

Ardom translated the brief but direct message. "You must raise the stone to the top of the arch." With that finished, the old man turned and followed the woman.

Quiet settled over the entire room and Jared began to survey his surroundings. Though he could not see them individually, he knew every eye was upon him. He could not see the stone, but the rope to which it was attached was hanging over the edge through a large metal ring. The other end ran through another ring near the middle and hung down the opposite side also out of sight. A metallic bar woven into the rope at one point kept it from falling to the floor below. There were no foot holds or anchors to use to keep the weight from pulling him off the arch if he made a mistake. He figured the slight bow in the platform might allow a little leverage as he attempted to pull it up. Regardless of whether he found secure footing, he felt his chances were slim to none to get it all the way up.

Here's hoping this last few mons of exercise and weightlifting have paid off. I'll have to rely on my legs, or I'll ruin my back.

Jared walked over, picked up the rope, pulled in several feet of slack before the line drew taught, then released it. Moving back toward the opposite side, he tested the stone's weight but was unable to move it. The arch appeared smooth, but the surface was rough enough to allow the shoes he wore to grip well. He walked to the far side, took hold of the metal bar, and pulled up the slack again. He then wrapped the rope around his back to use his weight as an anchor. The metal restraining bar fell behind him slightly with the slack, and he knew if he lost his grip the thing would become dangerous as the stone fell. Once the rope was tight, he leaned back and tried again. This time he felt the rope give a little as the stone shifted. He bent his knees and moved more of the rope around his waist. He positioned himself, then heaved again, pushing away with his legs. Again, the weight below moved slightly upward. He repeated this again and again, he slowly inched the stone upward. Since the excess of the rope fell off behind, he had no way to know how far he'd raised it, but felt he had a long way to go. His legs and arms were already beginning to ache, but he continued to pull the heavy object upward.

The vast crowd watched, and at first a faint hum of conversation filled the amphitheater. Those in the lower tiers on one side could not see the challenger but had noticed when the crystal moved and knew he had begun. For those on the opposite side and the higher tiers and balconies, it was far more interesting as they saw Jared hang outward at a precarious angle from the top. Betting and speculation as to the challenger's chances ran like wildfire throughout the crowd. A slight murmur ran through those assembled as the stone reached the first mark, the mark of Kalen. As it passed betting resumed, speculation changed, and the hum returned, a bit louder. At the second mark, which had been attained by the great hunter Ralym over seventy turnings ago, the assemblage roared in delight.

Kalen, over 1800 turnings ago, had been the first to lift an unbroken stone above the rulom. None had done so before and only five had done it since. Ralym had been the last of those five and had been both a great hunter and a beloved chief. The next mark was that of Dassai, the only female ever to exceed Kalen's mark, and another round of cheers arose as Jared passed it. Most of those gathered were now at the edge of their seats, intent on watching, all betting at an end. No sound could be heard as the stone neared the fourth mark nor as it passed, but amazed looks were exchanged by most as the outsider passed Eryom's score.

Jared's arms and legs burned as he continued to struggle for both altitude and balance. After a moment's pause between each pull to take in a breath, he surged back again and gathered in a little more rope. He knew he would not be able to do much more but also had no idea how far he had lifted it. Why the crowd had cheered a short time earlier he could only guess, but hoped it was because he had passed the mid-way point. It suddenly occurred to him that he would not only be in trouble if he lost his balance, but when he did get the stone to the top, he had no way of getting out of the position he was in. By releasing the rope, he would topple off the arch backwards, and if he moved forward, the stone's weight would carry him over the opposite side.

Jared brought the stone even with the inscribed mark of Lareth, which glowed slightly from its inset band of crystal. A longer pause than usual made many of those in attendance breathe deeply before a single pull brought it above the line. The room erupted into shouts and cheers, most likely because many realized that they might also see Talm's record exceeded. Only a few of the eldest in attendance had been alive when Ralym had set his mark. The next upward movement of the stone was slight, almost imperceptible. Again, an extended pause seemed to make the audience wonder if it would soon fall; yet another, more noticeable surge upward followed.

Jared knew he was at the end of his endurance but could not think of any way to solve this dilemma. He could try to lower the stone, but that would be giving in, and any hope of saving Shar'ya and the others would be lost. Then he had a sudden thought. The only instruction they had given was to get the stone to the top; they did not limit as to how. Jared closed his eyes and prayed for a moment before letting the weight of his body fall further backward. As he did so, the stone moved up slowly but steadily, drawing the multitude to their feet. Most of the spectators could see Jared's position and marveled at his courage and audacity. As more of his weight extended out over the open air, the faster the stone began to rise until at last, he dropped away from the edge and began to slowly descend.

He gripped as tightly as he could, and he was able to maintain his hold as he pitched downward until his feet were again below him. The jerk on his arms sent a jolt of pain through his shoulders and back, also reopening the wound on his side. He opened his eyes and found himself below the bottom edge of the arch and slowly descending. He was still twisting from side to side slightly but was able to see the opposite end of the rope and followed it downward to the crystal weight. He was descending very slowly and could now see he hadn't had the stone anywhere near the halfway point. He could also see that the crowds were on their feet and shouting, though he couldn't hear anything. The stone drew nearer, and Jared could see it clearly for the first time. It was indeed tear-drop shaped and had seven grooves running around its circumference at varying distances from its tip. The grooves were also at different depths and Jared realized that the Mulu-Daln did not expect the entire rock to reach the top. If he had lifted it a short way and let it drop there would have been less to lift. Ardom had translated the woman's words as strength of heart, might and mind. Part of the test was figuring out how, not with just brute strength, but also with strength of heart—as in not giving up.

Damn, by pitching myself off the top I may just have failed the test.

A room-shaking shouting burst forth from the spectators, and Jared saw many waving and stomping. This time however he had no problem hearing it, and though relieved to know he could still hear, was not sure whether the crowd was now friendly or angry. His hands and arms were becoming numb, and he was not sure how much longer he could hold on. As he neared the same level with the stone, he decided he had to try to get down more quickly. While trying to maintain his facing, he began to swing back and forth in the weight's direction. Like a trapeze artist he became a pendulum with a particular goal in mind, but his grip was deteriorating rapidly. His swinging was increasing his rate of descent, but not enough to get him down before he would lose his grip. He might be knocked loose when he hit the crystal but had to try.

The first time he passed the crystal, he did so from a few feet above and had to pull himself up a bit on the return swing. As he neared the apex of the outward point, he stuck out his foot and aimed as best he could. Momentum and bad timing caused him to hit the tip square-on with his upper back. The shock caused him to lose his grip with his left hand, and he strained to stay on with his right.

On the return trip, just as he regained his hold with both hands, his left shoulder hit again and despite the pain he heard a loud cracking sound. He was now too low to get another shot with his foot so decided to hang on, for as long as possible. His calculations were slightly off and on the next pass his head hit the crystal. From the incredible thud in his ears and cracking sound without, he was sure he had fractured his skull. As darkness began to close in, he concentrated on holding on, and did not see the large chunk of crystal fall away nor feel his descent rate increase.

Jared's trapeze-like stunts invoked a wild outburst of delight and controlled chaos from all who witnessed them. Each of the three impacts caused shouts of awe and amazement. The stone had risen, intact, to well past halfway, and all there knew that would not be matched for a very long time. Only a few of those present had witnessed the killing of Tasnaklet and so the Test of Courage was less real to the rest who had not seen it. Now, however, it seemed they felt they knew, for no one had ever jumped from the arch with intent.

As Jared hit the last time and the tip broke away, the spectator's chanting and stomping intensified. His descent increased and the rock quickly began to near the top. When it hit, the sudden jerk ripped the rope from Jared's hands just a few feet from the ground. Consciousness failed him an instant before he hit the chamber floor, and he lay there unmoving.

Cries of warning and disbelief ran through the watchers as the crystal above, now free of the challenger's grip, plummeted downward. Residual swinging left him directly within the path of the falling object, and the chaos of victory succumbed quickly to the silence of impending doom as the stone neared the ground. Impending doom, however, shifted just as quickly to awe and disbelief as the stone flared with green light and seemed to slide sideways, away from the helpless figure on the ground. The crystal hit with a loud, earthy thud, rolled for a distance, then stopped just as the green glow faded.

After several moments of continued silence, murmurs began to arise from the crowd. Many seemed to believe him dead and thus to have failed; others shouted he had succeeded even in death. A lone figure walked slowly up to Jared and knelt beside him. She placed her hand over the right side of his neck. Once again, the crowd became quiet as they waited, though most doubted she would find signs of life. As several voices cried out for her to make haste, she stood and called for the two guards to remove him; then slowly ascended to the top of the arch.

"The trial has been attempted, successfully completed, and yes, the Challenger lives." The chaos was no longer controlled.

News of the spectacle that had taken place within the Rulath-lom soon spread throughout the city. The Co-mural Atasta (Trial of Heart, Might and Mind) was the only one of the four that was optional within the Mulu-Daln rites of passage to gain acceptance as an adult member of society. Only those who wished to become warriors, hunters and leaders needed to pass the test of the second trial. Caution was used by the adults around the youth, children or others yet to take the trials, so as not to give away any secrets. A new mark had been set more than halfway up the arch, though no one yet knew what to call it. The fact that the rock had not been broken on the ground but by the challenger's head brought stares of disbelief from those who heard second hand. Jared leaping off the stone's final fall and the miraculous green light which seemed to divert it, illicited similar reactions.

The high chief of the Mulu-Daln sat in his chair and seemed to wonder at what he had seen. This child of the invaders was a great warrior and hunter. He had passed the first two tests beyond what any other Mulu-Daln had done, and had done so without preparation, and while wounded. He had challenged the musara, alone, to help others, which all the old lore said the invaders would not do. Most amazing however, was that he seemed to have the help of the

Hadara themselves. Crystals could not produce light on their own. They must have a source of energy to function, but the crystal of the trial had no such connection. The Faldara could not produce anything but darkness, so the only remaining answer was the Hadara. It was written that the Hadara appeared within the whitest of light, and crystals gave off white light when properly cut; but there was no record of the Hadara working on or through a crystal. The chief's concern faded as he made his decision and summoned a large man to his side. Carefully he whispered directions in the warrior's ear, then signaled for him to go.

Celebrations continued throughout the night in many homes and taverns while others went to sleep happy, knowing they had been alive when this great event occurred. Considering this people's animosity toward those not born of Mulu-Daln blood, they apparently accepted Jared's triumph as they would have one of their own.

Of all the trials, the second was also the only one where spectators were allowed to watch. The first trial, the challenge of the musara, was done alone though under the watchful eye of several hunters to ensure no one interfered. The third, which was the Trial of the Soul, took place within the dark halls of Ja'narom. It was just prior to this that the talisman of belonging is given to the challenger and infused with his or her blood. The fourth is a walk through the Chakra'tal by which an individual's status within the Mulu-Daln society is determined by the number of crystals he can illuminate.

CHAPTER FIFTEEN

Blood Bond

"First seek to be one with all around you.
Then you will become one with the One who made you."

Mulu-Daln Proverb

JARED REGAINED CONSCIOUSNESS several em-hars later, feeling better than he figured he should. He lay on the bed in the room he had changed in prior to the second trial, with a clean pair of pants on, but no shirt. His side, freshly bandaged felt slightly numb, but there was no sign of broken bones or soreness in his torso or limbs as he moved them. He had no recollection of how he'd finally gotten down but must have somehow hung on until he reached the ground. Still tired, he walked to the door and opened it, wanting to get on with the trials so he could get help to the others. Relaxing against a rail outside was a Mulu-Daln female, who turned when she heard the door open. A smile crossed her face when she saw him but she put her hand up to stop him.

"Konas umnaw pulota."

"I don't understand you," he said with a sigh. "I need to begin the third trial," he continued by holding up three fingers.

"Mala'num," she smiled knowingly, pointing toward the bed. "Hal vetwa mala'num."

Jared decided it was pointless to continue, closed the door, returned to the bed and stretched out. A short while later he was fast asleep.

A gentle shaking woke Jared from his slumber, and he opened his eyes to see Ardom standing over him. "It is time to begin the third trial."

"I'm ready," Jared replied groggily.

"Almost," was Ardom's brief but polite reply.

Jared looked at him for a moment, wondering what else he had to do, but said nothing and began to put on the clean tunic Ardom offered. A soreness in his shoulders and hands was now noticeable, along with an occasional twinge from the wound in his side. He did not allow Ardom to see any indication of his discomfort and followed the old man from the room. Upon entering the hall, Ardom handed Jared several cake-like biscuits and told him to eat quickly. Ardom was his sole escort, and neither talked as they made their way toward the next trial. This time they headed in the opposite direction around the second level balcony to a set of stairs leading upward. After passing one landing, they exited into a long, well-illuminated chamber with an ornate door at the far end. The chief, and numerous other richly dressed individuals lined the walls to either side, each gripping a spear in their right hand. As he and Ardom entered, they began tapping the butts of the weapons upon the floor. The tempo increased as he and Ardom crossed the room, and Jared felt as if he were in some surreal dream moving in slow motion.

Why am I here?

Jared had accepted the fact that he was not going to get back to Earth, but he had yet to figure out the answer to his thought. He had not chosen to be in the wastes of the musara, killed the kas-lu through sheer luck and barely escaped death during the Trial of Strength, though he still had no idea how he'd pulled that one off.

Yet these people treated him like some kind of hero.

Are people going to die everywhere I go? It would have been better if I had stayed on that miserable world of my birth.

Jared was caught by surprise at both his thoughts and by the intensity of the emotion connected. On Earth he had never considered there would be any more to his existence beyond work, occasional recreation and family dramas. Life had not been all that bad, but everything had changed in one moment. Now, walking the span of the long, narrow room, he began to recall all that had transpired from the time he'd arrived at the outpost.

My father once said there is a reason for everything that happens to an individual.

Jared could find no reason for being where he was.

Near the ornate door stood two individuals dressed unlike the others. In a less ornate, but far more ceremonial style of clothing and with very serious countenances, both were wearing headdresses vaguely like those the ancient Egyptians wore. For the first time since he had arrived in the subterranean oasis, he saw a sample of their writing on the jacket of a book held by the male just to the left of the door ahead. Script like that of the peoples of the Orient covered a surface of deep brown leather. The warrior who had bandaged his wound stood next to the male priest, seemingly out of place among the richly dressed members of the court. The woman to the right of the door was very advanced in age, but had keen, intelligent and penetrating eyes that followed Jared as he approached.

Ardom stopped several paces from the door and turned to address the woman. "Cha klans humara Ja'narom afturas."

"Ki sulet imbular," she replied.

Ardom turned to Jared and smiled. "Before you lies the door to the Ja'narom, or Chamber of the Soul." Ardom paused and gestured for the warrior to come to him. "To enter this sacred place, one must have claim to family within our society." Ardom continued despite the look of shock Jared gave him. "This is Kuma. He has petitioned his family on your behalf and now stands here to offer you a place within his family. Do you accept the honor he offers?"

"Yes," Jared said without hesitation.

Ardom turned to face the man. "Kuma, Som jul gelsim otriad tubas." A gasp of surprise came from many of those present as Ardom gave Kuma Jared's reply. They must not have expected such a quick decision from the child of the invaders.

"Su'los," Kuma said, taking a step toward Jared and withdrawing a fabric-covered item. "Ty'oln pwe asad togal."

"Thank you," Jared replied, knowing the other could not understand, but was surprised by a broad grin from the warrior. Jared slowly removed the covering and found himself holding one of the crystal spear tips.

"It is time for the Una Han K'lar," Ardom said, translating into Ilirian as much as he could.

"The what?" Jared asked, though not surprised when Ardom continued without answering.

"Hold the K'lar in your right hand and touch the tip to the palm of your other hand," Ardom explained.

A faint glow of pale white light emanated from the object as it touched his skin, and he held it up close to get a good look at it. The others in the room stood by patiently as he looked into the transparent, faceted stone. At the widest point near the base, a pulsing speck of light rested near the center and seemed alive. Tendrils of light flowed outward from the source in a spiderweb of branching capillaries to all other parts of the gem. For some reason he had the odd feeling he had seen something like this before, perhaps from a strong, long forgotten dream. Defensive thoughts played quickly through his mind as to the possible ramifications of his choices. Logic won out over his natural psychological urge at self-preservation, reasoning he was already in too far to quit now.

Raising his left hand above the K'lar, he paused a few moments before moving it downward toward the sharp tip. At the last instant before contact, he closed his eyes and took in a deep breath. A sharp pain shot through his hand and wrist, which caused him to draw his hand back quickly. Opening his eyes he looked at his appendage, which had a small bead of blood near the center of the palm, then to the crystal tip where sat another drop of his blood. For a moment nothing happened, but as another pulse of light emanated from the small stone's heart, several of the snaking tendrils near the tip reached out and seized the single drop of blood, and the crystal flared brightly. The droplet, as if consumed, vanished and the white light blossomed into crimson, pulsating rhythmically. Jared felt his legs weaken and fell to his knees, but did not lose his hold on the object. His head swam in a murky pool of half-remembered dreams, unrealized hopes and irrational fears. Vague shadowy shapes, some familiar, some completely alien, drifted among dark misty surroundings in which he floated.

His vision cleared slowly, and he regained full consciousness to find himself still on his knees in front of the door to the Ja'narom. Every person in the room was watching him intently as he struggled to his feet and faced Ardom. Rolling his shoulders and breathing deeply to further clear his head, he held the crystal out in front of himself. "What now?"

"The K'lar did not deny you. Somewhere within, you possess a part of the Mulu-Daln. Now you may enter the Ja'narom and face the Trial of the Soul."

"Deny me? What would have happened if it had denied me?"

"You would be dead," Ardom replied flatly.

"Oh!"

Jared felt a numbness in his left shoulder which he tried to massage.

"The sensation you feel is the beginning of the Suran K'lar Rhy'om," Ardom spoke, noticing Jared's discomfort. "As with all who take the trials and pass the Una Han K'lar, you will be given a Rhy'om, which is a mark upon your left shoulder indicating that you are Mulu-Daln, the family to whom you belong, and on rare occasions telling one's destiny."

"What causes the mark, or Rhy'om to appear?"

"Inside certain crystals dwell tiny organisms which many thousands of turnings ago our ancestors first bonded with, in a symbiotic relationship which gave us a true connection to this planet. They are what give us our identity and our peaceful society. The K'lar will not accept one it determines to be a threat to our laws, as they were created to be in harmony with the Rhy'om and to weed out those who would create chaos and misery."

"You mean anyone with a different opinion from those who rule?" Jared asked, feeling a wave of anger welling up inside.

"No," Ardom replied sternly. "If the Rhy'om did that, only a few would survive. Only those who would seek to cause damage or sow the seeds of bloodshed are rejected. Individual freedom and opinion are needed for a society to thrive, for ideas to flourish, and new knowledge to be learned. Perhaps it is not what you are accustomed to, but it is our way, and it works."

"So why was I accepted?"

"I cannot answer that! Unlike the K'lar, I cannot see the future. Have you ever willingly caused harm to another?"

"No."

"Then perhaps that is part of the reason. You will have to find your own answers from there."

That's no big surprise.

"Are you ready to proceed?" Ardom asked.

"Yes."

Jared stood rigidly in front of the large door as it slowly swung open to reveal total darkness, while Ardom spoke to the elderly female priestess. As the door silently came to a stop, the interpreter turned to Jared.

"Within the Ja'narom you will come face to face with that which gives you life. Finish what you have begun or die trying."

"Just my luck to die facing myself after surviving everybody else who's been trying to kill me," Jared started to step through the door when the face of his father came into his mind. He stopped abruptly, he stood rigidly and concentrated on the memories that flooded inward. Words he'd heard his father say came back from long forgotten childhood and teenage lessons.

"Son, I have never given in, nor allowed any outside influence to compromise my principles. Oh, I have made mistakes and learned hard lessons, but I stand firmly upon my beliefs. Whatever you choose to do, believe, or love, do so as if your very existence and your soul depend upon the commitment to see it through; no matter how you may suffer, or even die. For, whether or not you know it now, one day you will understand that we are not just sparks which flair brightly for a brief period in this universe, but are part of a greater whole, with far greater destinies."

"My father told me more in that statement than I ever imagined. Perhaps I should try to remember his council more often." Jared had spoken out loud, and though Ardom was not privy to Jared's thoughts, he smiled warmly at his honoring words to his parent, and as Jared stepped through the doorway, Ardom said a brief prayer for the newest child of the Mulu-Daln.

Taking one last look back as the door began to close, Jared saw his K'lar glowing in the tall, slender holder near the door. Not one of the witnesses spoke, and Jared wondered what they might be thinking as the last of the light faded. Several minutes passed before he tried to move, having hoped for some form of illumination, but when that did not happen, he began to feel along the wall to his right. Cold, uneven stone met his touch while the floor sloped gently upward, and a slight twinge of apprehension entered his mind. Previously he had been able to see what he was facing but now, caught in total darkness and unable to see what might be lurking, really had his nerves on edge. After what seemed like several hours, he let go of the wall and sighed angrily. He had walked a great distance but had encountered nothing. Standing where he was and fuming at the wasted time did little good, so he began to walk again.

A short while later, he rounded a sharp corner. The faint light within seemed to have appeared as he entered, but only enough to see vague shapes. He found himself in a large, half round chamber across from a broad flat wall. Cautiously, he moved away from the cavern wall and into the middle of the room. His vision became blurred by the appearance of a mist emanating from the center of the floor. Voices, some recognizable, some strange, began to come and go, intermixing from time to time, creating a noisy mess within his head. Jared tried to concentrate on the ones he recognized, and after a period of frustration was able to isolate some.

The first one he was able to decipher was council from his mother when he was leaving home for the first time, "I know you find it difficult to understand my faith in God, but if you only try, you'll be able to discern which is the best path to follow. Don't ignore all..."

"You are so strange to hang onto your parents' outdated beliefs, Jared." Cal's voice, one of Jared's best friends, blocked out the remainder of what his mother said. "It's going to stifle all the enjoyment of your life if you're not careful..."

"Someday you may be forced to make a choice which, no matter how you decide, will result in anguish and regret." His father's voice broke in. "A difficult thing to live with if your soul has no companion."

Caught up in the voices within his mind, Jared did not see the edge of the gaping rift until too late and toppled over the edge into darkness. The voices continued to filter in and out as he fell, twisting and spinning. From time to time, he heard his own voice asking various questions on one single subject.

Why should I believe? What should I believe? Why can't I believe?

But with all the chaos in his head, he was not even sure what the questions pertained to. He was falling and should be fearing for his life, but he had no such feeling.

Why? Perhaps it was all just a bad nightmare after all. God and faith, that was what it was, or was it? I have no idea what the Mulu-Daln believe. My parents wanted me to believe in God, but what is God?

"One who exists beyond the scope of your ability to comprehend. One who has moved beyond what you see to that which you seek."

The new voice drowned out all the others and penetrated to the very center of his being. "To evolve beyond that which you know, you must first believe in that which you do not know. The key to the portal which links you to that higher existence is hidden within that which gives you your life. It is not tangible to the physical shell you inhabit and cannot be found from without. Only when you can look inside with a faith strong enough to break the bands that create doubt, and fear will you know what potential you have and what destiny lies in store."

Total silence was all that remained after the piercing voice stopped, and Jared continued to fall for some time before suddenly finding himself standing in a small, rectangular room. On the narrow wall furthest from where he stood was what appeared to be a window, but the room had no doors or furnishings. Curious, he walked up to the mirror-like panel and attempted to look out, but only a gray/black haze met his gaze. He rubbed his tired eyes as he felt around the simple frame for some switch that might open the panel and allow him to continue, but he found nothing. The walls, light gray in color, had no seams nor was there any sign of a hidden panel to possible controls. Though no source was evident, the room was filled with a gentle light providing ample illumination. Only the floor, which was made of small gray tiles, had any texture, and Jared spent a good deal of time checking each one. He found them all firmly secured, and in frustration slammed his fist against the wall.

Where he had struck the dark gray panel of glass, faint ripples coursed across its surface like ripples in a pond. Upon closer examination he could see faint ripples in the walls themselves. He moved close to the window's outer frame on the right side and slugged the wall again with enough force to make his knuckles hurt. A moment later, ripple after ripple flowed outward from the impact area in ever growing circles. He stepped back, and began to rethink his situation, though no solution was immediately apparent. He eventually sat down on the floor, leaned against the wall opposite the window, and continued to ponder.

I entered this test in total darkness and walked for what seemed hours.

Jared sat silently, tracing the events of the past few hours in his mind.

I then entered a room in which I could see and there was no apparent danger, or obstacle. As I approached the middle of the room, I could no longer see clearly because of a mist clouding my vision. It was then I fell into a pit where I felt no fear and heard many voices, some from my past, some from my present, and others I did not know. Perhaps those could have been from my future, but the future has not occurred yet. How can I remember that which has not yet come to pass? The last voice said I must look within to find what I seek. I'm not sure what it is I seek, but if this truly is a test of the soul, then could it be that I am on the inside trying to look out?

Suddenly Jared's train of thought shifted into shocked realization.

Ardom said to succeed or die trying. I gave those words very little heed when he said them, but if I am now within, that means I am unconscious, and this is all within my subconscious. If I don't figure out the secrets of this place, my body will waste away and die.

Jared was beginning to feel weaker. He had begun the trial on a minimal amount of sleep and with only the few cake-like biscuits Ardom had given him on their way to the entry of the trial. Much time had passed since then, and though he knew his body was strong, it could not last more than two, perhaps three days without water and food.

If I am indeed on the inside, there must be a way to look out, but where should I look? My physical form is in a dark place with nothing to see.

Wait! The voice said the key to the portal lies within and I must look there to find my destiny. If I am on the inside, the key has to be here somewhere.

Jared stood and began to search again, scrutinizing every square inch of wall and floor. Though unable to reach the ceiling, he visually searched it, but again his efforts turned up nothing.

The word 'faith' kept popping into his thoughts, but he had been pushing it aside in his search for a tangible representation of a key. It occurred to him like a light going on in a dark room that he was still trying to find physical evidence of that which existed beyond sight, sound and touch. The voice had spoken of a portal, and Jared looked from where he was to the gray/black panel of glass that cast no reflection. He realized he'd responded to this situation in the same arrogant and blind manner most humans approach spiritual concerns; wanting or needing proof of their existence before accepting that such was possible or truly existed. He slowly approached the translucent panel and reached his hand toward it with his fingers rigidly extended.

"Faith strong enough to break the bands that create doubt and fear..." An echo of the words he'd heard so clearly earlier rushed into his mind and he stopped, standing perfectly still. Never had he come across such a difficult task, one so foreign, so beyond his experience.

Here he did feel fear and great doubt, for beyond that, he truly didn't know what he would find. If a race of beings far in advance of his own really did exist, how would he deal with that knowledge? If part of him had somehow come from them, and so connected him to them, thus giving him a greater destiny, how could he face them after all the failures he had known, with much guilt over past mistakes? His middle finger touched the surface, and it did not react or yield. He withdrew his hand slightly, cleared his mind, now wanting to know, determined to learn.

"If there is more than what I have known, I want to learn more. I want to believe!" The words no longer seemed forced, for Jared truly did want to know. This time when his finger touched the surface, it yielded slightly like a soft fabric. Again, he withdrew his hand and concentrated on all his parents had taught him. "Teach me what I should know, so I may know what I am to do." He reached out, touched the portal and felt his finger pass through the fabric.

A voice spoke briefly, but with firm intensity. "Belief must precede knowledge, and patience must prevail, for all things are revealed in their own due time."

Jared continued to move forward and watched as parts of himself vanished from sight. As his head penetrated, he was standing in another room of identical proportions though possessing a whiteness beyond anything he had ever seen. Turning to look behind, he again saw the portal, but this time it reflected an image of himself.

Is this all there is?

As if in reaction to his query, the mirror shifted and flared with bright light, then stabilized into a view of an incredibly beautiful landscape the likes of which he had never imagined. Gently flowing hills of unmarred green lay behind a tranquil city of white and transparent structures among which people of various races mingled and moved about their tasks, all dressed in blindingly white robes. Trees and plants of abundant and incredible variety grew everywhere in neatly groomed planters and gardens, some of which had leaves of the purest white. But it was the sky that impressed Jared the most. Though it felt as cool and comfortable as the blue skies of Earth, it was also white with an intensity beyond any description.

"What else would you see?" Jared was startled by the voice of a female, gentle but as deeply penetrating as that of the male voice he had heard before.

"What is this place?"

"An Oracle. It reveals insight into things that might yet come to be. It is not concerned with that which is past, and sometimes that which is seen is difficult to behold."

Jared took a deep breath and steadied himself. "I would see what it has to show."

"Very well. My love goes with you, and I bid you farewell," the woman replied and then all was silent. Immediately, Jared felt foolish for not asking her more about the questions that nagged him.

The scene of the strange world vanished and was replaced by a sight Jared was very familiar with. For a time, his view drifted over the city in which he'd been living when he was taken from Earth, circling like some soaring bird of prey in ever tightening circles hunting for its meal. The voice had indicated that the portal showed the future which meant that if what he saw were true, Earth remained as he had left it and someday, he might be able to find a way back after all. If he were there with Shar'ya, it might be worth a visit to see his family.

At last, he found himself over the city's largest mall where, after a few tight orbits, he came to rest at the outer perimeter of the parking lot. Further in, near the main entrance, he watched as many people came and went, while near him to his left a light-colored SUV pulled into a parking space and the driver got out, opening the rear hatch. Though he did not consciously move, his view drifted toward the vehicle and what the man was doing. Jared had only a moment to see the inside of a small brief case before the lid was shut and the man walked toward the mall with it. Inside had been several boxes wrapped like presents and a digital clock. Though no wires had been apparent, he suspected it must be some sort of explosive. Jared was merely an observer and since no further movement occurred, he simply watched as the man disappeared into the building.

Jared turned to his left and froze, his heart hammering in his chest. There they were—his mother, two sisters, and Shar'ya—walking into the mall...

Jared's breath caught in his throat, he felt paralyzed, knowing there was nothing he could do. Or was there?

He reached out, his hand pressed against the smooth, transparent surface, feeling its warmth. It did nothing to ease the tightening in his chest. As the moments passed, his frustration grew. He pounded his fists against the window, harder and harder, trying to make something—anything—happen. But it was useless.

Then Jared saw himself. His other self, getting out of a car near the mall entrance, walking toward the building. He watched, horrified, as his other self was stopped by someone—someone he didn't recognize—who started talking to him.

His voice broke through the silence, desperate and frantic. "Run! Get inside! Save them!" He screamed at himself, his heart racing. He knew what had to be done, but couldn't reach him, couldn't warn him. He could only watch as the moments slipped away. And hated himself for it.

"Fool! Listen! Listen to the promptings you've so long ignored. Ahhhh!" The last angry impact of his fists against the fabric of the screen created a huge burst of light and Jared was suddenly beyond the barrier, rapidly approaching his other self. He felt a shock as he merged with the other and knew he now had power to act.

"...I was so amazed..." The stranger was saying.

"Excuse me!" Jared darted inside just as a horrific blast sent him flying into a wall.

"No!" He screamed as he got to his feet and began to run toward an area of the mall filled with smoke and fire. Cries for help and painful wails came from all around as he made his way through the devastation. The blast had occurred in the food court and left many bodies scattered around. Jared recoiled at the thought that his presence on Earth would also bring disaster.

Was there nowhere he could go where suffering would not follow?!

As he searched for his family, he helped several of those who could move out from under the remnants of tables and other fragmented items. He received no answer to his calls but continued to search even though the smoke was beginning to make breathing difficult.

A small moan came from a raised area off to his left where part of the floor above had fallen in. A huge, reinforced beam lay across the area and as Jared moved around to the other side, his eyes filled with tears and an agonized howl of rage exploded from him. He paused only a moment before he overcame his shock and rushed to Shar'ya's side. The heavy concrete beam lay across her mid-section pinning her solidly to the floor. Terry and Sandra lay nearby, both unmoving, though Jared could see Sandra's chest rise and fall. Returning his attention to Shar'ya, he touched her face and felt a ragged breath brush his hand.

"Shar'ya, please don't die, I'll find a way to get this off you." He didn't know if she could hear him. He began to move away to find some implement to remove the beam when her gentle voice stopped him.

"No."

"What?"

"Jared, you must get Sandra out, there is little time, and you must hurry."

"I'm not leaving you."

"My love, please listen to me," she spoke through a spasm of pain and her green eyes flared brightly. "It is too late for Terry and me, but Sandra has a chance if you do not delay."

Jared looked at his younger sister and felt little in the way of compassion for the one person who had always made him feel worthless.

Why should he leave his wife for such as that?

The fact that this was only a vision of a possible future made no impact. It was too real and hit too hard.

With his eyes full of tears, he searched deeply into hers, and once again saw the strength he had come to know. He could sense her saying, "Do not sacrifice yourself in vain when you could save a life. Remember all we have seen and experienced. Continue to live and I will be with you. This is not an end, but a change."

"I cannot let you go! I will not allow this to happen!"

"Jared, please do not deny me, for I will not lose you to a moment of weakness. The others need you and you have a responsibility to them. I love you and shall always be near you. Go now and do what you know is right. Believe in that which you cannot see, for that is where I shall be waiting. Go, my love, and make me proud. Do not look back. Remember me as I was, for in that you will find strength."

Jared gritted his teeth, kissed her gently, then released her hand in response to the pleading in her eyes. Shifting sideways, he knelt briefly beside Terry and felt no pulse or breath, then kissed her goodbye. Moving to Sandra and scooping her up in his arms, he walked away, not turning to look back with his tear-filled eyes. He heard her faint voice one last time urging him to hurry, and he quickened his pace. As he came to the top of the stairs, he saw his mother sitting on a bench near the entry to the food court. When she saw them, she jumped up and ran placing her hand on Sandra's cheeks. Then, with fear in her eyes, she asked about Shar'ya and Terry. The look of pain was more than he could stand, and he turned away just as the entire ceiling above the food court collapsed, leaving the mall separated into two halves by a mound of rubble. Jared handed his sister's limp body to one of the paramedics coming onto the scene and walked away, as it all faded into nothingness.

Jared awoke to find himself laying on the floor of a small room with two doors illuminated by several of the small crystals in the ceiling. One door had no handle or latch. The other had a very ornate knob and heavy hinges. It took a moment to find the strength to get to his feet and he used the wall to steady himself. His memories of the vision were strong, and he determined then and there that even though he had no proof of the events coming to pass, he would never again seek to find his home world. His vow did not lessen the knowledge that fate might not let him avoid that which he had seen. The term "ignorance is bliss" took on a whole new meaning at that moment.

An intense thirst hit as he moved toward the door, followed by hunger pains and a need to relieve himself. Grasping the cool metal knob, he took a deep breath and turned it. A faint click sounded and the door pulled open freely and silently. Outside, only one individual stood, looking somewhat surprised that someone was coming out. His k'lar was the same as he had seen it before he entered, except that a long greenish shaft now hung beneath it about halfway to the floor.

"Indaru ast libak tys fe'androu." The male priest stated to which Jared merely shrugged.

"Stutar adin me'al," he said, holding up his hand and dashing to the opposite end of the room. Once there, he grabbed a cord set into the ceiling and pulled several times, all the while never taking his eyes off Jared.

Curiosity as to why the man regarded him so was set aside as the urge to urinate became nearly overpowering.

"Hey! I've got to go!" Knowing he would not be understood; he did a small pantomime as he spoke hoping to get his point across. That, along with the hopping motions he was exhibiting, seemed to get through.

The priest reached up and pulled the cord several more times, as if that would make someone hurry. Fortunately, it seemed to work as several others came through the door moments later, one of whom was Ardom. A broad smile came across the man's face as he saw Jared and increased his pace. Just behind came the chief and several of those who'd been in attendance when Jared had entered the trial. Ardom began to say something, but Jared cut him off as delicately as possible and said hurriedly, "Where is the restroom?"

Ardom let out a burst of laughter. "Follow me, Jared Ildae'Tuon, I will show you the way." Then he spoke in a whisper to the chief who also chuckled, then stepped aside as the interpreter led the younger man toward relief.

"Ardom?"

"Yes."

"What is the meaning of the term Ildae'Tuon?"

"That is Kuma's family name, which now belongs to you as well."

"I see," Jared said respectfully.

"Kuma's father, Namar Ildae'Tuon, is the brother of our chief and second in power to him only and is also the head of all warrior/hunters," Ardom continued.

"Any idea why Kuma chose to bestow this honor upon me?"

"It is said that he always desired a brother but has been gifted with seven sisters. In his Trial of the Soul, it is said he had a vision that a brother would come from the musara. Until now, few paid his claims much heed."

"Do all those who enter the Ja'narom see some type of vision?"

"No," Ardom said with a tint of regret in his voice. "Most simply see within themselves and must face both the best and worst they are capable of. To see within one's own mind can be a blessing or a curse, though I suppose it depends greatly upon that individual's point of view. I had no great vision and came to know that I would never be a great warrior/hunter as I had so long desired; that my destiny lay down a different path from that of my fathers. It took a great deal of time for me to come to terms with that knowledge."

"You are an enigma, Jared Ildae' Tuon."

"How so?"

Ardom smiled, "Have you ever killed a predator like the kas'lu before?"

"No."

"Perhaps formal training in combat?"

Jared shook his head, "No."

"The path…" Ardom began, a suspicious grin crossing his lips, "…that you took
on the great arch was, shall we say, unorthodox."

Jared grinned tightening his abdominal muscles, "Yeah, I suppose it was. He
grunted.

"And you have endured the Ja'narum, facing what you needed to in order to find
your way out. Most take at least twice as long and some never do."

"How long was I in there?"

"One and a half turnings of the daystar," Ardom said stopping in front of an
unremarkable door and pointed

"What," Jared groaned as much from a likely bladder fail as having lost more
than another full day.

"Do not despair, you still have time."

"That's easy for you to say," Jared said as he dashed inside.

"Kalla, are you sure?"

"Yes, the system came up this morning and no trace of the aircraft was found. Officially it has been listed as lost, and no further search will be conducted. Several more storms are forecast for that area and the prevailing thought is that the wreckage has by now been consumed by the desert."

"No trace of the craft has been found, Rehad. Do you still insist that it is necessary for someone to search the desert when not even advanced satellites can find it?"

"No, but you had better hope they do not somehow turn up in the future."

"You know as well as I that to survive that desert they would need the help of either a divine being, or the Mulu-Daln themselves. Do you believe either of those might happen?" Alrios asked sarcastically.

Rehad merely shook his head.

"Because if they should turn up, then I would calculate you chose the wrong people to tangle with."

Rehad retorted, "What exactly do you mean by that?"

"Perhaps I have given you too much credit for intelligence." Alrios produced a sinister smile, to which Rehad shot back a hateful glare.

Alrios continued, "There is much more out there than what we know. For example, the vessel he arrived in. It is not of the Commonwealth, nor any other world we know. You seek to possess its secrets and its powers. That is all the Guild seeks. But power without caution and wisdom leads to ruin."

"So, why did you join the Guild, old man?"

"I joined long ago when what we sought was regaining what had been lost," Alrios said with firm resolve. "I am forced to do much I loathe because those above have lost sight of the original vision and now stoop to terrorism and murder to reach their goals. What I do is no longer for my hopes of the Commonwealth regaining its former glory, but so those at the top can get a grip on the power they desire, but do not deserve. I do so because to spurn them would mean certain death for me, and my family. For them, I have become everything I hate," Alrios said bitterly. "If you've no more to plague me with, then get out of my house. If they do not turn up, then our task is done. If they do somehow survive, then you may do your worst, for I have lived under this threat long enough."

"If they do show up, I shall make you suffer," Rehad threatened. "No doubt about that!"

"If they survive, I believe I shall not suffer alone," Alrios shot back. "Good-bye, Rehad."

Kalla sat and listened to the two men, and for the first time in her life felt a twinge of fear. It didn't last long for she forced it down, but if the enmity between many of those she served continued to grow, then problems would soon arise regardless of how powerful the eminence was. She watched as Rehad left the room, seething, and Alrios returned to his seat. He sank back into his chair and stared at the painting on the wall below which she sat.

"There is little wisdom in angering him, Alrios," she said.

"Wisdom, Hmmm. If wisdom had been followed years ago, I might be living a peaceful life on a grand estate concerned only with my business and family. I have told no one this, but last night I had a dream that left me cold and filled with fear. It has been a great many years since I've dreamed anything I have remembered."

"Fear of death can do that."

"I no longer fear death," Alrios said with such conviction that Kalla was taken aback. "I fear that the person who now leads the Guild has become less than human. She is bent beyond any reason in pursuit of power and dominance and has allied with the worst of our race and other forces too evil to even describe."

"What was it you saw?"

"It's not what I saw that terrified me, but what I could not see," Alrios said, shivering noticeably at the memory. "Everything I beheld was consumed by a black mass which, though I could not see, I knew was alive and hungry for anything not of itself. Do you like blackness, Kalla? Are you fond of the dark? What about being forever trapped in an endless, black void? Never dying, never seeing again. Lost in a hellish void with no hope of release?"

Kalla's fear sprang up again, for she did not like the kind of dark he mentioned. She forced a laugh to keep Alrios from noticing her anxiety. "You have a very vivid imagination," she replied.

"Kalla, have you ever considered what your victims feel as they suffer and die? Have you ever put yourself in their place?" he queried.

"Perhaps long ago, but I don't remember a time when I cared."

"Well, you laugh now, but a time may soon come when you will wish you had; for in the last moment of my dream I saw that white ship consumed by the blackness."

"So?"

Alrios rubbed his tired old eyes. "If that vessel is destroyed, angering Rehad may be the least of our concerns."

"So, what are your plans?"

"Those are not yet ready for discussion."

Kalla rose from the couch and walked toward the door. "I think you put too much value on a dream."

"Perhaps, but I don't believe it will be long before we both know," Alrios said and then nodded as she pulled the door closed. He had not told her about his second dream wherein he saw five individuals emerge from a bright light and to which all existence converged. He did not understand its meaning, but he no longer feared death. What he had witnessed in the first dream was not death, but something worse, and he had no desire to follow those above him into a never-ending hell. He had chosen a new path, and it was now time to build again, instead of destroying and killing.

After leaving Alrios, Rehad felt some relief from the constant stress he had suffered since the white ship had first appeared. There really was no reason to believe that any of the passengers of that flight had survived the crash or exposure to the desert for four days. Only the Mulu-Daln could have interfered, but their hatred for all who were not of their blood made it most unlikely any aid would have been rendered. Even considering their tolerance of the resort at Torudal, it had usually been death to anyone unfortunate enough to stray onto their lands. Disposition of the white vessel would have to wait until after he made his report, and then he could take a rest from his responsibilities.

Traffic was heavy, and his transport was frequently stopped at congested intersections. As it usually did, the constant starts and stops began to irritate him. He preferred fast results and constant progress, but traveling by taxi, particularly in this city, was anything but, and soon became a drain on his patience. Suddenly unable to sit any longer, Rehad thrust the required credits at the driver, and exited the transport. He began to make his way toward his hotel but found the pedestrian traffic nearly as bad. Rehad had spent enough time in Tyris to know this was unusual for the city. He glanced across the avenue and found it to be no better, so struggled on as best he could while finding respite in a shop for a time. Twice he found himself in a disagreement with someone he'd collided with, and before long had a headache and was more irritable than usual.

Upon reaching the intersection, he discovered the reason for the problem in the form of maintenance work being performed on the north/south crossing tunnel. The sidewalks and one lane on each side of the connecting street were also blocked off, though he saw little that would pose a threat to most pedestrians. Some of the manholes and access plates were open, and a few workers moved about carrying various tools as he watched, waiting for his turn to use the east/west crossing. Crowds diverted by the infuriating city worker's labors made what should have been an enjoyable afternoon a true trial of patience. The fact that the downtown city blocks were so large made the effort even more objectionable when he realized he would have to go beyond his hotel, then a block south before coming back nearly a block before he could rest.

Most of the problem resulted from the fact that the designers of Tyris had planned poorly when the city was first built. Many of the crossing tunnels were too narrow to allow for heavy traffic in both directions, so pedestrians were allowed to move in one direction at a time only. Many had been replaced in some sections of the city, but he was just unfortunate enough to choose a hotel near a bunch of old ones. Finally, it was his turn to cross and he moved as fast as he could while trying to avoid any complications. He had to fight hard to control the urge to hit various idiots who got in his way or held up the progress of the mass of bodies he was trapped in. It was at this point he first felt the hackles raise on the back of his neck. He felt eyes upon himself, and could not shake the feeling, though when he looked about, he could find no one who seemed to be paying him any attention. In this dense crowd however, there was no way to be sure.

Once out of the crossing, he leaned up against the wall of the corner building and surveyed the area within his view. A good deal of time went by with no evidence of any threat, so he moved off again to the west. He had only taken a few steps when he noticed Kalla's dark-haired female acquaintance named Valeris, and a tall dark-haired man in Sha'Luralian-cut clothing disappear into an alley. Rehad had not been able to get a good look at the man, but his height was about the same. Kalla said Valeris had a desire to make the trader her own.

"Bah! Females and their stupid need for bonding," he spat out loudly enough for many around to hear. He ignored the various looks sent his way and headed for the alley. His internal danger signal told him that Alrios may have been wrong. The old fool had assured him those two had been on the flight, but foul-ups had happened before, and their slipping past Alrios's grasp was not impossible.

Rehad had to be sure, for one more failed assignment would be fatal! Since neither the trader nor Valeris had ever seen him, he would not likely attract their attention by taking a short cut through the alley. Rehad nonchalantly looked into the alley upon reaching it and saw the two people slowly walking and talking. He carefully moved into the narrow back street and began to head toward his hotel. Neither of them seemed the least bit concerned that they might be in any danger, so he made no effort to hide his presence. He closed to about half the distance when they turned down a branching alley.

Hastening his steps, he stopped cautiously at the edge of the inter-section and peered around the corner. They were still walking as if they were in a park among summer gardens. Rehad again began to follow, but this time more cautiously than before. He had not taken more than a few steps before he again felt the hairs on the back of his neck stiffen and a shiver run down his spine. The two ahead of him gave no indication that they were aware of his presence, so he spun around in time to see a dark silhouette in the shadows on the far side of the intersection.

His eyes grew wide as Valeris stepped into view holding an energy pistol in front of her. He opened his mouth to speak, but had no time to make a sound as the weapon went off. He felt pain swell in his abdomen, and then all feeling vanished from his legs. A moment later he toppled to his left and hit the ground hard. Sparks of pain shot through his already aching head and moisture clouded his vision. He managed to roll onto his back with extreme pain in his lower torso. It was just in time to see the woman walk up and stand over him, wearing a satisfied smile.

Rehad was stunned. He had been sure the old man was behind this, but then Valeris had never been told about any of them, except for Kalla who was her old acquaintance.

"Why do you attack me?" he stammered out as his lifeblood ebbed away.

"This is the fate of all who interfere in my affairs," she growled.

"I've no idea what you're babbling about, woman," Rehad choked out.

"Well, if you must play stupid, I will indulge you. You had the trader named Jared Chandler killed. That was not a nice thing to do, I had chosen him." At this point her eyes grew large and wild. "He was mine to do with as I pleased. I do not like it when anyone gets in my way."

This woman is insane.

"You robbed me, and that I can't forgive," she spat.

Rehad began to feel cold and knew the end was near, but also knew he was far more fortunate than he would have been if the Eminence had had him eliminated. The only downside was that he was now dead, and he no longer had need to fear. As he drew his last breath, he smiled at the woman to show he left with no regrets.

Valeris looked into the man's eyes and grew even more angry at the peaceful, contented smile. She didn't realize he was dead. She pointed the gun at his head and pulled the trigger.

She walked away. "I do not like being lied to either."

Still grumbling at her loss, Valeris left the alley.

About the same time, far off at the spaceport, startled workers and curious travelers watched as the white ship came to life, rose and pivoted one hundred eighty degrees. In the port control center, a voice asked for priority clearance to depart from a vessel everyone had thought empty since the disappearance of the ship's master. The request had indicated it was an emergency, and the astonished control tech gave clearance before he thought to ask a supervisor if any hold had been placed on the ship.

Many rumors had developed over the preceding days as to where it was from and what lay inside or what secrets it held. Orion was not within range to watch the Companion's progress, but had been able to sense the few times danger had arisen. Interfering was not permitted, and if the Companion wished Orion to wait here, it would do so. Yet now the time set by the Companion for Orion to come had passed and the ship would do as requested.

Once clearance was received, Orion moved out of the hangar and onto the apron. Waiting briefly as a freighter passed, the ship then moved onto the taxiway, turned forty-five degrees to the left and proceeded to the runway. Orion would have preferred to just take off from where it stood, but traffic overhead made that unsafe. As Orion moved onto the runway, it again contacted the control center and requested departure clearance. As it had done on arrival, the ship drew attention from anyone within visual range. Moments later the authorization came, and after making sure the path ahead was clear, the ghostly white vessel shot away, leaving more unanswered questions in the minds of all who witnessed the event.

"There is much to celebrate this day, Jared Ildae'Tuon," Ardom stated as Jared prepared for the final trial. Ardom told him it was not really a test, but a formality to determine a person's beginning position or status within the Mulu-Daln society. Those with high aptitudes and reasoning abilities always scored the highest and were trained for leadership. Often those who did well in the trial of strength would do poorly in the trial of acceptance and be limited to a warrior's life with little chance at leadership, but occasionally there were those who overcame their obstacles to move beyond their initial rank. Most of the time however, those entering the hall of light illuminated between one third and one half of the crystals, which placed them into the central majority of normal citizens. It was from this group that the artisans, tailors, cobblers, craftsman, and other trades came from. Healers, keepers of the holy records and chiefs, had to illuminate more than two thirds of the crystals to be given their positions. It was the only one of the four trials not kept secret from the uninitiated.

"I will celebrate only when those I set out to help are safe and I have my mate with me again."

Ardom opened the door to the hall of lights. "Then shall we proceed?"

"Absolutely!" Jared stepped into the dimly lit, narrow stone hallway. On either side, raised platforms lined the walls—each about the height of a bench with symmetrically formed crystals embedded in them. Grooves, carved horizontally into the stonework, separated each pair of crystals into rectangular sections. The whole room felt meticulously designed, each detail deliberate, as if it was waiting for something.

Ardom told Jared he should take them slowly, one at a time, waiting for the crystals to light before moving on. If only one lit, or both crystals in a section did not illuminate, the trial would end, and the priest would validate the score and announce it to the court and family involved. The door closed and he walked to the edge of the first section, pausing to gather himself for possible disappointment.

Anything is possible.

He clenched his fists and took a deep breath. He stepped forward onto the brown stone tile. Almost instantly the two crystals flared into bright life eradicating many of the shadows within the chamber. After looking both left and right, he stepped into the next square where again the crystals lit almost immediately. A total of thirty crystals in fifteen sets ran the length of the room and with the first four down he realized that if he could get at least three more he would be within the one third to half score and not be a disappointment to his new family. It was the least he could do for the young man named

Kuma who had given him the right to finish the tests. Stepping into the third section, the crystals again illuminated, but there was a slight delay between the time he had both feet planted on the tile and the moment the crystals lit up.

Jared decided to count to ten before moving on and wondered what gave these shards of stone their ability to see a person's potential. As he stepped into the fourth section, a twisted vision of some old man sitting in a control room somewhere flipping switches arbitrarily as someone walked through this seemingly useless test came to mind. Again, the illumination occurred but the time lapse increased a bit more. In the fifth square the lights took several seconds before lighting and Jared realized he was not likely to get much further. He had however made it to the one third mark, so was within the range of the common people. Section number six took nearly half a minute before they showed any sign of life. Counting to ten again he then stepped into section number seven which took about the same time before the crystals illuminated. He was now one crystal short of the half-way point and was beginning to feel as if he might just make them proud.

Jared stood for nearly two minutes in section eight and was just about to turn around and leave when one of the two crystals lit followed moments later by the other. He had done it, passed the half-way point and moved beyond the common people. Jared stopped and considered the thought that had just passed through his mind.

"Beyond the common person," he said softly to himself. "I can't believe I'm doing this. If I start believing that I belong in a station or rank above others, I will become like those I loathe." He turned his back on the remaining crystals and walked toward the door.

"I did not come here seeking power, or fame. It wasn't even my choice I'm here at all. I know not what this place is supposed to prove, but I will not compromise my principles. I will not fall to pride," Jared said, then paused at the door. "Thank you, father."

He pulled the door open and hurried out without looking back. Not knowing how far he might have gone would probably haunt him for a long time, but he decided that was better than being consumed by a desire to be above or better than any other living soul.

The door swung slowly shut behind him as both Ardom and the attending priestess approached.

"You look troubled, Jared Ildae'Tuon."

"Ardom, of all the trials I have faced, that had to be the most foolish and shallow. I'm not so sure I want to be part of a society which holds things such as station or rank, or whatever you choose to call it, in such high esteem."

"You misjudge us, my friend," Ardom said with no trace of anger or hurt. "The trial of acceptance is the simplest of them all, but also the easiest to fail."

"I don't think I follow you."

"What is not told to the uninitiated is that it is a test of character," Ardom smiled brightly at the young man standing before him. "One which you have passed as have all those who lead our people. You chose a path in which you sought not to set yourself above others for glory, fortune or power and that is what makes the most desirable leaders. If you doubt my words simply look into the chamber of light."

Jared walked back to where the door now stood open, gazed in past the smiling priestess and beheld every crystal illuminated so brightly it hurt his eyes.

CHAPTER SIXTEEN

Reunion

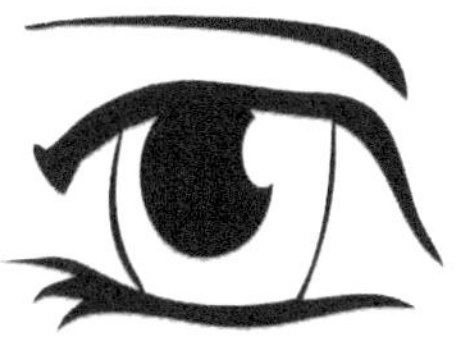

"It is through the eyes that the soul can be seen,
even by those who know not what to look for,
or even believe in its existence.
It is through their eyes that we see others,
and it is through our eyes that others see us.
The eyes cannot lie, for in them lies all truth."

JARED FOLLOWED ARDOM to the throne room where numerous long, low-set tables had been erected and covered with colorful cloths. As they entered, the rather loud conversation faded, and all eyes turned in their direction. He noticed Kuma seated to the right of an older man who sat at the head of the center-most table, and it was in that direction Ardom led him. Jared guessed Kuma's mother and seven sisters sat next, arranged by age, or so it appeared. Everyone wore a shirt or dress with a cutout, which revealed a colorful tattoo on the left shoulder and chest, even on the women. Jared wore a similar tunic, but the mark Ardom said would eventually appear was not yet more than a faint discoloration on his skin.

Most of those in attendance had a K'lar stone hung from a chain or thong about their necks. Only the warrior/hunters had K'lar spears instead of pendants, but regardless of the individual's occupation, the stones served as both their identification and key in or out of the city.

Ardom escorted Jared to the base of the raised platform which had before been occupied by the throne but was now replaced by a table for the chief and his family. The translator told Jared that each table would be presided over by the family head. Next would be those of his family who had attained the status of high office, then those who had won the right to be called warrior, and finally all others. All of Namar Ildae'Tuon's daughters had chosen careers other than warrior, two of whom had become respected teachers in their chosen crafts.

As they reached the steps to the raised platform, the chief and his entire family rose, followed by the remainder of the room. Jared glanced over his shoulder in both directions, a bit uncomfortable at the show of respect.

"Inas, na eridom tugal ya'ruliat sar fendemna ilyra osri polu ta na tetrial imrukutae." The chief spoke so the entire room could hear him.

Ardom quietly translated for Jared, "This day, we celebrate not only a passage into acceptance, but part of history which shall not likely be matched in our lifetimes."

The chief continued, "Ulmat'e, faslu ta tumak'e sa'dulsa, Jared Ildae'Tuon imora suklo na tal Hadara."

Ardom said, "Here stands, tried and accepted as a warrior, Jared Ildae'Tuon, truly blessed by the Hadara."

Just before Ardom finished, the room erupted into chants of "A'tae, A'tae, A'tae," which Ardom explained as something akin to 'hurrah.' When the chief indicated he was ready to continue, the boisterous crowd quieted. The chief then signaled to the left side of the dais and an elderly priest appeared from a side access carrying a long fabric-covered object. Upon reaching the chief, the elder handed him the bundle and withdrew as solemnly as he had entered. The chief then raised it above his head and pulled off the covering to reveal a Mulu-Daln spear, which to Jared's surprise created total silence in the room.

"Why the silence?"

"They have never seen the likes of it before," Ardom replied.

"What? But all the warriors carry similar spears."

"Yes, but none of us has ever seen a K'lar with any but a black shaft," Ardom said as he gazed at the crystal tipped, dark green shafted spear. "One does not normally attribute a weapon to the giving of life, but it is as unusual and unexpected as you have been to my people." Ardom smiled at Jared, then rephrased his statement, "Our people."

"Jared Ildae'Tuon, sutal ta ke-nomat'e."

"He has requested you to ascend and claim what is rightfully yours," Ardom repeated.

"This has taken a lot longer than I hoped it would. I fear that..." Jared said quietly but was unable to finish when Ardom held up his hand and smiled.

"Go, and do not fear, for time is no longer your enemy."

Jared didn't have time to think on Ardom's remark as he climbed the five steps up to the chief and stopped a few feet away. Once Jared was still, the chief held out the spear. He reached with both hands and firmly gripped the green shaft. The leader of his newfound kith did not immediately release the spear and smiled broadly. "Luma plouta itolas ke'nomat'e."

Jared looked toward Ardom, who simply pointed at the main pair of doors. Looking in that direction, he watched as the two warriors standing ceremonial guard pushed them open. Jared's jaw nearly hit the ground, and many audible gasps sounded as a young, tall, dark-haired woman with vivid green eyes stepped into the room.

Jared let go of the spear and his arms dropped to his side about the time Shar'ya noticed him on the other side of the room. She did not hesitate. She yelled his name and broke into a headlong run. Again, the room's other occupants began chanting "A'tae, A'tae, A'tae," though neither Jared nor Shar'ya seemed to hear any of it. Ardom looked at the chief, who was smiling more intensely than the old interpreter had ever seen. He had reason to. Never had a prior chief of the Mulu-Daln had both a warrior the likes of Jared Ildae'Tuon to award the spear to, plus a visit from a child of the Hadara in his court at the same time; and now it was clear the two were well acquainted.

Kuma was smiling as well, for now that his claim was vindicated, he also would be able to be joined to his chosen. Much to his surprise, Turi left her father's table and came to sit on the floor next to him. Kuma glanced at the old Sudar'mi family patriarch, who acknowledged the young warrior with a serious but respectful nod of approval.

Stepping off the dais, the chief walked to the embracing couple and placed his hand on Jared's shoulder. He set her down and turned to the chief, who again held out the spear which Jared took saying, "Thank you!"

"Omnopa di'al suptos endinar," the chief said so that all could hear.

The room became deathly quiet with everyone looking toward Jared. He had no idea what to do and was beginning to feel very uncomfortable when Ardom stepped up behind him saying, "You are the one being celebrated and the feast will not begin until you say so. That is what they wait for."

"What exactly should I do?"

"Raise the spear high above your head, tip toward the ceiling and then let it drop. The blunt end hitting the floor will produce a loud snapping that will release the attendees from the formal giving of the spear to the freedom of the feast."

"Jared, what's going on?" Shar'ya asked, both curious and confused.

"I'll tell you later, but right now, just enjoy yourself," Jared replied.

Doing as Ardom instructed, Jared raised the crystal weapon as high as he could. Shar'ya's head followed his motion, eyes wide with curiosity, then inhaled sharply as he let it fall.

Striking the floor, the shaft created a resounding tonal ring no one in the room was expecting. Shar'ya's eye color intensified for the duration of the sound. The Mulu-Daln who did see were left in awe.

Three em-hars later, the Mulu-Daln were still going strong, enjoying entertainment, laughing at comedy and chatting. Ardom happily spent most of the time talking to and translating for Jared and Shar'ya. During their conversations Ardom explained that children born with green eyes were a rarity among the Mulu-Daln, and they were usually considered as special gifts from the Hadara. Shar'ya however, had far more intensely green eyes than any of the desert people had yet seen and all believed her to be truly blessed by the Hadara. It was during this conversation that Jared learned how the chief had sent out a search party immediately after Jared had succeeded in the second trial. Jared asked about the others who'd been with her at the crash site and Ardom was more than happy to explain. Shar'ya had been brought into the city because of her obviously blessed state, but it wasn't until she mentioned Jared's name, when Ardom went to see her, that it was realized she was the one he was so concerned about.

The remainder of the survivors were currently at a nearby surface oasis being cared for by Mulu-Daln healers and protected by a full pack of warriors. The Mulu-Daln had let Jared in because he'd proven a great warrior and defender of others, and Shar'ya for her perceived connection to the Hadara. The others, however, were mere children of the invaders and would under no circumstances be allowed into the city of the one blood.

Jared also learned more about his new family and about Kuma and his plight, which existed from the time of his trials until Jared's appearance. Kuma had been unable to be joined with Turi Sudar'mi because nearly everyone considered him a bit addled. He'd claimed to see a vision during his Trial of the Soul in which he would finally get a brother who would come out of the musara. Kuma's troubles had fortunately not carried over to his sisters, two of whom were betrothed and would soon be joined forever. Jared had been brought up to believe that a marriage was only in force for the span of one's mortal existence. One of the strongest beliefs among the Mulu-Daln was that their deity, the Hadara, followed the same rules set for the faithful. Joining forever was important and necessary for those of the one blood because it was also important to the Hadara.

"Ardom, the passage you quoted said '...a man and a woman should be joined for it is required of them to fulfill their stewardship. Now let not any tarry lest they be lost, for joining is only given while they dwell within a shell of flesh and blood'." Jared paused to consider his question carefully. "Why is it believed then that joining exists beyond this life?"

Ardom did not immediately respond to Jared but instead called one of the elderly priests over and relayed Jared's question. The old man considered Jared for a moment before he spoke, then recited a lengthy answer to Ardom.

Ardom apparently asked the priest to repeat several parts before returning his attention to Jared. "I will quote Ty'nom's reply as closely as I can. We take the writings of Su'mal as they are written as I quoted, but it is also written elsewhere that the Hadara makes not rules that are arbitrary or needless. What was true in ages past, is true for today and forever, for the Hadara changes not. We exist in our mortal state for a brief time, but the written word talks of 'forever' many times and that if our lives and deeds warrant it, we shall one day return to live with the Hadara. Though it does not specifically say we shall be joined after this life, it also does not say we shall not. It only specifies that we must fulfill the right of joining while here. To read more into that statement would be wrong and presumptuous and would attribute inconsistency to the Hadara. Forever is the Hadara, and so are the Laws and Requirements which guide us through this life and through the next."

"That makes a great deal of sense," Jared said solemnly. "I can see why so much confusion exists on my world, because of the people who put their own twist on similar words. I never met anyone who looked at deity both spiritually and logically."

"The Hadara is all things and can do all things, because the Hadara has experienced all things. In creation, the Hadara is the ultimate architect, the pre-eminent artist, an unmatched scientist who knows all the secrets of genetics and matter," Ardom replied with great conviction. "That is why the Hadara has moved beyond where we are, to a place we cannot see, but aspire to. The Hadara has given us only what we need to know to make the right choices, for to give us too much before we have proven worthy of the responsibility would be like letting an infant play with a knife," Ardom finished with a smile.

Ardom had given Jared much to think about and he noticed that

Shar'ya also seemed to be intrigued by the translator's words. The topic of discussion changed suddenly as all in the large room turned their attention to the main doors and to a trio of acrobats entering. Jared watched for a time, enjoying what he saw, for the nimble trio was indeed good, but he eventually found himself surveying the room and the people within. After listening to the many things Ardom had said, he realized there might be more connecting his home world to these people than he could have ever imagined. For if indeed there was a God, then the Commonwealth, its neighbors and Earth all shared a common past and likely a common future. Perhaps that was why all those he had so far encountered were, in appearance and belief, not so different from the mixed-up masses of Earth.

"Ardom?"

"Yes."

Jared yawned. "How much longer will this party go on? I sure could use some sleep."

"Any time you wish. It was yours to begin, and it is yours to end."

"I suppose I end it the same way I started it?"

"You catch on quickly, Jared Ildae'Tuon."

"What if there are those who wish to linger longer?"

"Then you may simply rise and leave. No one will be offended, and many may appreciate the gesture. After you leave, they are then free to do as they wish."

"Thank you, Ardom, for all your help."

"You are welcome."

Jared leaned to his left and kissed Shar'ya, receiving a smile and a hug for his efforts. He then took her hand, rose and stepped away from the table. All activity stopped as everyone's attention turned to them.

"Ardom, please let the guests know that I retire to get much needed sleep, but that I wish them to continue as they would, with my blessing and thanks."

Jared retrieved his K'lar and led Shar'ya to the main doors as Ardom translated his words. Ardom finished as one of the guards was opening the door for them and the room again erupted into A'tae's.

As Namar had indicated earlier during the feast, a warrior was waiting outside the throne room to show Jared back to his rooms in the Ildae'Tuon family compound. The walk had been uneventful, and the few Mulu-Daln they passed were both friendly, respectful and very curious. Jared realized the curiosity was primarily directed toward Shar'ya and her unusually green eyes.

Jared carried his spear as their escort did with hand downward, thumb to the front, the shaft tucked behind his shoulder and the tip overhead. Now that he knew Shar'ya and the others were safe, he relaxed and was beginning to enjoy these unusual people. Shar'ya did not speak while they walked, other than asking where they were going. For the remainder of the time, Jared filled Shar'ya in on most of the details of his journey, except for the trials, which he covered only vaguely or understated, not wanting to frighten her.

Down the ancient dusty halls of the deserted temple, the echoes of footfalls thrummed as an old man hurried with his message. His face beamed with a smile for this news would not bring pain, as those of the past weeks had. He wasn't supposed to look at them, but since no seal had been used, he read it to see if he should prepare for the Eminence's fury. He found that neural suppressants made life far less traumatic when she was in a bad mood. He had been in her service for most of his life and had at one time been her lover. Though she later spurned his affection, he hadn't wanted to be apart from her, so had sworn his loyalty and service to her for the remainder of his life. She had not always been as she was now, consumed by her plans and dealings with pathetic followers, who seemed to fail her at every step.

He'd never failed her and was determined that he never would. He felt deep inside that she loved him too but had been taken from him by her need for success. If that was what she desired though, he would do all he could to help her achieve it. He approached the tall set of doors to her chamber, paused before it a moment and took a deep breath. A fit of coughing racked his frail frame due to the disturbed dust he inhaled, and he clung to the doorknob tightly to keep from falling. He glanced at his withered hand and grimaced, being again reminded that he had grown old and ugly while she had aged with grace and beauty. He often wondered why he had been cursed to grow old and shrivel into a ghost of his former self while she remained untouched by time.

Finally in control of himself, he saw the red light wasn't on, so he opened the door and walked toward the curtain that separated the room into two halves. Stopping a few paces before it, he again paused before speaking. "Your Eminence."

"What is it, Pedrosh?"

"I have a message from Sha'Lural along with other news."

The growl that issued forth from the other side of the curtain made the man wince. "Read it," she said.

She had never asked him to read her communications before, but he also knew not to disobey. "In'dros reports that a large portion of the planet's population is now crying for the local government to seek help from the Commonwealth by petitioning for membership. The governor's reluctance is creating a great division among various factions, and her previous popularity is dwindling. Most of the planet's infrastructure has collapsed due to insufficient supplies reaching the former colony. Commercial transport traffic has effectively ceased due to intense pirate activity."

"It's about time," her voice sounded pleased. "Continue."

"Reports from Central News Agencies indicate that the Commonwealth has dispatched a security task force to help prevent similar occurrences of pirate activity among the mid-rim worlds. Critics within the Commonwealth are saying this is a foolish move by the council as it will weaken patrols in other areas. Proponents of the plan say the move will strengthen relations with former member worlds and that outside threats are unlikely."

Pedrosh read with little emotion but nearly dropped the documents as the woman stepped from behind the curtain. Memories and long subdued feelings sprang to life in the old man.

"Those fools who play at politics wouldn't dare risk their precious defenses on that backwater planet, and that will lead to their eventual downfall as well. Is there anything else?"

"Yes," he turned away from her to hide his eyes. "A statement issued by the trader's guild this morning indicates that unless pirate activity in the outer-rim worlds can be curtailed, they will put a quarantine into effect to protect their members."

"That could be of benefit. It might help to save much expense," she said intensely. "Has there been any news from Rehad?"

Fear entered the old man's mind as he answered. "No, your Eminence."

"It is well past the time for his report," she replied more calmly than he had expected. "Send an inquiry to find out what the delay is."

"Yes, your Eminence," Pedrosh said with a respectful bow, then turned and walked from the room, and began to weep.

Once he left, the woman reentered the room lit by several Sova lamps which illuminated the once richly adorned walls. A large bed, a wooden free-standing closet, a soft couch and a trunk were the rooms only other furnishings. A mirror set at the end of the built-in bath allowed her to see and wallow in her self-admiration. She often gazed at her features as much out of fear as vanity, for she knew all too well how fragile her facade was. Without the vanseed, she would be just like every other aging being around her, and that was not acceptable. She had once been destined for greatness, but it had been stolen from her. She would not let that happen again. She considered the situation at Sha'Lural and decided that even if Rehad failed, there was little the trader and his white ship could do to foul things up if they did survive.

Next, she opened a small panel in the rear wall behind her clothing and switched on the small comm unit within. She gave her servants a great deal of responsibility, but there were some things she let no one else know. She knew that regardless of their promises of loyalty and commitment, she could trust only herself. She flipped the selector switch from the voice comm setting to message comm, she began to type, reciting her words aloud as if to convince herself things really were going well.

O.R.O.S.
Routing: 17-5879-326-000-TR905169980
ID code: 890654-009082-803080-143984

Lolis:

Let the situation on Sha'Lural brew on its own. There is nothing more you can do. It is doubtful there is anyone foolish or brave enough to attempt getting a shipment through to the planet. I have need of your services now at target two. Depart immediately but leave most of the T.A.G.S. behind to discourage any who might try. I know you just received them, but better some of them sitting around, rather than you, when there are better pickings elsewhere.

RKX

With that accomplished, she shut the comm unit down, closed the access door and returned to the mirror by the bath and studied her reflection for several moments before departing. It was time to return to the plague of civilization and other tasks for now, but the time would soon come when she would have what was rightfully hers. Then all those who dared to defy her would know just how insignificant they truly were.

Jared was amazed at the scope of his room in the Ildae'Tuon household. It was more of a condominium, with a living room, kitchen, bath, and practice rooms as well as two bedrooms. They looked through each of them, then returned to the larger of the two bedrooms. The need for sleep overcame Jared, he sat down on the edge of the large bed, and he fell back.

Shar'ya, however, was still full of awe and curiosity about the Mulu-Daln and their strange underground city. She walked to the large sliding glass door, opened it and strolled out onto the ample balcony. She was four stories off the ground, well above the Ildae'Tuon compound's outer wall and had a good view of the surrounding city. Buildings extended beyond her view in all directions though they became only fused black masses in the dim light of the night. A pale glow, like that of a moon at midnight emanated from the smooth surface high overhead casting eerie shadows below.

Lights shining from a few other windows at various distances almost looked like stars. The walls below, covered by some climbing plants, took on a sinister air as they shifted gently in the soft breeze that wafted past her. She glanced back inside to where Jared had fallen asleep and smiled contentedly. She decided he would have to be moved to a more comfortable position, or he'd likely end up on the floor. He had told her a great deal about how he came to be here, but she felt there was much he'd left out. He seemed sad at certain points in his story but had related nothing to elicit sorrow.

She looked back out again and gripped the edge of the balcony, wondering if she should tell him about her dream. Erith had once told her not to discount the importance of dreams, but this one had been strange. She did not want to give him the impression she was addled by bizarre or crazy visions. She finally decided to forget it, because as far as she was concerned there was no way it could be a prediction of the future. After all, the odds of being able to stop a stone that large from hitting him was impossible.

A faint click made her jump and she backed away from the railing, but relaxed as the compound's main gate opened, then closed. Two individuals walked slowly toward the main tower to her left, talking and laughing. About halfway across the courtyard, one of them stopped short and looked up toward her. After getting the other's attention, they both looked up at Shar'ya and waved cheerfully. They seemed pleased when she waved back, then went on their way.

Shar'ya had not been able to see their faces in the dim light and didn't know anyone here, so was at a loss as to why they had treated her as if they knew her. She stood a moment longer, wondering about it, then turned and walked back toward the bed.

At the edge of the bed, she knelt and watched Jared's chest rise and fall and, as she had so many times over the past mon, considered all that had happened. She wondered how many times the same fears would pop up. Would she ever really be all he needed? When would the faces of those she knew on Sha'Lural stop haunting her dreams? If the time came where she needed to save him, would she be able to? One nagging fear tormented her above them all, that she might fail or disappoint him, and he would send her away. A large part of her said he would never do that, but memories of things she had seen while growing up persisted and would not be easily silenced.

Tears formed in her eyes and coursed down her cheeks, born partly of happiness for today, but also with sorrowful memories. The slender, green-eyed girl had never been taught what love was. No one had ever explained its many intricacies and mysteries. Yet, somehow, she knew that she had found more than a bondmate who took her out of the hole she had called home. Like the fabled Su'lara which when put together gave its wearer insight, Shar'ya had found the other half of herself. All she had to do was hold on tight. She lay down next to him and fell fast asleep.

Jared groaned in response to a noise outside but did not immediately open his eyes. Once again, he was being robbed of a full night's sleep by something beyond his control. Shar'ya's head lay tucked into his shoulder, her right arm across his chest and he could feel her breath on his neck.

"What now?" he said in almost a whisper.

"Mmm..." Shar'ya droned dreamily.

Jared smiled and stroked her cheek, then spent a few minutes trying to ignore the considerable hubbub coming from the city. Finally, he opened his eyes, he found the room still bathed in the darkness of night though he wasn't sure if it ever really got light. Whatever was going on, at least it was not because of his presence in the city, or someone would have been knocking on his door. Slowly he swung his feet out and sat up, trying not to disturb the peacefully sleeping girl. After a few stretches he rose and headed for the bathroom.

Finally roused from her deep sleep by the nearly constant din from outside, Shar'ya awoke. Mild alarm gripped her momentarily in response to her often-disagreeable dreams. His shirt, resting on a chair nearby, arrested that emotion and she sat up looking around the dark room. She glanced toward the window and noticed a bright line of light along the edge of the thick curtains. She stood and walked up to the draperies to look out. What she witnessed was so overwhelming she let out a squeal of delight.

Jared dashed into the room. "What was the scream for?"

"I..." Shar'ya motioned toward the draped window.

So, you pointed to the curtain, I take it the cause originated out there?"

"Uh," she began, "I think its day, but..." She shrugged. Jared walked over to the drapes and flung them apart.

Like his mate, Jared was taken totally by surprise by the sight that met his eyes. It was indeed as bright as mid-day on the outside, but unlike the simple yellow/white light of a star, the city of the Mulu-Daln was filled with a kaleidoscope of color. From overhead, rainbow-like hues streaked downward in random arrays touching every surface. Plants, which had until now been seen only in darkness, filled the immense cavern with an array of color to match that of the cascading light. Crystal inlay which had appeared as nothing more than diamond-like trim on so many buildings, now shimmered vividly in the light, pulsing and dancing like neon volcanoes. Leaves predominated in green, but some of aquamarine, violet, yellow and crimson were mixed in beneath dense growths of multi-hued flowers.

From their balcony, they could see the streets outside the walls of the Il'dae Tuon compound, where people were milling about. Some of them pointed toward the ceiling of the cavern in excitement and awe, which was curious, as if they too had never before seen such a sight. Even the citizens' clothing seemed to have elements that reflected the various light values.

"Wow." Jared barely breathed the word.

"Have you not seen this before?" Shar'ya asked, sounding surprised.

He slowly shook his head, "No. I think I slept through the entirety of yesterday." He paused a moment then looked at her. "When I first arrived, it was night, then realizing they wouldn't help me unless I completed their trials, I chose to just get them over with."

His expression became pensive. "I had to sleep after the second trial. When I began the third, we didn't go outside." He stopped and looked at her, "Well I guess outside is relative, considering outside of here…" He threw his arms out, "…is technically, still inside."

Shar'ya smiled.

A moment later a knock sounded. Jared headed for the main room. A stiff yawn hit him which he endured then opened the door.

"Greetings," Ardom said cheerfully,

"Good morning," Jared returned gesturing for the interpreter to enter. "I must say that your mornings here are, amazing."

"While that is generally true, and this is indeed what one of our best days should look like, this display is premature."

"Why is that?"

"It is unusual to have one in the middle of the night. It is, in fact, only a little before star rise."

"I beg your pardon? Then, how…?" Jared said, suddenly confused.

"The actual rise of the daystar is not for some time yet, so the city should not be illuminated."

"You mean that your days here follow the daystar outside and are not created artificially?"

"Oh yes, and the plants and crops would not survive on artificial light."

"Wait a minute…if light can get through the dome, then how do you keep the outsiders from finding the oasis? Surely a translucent dome of that size would be nearly impossible to hide," Jared asked, incredulous.

"The dome is not visible from the outside because it is buried under many jai of rock."

"You've got a glass dome buried under many jai… er, feet of rock, and it still manages to get all that light down here?"

"Yes! The dome is connected to the surface by many conduits of unflawed crystal formations. The light is transported down, unfiltered for our use without revealing our location to those not of the one blood."

"Ah, like light fibers," Jared was impressed. "Those must be some big filaments!"

"If you are interested, I can arrange a tour of our maintenance stations."

"I'd like that, but if this isn't normal, could there be a problem?" Jared asked with genuine concern.

"We are checking that possibility both here and above. It is unlikely the cause is within the caverns since the dome system only transmits light, it cannot create it. We should know soon if there is something else outside producing this night turned to day."

"Ardom, while we wait, I need to talk with you about our departure."

"Yes, I knew that would come up soon."

"Um, I would love to spend time here and get to know my new family! I honestly would, but I came to this world to get help for another. I've already been gone longer than I intended, and many people continue to suffer while I delay. I hope you understand."

"I knew when you came that you would not stay. I did not know to what extent you would affect my people, but felt there was much of worth in you, even from our first meeting. We have for so long considered all who are not born of the musara as undesirable and dangerous. You have made some of us begin to reconsider those feelings, that perhaps there may be others like you out there."

"I'm nothing special, Ardom," Jared was embarrassed. "There are a lot of good people out there, but unfortunately there are probably just as many bad ones who would cause you misery or destruction. I hate to say it, but as a race of intelligent beings, we tend to behave in ways that lack insight."

"Special to the whole of creation, perhaps not; but you are to those whose lives you have touched here and maybe even a few more out there," Ardom pointed heavenward. "You have become more than you know! You have made yourself part of our history and shown that no mark is too high to reach. You are one who walked out of the musara and became a brother to one who had no brother. You have slain Tasnaklet and avenged many whom it killed. You have passed the Trials in ways few others have done, and in all that, not once did you utter a complaint or unkind word, even while wounded."

"Ardom…"

Ardom held up his hand, letting Jared know he was not finished. "All I have said would have been for naught if you had failed the fourth trial. You wonder why you are here, don't you? What purpose there is for all that transpires? Why, of all the trillions of people in this universe, you are here now, and asked to go through what is thrown your way? I believe I know the answer to that, but it is not for me to tell you. I'm not sure I can even give it words. I will tell you this however, Jared Ildae'Tuon, that I do not believe it is by accident or chance you are here."

Shar'ya stood by quietly and listened to the elderly man speak, drinking in his every word. He spoke with great conviction and love for Jared, but she knew they had not known each other for more than two days. He mentioned the trials as Jared had, but as if they had far greater significance and had been a far more serious challenge than her mate had let on. From her point of view, he had every right to keep things to himself if that was his choice, but she wished he would allow her to share in all he did and felt. She wanted so much to be part of that 'him' too, the deeper, innermost part.

Jared changed the subject in an obvious attempt to avoid further discourse on his reason for being, and asked Ardom more about the tattoos on all the adult Mulu-Daln just as a young female warrior jogged up.

"Ati nasma sen olufas," the girl spoke quickly.

'Tes'yat bidwom, umopae ta nolu," Ardom responded.

She said, "Sask to imnon redah."

"Olerim towe kuldara," Ardom waved as she dashed away. "The warriors have indeed found something, and she said it is quite a sight. Would the two of you like to come and see it?"

"Sure," Jared replied, glancing at Shar'ya to make sure she agreed. Her enthusiastic smile and rapid nodding confirmed she was ready as ever.

"Good, then we must be going, because there is no way to tell how long it will remain." Ardom turned and headed out.

"Did you bring anything with you?" Jared asked her.

"Only what I'm wearing."

"Okay, let's go," he grabbed his spear and took her hand.

Ardom led them out of the Ildae'Tuon compound and onto a main street lined with businesses. Despite the apparent early hour, the citizens were making the best use of the unusual situation and conducting brisk transactions as if it were any normal day. Once again, they drew considerable attention as they wound their way through the city's streets. No transport system existed in the city despite its size and none of the populace seemed to mind. Jared however, felt one was needed, at least for traveling longer distances. After considerable time, the three entered a large door set into the side of the cavern wall and began to ascend a winding stairway. At first, he figured they would exit the way he'd entered, but it was a different route.

Shar'ya walked silently until they were away from the crowds, then spoke to him softly. "Are we going back?"

"Are you referring to Tyris or to the city below?"

"Tyris."

"Yes. Well, at least as soon as we can. We need to get back to Sha'Lural as quickly as possible with the stuff Harin asked for, and with whatever we can for those poor people in the lower city. I like the leather look on you," he said offhandedly.

"Huh, oh the skirt," she smiled. "You like it?"

"Yup," he shot her a smile in return. "It even goes well with the wild look you have your hair done up in."

Shar'ya gasped and reached up, trying to straighten the ponytail she'd put it in the night before. Jared never complained about her hair in the morning but always complimented her about it after she had time to comb it out or put it up. Since that's what he liked, it's what he got, and she liked it that way better too. She would never go back to the tangled mess she'd had when he found her. She was not sure if she should take him seriously, since he never said anything about her unruly morning hair. Exasperated at her unsuccessful attempts to get the tail straight, she pulled out the thong and shook her head. Then she stared straight ahead, a noticeable temper setting into her features at her disheveled looks.

Jared watched as the young woman struggled; it was his turn to smile in bemusement at her predicament. He just could not stand to have her upset, so he reached up and ran his hand through her hair.

"So pretty," he said softly. Then, he returned his attention to the path ahead.

Shar'ya walked on for some time staring at him in surprise, wondering why he was so unpredictable. Though it took a little while, her smile returned as she realized all the other reasons did not matter, because he thought she was pretty, even when she was less than her best.

Finally, the stair opened onto a broad flat expanse, lit much like the city below and full of people milling about, waiting to get a glimpse of the marvel outside. Ardom motioned them toward another door on the opposite side of the chamber. A warrior standing guard at the door opened it as they approached, and they entered a long hall with what appeared to be a blank wall on the other end. After about a hundred feet, Ardom stopped and turned to Jared.

"Would you like to use your K'lar for the first time?"

Jared had forgotten the spear was also a key and nodded to the elder that he would. He began to look for the opening. It took him awhile to find it as Ardom waited patiently and Shar'ya watched curiously. Once he was confident it was the right niche, he leveled the weapon and pressed the tip into the hole. As he had heard before, a faint grinding sound preceded the door's opening. Before him lay a black starfield uninterrupted by clouds, with a multitude of people staring up at a huge, glowing, white bird-like shape which hovered motionless in the air.

Jared looked to his left in time to see a tear slip down the old translator's cheek. Why would a ship cause such...? His thought was cut off as he realized it was Orion who was responsible for the illumination of the city below.

"Orion." He hadn't realized he'd spoken out loud and found both Ardom and Shar'ya looking at him.

"You know what this is?" Ardom asked unbelieving.

"Yes, it's called Orion. It's my ship."

Ardom was dumbfounded, and failed to notice the chief walk up until the great warrior clamped his hand upon the older man's shoulder. His delighted expression faded somewhat upon seeing the elder's shocked countenance. He looked at Jared. The newest Mulu-Daln solemn-faced as well, though Jared was only concerned with not offending his new family. The chief turned back to Ardom and broke the silence.

"Ardom?"

"Suvala," the translator said almost imperceptibly.

"Etas, Ardom?" the chief asked.

"Uminat sui talud havuta na ke tenast far umbra taguot soca tal urisma foradom." Ardom's words grew in strength as he spoke, raising the chief's eyes as well as all others who were within hearing.

Jared did not have time to find out what Ardom had said, but its effect spread rapidly throughout the mass of people. Beginning with the Chief and Ardom, everyone began to step back, and a lengthening path through to the center of the surface pavilion slowly formed. Jared and Shar'ya began to walk along it, and as they did so, they were followed by silent, respectful looks.

At the center of the oasis, they stopped and looked around in all directions. Considering the multitude, the silence was total. The Chief, another elder and Ardom had followed, and the latter now approached Jared.

"If you do not mind, Jared Ildae'Tuon, may I see your left shoulder?"

"Sure," Jared replied good-naturedly, then proceeded to pull his shirt from his shoulder.

Ardom moved close and studied the complex patterns the K'lar had formed in the young man's skin and wondered what it might mean, for he had never seen so much on one individual. "I hope someday you will return, my friend."

"What does it all mean?" Jared asked, looking at the tattoo and seeing it in its entirety for the first time.

"I can tell you what each element means to us, but I cannot reveal the message that lies within its whole. Only experience can do that. Patience, knowledge and wisdom will make it all clear when the time is right."

"I guess that'll have to do. Anyway, it's more than I've received in the past."

Ardom told Jared about each of the four marks which made up

his 'K'latura' or Mark of the K'lar. "This is the symbol of the Family Ildae'Tuon," the translator said, tracing the pattern of an 'S' which nearly formed a figure eight. "The spear is the symbol of the warrior/hunter." He glanced at Jared as if he should know that. "The star signifies strength and hope, and the crescent is for honor and justice," Ardom said then stepped back. "The crescent also was the mark of Dasan, first great chief of the Mulu-Daln."

"Thank you," Jared said to Ardom, as he would a father. "Tell them good-bye for me."

"I will," Ardom said, handing him a folded bundle. "The others you sought to help wait at the Fosati Oasis to the NW," after which he walked back toward the chief and the other elder.

Jared glanced up toward Orion, then back at Shar'ya, expecting to see joy on her face, but was met by a countenance of pain and grief. He took her hand, pulling her to the center of the clearing directly beneath the ship. "Shar'ya, what's the matter?"

"You entrusted me with the wristcomm and I no longer have it."

"What happened to it?"

"It's band was broken when I was trying to get through a tight place in the underside of the transport. I was unable to reach it afterward." Shar'ya's eyes were downcast. What was worse, she'd forgotten to tell him in all the excitement.

Jared could not figure out why the loss of the wristcomm would create such trepidation. "Well, better it lost than you," he said softly, then turned his head upward toward the ship.

He struggled with the realization that her perception of relationships was marked by what she had seen in the worst places on Sha'Lural. Materialism and selfishness she had viewed in others made her believe that objects held far greater value than she did. She had come to believe that failing another, particularly a bondmate, was the worst thing she could do, for it resulted in being cast off. She still saw herself as just one of so many disposable items who's worth depended on the whims of the possessor. His statement, as they often did, left her confused. He hoped she would soon begin to realize that she was priceless, and far more valuable than a wristcomm.

Moments later, the crowd watched in enthralled silence as Jared and Shar'ya rose into the air, carried by Orion's localized magnetic stasis field. Despite the interesting technology they possessed, the Mulu-Daln remained a very spiritual race. Locked into customs and beliefs handed down for many generations, they viewed the white glowing ship as a manifestation of the Hadara. Jared had witnessed enough in the last few days to be aware there was far more to the universe than what he could see, feel, or hear. Little by little a picture was forming in his mind, laced together from all his recent experiences, built upon a base formed in his youth. Many viewpoints he'd heard on Earth now seemed shallow and arrogant. Much of what was taught about God now felt more alien than this planet did. Unbound from the fetters of narrow-minded clergy trapped in age-old convention, and misguided scientists refusing to see the wonder of a power beyond their comprehension, Jared began to grow within.

For a few moments after Jared and Shar'ya vanished inside the ship, it remained hovering; then it's ever-present hum grew subtly louder, and it gracefully moved away to the north.

Ardom exchanged glances with the other two men as the crowds began to disperse amid excited conversation and awe.

"Ardom, you told him the meaning of his K'latura?" the elderly priest asked.

"Most of it," Ardom replied somberly.

"Why? He has a right to know all," the priest said, sounding a bit perturbed. "What was not told?"

"I told him the meaning of all the symbols within his K'latura. What I left untold was the significance of the color. I doubt any Mulu-Daln has ever been marked so decisively before, nor is likely to be again."

"Why? What color predominated?"

"Green," Ardom replied flatly, to which the priest's eyes widened.

"To what proportion?"

"The entirety," Ardom said, looking at the priest intently.

"The complete K'latura? A sign of life, and sacrifice..."

"Yes, and he has enough to worry about without the burden of knowing just how much it may cost him."

THE END
of Book 1

Acknowledgments

I WOULD LIKE TO THANK Andy Lewis for his unwavering support and creative inspiration. His contributions—through countless drawings and animations—brought many of my concepts to life.

To Debbie Ihler Rasmussen, a dear friend, and my meticulous Content Editor, who spent untold hours guiding me through the nuances of the written word—your insight and patience were invaluable.

To Francine Platt of Eden Graphics and her team, whose artistic vision and skill in cover design brought my ideas to life so beautifully—thank you for capturing the spirit of this work.

To Kaylin James, for her ongoing costume design, unparalleled creativity, and unmistakable flair—your work added depth and character in ways only you could.

Special Thanks

TO MY EXTRAORDINARY WIFE, DIANA—Thank you for being my steadfast partner through every step of this journey. You edited and proofread with care, nourished me body and soul, and—perhaps most importantly—stood by me through every emotional high and low. Your belief in me never wavered, even when mine did. Your encouragement and patience made this book possible in more ways than words can express. The way you meet challenges with grace, humor, and deep empathy speaks volumes about your strength and the depth of your care. You bring balance to the chaos and clarity to the fog. I'm endlessly grateful for the way you show up, every single day.

Thank you also to my wonderful daughters Naomi, Emily, and Jennifer for your consistent eagerness, positivity, and support. Your energy helped keep this project moving forward, and I'm deeply grateful for each of you.

To my grandsons Daniel, Tim and Acie for helping to keep me young in spirit with your enthusiasm for this story.

To my good friend Andy for helping with design, concepts and other art which helped inspire my creativity.

About the Author

JAMES CATLIN is a master model builder renowned for his meticulous recreations of model railroad trains, capturing every detail with precision and artistry. An autistic creator, James has faced and overcome unique challenges, channeling his determination into his craft and storytelling. In his workshop—a space filled with tools, imagination, and the melodies that inspire his creativity—James brings his passions to life. Music becomes his muse, facilitating not only his intricate model-building but also his ability to craft the captivating stories he shares with his seven daughters. *Trials of the Elected* marks James's literary debut, introducing readers to his vivid imagination and keen eye for detail. With many stories already queued up, he is eager to share his worlds of wonder and magic with an even broader audience. James's dedication, resilience, and creativity shine through in all he does, offering a powerful reminder of the beauty that comes from pressing forward and creating something extraordinary.

A HOME AMONG THE STARS

Awakening

BOOK TWO

"DROP OUT OF NULL SPACE as close to the planet as you can. That way there will be less time for any pirates that are likely around to reach us," said Jared.

"Understood. ETA to NS phase field termination is 2.7 al–ems."

"Right, and we'd better get the shields up as soon as we make the transition."

"Confirmed."

Shar'ya walked onto the bridge with his breakfast. "Would you like to eat now?"

"Sure, it's as good a time as any," he said with a smile. "But you had better sit down and strap in. We may be in for a bumpy ride if we come across any bad guys. Um. Or should I say bad girls?"

"Okay," she climbed into her seat.

"Time to transition?" Jared asked in Adarian.

"2.1 al–ems."

"Thanks for the food," he said, going back to Ilirian.

Shar'ya smiled, "You're welcome."

"Have you seen our guest this morning?"

"Yes, I took her some breakfast before I came here."

"How's she doing?"

"Same as yesterday, very opinionated."

"Transition in 1 al–em." Jared turned to her, "This is very good. I don't recall ever trying it before."

"I kinda made it myself. Sort of a combination of tusa cakes and a modified tamni'var sauce."

"Really?" he said with raised eyebrows. "What a gem."

Shar'ya looked at Jared quizzically but remained silent. She busied herself with a small 3-D puzzle they bought on one of their shopping excursions while in Tyris.

"Transition in .3 al–em."

Jared finished his meal quickly, handed the plate to Shar'ya and turned his attention to the console. Ten em before the phase field was dropped, Orion alerted the pair, after which Jared needlessly translated it for her.

"Phase field shut down initiated."

Dropping smoothly from the blackness of null space, Jared and Shar'ya watched as Sha'Lural suddenly appeared with Lural prime behind it in the distance. Immediately, Orion raised the kinetic impact shields and began to scan the area around the planet.

"Head directly for the planet," Jared said as he watched out the viewport for anything in his range of vision.

"Understood."

"Any ships out there?"

"Twenty-three."

"What!" Shar'ya squeaked in surprise and looked at Jared.

"Tactical display," Jared requested, sitting up straighter in his seat.

Jared listened and watched intently as twenty-two equally sized blips and one larger blip appeared on screen.

"Eight class E vessels at 349 degrees, 403.093 ald distant. 12 at 352 degrees, 405.831 ald distant. Two at 208 degrees, 367.003 ald distant. The latter appear to be in pursuit of a single class C vessel which has sustained considerable damage."

"Damn. I was hoping to get down without tangling with any more pirates than absolutely necessary. If I remember right, the pirate ships we encountered before were class D types."

"Correct."

"The most we ever came across at one time was three."

"Correct."

"Can the transport escape?"

"Unlikely, scan shows the class E vessels as having superior speed."

"Aha. All right, bring us around to 208. Start power up on weapons."

"Understood."

"Recommendation on weapons power setting."

"Plasma flair will destroy class E vessels, but class C vessel will be caught in the blast area."

"What about a base flair?"

"Standard flair has eighty-nine percent chance of disabling target on first hit. Probability of destruction of craft on first hit is three percent."

"Then target the first one and fire as soon as possible."

"Understood. Core charge increasing. Remaining class E vessels are now approaching."

"At our current speed will we be able to get both on the first pass?"

"No. Current velocity will carry us well past targets before a second burst can be fired."

"What is the velocity of those pursuing us?"

"Equivalent of setting 36."

"Reduce speed to 40."

"Complying. Core charge at one hundred percent."

"Fire."

"Complying."

A bright flair of light leapt from the prow of the Orion and struck the closer of the two small craft and enveloped it for a moment causing system failures and exterior structural damage. From the distance the flair was fired, the small attack craft was not visible to the naked eye, so Jared relied on Orion's scan data. The damaged vessel veered to port and appeared to be running, so Jared ignored it.

"Target number two and fire."

"Complying."

Again, a bright flash shot forth, unerringly hit its target and enveloping it in a cocoon of plasma energy. Pieces flew off, some glowing brightly but this time engines failed as well and the craft began to tumble out of control. Jared made a fist and shouted, "Yes!" just before a violent shudder ran through the entirety of Orion.

"What the hell was that?!"

"A high impact explosive warhead encased in an ion shielded container hit the aft shield."

Frustrated, Jared asked, "Why didn't you warn me about it while it was incoming?"

"The ion shielding creates a variable magnetic resonance which makes the unit difficult to detect. Projectile was not detected until .25 ald distance."

"Oh great. You mean you can't see them until too late?"

"Incorrect. The initial one was not detected because required parameters were not known."

"Are they known now?"

Orion did not respond immediately, but veered right suddenly, pinning both occupants of the bridge back in their seats. Moments after, another, though somewhat lighter shudder rocked Orion. "Yes."

"What's the status on the other transport?"

"Continuing to run from the area, but speed is decreasing."

"Are any of the attackers harassing it?"

"No, all are converging on our position."

"Any more of those, Ahhh!" Jared groaned as Orion veered again, another blast rocking the hull. "Status report."

"Attacking vessels converging from various directions. Projectiles are proving difficult to avoid."

"No kidding!" Jared said intensely. "Can we fire to the aft?"

"Yes. Maximum power available for aft flair is thirty-five percent."

"We could out-run these clowns, but that would leave the other transport at their mercy. Prepare to fire aft."

"Star flair charge at maximum."

"How many will it affect?"

"If their course remains unchanged, three."

"Fire, then come about 180."

"Complying."

The plasma ejection and resulting blast was not visible from the bridge, but a shrill, grating and angry voice cut into the tension and both Jared and Shar'ya turned to look at its source.

Ceralia suddenly walked onto the bridge. "What in the name of E'rund is going on? If you are the idiot piloting this wreck, I demand you stop before you cause injury to a...." She was tossed roughly aside as another proximity blast shook Orion."

"I suggest you take a seat, lady, before..." Jared ordered.

"How dare you talk to me like...." Ceralia snapped back with indignant anger.

"Sit down and shut up, you spoiled Prima donna, before I get up and throw you out the air lock!"

Ceralia obeyed, but not without a good deal of anger and shooting Jared a piercing look. As her rear touched the seat Orion weaved again nearly pitching her sideways out of the chair. "I want to know what's going on?!"

"What's going on is that somehow, minions of those responsible for your family's death have found out you're alive and are trying desperately to kill you and us as well. Now unless you have any more stupid questions, do us a favor and remain silent!" Jared raged back.

He barely noticed Shar'ya looking at him in bewilderment. "And I suggest you put on the safety restraints." He didn't have time to make sure the royal obeyed, but heard the distinct snap of the buckles.

"How many did we get?" asked Jared.

"Three."

"Status of remainder."

"Four are aft, three others have now turned on the transport and the remainder are moving away on arching courses. Three more VMR projectiles have been fired."

"Do we have time to get off a shot before the, um, VMR's reach us?"

"Yes."

"Okay, let's waste the four behind us and then help the transport. Fire."

"Confirmed."

Orion released the plasma bolt and pitched hard to starboard just as two of the VMR torpedoes found their mark and the third went off in close proximity. The first sent a violent shudder through the ship and since Orion had used much of its available power for the last shot, part of the aft shield collapsed. The second one hit the magnetic envelope and detonated, ripping a hole through the port wing pylon. A violent jerk ripped through the ship, causing Ceralia to lose consciousness.

Jared knew that if anyone had been unsecured, they would not likely have survived.

"Status."

"Aft shield down. Port shield at twenty percent. Starboard shield at seventy-three percent. Fore shield ninety-seven percent. Structural damage to port pylon. Plasma patching initiated. Twenty-three percent power available for weapons."

"Why is it so difficult to avoid those damn things?"

"Avoiding a few is not difficult, but eleven coming from various directions is."

"You had only indicated three."

"Tactical error. Scanners were on tight beam to increase accuracy of tracking known projectiles; avoidance percentage is seventy-seven percent."

"Okay, so you did a good job," Jared said affectionately. "Any recommendation on how to off these troublesome insects?"

"No."

"What are their locations?"

"Three are still attacking the transport, it is attempting to evade but is sustaining heavy damage. Remaining ten are pursuing but falling behind."

"Any more of those projectiles?"

"None detected at this time."

"I don't know what to do," Jared said, becoming frustrated. "I doubt we could survive another barrage like the last."

"Too bad we can't fire at them from the front...." offered Shar'ya.

"Wait, that might just work." Jared brightened. "Orion?"

"Ready."

"Is it possible for you to pivot on your Z axis 180 degrees without changing our course?"

"Yes, however it would also reduce speed sufficiently for them to overtake this vessel."

"Is there enough power for a star flair?"

"At half maximum yield."

"That will have to do." Jared's eyes widened and he rubbed his hands together. "Right. Okay, transfer all remaining power to weapons."

"Complying. One hundred percent of power reserves rerouted to weapons."

"Good, initiate maneuver and fire as soon as complete."

"Complying. Data indicates the transport will get caught in the edge of the blast zone."

"We'll just have to hope their luck holds out."

As Orion spun 180 degrees, its speed dropped off dramatically. The TAGS suddenly gained on them. The brightness of the plasma energy release was enough to cause both Jared and Shar'ya cover their eyes. Orion's power was nearly spent and it accelerated slowly back toward the other transport.

"Orion."

"Ready."

"How are you?"

"Functional."

"That's not what I meant."

"Explain."

"How do you feel?"

"Unable to answer, insufficient parameters and data references to formulate comparative information."

"You hurt, don't you?'

"I am at less than my full potential."

"I am sorry, my friend."

"Apology noted. Friendship remains unchanged, companionship is worth much risk."

"Yes, friendship remains unchanged," Jared repeated solemnly. "Please show me tactical."

"Three class E vessels remain, powerless and drifting near the last blast area. Two contain life signs. Three other class E vessels are rapidly retreating on a course of 075 degrees Z-21. The transport is also unpowered and drifting, atmospheric integrity has been compromised in several areas. Seven life signs detected."

"Do we have sufficient power to dock and get the survivors off?"

"Yes. Power recharge is now at twenty-three percent."

"Alter course to rendezvous with the transport, but make sure all scanners are on the lookout for other hostile vessels."

"Complying."

Jared rested his head against the seat. "Try to establish radio contact and inform me as soon as we get within docking range."

"Understood."

Orion began trying to raise communications with the damaged transport and swung gently to the right, heading toward it.

Shar'ya had remained quiet during Jared and Orion's interaction during the battle. She had often expressed to Jared that she felt a kinship to the ship, perhaps even greater than Jared himself. He noticed her wipe away a tear.

Jared had Shar'ya get the anti-grav stretcher and then he helped haul the unconscious Ceralia back to her quarters. Unfortunately, she came to not far from her door.

"Wha… What's going on? Why am I on this…" Her eyes locked onto Jared. "You…"

Jared looked at the blonde quizzically.

"Your disrespectful verbal abuse will not go…"

"Verbal abuse?" Jared growled. "I'll give you verbal abuse, you thankless guren! It was you who came bursting onto the bridge demanding to know what fool was driving the boat, at the very moment I was trying to save your arrogant hide." Jared barely paused for a breath and even Shar'ya was wide-eyed at his intensity. "I could have left your miserable, worthless butt on the deck to flop around like a beached fish, but nooo, I gotta try and help lug your fat carcass down here so you'd be nice and comfy in your bed. And what do I get for my troubles? More verbal tar sludge from your black pit of imperial flatulence!"

Ceralia was left speechless as Jared stormed back toward the bridge, though somewhat wobbly on his crutches. Finally, she caught her breath and looked at Shar'ya with hurt in her eyes. "I'm not fat."